UNIVERSITY OF NOTTINGHAM

60 04317780 0

KU-393-050

JOSEPH ZALMONAH

JOSEPH ZALMONAH

A Novel

BY
EDWARD KING

AUTHOR OF "THE GENTLE SAVAGE" "THE GOLDEN SPIKE" "MY PARIS"
"A VENETIAN LOVER" ETC.

UNIVERSITY LIBRARY NOTTINGHAM

*" And the children of Israel sighed by reason of the bondage,
and they cried, and their cry came up unto God."*

THE GREGG PRESS / RIDGEWOOD, N. J.

First published in 1893 by Lee and Shepard
Republished in 1968 by
The Gregg Press Incorporated
171 East Ridgewood Avenue
Ridgewood, New Jersey, U.S.A.

Copyright© 1968 by
The Gregg Press, Inc.

Library of Congress Catalog Card Number: 67-29271

Printed in the United States of America

T/DE 5.56B5
Counter

SMITH (<u>Sir</u> William).

A smaller classical dictionary. Ed. by E.H. Blakeney.
(Everyman's Library).

8vo London, (1910).

15,135.

KING, Edward, 1849-1896

Joseph Zalmonah.

1 - JAN 1972

298462

398613

PS 2174.K3

0

Shon

Amer Studs.

AMERICANS IN FICTION

In the domain of literature the play may once have been the chief abstract and chronicle of the times, but during the nineteenth and twentieth centuries the novel has usurped the chief place in holding the mirror up to the homely face of society. On this account, if for no other, the Gregg Press series of reprints of American fiction merits the attention of all students of Americana and of librarians interested in building up adequate collections dealing with the social and literary history of the United States. Most of the three score and ten novels or volumes of short stories included in the series enjoyed considerable fame in their day but have been so long out of print as to be virtually unobtainable in the original editions.

Included in the list are works by writers not presently fashionable in critical circles—but nevertheless well known to literary historians—among them Joel Chandler Harris, Harriet Beecher Stowe, Thomas Bailey Aldrich, and William Gilmore Simms. A substantial element in the list consists of authors who are known especially for their graphic portrayal of a particular American setting, such as Gertrude Atherton (California), Arlo Bates (Boston), Alice Brown (New England), Edward Eggleston (Indiana), Mary Wilkins Freeman (New England), Henry B. Fuller (Chicago), Richard M. Johnston (Georgia), James Lane Allen (Kentucky), Mary N. Murfree (Tennessee), and Thomas Nelson Page (Virginia). There is even a novel by Frederic Remington, one of the most popular painters of the Western cowboy and Indian—and another, and impressive minor classic on the early mining region of Colorado, from the pen of Mary Hallock Foote. The professional student of American literature will rejoice in the opportunity afforded by the collection to extend his reading of fiction belonging to what is called the "local-color movement"—a major current in the development of the national belles-lettres.

Among the titles in the series are also a number of famous historical novels. Silas Weir Mitchell's *Hugh Wynne* is one of the very best fictional treatments of the American Revolution. John Esten Cooke is the foremost Southern writer of his day who dealt with the Civil War. The two books by Thomas Dixon are among the most famous novels on the Reconstruction Era, with sensational disclosures of the original Ku Klux Klan in action. They supplied the grist for the first great movie "spectacular"—*The Birth of a Nation* (1915).

6004317800

Paul Leicester Ford's *The Honorable Peter Stirling* is justly ranked among the top American novels which portray American politics in action—a subject illuminated by other novelists in the Gregg list—A. H. Lewis, Frances H. Burnett, and Alice Brown, for example. Economic problems are forcefully put before the reader in works by Aldrich, Mrs. Freeman, and John Hay, whose novels illustrate the ominous concern over the early battles between labor and capital. From the sweatshops of Eastern cities in which newly arrived immigrants toiled for pittances, to the Western mining camps where the laborers packed revolvers, the working class of the times enters into various other stories in the Gregg list. The capitalist class, also, comes in for attention, with an account of a struggle for the ownership of a railroad in Samuel Merwin's *The Short-Line War* and with the devastating documentation of the foibles of the newly rich and their wives in the narratives of David Graham Phillips. It was Phillips whose annoying talent for the exposure of abuses led Theodore Roosevelt to put the term "muck-raker" into currency.

While it is apparent that local-color stories, the historical novel, and the economic novel have all been borne in mind in choosing the titles for this important series of reprints, it is evident that careful consideration has also been given to treatments of various minority elements in the American population. The Negro, especially, but also the Indian, the half-breed, Creoles, Cajuns—and even the West Coast Japanese—appear as characters in various of these novels or volumes of short stories and sketches. Joel Chandler Harris's *Free Joe* will open the eyes of readers who know that author solely as the creator of humorous old Uncle Remus. And there is a revelatory volume of dialect tales, written by a Negro author, *The Conjure Woman* by Charles W. Chesnutt.

In literary conventions and the dominating attitudes toward life, the works in the Gregg series range from the adventurous romance illustrated so well by Mayne Reid or the polite urbanity of Owen Wister to the mordant irony of Kate Chopin and the grimmer realism of Joseph Kirkland's own experiences on bloody Civil War battle-fields or the depressing display of New York farm life by Harold Frederic. In short, the series admirably illustrates the general qualities of the fiction produced in the United States during the era covered, just as it generously mirrors the geographical regions, the people, and the problems of the times.

PROFESSOR CLARENCE GOHDES
Duke University
Durham, North Carolina

December, 1967

EDWARD KING

Edward King was born in Middlefield, Mass. in 1848. At the age of sixteen, he started work for the *Daily Union* and then took a job with the Springfield *Republican*. In 1870 he joined the Boston *Morning Journal,* covering the Franco-Prussian War and the bloody Commune uprising in Paris (March - May, 1871). His European experiences provided the basis for *Kentucky's Love* (1873). *The Great South,* published in 1875, was the result of a trip through the American South, where King observed the devastation caused by the war and the Reconstruction. He then was correspondent for the Paris bureau of the Boston *Morning Journal,* and witnessed the Carlist Wars in Spain and Russo-Turkish War in the Balkans. In 1880 he published *Echoes from the Orient,* a travel book, a blank verse romance called *Venetian Lover,* and *Europe in Storm and Calm.* Returning to America in 1888, King worked for the New York *Morning Journal* and *Collier's Once a Week.* He died in 1896.

Joseph Zalmonah (1893) is King's best work. It is an account of the brutalized, degraded conditions under which Russian-Jewish garment-makers lived and worked on Manhatten's Lower East Side. *Joseph Zalmonah* anticipates the "muckraking" novels such as Sinclair's *The Jungle* and *King Coal,* Lincoln Steffens' *The Shame of the Cities,* and the works of David Graham Phillips: novels and essays which concentrated on the exposure of abuses which had crept into American life with the spread of industrialism and the growing power of financial tycoons. King, like these writers, and unlike Thomas Bailey Aldrich, concentrated on writing in a fast-moving, reportorial style, instead of striving for artistic form. *Joseph Zalmonah* is nevertheless a well-written story, powerful and moving, not just an exposé or a sociological tract. The atmosphere is one of unrelieved suffering: There is a wildcat strike, a lockout, a rigged trial, a fire in the "Sweater's Hell," cold, hunger, typhus, violence, and betrayal among both the oppressors and the oppressed: "Seventeen hours a day, and three dollars a week, refuse to eat, and a pile of unfinished garments to sleep on!" (page 352). *Joseph Zalmonah* is also one of the first, and best novels which explored the culture and personal lives of the New York Jewish population which was concentrated in the Lower-East Side ghettos. King was particularly interested in the Russian and Polish Jews who had escaped the pogroms which followed the assassination of Alexander II in 1881, only to die of disease, malnutrition, and overwork in the New York sweatshops, denied the opportunity of assimilation into the stream of American life. There was an important Jewish labor movement with which King was acquainted, a movement which had its golden age between 1901 and 1918, culminating in the "great revolt" of 1909, in which 60,000 cloakmakers struck. Although King did not live to see this strike, it is foreshadowed in *Joseph Zalmonah.*

King's point of view is that of the sympathetic outsider, who respected the cultural richness and deep religious traditions of the Eastern Jews; their patience, faith, and loyalty. He paints a vivid imaginative picture of the half-oriental, half-slavic origins of these emigrants who brought memories of "the oppressor in his fur cap and jackboots," as well as of the "still, mystical evenings in autumn, when the last warm hazes lay along the level lands."

F. C. S.

CONTENTS.

iii

JOSEPH ZALMONAH

CHAPTER I

ENTER JOSEPH

Miryam stood on the high platform of the Bridge promenade, near the New York side, clapping her hands with
childish glee, as she looked at the vast and splendid panorama of town and bay, and the swaying and darting
throngs of ships and steamers.

A soft violet haze filled the air, and lavished its enchantment on the mighty ranks of tall buildings, on the taper-
ing forests of masts, and on domes and spires which
marked the line of Broadway.

The dull red shaft of the Produce Exchange, séen under
the glamour of the hot summer afternoon, was as picturesque as the Golden Tower at Seville. A " tramp " steamship, rusty and wave-battered, came crawling along the
silver pathway of the waters, and, touched by the omni-
present glory, was straightway as romantic as an ancient
caravel.

Snarling and fuming little tugs bounded over the waves,
their hoarse throttles barking not unlike the bulldogs
which the sturdy craft resemble. Past the Battery came
an "Annex" ark, wheezing majestically, and muttering
sharp warnings to the sailboats fluttering near its bow.
And in the tiny haven just above Fulton Ferry dozens of

1

oyster-boats, with their sails neatly knotted at the sum-
mits of their slender masts, were rocking gently, as if
cradling their owners to sleep after the day's toil.

"Oh! look!" cried Miryam suddenly, dancing up and
down, with her black curls floating in the breeze, "I
thought the great statue moved its arms! It seemed to
beckon to us! I believe that if I should spread out my
arms and jump over the railing, I could fly away to it as
easily!" —

And the child seemed ready to suit the action to the
word.

"Be still, Miryam!" said David, tugging at the child's
dress, as if he feared that she might try to fly. "A nice-
looking angel you would make, with that patched petticoat
and those black stockings! No, you would simply get
smashed on the deck of a ferry-boat down below there;
and who would take your place in 'Holofernus' this
evening?"

"I don't care about 'Holofernus,'" said, the girl-child;
"and as for the dull, ill-smelling old theatre, I wish I had
never seen it, even though it does give me a living. What
I want, David," and she turned a pair of yearning black
eyes full upon her companion, "is light — air — perfume
— space! Oh, if I could only fly out across that grand
scene below there!"

"You frighten me, child," said David, with a percepti-
ble quaver in his voice. "That is all the gratitude one
can expect of children. I rescue you from a den in which
you had bad air, little food, and long hours of cruel waiting
daily; I bring you to my theatre, and teach you to act in
my plays; I make you an artist, and give you an independent existence, and what is my reward? You want to
fly away! And I suppose you will do it just when I need
you most; but not through the air. You will be taking

the Chicago express some day with the dark-faced fiddler from Moscow ! "

Miryam's girlish face clouded : she looked curiously at David, as if doubting that he could be in earnest ; then she began to cry. David drew down the corners of his mouth, and tried to look sad ; but suddenly a roguish smile crept over his cunning face, and he held out both hands to the child.

" How can we quarrel ? " he said. " And on this day of all days ! Forgive me, Miryam, and dry your tears ; for Joseph will be here in a minute, and if he thought that I had made you cry, he might take you away from me."

And, coming closer to the slight girlish figure clinging to the railing, he placed his arm about it, and Miryam looked up in his face, smiling through her tears.

" Sunshine sparkling in the morning dew ! " said David gently, gazing admiringly at the pretty child. " You have furnished me with an inspiration for that new song which I must write for ' The Beautiful Shulamite.' "

" When shall I be old enough to play the ' Shulamite,' David ? " inquired the girl eagerly.

" Never, I hope, my child. Leave that to the actresses who no longer tell how old they are. Remain a child, and beautiful — forever."

Miryam said nothing more, but gazed steadfastly at the sun-burnished water below, and David himself gradually fell into a kind of day-dream, from which nothing came to awaken him for some minutes.

From the immense height at which they stood each detail of the colossal picture before them gained fresh charms. The exquisitely luminous and ethereal dome of the sky seemed to Miryam, when she looked up, but a little way above her head, and she could fancy herself poised in

mid air, like some bird of tireless wing. Directly beneath
them the water was of a deep, dark blue, veined with small
white threads of foam; farther down the bay it was like
the silver in *repoussé* work, catching and reflecting every
light thrown upon it. Near the base of the gigantic statue
a few white sails were fluttering, like swallows around a
house wall; and beyond it two or three gaunt black steamers lay at anchor, making an ugly shadow against the
faint blue of the Jersey shore. Those flitting sails! they
awoke in Miryam's innocent heart a delicious pain — a
vague longing for the romantic and unknown, which
wrested from her little bosom a deep sigh. The home-
sickness which she had first felt when, a tiny slip of a girl,
she had landed in New York, was revived for a moment;
then it died swiftly away, as if the keen American air had
banished it.

David and Miryam were members of the vast colony
of Russian and Polish Jews which has taken possession of
whole quarters of the metropolis since the " persecution "
began anew in Russia. David was the son of a Roumanian
father and a Russian mother, and had grown up to boyhood
in a little town not far from Odessa. He was of a studious
turn, and his family was anxious that he should become a
rabbi; but he manifested an unconquerable disposition for
the stage, and had just joined a strolling company when
the persecution smote him. He was banished without even
time to see his old father and mother in the muddy little
town of his nativity; and he and his companions, half
starved, and thoroughly downcast, migrated to Hamburg.
There two of them died of hunger, one of the cholera, and
a fourth hanged himself in despair.

But David was destined to survive. By singing comic
jargon songs to the German officials he managed to earn a
few pennies for food. One day a tall, lean man, with dense

black beard and hair, made his way through the throng of
refugees to David, and said, —

"I am going to America to open a theatre for our people.
I have heard of you: will you go with me? We may
starve; we may make a fortune: will you sail to-morrow?
Come! don't linger here! You know our proverb: 'Before the sun rises, the dew may eat your eyes out.'"

"Yes," said David, who yielded to no one in his knowledge of proverbs; "and I know another one. Rabbi Gam-
liel said, 'He who hath a trade in his hand is like a
vineyard that is fenced about.' I am not afraid; I will go
with you to America."

The black-bearded man's eyes twinkled. Before nightfall he and David were on their way to the land of the free,
and David had been engaged to write, i.e., to rearrange the
old Hebrew tragedies, pastorals, and farces, which form
the stock in trade of the modern theatre as known to the
Russian and Roumanian Jews. "We shall get a living,"
said David. "God will help us. As the wise saying hath
it, 'He sits and feeds the whole world, from the horns of
the unicorn to the eggs of the vermin;' and why should
he not feed us?"

David's confident prediction proved well-founded; he
prospered in New York, so that he was able soon to buy out
the black-bearded man and manage the theatre himself.
But he found abundant misery everywhere around him; and
one day, when visiting a woman from his native town who
had been struck down by disease while toiling at the sewing-machine in a pestilential den in Hester Street, he had
acceded to her dying request that he should take care of
her little daughter, Miryam, until she could care for herself. David closed the poor woman's eyes, was mourner
at her funeral, and took her desolate child to share his
humble lodgings in a cock-loft of the dingy barracks which
served as theatre.

Miryam slept on a pile of well-worn costumes, behind a little curtain, and her food was bread and cheese; but she grew strong, and, when her grief was somewhat assuaged, the maid of twelve proved as pretty as a meadow violet. So David at once made her a member of the theatrical company, and she already had a dozen Israelitish heroines in her repertory.

David, as chief writer for his own theatre, brought out a new play every few nights; and sometimes his company, recruited from the more intelligent artisans in the colony, and their wives and daughters, with a little sprinkling of "professionals" like himself, would grumble at the hard work imposed upon them.

On such occasions David would quaintly say, "Those who eat must work! And how shall we get food except by exertion? We are not like Rabbi Chanine and Rabbi Oshain, who used to sit every Sabbath evening and study the book of Jetzirah, and then created for themselves a three-year-old calf and ate it!"

And the company, weary of this sempiternal repetition of the fable of the wise men who evolved the calf out of their inner consciousness, would go on earning its daily veal with renewed and stimulated industry.

Meantime, David's old father and mother died in Russia, just as he was preparing to bring them out of bondage. He was now alone in the world; so was Miryam. David was thirty; Miryam was twelve. She called him father; and he called her daughter.

David was a lean, lank son of Israel, dark-haired, dark-eyed, with regular features, and a melancholy mien which seemed to indicate meekness, but which concealed a will of iron and nerves of steel. Despite the theatrical smartness of his cheap, but well-fitting, clothes, there was a quaint and Oriental air about him, which perhaps came from his long association with the mystery plays and farces of the Hebrew stage. He looked like a shepherd from the Syrian slopes, masquerading in a Bowery sixteen-dollar suit. He was temperate, honest, pure, and stocked with stage lore and a knowledge of the archaic music so common in the Jewish theatre.

Miryam was a superb example of girlish beauty of the Southern Russian type, and the brilliant complexion and full lips of rose-like redness testified to her Semitic origin. Not even the slow starvation of her babyhood, in the black desolation of the village in the "Pale" in Russia, and the misery and want which she had known in Hester Street, had been able to dim the passionate glow of her dark eyes, or to destroy the delicious curves of her symmetrical though immature form.

From the tender age of eight until she was eleven Miryam had known all the tortures of the sweaters' dens, in which her poor mother had lived and slaved sixteen hours daily. All day long the little Miryam, whose mother would not trust her to play in the street, sat in an atmosphere of such foulness that when fresh air was admitted into the room by the opening of a door, or that very infrequent event, the raising of a window, it influenced her as a draught of strong wine would have done. Hour after hour the poor woman toiled, sewing on buttons, until the shadows of night came, and hunger came with them to young Miryam. Then the mother produced from her pocket a crust of bread, moistened it in bitter coffee made in a crockery pot on the stove, and with this frugal meal Miryam retired to a pile of unfinished garments. Upon this rude couch, with fluff and dust choking her poor lungs, the child fell asleep, to be roughly awakened two or three hours later when her mother, broken and bent, was preparing to creep home to their comfortless couch. At home they slept,

often without removing their garments, so worn out were
they both with fatigue, and long before dawn they were
afoot again, crawling through the dark and chilly streets
back to their toil, for which the mother received but three
dollars and fifty cents weekly.

Once only had the mother been persuaded to allow Miryam to attend a Jewish school, kept by a hump-backed
little man in an attic which was too hot in summer and too
cold in winter. One day Miryam came home with some
strange notions which she had learned while talking with
other children in the street, and the frightened mother at
once withdrew the child from school.

And so Miryam would have continued to live on bread
and coffee, and to sleep on the dusty and fuzzy piles of
ready-made clothing, until she had contracted some dread
disease, and been carried off by it, had not the mother one
morning fainted at her work. The weary hands could no
longer pull the needle; the worn bosom no longer rose and
fell to the labored breathing. "Keep me my place if you
can," said the poor woman piteously, in the intervals of
her struggle for breath, "and I will try and get well soon!"

"We keep no places here," said the contractor, with an evil
grin. "When a horse falls down, the driver gets another,
and puts it in the same place, and that is all there is of it."

So the poor woman was borne away and died. Then
came Miryam's liberation from the foul air and dust; and
ever since that time she had displayed unbounded pleasure
in being under the open sky, or on heights, or on the river
when cool breezes were blowing. Even the thought of
Hester Street made her shudder.

The image of her mother, lying peaceful, and with a
smile on her worn face, came back to the child as she stood
watching the great moving plain of water beyond Govern-
or's Island. She thought how bitter that smile had been

in life, because the poor mother had been sorely disappointed at the hard lot which had fallen to her in America; and how triumphantly sweet and tender the smile was after death had touched the mother's face. It was a mystery; she could not fathom it, and she was turning to David with some childish question concerning it upon her lips, when she saw a thin figure wearily approaching, and gave a cry of delight.

"Here is Joseph!" she said; and jumping down she ran to him and kissed his hand with a pretty and caressing movement which had something of reverence in it. David also turned hastily, and held out his hand joyously, saying, —

"Yes, it is Joseph, and with a smile upon his face. I like that better than the frown I last saw there."

Joseph looked sharply at David. "Do you want me to smile," he said, "when I am crazy with desire for things which I can never reach?"

"I don't like the frown," said David, "and 'to desire too much is remorse.' 'The camel desired horns, and his ears were taken from him.'"

"But my desires are not selfish ones, David. They are for the good of our poor people, and I was taught to believe that here they would be realized — here! in the land of liberty and plenty! And what have we found here? A slavery more dreadful than that which we left at home!"

The speaker struck the railing fiercely with his right hand, as he said these words, and his eyes sparkled. In a few moments he would have burst forth anew, but Miryam hastened to his side, and, laying her pretty head against his arm, looked up into his eyes with a gentle smile, saying, —

"Ah, Joseph, not to-day! Don't think upon wrong and suffering and weariness to-day! Think of your wife and

the little one who will soon be with you — who are hasten-
ing to you over the shining water down there."

A smile stole over Joseph's sombre features, as the sun
sometimes sends a vagrant ray into the edge of a forest.
" How she says that, the little actress ! " he cried. " David
has already given her the trick of the trade ! " Then his
manner altered suddenly. He approached the railing, and,
gazing out over the water, the islands, and the faint line of
blue shore behind them, he murmured brokenly, —

"Yes, they are coming — they are almost here ! My wife
and my child ! And to what are they coming ? To the
graves of all their hopes ! "

David glanced at Miryam, who was alarmed at this unusual sternness of manner; and he made a slight gesture
to indicate that she should leave the duty of comforting
Joseph in his hands.

" See, Joseph ! " he said briskly. "It is already half
past two. As they came into the bay early, they have finished with the health officers long ago. The ship is moving
up the harbor. At any minute you may see her. Cheer
up; drive away those dreadful fancies ! Be ready to welcome your wife, your child."

"David ! " said Joseph, facing him suddenly, "do you
mean to say that our misery is not real ? "

"No, no," answered the ingenious David, seeing that
Joseph would drive him to a discussion, and then corner
him, unless he fenced himself off with a proverb; " but
remember that 'to be patient is sometimes better than to
have much wealth ! ' "

Joseph did not reply, but extended his arm, and pointed
to a black mass now coming into full view beyond the
lines of green and gray on Governor's Island, and moving
slowly past the great statue. This was an ocean steamship, a huge Glasgow liner, bound in and working up

across the shining water with cumbrous and ungraceful action.

"The ship! the ship!" cried David. "There they are! I know the old ark by her bow. Shall I ever forget the days I spent in that craft! Come, Joseph! they will be able to land to-night. Come, man, and welcome your family!"

"A bitter welcome!" said Joseph, as two tears rolled down his face. "A welcome to slavery and sorrow! A welcome to the living death."

He spoke with such terrible earnestness that David and Miryam fell back aghast. Volcanic forces were at work in the man's soul.

Joseph was tall and gaunt, with delicate features marked with a certain shrewdness, which had been refined and spiritualized by melancholy and suffering. His hair was coal black, and fell down upon his shoulders; a black mustache shaded his sensitive and nervous lips; his cheeks were beardless. His eyes were the singular and compensating features in his physiognomy. They were azure blue, profound, pellucid, frank, and fearless. There was the calm of greatness in them.

The chin was not strong; the brow was low, but marked with power. Joseph's limbs were thin; his frame was bowed forward, and there was a faint flush in his cheeks. His hands were marked and scarred with toil. He was neatly, but plainly dressed, and would have passed unnoticed in the streets had it not been for his wonderfully luminous eyes and the deep sadness of his expression.

Joseph took off his hat, and turning his back to the ship leaned wearily against the railing, with his arms spread out upon it, and his head bent forward.

Standing thus, in bold relief between sea and sky, it seemed· to David's active perceptions, always acutely open

to the picturesque and theatrical, that Joseph bore a re-
semblance to an old print which he had once seen of the
crucified Nazarene — the Jew who willingly suffered for
the sins of his fellows twenty centuries ago, and who was
denied by his countrymen even when his agony was most
bitter. But the reddish glow which had lingered around
Joseph's dark head for a moment vanished, and with it the
fancy went from David's mind.

"Come!" said Miryam. "We have seen the ship; that
was what we came up here to see, and now let us go and
welcome the greenhorns! Come, Joseph! are you dreaming?"

"I wish it all were only a dream," said Joseph sadly.

CHAPTER II

MALCHA IN THE LAND OF PROMISE

WHEN the three friends, after a fatiguing walk of an
hour through crowded streets, losing their way and finding
it again with infinite difficulty, at last came out upon the
fresh green expanse of the Battery Park, and felt the cool
breeze of the harbor upon their heated faces, the steamer
had already sent off the greater portion of its immigrants.

The gloomy interior of Castle Garden was crowded with
them; and men, women, and children were straggling about,
vainly trying to obey the orders shouted at them in half a
dozen languages.   In one dark corner a dozen long-bearded
old men had thrown themselves down in the dirt together,
and were gazing up at the whitewashed walls of the time-
worn fortress with as melancholy air as if they were prisoners.   Black-hued and tawny-skinned women, with quaintly
dressed little children clinging to their skirts, sat on their
bundles of household gear, and looked around with frightened eyes.   The portal to the Land of Promise was so
different from the image which they had formed of it!
During the long days of steaming across the summer ocean
they had beguiled the way by picturing to themselves an
exquisite garden park, with some old and picturesque castle
frowning upon it from a commanding eminence.   Into this
pleasure-ground they would be doubtless ushered up long
flights of marble stairs, leading from the sea; and, after

pleasant partings there with their fellow-voyagers, and joyous meeting with their friends awaiting them, they would go merrily forward in pursuit of fortune, and perhaps of fame. But this gloomy place into which they were almost driven, as if they were sheep or cattle! this circular tower, which seemed like the anteroom to some penal institution! — how sadly did it differ from their vision! Was it possible that it was the gateway to Liberty ?

These thoughts were in Malcha's mind, and brought a mortal sadness to her pretty face, as she stood near one of the unpainted wooden railings, with little Zipporah wailing at her knee. The poor wan girl child was hungry and afraid, and Malcha was in much the same condition. Everything around her seemed black and unlovely ; and now for the first time a fear that Joseph might not come to meet her stole into her heart. Perhaps he was ill, or had mistaken the day ! And what could she do alone in a great city, with Zipporah clinging to her skirts ? The formalities of landing had already alarmed her ; and now the absence of the beloved face increased her apprehension so that it was almost intolerable. She stooped and raised little Zipporah, and mingled her tears with those of the child.

How long she stood so she never knew. It might have been half an hour, for she lost all sense of what was going on around her, as before her arose a scene she had lately witnessed. It was the gathering of the immigrants on the lower deck of the huge black steamer, to see the mammoth statue of Liberty, serene and imposing on its little island amid the tranquil waters, as they came into port. How the poor souls huddled together and cheered ! How they held out glad and welcoming hands to the vast bronze impersonation of the supreme blessing of human life — the liberty so sighed for, prayed for, fought for, in the countries which they were now forever leaving behind them! What ineffable and mysterious inspiration seemed to pass into the hearts of these worn victims of oppression, as the steamship came abreast of the statue! How old men took off their hats, and all unconsciously stood erect, as if for the first time in their lives they felt free to assert their independence! How the eyes of wan mothers glistened as they held up their offspring to greet the mighty symbol of freedom and refuge from tyranny! Verily Malcha had, for one moment, felt such a pang of ecstasy then, that it repaid her for all the sorrows and persecutions past. But now!

Now she was hungry and tired and afraid. A huge Italian woman, her arms filled with screaming olive-colored brats, jostled her rudely; Norwegians and Danes and Arabs paused to ask her questions, which of course she did not understand; and when finally an official charged down upon her with a volley of inquiries, each of which to her unpracticed ear sounded like accusations, her tears flowed more freely, and she could only murmur "Joseph."

At that instant a hand touched her lightly on the shoulder. Her heart leaped with joy, and she turned eagerly, certain that she was to look upon the longed-for face. No, it was David; whom she did not at first recognize in the transformation due to American garb. But in a minute she was certain of the features of her dear old friend, — he who had known her as a girl in her father's house, — and she bowed her head on his shoulder and sobbed out her relief, and asked for Joseph, while little Zipporah joined in the refrain.

David did not at once answer the poor wife's inquiry for her husband. He smoothed the small Zipporah's tangled hair, and remarked in his soft, tranquil tones, "Rabbi Akiba said, 'It is well that man should be afflicted, for his distresses atone for his sins.' But the rabbi did not say that

affliction was necessary for woman.   Cheer up, Malcha ꞌ
you are in your new home at last ! "

"And where is Joseph ? "

"We will go to him at once.   Give me the child.   The
bundles may stay here for the moment.   Joseph is seated
on a bench outside, in the park.   The sun gave him a little
knock on the head as we were coming here.   And my
friend Miryam is attending him.   There now, Malcha ! "

And David gave a cry of surprise and expostulation, for
Malcha had seized the child, and was running like a deer
toward the exit, wild with fear lest the beloved Joseph were
in danger.   He managed to stop her, and save her from
crushing herself and Zipporah in the struggling throng ;
and, after much persuasion and many proverbs, he succeeded
in piloting her safely into the park, and to the bench where
Miryam sat, rather dejectedly supporting the forlorn
Joseph's head upon her shoulder.

A little pang of jealousy shot through Malcha's heart
at this spectacle, but it was speedily dispelled by David's
many explanations.   "Joseph has been overworked; you
see all our poor people have to overwork ; and his strength
gave out.   Then the excitement and the sun wearied him,
and — he is so glad to see you."

"Yes," said Miryam; "the work and the worry about
our poor people are killing him."

Malcha did not quite understand this, nor did she hear
all of it, for now Joseph had revived; his arms were around
her, his kiss was on her brow, and the child was clinging to
him.   David and Miryam said nothing while the reunited
pair babbled their joy, and David was just about to return
to Castle Garden to secure the few bundles which composed
Malcha's baggage, when he was accosted in jargon by a
small red-haired man, with a cracked voice, who assumed
a mysterious air, and beckoned him aside.

"Ah ! Ben Zion !" said David, "what brings you so far
out of your beat ? Have you made your fortune, and are
you already going back to fight against the Czar ? I see
you have brought your carriage. Perhaps you have come
to ask us to take a drive with you ? "

" Always laughing, David ! " answered the cracked voice
querulously, emerging timidly from the recesses of the
red beard and mustaches, and provoking a smile by its
quaint cadences. " Heigh ho ! I see that you play-actors
have no idea of the hardships of real life. I understand
that you had a caricature of me on your stage the other
day, in that play you wrote about the Polish Jews in the
Bowery. Ah ! David, David ! I might get heavy damages
against you ! " and he threw back his opened palms above
his head, and shook them playfully at David.

"What ! you old miser ! " cried David, a little disturbed
by this accusation, to which he was bound to plead guilty.
" I give you an advertisement worth thousands of dollars,
and you want to sue me for damages. Ah ! Ben Zion ! you
do not belie the race of pedlers to which you belong ! "

" Pedlers are their own best advertisements, I have
heard my grandfather say," replied Ben Zion, whose eyes
twinkled merrily, and who did not seem very angry. "And
now to business ! " he continued, lowering his voice. " I
have heard that Joseph's wife was coming out on this
steamer, and so I brought my wagon to take her baggage
to the house for her. Do you think, David," he said, "that
Joseph would accept that little service ? I know that he
has none too much money — for he gives away much. And
the strikes and lock-outs ! Ah ! happy am I that I have
no wife nor daughter obliged to pull a needle ! "

" Why, yes, Ben Zion ! " cried David heartily. " Joseph
and Malcha here will thank you for your offer, which I will
accept for them." And Ben Zion tiptoed forward, holding

his greasy hat in one hand, and saluted Joseph as if that forlorn and fatigued personage were an emperor.

Ben Zion was a pedler, and dwelt in a cellar in Hester Street. By dint of seventeen hours of unremitting toil daily, he managed to keep the wolf from entering his damp and gloomy abode, although the creature often enough showed his fangs at the door. The little man had a wiry frame, on which there was not a superfluous ounce of flesh. His features, of pronounced, Hebraic type, were framed so grotesquely in the bright red hair and untrimmed red beard that every one's first impulse on beholding Ben Zion was to laugh. A pair of full and red lips, slightly open, displayed even white teeth; and two black eyes twinkled with a shrewdness which showed that their owner rarely got the worst of a bargain. He had been in America five years, and had learned the rudiments of English. His "declaration of intention" to become .a citizen was long ago made; and now and then, when standing behind his push cart in the "Pig Market," he ventured to express himself on political matters as if he were already an independent voter.

At two in the morning Ben Zion arose, ate a lump of bread and a pickle, and pulling into shape the garments in which he had slept, he propelled his little cart to the Grand Street Ferry. While waiting for the boat, on fine nights, he lay on his back in the cart and studied the stars. Once across the river, he trundled away to Wallabout Market, where he bought carrots and onions; and with his savory load he hastened back to Hester Street, to meet the current of frugal Jewish housewives seeking provisions for the midday repast. Ben Zion was an artist in peddling; he knew exactly how often to move his cart, so that the admonishing club of the policeman should not gall his shoulders; and it was indeed a mouldy carrot or deteriorated onion which he could not force the sale of. In the afternoon he reappeared with the cart gayly decked with cheap stationery and trinkets, in which he did a tidy trade until four; after which he locked up his cart in the cellar, and betook himself with a little pack to Fulton Street. Here he sat on a broad step, with a stock of useful articles spread out beside him. He folded his hands, and assuming the dignity of a Hebrew prophet in lamentation, he softly murmured from time to time, "Shoe-strings! Shoe-lace-us! Col' buttons!" The grand air and the assumption of indifference were profitable strokes of acting. Ben Zion did a good business with the hungry throng of home-hurrying Brooklynites. In warm evenings he sold "hokey-pokey" in East Broadway, and went early to bed in a stone recess in the cellar, where friendly rats scampered over him at intervals, without disturbing his slumbers a particle.

Such was the daily life of Ben Zion, poor waif from a muddy town within the Jewish "Pale" in Russia, landed upon American shores with scarcely a dollar in his pocket, started in his humble business by the charity of his fellow refugees, but esteeming himself the happiest of men. Ben Zion looked with genuine pity upon the toiling thousands of cloak and clothing makers; perhaps in his secret heart he cherished a contempt for them, because they seemed to fall with such readiness into the snare of the sweaters. "But there! poor things!" he would say, "they were not born with figures in their head, as I was! We cannot all be in commerce!"

For Joseph, because of what he had done to ameliorate the sad lot of the sweated toilers, Ben Zion had an intense respect, which would have reached veneration, had it not been kept in check by the so-called "socialists." These somewhat incoherent enemies of the established order of things were also Joseph's enemies, because he brought peace rather than a sword into the treatment of disputes between capital and labor ; and they never tired of speaking ill of him.   Ben Zion listened to them, but his heart yearned to Joseph, and he would not believe the inventions of his enemies.

It was to manifest his affection for the unselfish and courageous leader that Ben Zion had jogged down to the Battery Park, to save Joseph and Màlcha any expense for transportation of baggage.   At the same time he intended to do a stroke of business; for, as he informed David, " the American boys stone our people when they appear in the streets with their Russian flat caps on ; so I have brought down a few nice second-hand straw hats, very cheap ! " And his assistant, who kept watch over his cart while he talked with Joseph, was at that moment reaping a rich harvest by selling these hats to refugees, old and young, as one by one they straggled away from Castle Garden.

When David and Miryam had gone with Ben Zion to secure the baggage, and Joseph and his wife and child had no witnesses save an occasional indifferent passer-by, Joseph's energy returned, but a mortal sadness settled upon his face.   How could he tell his wife of the horrible slough of despair into which he and the greater part of his brother and sister refugees had fallen ?   He had not dared to tell her the truth in the letters sent to her in Russia; nor, indeed, had he ventured to write often to her, lest some chance sentence in one of his letters should be made the pretext for persecution of the dear patient wife and her friends and relatives.   And when he learned that her father had at last consented that she might join him in America, much apprehension for the future was mingled with the rapture awakened by the thought of reunion.   And now she must know the truth : she must be told that the misery into which they had fallen in New York was almost as deep as that which they had left behind them.

"Except," thought Joseph, "that here we have nearly
absolute personal liberty — and that is a great deal."

While Joseph, with little Zipporah's olive cheek laid
lovingly against his pale face, talked to his wife of every
thing except the one topic which lay so heavily upon his
heart, Malcha's eyes were busy with the strange new landscape, the tall buildings, and the people who seemed hast-
ening to some rendezvous upon which their very lives
depended, so serious and preoccupied was their air. The
sinuous trains crawling to and fro on the high skeleton
platforms; the mottled row of houses beyond them; the
pretty sweep of lawn in the park, with its fringe of trees,
behind which arose the reddish walls and dome of the
Washington building; the Battery terrace, with the water
lapping against it lazily, save when some huge craft passed,
and sent a procession of scurrying wavelets to the shore;
the ferry houses, with the endless processions of people and
of huge rumbling drays and clanking beer wagons to and
from them — all these things were new and strange to her;
and in spite of the brilliant sunshine, and the cloudless
blue of the heavenly vault, she felt a strong depression,
against which she tried in vain to rebel. Everything was
so full of light and life and action! She longed for a
comfortable shadow into which she might creep for a time,
until she had gathered a little more courage for her entry
into the "promised land."

One glimpse of the sweaters' hell was caught by Malcha,
despite Joseph's unwillingness to unveil its horrors so
early. That was when he told his wife the story of
Miryam and her mother, and how David had taken pity on
the poor, deserted girl. But Malcha did not ask him to
tell her more, and Joseph's heart sank within him when
he reflected how soon she would find out everything for
herself.

When Ben Zion and the others came back with the bundles, Malcha was trying to place in her husband's hands the small store of roubles which her worthy father had sent him, but Joseph made her keep it. This tiny sum, and the price of Malcha's journey with little Zipporah to America, represented the good man's contribution to their future prosperity. "I can do no more," he had said; "the Russian government will soon take from me all that your mother and I have managed to save." And so, indeed, it proved ere long.

"The little girl has fallen asleep," said Ben Zion. "If I might suggest, let us put her in the push cart, and cover her with this bit of cloth. She will ride nicely so." This was done, and the party made its way to the East side, through streets which to Malcha seemed endless, and in which they encountered rough people, who jostled them and called them "Sheenies," affixing to this descriptive epithet a bewildering collection of variegated profanity which was not without a touch of the grotesque. Here and there a half-grown youth threw a stone, or a hulking bully made a derisive gesture; but these things, which made Malcha's heart beat faster, and her face turn white with apprehension, seemed to have no effect on Ben Zion or Joseph.

At last they came into East Broadway, where David and Miryam left them; and, just as Malcha's force was failing, the little cart stopped in front of a tall, grim, old mansion which had seen better days, and which still had about it a curious air of faded gentility. Hebrew signs covered the front of this building, and the jargon which was Malcha's native tongue was heard on every side. Multitudes of children were screaming, dancing, and jostling each other; but the men and women whom they met were pale, bent, and silent. The men seemed half-asleep, as they staggered along beneath the weight of huge piles of clothing, from

which arose the faint, nauseating odor of dyes and hot
pressed cloth ; the women's faces were drawn and worn,
and some of them had a wild look, as of persons half crazed
with long vigils. Young Polish and Russian girls, with
heads bent and eyes half closed, were toiling at sewing-
machines in a basement into which the afternoon sun was
sending some scorching rays.

"Well, well," said Malcha, who was beginning to feel a
bit more cheerful at the sound of her own language in the
street, and the sight of it upon signs, "at least there is
work for everybody here! And that is better than in
Podolia, is it not, Joseph?" she said, thinking of the
throngs of half-starved, unemployed, and persecuted Hebrews in the town whence she had come, in the far-away
Russian province.

"No, Malcha, no," answered Joseph in a low, fierce voice,
taking his wife's arm, and aiding her to climb the steep
steps to the old-fashioned door.   "No, it is not better here
— not at present. But don't ask me how or why to-day,
my love ! "

As Malcha went up the steps, she caught sight, to her
astonishment and delight, of a familiar face. It was that
of a young girl who had been her neighbor at home — a
beautiful, voluptuous face, with exquisite features set in a
picturesque frame of coal-black hair. Malcha nodded and
waved her hand impulsively in recognition, and would have
paused to speak with her, but the girl hastily turned her
face and glided away.

"See, Joseph, see ! " cried Malcha, "there is Shiphrah,
the pretty Shiphrah from our own town ! our old neighbor !
Joseph, do run after her, and tell her that I am here ! "

"Hush, Malcha ! " said Joseph, hurrying his wife into
the ·house, and taking the sleeping Zipporah from Ben
Zion's arms, "do not speak of that creature ! Do not

say that you have seen her! She is lost forever! I do not blame her: she is but one of many victims; but to you she is lost — lost!"

"Oh, dear!" cried Malcha, bursting into a passionate fit of weeping; "how terrible! And what is the meaning of all this mystery, Joseph? And why are you so sad?"

"Not to-day, love, not to-day," said Joseph, trying to smile. "Let me welcome you to our poor little home. See! you have already brought the sunshine into it."

And at that instant a vagrant ray streamed in at the open window of the room which they were just entering, and enveloped in golden glory the young parents and the sleeping child between them.

CHAPTER III

BAUMEISTER IS REPELLED

WHEN Malcha awoke next morning, she might almost have persuaded herself that she was still in her humble village in the Jewish " Pale," in the Russia from which she had been compelled to flee. For in the plainly furnished room many simple memorials of her old home, unpacked from her bundles by Joseph's loving care, were placed where she could see them as soon as she awoke.

Little Zipporah was nestling at her side, and smiling at the long rays of sunshine which slanted into the room through dusty blinds; and outside Malcha could hear two highly pitched female voices talking in her native jargon.

" I tell you," said one voice, " he is as thin as a spring snow-drift, and he will kill himself running after those poor fools of cloakmakers."

" Yes; but, my good woman, doesn't he make his living that way ? and shouldn't we all work for our livings ? "

" A pretty living you would make," cried the first voice, rising to the sharpness of a piccolo in its intense earnestness, " if you did missionary work fifteen hours a day, and then gave to the poor whatever it brought you in. I tell you he goes hungry, and I know it. And now that his good wife is here, I have a mind to tell her, so that she can put order in the head of this dreamer."

Malcha sat bolt upright in bed, and put out both hands,

as if she would ward off the words she had just heard. They were talking of Joseph — her Joseph, from whom she had been separated for two weary years. And he was in trouble, in poverty, and — what did she hear? — doing missionary work for the poor!

A proud and satisfied look came into her face. So now she understood many things. Now she could comprehend why Joseph could not send her the money to bring her to America, and why her relatives had been compelled to advance it. Now she saw why Joseph was so preoccupied; why he had been so sad and quiet at their meeting after so long a separation; and why he had arisen long before dawn, saying that he had some business among the working people.

She had noted the hectic flush in his cheek, the intense fire in his eyes, his poor and scanty clothing, and his hands calloused and stained and scarred with toil. And now, as she lay back upoñ her pillow and thought anew upon those poor hands, her eyes filled with tears. She had dreamed of another lot than this in America for her Joseph.

"Must we forever be driven on and on, without rest, without help, without consolation ?" she sighed; and closing her eyes she seemed still to feel the rocking and swaying of the great steamship, and to hear through its rigging the hissing and screaming of the gale which they had encountered just off the Banks.

But as the hours passed, and Joseph did not return, Malcha arose and dressed the child and herself, and began preparations for breakfast. The small and ill-lighted kitchen, with its range and utensils, which, to Malcha's Russian eyes, were decidedly novel and complicated, was soon fragrant with the aroma of tea.

Malcha had brought with her a little parcel of the delectable herb, sent as a peace-offering by her mother, who had long disliked Joseph because he was not a very careful observer of Hebrew religious customs, but who had finally yielded to her daughter's point of view. After a little searching, Malcha found a loaf of bread, somewhat nibbled by adventurous rats, on a little shelf; and to this simple repast she invited the small Zipporah, the two contentedly munching and drinking as if they were nobles at a feast.

Presently Joseph came in, and the tears sprang to Malcha's eyes as she noted how thin and wan he was. His eyes were strained and weary; his back was bent, as if beneath a load of care, and there was an unquiet look on his face which Malcha had never seen there before.

She threw her arms about her husband's neck, and drew him down beside her at the little table in the kitchen, where she and the child were eating. Joseph placed his hand caressingly on his wife's head, and gazed at her tenderly for a moment; then he said, —

"I have been saving a poor woman from being put into the street by a pig of a landlord who would not listen to reason. But I made him behave more decently. If I had not had this to do, I would not have left you."

"Don't talk now, Joseph," said Malcha, "but eat."

"Eat?" he said with a quaint smile. "What is that? I don't eat any more. But perhaps I shall change my habits, now that you have come."

Malcha secretly vowed that he should, so far as neglecting his health was concerned, and she rejoiced to see him presently eating the bread and drinking the tea, and with the ravenous appetite of one who had not broken his fast for a long time.

"There is no sugar for the tea," said Malcha; "perhaps there is still a little in my valise. It was better to carry our own tea and sugar in that dreadful steerage."

"No, no, Malcha," said Joseph, rising hastily, with a

faint blush on his cheeks ; " I was very thoughtless ; I have not provided the necessary things : let me go at once and get them."

" Nothing of the sort ; and you up at four to keep Mother Levitsky from being put on the sidewalk without, God knows, even a three-legged chair to sit on. No, no ; not while Ben Zion has two legs ! Let me do the errand for you."

And the surprised family turned to see their unpretentious friend of the red beard and the cavernous voice stamping across the room, bearing in one hand an immense bunch of savory new vegetables, and in the other a little packet of fish, which gave forth a curious and somewhat unpleasant aroma each time that the lively Ben Zion gesticulated with the hand containing it.

"I said to myself," continued Ben Zion, " ' A small fish stew,' says I, 'is just the thing to comfort the heart and keep the courage up ; and Joseph's wife may not have time, with all her unpacking ' — so if I can turn to and cook it for you, or if Joseph's wife would condescend, now — and what can I bring you from out there ? " he concluded, pointing with the fish to the street.

" My dear friend," said Joseph, " you are kindness itself ; but you are poor like ourselves, and we cannot allow you to pillage your push cart for our benefit."

"Dirt cheap ! I tell you that *was* a bargain !" cried Ben Zion, holding the fish flat in the palm of his hand, and shaking the palm violently. " I bought 'em in Fulton Market, where they were going to throw them away, those fish ; and they are still as good as gold ! And I says, ' A nice little fish stew — just the thing ' " —

Joseph's eyes twinkled ; and, as he accepted and laid Ben Zion's gifts away, a smile stole over his weary features. The fish were carefully placed at some distance from the

vegetables, and when Ben Zion had been despatched for the
sugar, Joseph said, —

"I think he has come to bring me some news. The
savory presents were only a pretext. Perhaps if you hear
what he has to say you will understand a little better" —

"I understand already, my husband, that you are sacri-
ficing yourself for the poor of our people. But why do
they remain poor after they get here? I thought that this
was the land of plenty."

At this Joseph drew so long and dolorous a sigh, that
Malcha forebore to question him further; and presently
Ben Zion burst in again with, "Here's the sugar! And
what's this I hear! Another lock-out at Freier and Monach's!
Well, well! what will the poor needle shifters do now?
They can't eat dust, and what else can they get? Well,
God be with us, as the fox said to his wife when the hounds
were after them! And, Joseph, I thought you might like
to know" — he glanced at the wife and child, and paused.

"You may speak before Malcha. I have no secrets from
my wife," said Joseph rather sharply.

"Of course. It was only to say, Joseph, that I saw one
of those fools of Socialists last night, and he said" —

"Well, out with it, man! What did he say?"

"He said that you must come over to them, or they
would fill your road so full of rocks that you would find it
hard walking. They say that you are too mild, Joseph,
and that it is better to use force."

"And what is your own opinion, friend?" said Joseph.

"Ah!" said Ben Zion, scratching his red head reflectively, "that is a grave question. I don't say that if I had
a capitalist in a corner, I wouldn't squeeze him. But to try
driving a good many hundred capitalists into a corner is quite
another thing. They say in this country that every man
can get his rights under the law, if he works hard enough
for them. I don't know how it is" —

"But you would not advise me to incite my poor oppressed countrymen to riot, even if the Socialists were willing to lead them ? "

"What! Those cattle ! They would run away when the
fighting began, and leave you and your followers to be
locked up. That is what I think. But they are going to
send Baumeister to argue with you on the subject. They
say that he imposes his will on everybody who listens to
him. But I must be off! Good-by, Joseph ; I thought I
would post you." And bowing to Malcha and the child, he
withdrew, but a moment afterward thrust his head in at
the door with the cry : —

"Don't forget to sample them fish. They was a great
bargain."

Joseph went on munching his bread and drinking tea,
and looking thoughtfully at the ceiling ; and Malcha, a
little reassured now that she was once more sharing her
husband's confidence, busied herself with household duties.
An hour after Ben Zion's departure Joseph was still
in the same attitude, with an empty teacup in one hand,
and a crust in the other, when there came a loud knock at
the door. Joseph arose and opened it, and ushered in a
tall, ungainly stranger, who bowed politely, and said with
a self-conscious air : —

"I am Rudolf Baumeister. Am I speaking to Joseph
Zalmonah ? "

"That is my name," said Joseph, politely motioning the
visitor to a chair ; "and there is my wife, and that is my
child Zipporah. They arrived yesterday from Russia, and
they think that they have come to a land of promise. I
trust that Mr. Rudolf Baumeister, the eminent Socialist
leader, has not come to say anything which will undeceive
them."

The visitor winced at Joseph's remark, and muttered

that he should be sorry to see any one else undeceived as he himself had been. "Perhaps I am disturbing you?" he added; and while Joseph assured him that he was not, his gaze wandered over the small and ill-furnished room, with Malcha's poor valises still scattered about it; with the humble bed, the two or three rickety chairs, the little shelves of white pine, with Karl Marx's "Kapital," and an odd volume of Turguenieff, and one or two Hebrew books standing dejectedly together, as if discouraged because their owner did not find more time to commune with them. His thin lips curled slightly as he observed the blackened entrance to the small kitchen, and as he scented the heavy and rancid odors which came in from the street.

Malcha felt an invincible repugnance to this man. It seemed to her that if she remained in his presence a minute longer she might quarrel with him. She caught Zipporah up in her arms, and, with a faint murmur of apology, opened the door and went out; nor did Joseph make any effort to detain her.

Baumeister was well, but plainly dressed, and his long nervous hands bore few marks of toil. He laid these hands flat down upon his knees, and seemed consulting them while he was waiting for Joseph to reopen the conversation.

But Joseph said nothing, and continued to munch fragments of the bread crust. At the same time he was carefully studying his visitor with a cool and patient analysis which was slightly disconcerting.

He was not pleased with his examination. Baumeister belonged to that class of men which is profoundly egotistical, without knowing it — the class which is always serving itself alone, while professing to serve others. The forehead was high, and crowned with blond hair thrown carelessly back. The gaze was shifting, and at certain moments the eyes had a wild look, like that of an animal about to attack.

There was an ominous wrinkle between the brows of this young man of thirty, which seemed to indicate a perplexed condition. It also gave a sinister look to the face. People who found Baumeister gazing intently at them felt a little shudder, and turned away hastily. He was uncanny.

And yet he was gracious, and almost charming, when he began to talk to Joseph of the business which had dictated his visit. "You speak of me as a Socialist," he said caressingly, "but, my dear overworked enthusiast, you are one yourself, without knowing it. The only difference between us is that you have not taken the Hannibal oath of eternal hatred to Rome. In other words, you do not regard Society as the enemy against which one must always fight : you are trying the persuasive processes; but they will not work ! When they have all failed you will enroll yourself with us. And perhaps you will pardon me for suggesting that, in view of your recent and complete failure to get higher wages for the men whom you have banded together, the time to join us is now ! "

He arose as he said this, and held out one hand with such a magnetic gesture of friendliness and fellowship that Joseph was strongly moved. But he kept his place opposite Baumeister, and took another bite of the crust.

"Who tells you that we have failed in our struggle for fair wages ? " he said, a moment later. "It is too early to form any conclusions about that matter."

"Indeed ! " said Baumeister with a sneer, "I should have thought that the insolence of Freier and Monach in decreeing a lock-out as the only response to your starving strikers was a pretty conclusive proof of failure. You ask for better wages, and the brutes offer you starvation. That is the response of Society — and yet you persist in clinging to Society's skirts ! But the day will come when you will be undeceived."

"Perhaps so," said Joseph; "but I do not agree with you that the greed and brutality of a few hard taskmasters are to be attributed to Society. They are able to tyrannize over us because Society is not vigilant enough. Now, I mean to wake up Society to a knowledge of the truth. Then we shall see if the wrongs will not be righted. If not " —

"What then ? " said Baumeister.

"Then you may renew your invitation. For the present I do not see my way clear to accept it."

"Poor youth!" murmured Baumeister in his softest tones. "How cruelly you will be undeceived! Society will turn upon you and rend you ; will not redeem its lying promises ; will put you in prison, and forget you there, if you are too bold. Did you ever hear of persuading a tiger ? or coaxing a boa-constrictor to let go its cruel hold ? Bah ! your bones will be cracked, and Society will suck the marrow. Come, man! throw persuasion and such idle expedients to the wind, and rally to the ' party of force ' ! With us alone victory rests ! "

Joseph arose and laid his crust of bread upon the table. His face was pale, and his eyes glowed with a strange light, which seemed to envelop and to awe Baumeister.

"No," he said with a sweeping gesture which put away the tempter from him, "I will not believe in your doctrine until the other means have been given a fair trial! I will appeal to the press, to the Legislature, to the country! I have been hearing and learning ; I believe there are hands ready to help us — we shall beat the sweaters, and destroy their slavery! But not by the means which you propose. How do we know that you are sincere ? No! Let us try the proper means first ! "

Baumeister arose now, and the wrinkle between his brows grew deeper, and his face clouded ominously. " I was told," he said, "that you are an obstinate man, and

now I am quite sure of it. Listen to me! Our associa-
tions in this city are numerous and powerful. We will
have nothing to do with appeals to the capitalistic legisla-
tors, or the bloated officials enriched by coining the blood
and sweat of the people! Do you understand? We will
have nothing to do with them. The concessions which we
gain from Society must be wrung from it by force! And
you will have to come to our way of thinking. Perhaps
we can find means to show you that we have power —
enough even to restrain you from coquetting with Society.
Good-day! I will see you again when your mind has been
changed by cruel experience," and he took up his hat and
turned to go.

"Stop a minute!" cried Joseph in a clear, ringing voice,
which caused Baumeister to turn in astonishment.

Joseph stood erect before him, white and tremulous, but
with resolution in his gaze. "Listen to me! and, when you
have heard, go and tell those who sent you what my message is. I came here five years ago, with a gold watch and
twenty-five roubles in my pocket as my whole fortune.
Like so many others of our poor refugees, I fell into this
hell of misery in the sweaters' dens! Do you know what
I have suffered? Look here!" he cried, pulling up his
coat-sleeve, and showing his emaciated arm. "Look at
that! look at my face and chest! All this in the short
space of five years! Do you know that I have worked at
making knee-pants for sixteen hours daily, under a hot
roof, with the thermometer at ninety degrees? Do you
know that I have fainted at the sewing-machine time after
time from hunger and exhaustion? Do you know that the
man next to me in a sweater's den in Hester Street, a good
young fellow from Wilnau, — he had red cheeks when he
went into that hell, — worked without rest or dinner or
supper for day after day, until he fell down at the machine,

and I took him to the hospital, and he died there, talking of green fields and fairy tales? Do you know that the girls who worked in the room with me slaved seventeen hours every day, for a dollar and a half a week? and that the slave-driver abused and insulted them besides? Do you know that I have been so starved and enslaved that I was ashamed and afraid to have my wife come here, to see my dreadful condition? Do you know that this meal of bread and tea is the most substantial one that I have tasted for days? If you know all these things, you can understand that I have been tempted to violence quite as much as you, Mr. Rudolf Baumeister, with your half-dozen steins of beer and your comfortable supper every evening. And now I tell you once for all — our paths separate here! If I had to go through again all that I have suffered in these last five terrible years, I would not yield to the temptation that you lay before me, and I would scorn and spit upon your conspiracy. Go your way, and let me and mine go ours!"

"Poor deluded Joseph," said Baumeister, with an evil smile. "I wish I could remember all this fine tirade. I should make a sensation by repeating it. I think we understand each other."

Joseph closed his eyes, and did not open them until he heard the door creak softly. Baumeister was gone.

Presently Malcha came in with the child, and little Zipporah clung to Joseph's legs, and asked him why he had been shouting.

"At a silly man, my dear," he answered. And when Malcha said she had watched Baumeister's exit, and that he had looked as black as the Devil deprived of his prey, Joseph smiled and said, —

"Either he is a fool, or I am one. Time will decide." And he asked for some more tea, and began munching his crusts of bread again.

CHAPTER IV

THE WORLD IS A WEDDING

MALCHA opened her eyes widely, and hesitated, as, cling-ing to her husband's arm, she turned a corner whence she could see the glow and glitter of Grand Street in its Saturday night gala dress. She had never seen a really large city before: the momentary glimpses which she had had of Hamburg and Glasgow could scarcely rank as views; and the hurrying throngs, the floods of electric light, the incessant yelling and bawling of the children, the squeaking and clattering of the elevated trains, as well as the uncouth language and straggling gait of some drunken ruffians who passed near her, alarmed her more than she cared to say. A look at the diminutive Zipporah, who had blotted herself almost out of sight in her mother's voluminous skirts, convinced Malcha that her fright was shared by her offspring.

Br-r-r! Clang! Clang! Clang! There was a rush of wheels rebounding from the irregular pavement, and send-ing forth showers of sparks; there was a vivid accom-paniment of horses' hoofs; then a fiery dragon seemed to hurtle forward, followed by a motley throng. Malcha turned to flee. It seemed to her that if she remained longer in that spot she might suffocate.

Suddenly she felt a gentle pull at her arm.

"Come along, Malcha," said Joseph, "unless you prefer

be late at the wedding. What! Are you afraid? The fire-engines will not eat you. They are very useful. We may need them at any time."

And he told her how great conflagrations from time to time ate out the hearts of populous districts, leaving dozens of families homeless, suffocating poor people in their beds, ruining the precious stocks of starveling mechanics, who could never get up in the world again. He told her how the firemen came bounding to the houses in flames, and how they smashed windows and hacked away doors, and bravely risked their lives to save men and women stupefied by the smoke; but how the city never by any chance seemed to do anything to protect its inhabitants against the dread contingency of fire. "A few more solidly built houses," said Joseph, "and a few less fire-engines, and we should get along just as well."

It was Saturday, the evening of the day after Baumeister's visit to Joseph, and the Jewish Sabbath. Neither Joseph nor his wife paid much attention to the ordinary observances of the Hebrew church calendar, although Malcha still had a yearning toward them. Joseph's "emancipation," as he called it, dated from the beginning of his earliest readings in general literature; but he now and then was seen in a synagogue, and was a close attendant on the wedding festivals in the humble class whose cause he had espoused. "I never see them laugh anywhere else," he once said to David. "At your theatre they sit as solemn as moujiks in a row, waiting to be whipped. But then you always play such terribly doleful pieces, that your theatre is like the valley of Lamentations!"

Malcha was glad to go to the wedding — if for no other reason, that she might see lifted from her husband's brow the cloud which had been there since Baumeister's visit. But had she been alone she would certainly have fled in terror before the accumulated obstacles of Grand Street.

Beneath the glow of double lines of electric light two steadily moving columns of people on either side of the street presented themselves to Malcha's vision. There was nothing in the types of humanity seen in them to surprise Malcha; for most of them were German or Austrian, or Polish or Russian, Jewish or Italian. Here Demos from beyond the sea holds complete control. The American of the Eastern States, the suave Middle-States man, the nervous trader of the West, are rarely seen in Grand Street. An American name upon a sign looks as odd as the Hebrew lettering would seem to the inhabitants of a quiet village in Western New York. Malcha saw with astonishment the hundreds of young men and women of her own race, stepping briskly along, some of them making a brave display of finery. They spoke the jargon of her native province; they were unchanged, save in a nameless something in the demeanor, which seemed to be communicated by the air of the New World. No trace of their old servile attitude was to be found. "They walk," said Malcha to Joseph, "as if they already owned the country."

"Everybody walks that way here," answered Joseph. "But it does not have much to do with owning the country in fact, I can tell you. Especially in the case of our people." And he sighed.

After a long walk, at the end of which little Zipporah insisted upon going to sleep, still clinging to her mother's skirts, and had to be committed, an inert mass, to Joseph's sheltering arms, they reached a narrow door in a rickety looking block, and climbed a steep staircase, at the head of which a small doorkeeper, armed with a police club, suddenly loomed up like a Jack-in-the-Box, and extended his hand, as if to take the guests' invitations, and scan them.

But his stern features relaxed into a broad grin as he saw
Joseph, and, patting him in a friendly manner on the
shoulder with the club, he escorted the little family to a
rickety settee just under the lee of a platform on which
stood a small piano, at the upper entrance to à long dancing hall with waxed and polished floor. Here he begged
them to remain until the arrival of the wedding party.

The cushioned benches on either side of this hall were
occupied by various dark-haired mammas and their brown
daughters, some of whom were dowered with lustrous
Jewish beauty; with groups of children who talked in soft
voices and made profuse gestures, and who now and then
slid into the middle of the room, and gradually warmed up
to a boisterous game, which provoked peals of laughter.

When the confusion was at its height, the small policeman came rushing in, and, pounding violently on the floor
with his club, cried, "*Set* down!" an injunction which
the children instantly obeyed, only to disobey it again the
moment the policeman's back was turned, so that they
seemed to be playing at hide-and-seek with him.

Presently the piano and the violin on the platform behind Joseph and his family ventured to hold sweet and
rhythmical discourse, and the young girls began waltzing
together, their willowy bodies turning and swaying gracefully to quaint measures which had a gypsy twang. The
girls were nearly all Russians, although here and there the
sparkling eyes and handsome forehead of a Polish damsel
were to be seen. Most of the faces would have been pretty
had it not been for the shadow of hunger upon them —
hunger for the decent food which they never succeeded in
getting; hunger for a richer and a better life than the
horrible sweaters' hell of eighteen hours of daily toil.

There was a baleful glitter in the pretty eyes of some of
these girls. It augured bad things if they were ever to be

allowed the chance to avenge themselves on the Society which had kept them so cruelly down. There were lines in their faces which seemed furrows left by tears.

Half an hour passed thus, Joseph sitting musingly silent, with little Zipporah clinging to his knee, and Malcha attentively examining every living object which came within her scope. The dark-faced violinist, a diminutive man with a handsome, sensual face and soft, caressing manners, attracted her attention, and he looked at her curiously, as if he would claim an acquaintance. But she could not remember that she had ever seen him before. She was about to ask Joseph if he remembered such a man, when the masculine members of the bridal party came hurrying in, and at once grouped about Joseph with apologies. Already eight o'clock, was it ? And the wedding appointed for seven ! But at the last minute Wolf Zablinski, the bride's father, could not be found, and they could not proceed without him ! Some one had finally located him at his carpenter's shop, where he had gone to give directions about the business of the morrow, entirely forgetting his daughter's nuptials. Now all should proceed in good order.

The ushers were neatly dressed in black, with white vests and ties, and the lapels of their coats were decorated with enormous badges. They carried tall hats in their hands, and were fond of grouping themselves at the side, near the damsels on the benches, and discussing gravely together, or striking attitudes, in all of which the badge figured for its full value.

And now came the rabbi, plainly dressed in a frock coat, a pair of striped trousers, and a hat which could certainly have furnished abundant reminiscences of 1830, if hats could speak or write. The rabbi bestowed his box of marriage paraphernalia in a corner, carefully hung the wonder-

ful hat on a nail inaccessible even to the tallest of the
children, and clothed his cranium in a small skull-cap.

He then received the greetings of the members of the
bridal party, extending to each his hand with frosty dignity,
and seeming quite relieved each time he got his hand back
again, as though he suspected some one of the party of a
design to purloin it.   Meantime the piano and the violin
were getting quite religious, and played so slowly and
mournfully that they disorganized the dancers, who resumed their seats.

In a small carpeted room, separated from the main hall
by a little antechamber, sat the bride, supported on right
and left by her mother, her aunts and cousins, and with
her brothers and sisters near her.   A dozen great candles
shed a steady light upon this little company of white-robed
women and children, and brought out in strong relief the
anxious look in the bride's plain, wholesome Jewish face.
The women talked in an undertone, and were doubtless
criticising the dress and demeanor of the male members of
the party, while the children hitched restlessly on the little
stools, and longed for the procession to begin.

At last it was coming!   Joseph and his family came to
offer their congratulations to Liza, the bride, and then to
follow in her train.   And now came the " chuppah," the
four-cornered canopy, supported by rods held in the hands
of the ushers, with the rabbi leading the way, the bridegroom, a slender young man in evening dress, following in
the wake of Wolf Zablinski, the carpenter who had forgotten that it was his daughter's wedding day.

And when this goodly company of men, their faces aglow
with the excitement of the occasion, and their costumes
glittering in the candlelight, came opposite to the women,
and halted for them to join the procession, poor Liza, the
bride, felt ready to faint with pride and delight.

She arose, and, guided by the bridegroom, took her place beneath the chuppah, whereupon the whole company set forth, and returned, with the gleam of its candles reflected in the polished flooring, to the lower end of the hall.

The rabbi took off his skull-cap, folded his left hand over his right, as if still apprehensive that some one might get it, and emitted from his lips a long ululation, followed by a gush of sibilant phrases, the whole in a high key and a strained, unnatural voice.

Holding his head thrown back, and keeping his eyes closed, he continued the weird chanting for some time, and the little company whispered to each other that "this was ancient Hebrew." The bride stood up, quite radiant, in the centre of the company, and the glare of the candles gave a blue-black lustre to the massive dark braids of her hair, crowned with orange blossoms.

At last the rabbi came out of ancient Hebrew and down to earth and to modern times again, and performed the simple ceremony with the wonted accessories of the goblet of wine, from which both bride and bridegroom drank, the rabbi crushing the glass afterwards under his heel, that no man might say thereafter, " I have drunk from their wedding glass." And at the close he handed the bride her marriage contract, duly signed and attested, with the remark, " Take care of it. It is good for one hundred and twenty-five years ! " at which time-worn joke even the wearied features of Joseph shaped themselves into a smile, and he remarked, —

" The bride is evidently not employed by the sweaters, or she would not expect to live one hundred and twenty-five years ! "

Then there were kissings and hand-shakings; and just as the bride and bridegroom were returning together to the inner chamber, beneath the august canopy of the chuppah,

David appeared in their path, accompanied by little Miryam.
Joseph and Malcha beckoned to them, but at that moment
there was a loud crash of cymbals on the musicians' platform. This was the signal that the wedding was over and
that dancing might begin, and in another minute the
fat mammas and the lean daughters, the bearded papas and
the sallow sons, and even the olive-cheeked children with
the preternaturally aged faces were off in the voluptuous
whirl, floating, circling, and returning upon their airy steps
like veritable sprites of air.   When at last the elders
sank panting and palpitating upon the benches, the children, more especially little Simon, aged four, a strapping
baby boy with a voice like a young tornado, and tiny Sarah,
an ethereal child with dark ringlets and the blackest of
eyes, seemed determined to keep it up ; and young Baruch
a carpenter's apprentice, who had been in the country for
five years, and had already learned to " talk Bowery," and
a fat girl in a red gown, seconded the children in their
noisy sport.   Baruch and his partner thumped against
the rabbi so ponderously that the good man fled precipitately.   Simon and Sarah waltzed in and out through the
bridal party with such fantastic steps and such merry peals
of laughter that the short policeman once more rushed
upon the scene with dramatic flourishes of his club, and
loud cries of *"Set* down ! " This ruffled the temper of
Baruch, who had already acquired the American impatience of restraint; and depositing his partner on a bench
he sprang for the policeman, and, disarming him of his
baton, cried, —

"Set down yourself, you big chump ! You ain't goin'
to do no settin' down here, see ? Now go and lose yourself ! "

And blows would have followed words, had not Joseph
at this juncture interposed, and reminded the pugnacious

Baruch that he would lose his share in the excellent
supper soon to follow, if he indulged in fisticuffs. Upon
this order was restored, and Joseph and Malcha managed
to reach David and the little Miryam.

"'The world is a wedding,' says our Jewish proverb,"
remarked David, when they were near enough to hear.
"And indeed it seems true, when I think of the number
of matings I have seen in this very hall. Ah! the rabbi's
business is never dull! And the untyings are rather brisk
too, I am told. Well! well! 'all the blessings of a household come through a wife.'"

David was in the best of spirits, and joked and laughed
so freely that all eyes were turned upon him. But Miryam
was sombre and disturbed by some sorrow, and from time
to time she looked upon Joseph with a strange, far-away
gaze, as if she were dreaming. And when Malcha drew
her aside, and sat down in a corner to chat, the girl leaned
her head upon the friendly shoulder and began to weep.

"What is it, Miryam?" queried Malcha. "What ails
the poor heart?"

But nothing would Miryam answer until, half an hour
later, she confided to Malcha that she had overheard a
member of the theatrical company making threats against
Joseph, and saying that he would be "done up" yet,
because he interfered with the plans of the "force party."
Malcha listened with a new fear growing in her heart, but
with a robust confidence that Joseph would be able to
triumph over all his enemies doing battle with that fear.

While the women were endeavoring to console each
other, Joseph and David climbed a second flight of rickety
stairs, in search of a man whom David wished to see. "We
shall find him in his lodge-room," he said. They paused
in a shabby antechamber, and knocked at a rude door in
the rough brick wall. A little wicket in the upper half of

the door opened, and disclosed so comely a face and such
a magnificent pair of black eyes that for an instant Joseph
was as dazzled as if he had been looking at the sun.

The wicket was instantly closed.

" Whew ! " said David with a whimsical grimace. " That
is Bathsheba. What is she doing there ? "

The door now swung open, and David and Joseph entered a long room almost the counterpart of the dancing-
hall below. It was roughly furnished with an old desk
and a few chairs which had once been ornamental, but
which would then have fetched in the auction-room hardly
a dollar for the lot of two or three dozen. In these chairs
were seated a score of dark-haired, pale-faced young men,
all of whom seemed overcome with fatigue. They were
neatly dressed, but their thin features, their scarred fingers
blackened with toil told the story. These were the unhappy " sweated " workers whose lot Joseph was striving
to ameliorate ; and they had come from their day of crushing work direct to the lodge-room to hold their weekly
meeting. There were some among them who could fight
off sleep no longer, having been up and at work since four
in the morning ; and, lying motionless in their chairs, they
looked not unlike the victims of some enchantment which
had condemned them suddenly to immobility. Their sleep
was so dense, it was the expression of such utter fatigue,
that it was almost frightful. It hurt Joseph to contemplate it.

The "lodge" was one of the innumerable Hebrew co-
operative institutions which do so much credit to the heads
and hearts of the Jewish population ; and each of the poor
waifs from Russia who owned membership in it felt that it
gave him a better grip on the future, and a partial guaranty against want. The meeting was just over, and David
found his man, and had a brief interview with him.

Meantime Joseph was contemplating the face which had so dazzled him when he caught a fleeting glimpse of it through the wicket. He could not have taken his eyes from the face if he had wished to do so. A subtle and mysterious enchantment seemed to flow from the woman's gaze, and to envelop him like a garment, as she turned her great dark eyes to him, and appeared to take a mischievous pleasure in compelling him to look at her.

The woman was standing near the door, and talking in an undertone with a tall youth, mostly legs and shoulders, who listened reverently to her. She was of medium height, exquisitely proportioned, and with the full and rounded outlines so common to Jewish beauty. Her face was faultlessly perfect, save for the note of sensualism in it, which jarred on one's sense of propriety. It took away the ethereal grace which should have been seated on such a divinely beautiful low brow, in such star-like eyes, and on the dainty lips and voluptuous chin. The black hair was combed smoothly down in the sweet old fashion universal before a perverted generation knew the folly of " bangs." The noble form was draped in a long silk coat lined with gray fur, which, thrown back from the shapely shoulders, disclosed a plain and inexpensive robe, from the hem of which coarse shoes peeped out. The hat which crowned the Juno-like head was neither new nor in the fashion, and in both cloak and hat there lay the confession of pinching poverty; for it was in the early summer, when furs were no longer tolerable, and when a fresh spring hat was an imperative need for every woman. Despite the dinginess of her attire, the splendid creature held herself as erect as if she were a queen, and Joseph were a courtier offering homage.

Joseph felt a sense of relief when David was ready to go, and when the enveloping gaze was lifted from him.

"What glorious eyes, eh?" said David as they went down-stairs.

"Who is that woman?" asked Joseph slowly.

"Bathsheba. I thought I told you. I forget her other name. She is the wife of the dark-faced fiddler whom you saw on the platform down-stairs. Yes, she is one of our own people. Her father is very rich, but has cut her off altogether because she insisted on marrying the fiddler. She married him — at a loss, so the gossips say, of a hundred thousand roubles, and they came here. At first he made a good living; now it is not so good. A nice misery ahead, eh? Well! well! 'the world is a wedding,' as I said before, and 'a myrtle in the desert remains a myrtle still.' Bathsheba is a proof of it. And is she not a fine-looking witch? I am sure that with those eyes she can see into our souls, and can read the secrets of fate. She is ambitious. They say that she is a Socialist. I'll venture to say that she was talking Socialism to that tall youth when we came in. What do you think of her?"

"I think that if she talks it with her eyes, it will be more effective than if she preaches it with her lips."

Then they went back into the dancing-hall, and rejoined the wedding party.

CHAPTER V

"JUDITH AND HOLOFERNUS"

SOFT, brooding music of flutes and violins, now murmuring as in prayer, now long drawn out as in lamentation, filled the air, and seemed to the wearied Joseph and Malcha like some strange incantation to charm them to repose.

They were seated, with little Zipporah between them, in one corner of a huge, rambling box in that old-fashioned theatre in the Bowery in which David was chief artificer of the plays. David had invited them on the evening of the wedding, and had won Joseph from his melancholy, and from his determination to engage in no amusement, by telling him that his presence would aid the cause of the Benevolent Union, which had purchased the house on that particular evening, and was giving a "benefit."

"For benevolence, you know," added David, falling back, from unconscious habit, upon an ancient proverb, "is one of the pillars upon which the world rests."

Joseph did not need to be told what benevolence was, for he had been exercising it all day, even to the minute before going to the theatre; and it was because he gave his last half-dollar to a needy pedler, who professed to be starving, that he and his were obliged to walk to the theatre. "Never mind," said Joseph, "to-morrow I shall have some money returned to me." And he would not let Malcha use any of the tiny store of cash which she had brought from Russia. "We will keep that for emergency day," he said.

Malcha smiled faintly, and it seemed to her as if that day were not far off.

The house was in shadow. From the sole gallery came rustling and murmurs, interspersed with occasional laughter and guttural remarks in jargon, which proclaimed the presence of a strong contingent of juvenile cloakmakers. Those pallid, sharp-eyed, thick-lipped, lean and scrawny slaves of the needle managed to scrape from their miserable pittances money enough to see most of David's new plays.

But now and then, when the piece was unusually long and exhausting, this juvenile contingent, having been out of bed since four in the morning, fell asleep, and then the snoring of the lines of sleepers interrupted the tirades of Hebrew heroines and the songs and recitatives of Jewish generals of olden time.

A faint odor, too, as of new cloth which is stirred and handled, characterized the throng in this gallery. This was not wonderful, inasmuch as the overworked band certainly passed seventeen hours out of every twenty-four in the "sweaters'" shops, where the huge piles of freshly made garments sent up a rank smell, poisonous to the lungs, yet carefully confined to the room, in which windows were rarely thrown open save in the excessive heats of July and August.

In the parquette there were thoughtful faces of men and women making their first experience of poverty ; men and women who found in the newly created theatre — in which the panorama of ancient Jewish life was slowly unrolled before them — much consolation for their woes in exile. Some of these faces were delicate, almost aristocratic, and accorded strangely with the poor and shabby garments which their owners wore.

Others were sordid, cunning, malicious, Oriental in feature, and almost wolfish in their manner of looking about, as if in search of prey. There were jolly families which had known how to remain jolly after being brutally expelled from their homes in Russia, marched in manacles across the frozen wastes, or herded in fourth-class cars like cattle until they reached the frontier, when they began an era of wandering in misery and affliction which might well have broken the courage of a stouter folk. Landed in America, and hurled upon a labor market ten times overstocked by oppressed beings like themselves, they yet managed to get a living, and, on rare occasions, to patronize David's establishment.

Scattered through the audience were lean, bilious men with dark flowing beards, and eyes which had a fierce glow. These were the Socialist scribes and agitators who keep up a constant crusade against capital, and who print in their tiny Hebrew papers, issued from the recesses of some East Side street, strange prophecies as to what the "party of force" will do when the time shall come. In the best corner seats sat "contractors," magnificent in new and comfortable raiment, and wearing an air of complete innocence, as if the blood of the oppressed did not cry to Heaven against them.

Nothing pleased David better than from time to time to put upon his stage a local play, in which real life was copied with as scrupulous fidelity as was consistent with freedom from criminal libel. In these plays he pilloried "sweaters" and "contractors," and pictured the horrors of the dens with such force that on one occasion a contractor left the house precipitately, fearing that if he stayed a few moments longer the audience would rise against him.

In the less expensive seats were lines of young girls, delicate of form, and with bowed frames and pale cheeks which told of prolonged toil. Their intensely black hair and eyes, their red lips, and a certain indefinable Orientalism in their features, proclaimed them as Hebrews from Southern Russia. These pretty creatures were, like the youth in the gallery, almost worn out with labor. But they managed to bestow feverish attention on every detail of the play the moment that the curtain was raised.

All these types were recognized by Joseph's practised eye as soon as the lights were turned up, and the baker's dozen of musicians in the orchestra began a curious prelude, full of quavers, to the romantic historical opera of "Judith and Holofernus," in four acts and ten scenes, with musical interludes and dances.

The old musicians bent lovingly to their work. There was one violinist with silvered hair who especially interested Joseph, for he worked with as great solemnity and pious fervor as if "Judith and Holofernus" were a holy mystery play.

And now the curtain rose, and Malcha uttered a little cry of delight, for she had never seen anything like this in Russia; the Jewish jargon theatre is not yet twenty years old; nor was she prepared for anything so poetical and charming.

In the centre of the stage stood an old man with long white hair and beard, and clad in robes of dark hue. He was addressing, in impassioned strain, reproaches to a comely woman robed in white and seated on a rustic bench, with her eyes raised to heaven with an expression of profound melancholy. The old man was Zachariah, a veteran general, and the comely woman was Judith, or "Yee-hu-diss," as the actors called her — his only daughter. Judith was, it seemed, constantly in prayer and trance, and the woful sadness which weighed her down had excited her father's apprehension. When questioned, Judith's only answer was that she must go forth into the camp of the besieging enemy, the haughty Assyrians, and that her mission could not be explained. In a wild rhapsody Judith then sang of her faith in Jehovah, and her belief that he would rid the beleaguered city of its enemies. Zachariah believed this to be madness, and shook his palms in the air, and shrugged his shoulders, as in his quaint jargon he informed his daughter that he must bring her case before the Sanhedrim. Judith continued her rhapsody, and her father went away wringing his hands, while the violins and flutes furnished a wailing accompaniment to his foreboding cries.

The curtain fell upon Yee-hu-diss and her melancholy, to rise again in a few moments disclosing the arrival of the Assyrian general-staff in a little nook overlooking the besieged town. Priests of Baal, fearfully and wonderfully attired in multicolored garments, and with yellow flax for hair and beards, brought in a monster image of their deity, and danced around it, chanting barbaric prayers, until they fell down from exhaustion. Then a tremolo of violins, accompanied by the grr-grr of the bass-viol, announced the *entrée* of " Holofernus," as he is called in the jargon. On he came, with his guard of bloodthirsty spearsmen, and his generals in matted beards, rolling their eyes in ferocious fashion.

"Holofernus" was a mighty figure of a man. He looked like the copy by a Hebrew artist of the form of an Assyrian king on some old sarcophagus. His shapely head was ornamented with a long and rippling black beard, which came to his waist. His brazen helmet was adorned with a fiery plume. His scarlet mantle was thrown back to disclose a corselet supposed to be proof against Jewish javelins. His long sword, upon the hilt of which one brown hand rested, was richly ornamented. His generals were less expensively, but properly costumed. The black-bearded projector of the theatre had at the outset invested a little fortune in costumes, and many a long-established theatre "up-town" could boast of no better wardrobe than this infant Hebrew histrionic institution.

Holofernus held a council of war, and had brought before him the child Jochanan, a Jewish captive, whom he threatened with all sorts of indignities because he would not worship Baal. But the child stood firm for the true God; and his simple eloquence, naïvely expressed in the jargon, brought down thunders of applause from the youthful knee-pants makers in the galleries.

The curtain fell once more; and when it arose again, the audience saw before it the "Sanhedrim," with the High Priest seated upon the upper seat, and the attendant priests ranged on lower benches. This venerable assemblage was composed with the greatest effect, for David had a Titian-like eye for grouping. The holy tribunal was personated by rude and ignorant men, many of whom worked at their trades by day, and added to their slender incomes by figuring at the theatre in the evenings. But the magic of artistic discipline had fashioned them into a better *ensemble* than one often sees in grand opera, where the supernumeraries get nothing like the training which David bestowed upon his.

Solemnly, in ancient Hebrew, the Sanhedrim sang a hymn, all the priests folding their hands and raising their eyes. As the last words were on their lips, Zachariah appeared, leading his trembling daughter Judith, who was to be judged by the Sanhedrim. What wicked motive lay hidden beneath her resolve to go forth among the besieging heathen? Judith in a dramatic recitative explained that she was called of God, and that she would do valiant deeds for Israel. Then the High Priest declared his faith that Judith would not betray her people. Coming down

from his lofty seat, he placed his hands upon the hands
of Zachariah, held above his daughter's head, and invoked
the divine blessing.   Then the Sanhedrim dispersed, inton-
ing its chant in ancient Hebrew.   And the whole audience
remained silent, as if reverential in presence of the heroic
memory of the woman of Bethulia, of whom all had heard,
and whose name was in the calendar of national heroines.

The next act dealt with life in the camp of the besiegers.
To the sound of the merriest music Mufti, the eunuch, and
body-slave of Holofernus, arrived, marshalling four yellow-
haired soldiers, to whom, in his quality of court jester, he
administered a sportive drill, which consisted in counter-
manding one moment the order he had given the instant
before, a proceeding eminently pleasing to the cloth-per-
fumed youth in the gallery.

Mufti was a triumph of David's imagination.   There
was something suggestive of the earliest illustrations of the
Bible in his grotesque accoutrements, and in the bulbous
head, the parchment face sown with comical wrinkles, the
puffy lips, from which depended little braided fragments
of mustache and beard.   Only an artist tinctured with the
mediæval spirit could have produced Mufti, the bibulous
slave, whose amusing capers relieved the attention of the
spectators, when the drama was getting too serious.   And
Mufti's laugh! It had a goblin-like character, an eërie
quality which made one shiver while he smiled at the buf-
foon's antics.   When Mufti came forward to the footlights,
and, stepping out of the historical play, sang, now in guttural
tones, now in highly pitched key, a "topical song" which
discussed every-day occurrences in East Broadway and in
Hester Street, the roar of applause was loud and prolonged.

Suddenly Mufti paused in his song; the words seemed
to stick in his throat; his knees knocked together. He
heard Holofernus calling him, and a moment later that

valiant general made his appearance, slightly the worse in
equilibrium, and the better in valor, for numerous potations
of strong wine. Holofernus, surrounded by his concubines,
dancing-girls, and soldiers, was in a terrible temper, and
was determined to cut off a few heads before relapsing into
a drunken slumber. Advancing to the footlights, he sang,
in a tremendous bass voice which seemed fairly to shake
the little old men in the orchestra at his feet, a song, the
refrain of which was "Blood! Blood!" Rolling his eyes
and tearing his beard, he rushed to and fro, brandishing his
sword, and making terrific passes at Mufti and the girls.
And every minute or two it was Mufti's dangerous mission
to fetch him a fresh skin of wine, the contents of which the
giant consumed with the ease of a company of politicians
doing a few "cold quarts" when work is dull and money
is easy.

Who should calm the furious savage? Who *could* do it —
who — save the beautiful Bethulian woman captured that
day just outside the lines — the woman to whom Holofernus had taken such a mighty fancy, that all the concubines,
feeling their Assyrian noses out of joint, were already plotting to destroy? Who but Judith, the lovely creature who
seemed to humor all Holofernus's fancies, and to respond
to his drunken advances? The terrified camp followers
whom Holofernus was on the point of immolating implored
Judith to save them. She persuaded Holofernus to lean,
leering like a wine-maddened satyr, on her shoulder, and
to be led to a couch, where he sank in a few moments into
dreamless slumber. The captive boy Jochanan recognized
Judith, and, believing that she had sold herself to the
enemy, spurned her from him with contempt, all of which
Judith endured for the cause's sacred sake.

Joseph thought that he recognized a familiar voice when
Jochanan spoke, and, looking more closely, he discovered

his little friend Miryam in the boyish habiliments of the
captive. He marvelled at the training which had in a few
months transformed Miryam from a gawky and frowsy girl,
turning half somersaults on piles of new clothing in the
sweating den, into this winsome actress, who was daintily
pretty in Jochanan's robe and cap. The child felt that he
was watching her, and a great throb of joy stole through
her being, for she looked upon Joseph with reverence.

While Joseph was contemplating Miryam he felt a curious sense of being himself contemplated, and, raising his
eyes suddenly to the upper box on the other side of the
theatre, his heart gave a sudden and unfamiliar leap which
surprised him, and brought a faint color to his pale cheeks.
For there sat the strange woman, Bathsheba, the handsome
wife of the dark-faced fiddler, and she was gazing at him
as she had looked when he entered the "lodge-room"
where he first saw her, with a gaze that seemed to envelop
him and take possession of his being. Instinctively he
turned to Malcha, to see if she had observed the disturbing
influence. But Malcha as yet gave no sign of a knowledge
of Bathsheba's existence, and Joseph remembered, with a
slight feeling of guilt, that he had told his wife nothing
about her.

Bathsheba was not alone. She was escorted by an elderly
man with a hair-dye complexion and a fringe of whiskers
which seemed a misfit for his features. In this singular
being Joseph recognized the owner of several houses in
which the victims of the sweaters were herded together
like animals — a mean landlord, who treated his victims
with the utmost cruelty ; and his gorge rose at him. What
was Bathsheba doing in his company? Joseph found himself strangely curious to know this.

He tried to concentrate his attention upon Miryam as
Jochanan, the captive boy, but the eyes of Bathsheba

seemed imperiously to claim him. He looked up at her again, and in her gaze he could see a sudden gleam of triumph, which gave him a small heart-pang.

Hugging to his breast little Zipporah, who had fallen asleep, he retired into the shadows in the box, and from his sheltering obscurity watched the drama as it slowly progressed to the grand culminating scene.

Judith was still in the camp, despised by Jochanan, hated by the Assyrian brood, contemned and spat upon by the concubines and dancing-girls, who envied her the strange power which she had obtained over their master. Her aged father, who had wandered out incautiously in search of her, was brought in, bound with ropes, and mocked and insulted by the pagan soldiery, who called him a spy, and demanded his life.

In his extremity the old man fell on his knees in prayer; and while busy with his supplications, the Assyrians danced round about him, calling him rude names, and buffeting him with the palms of their hands. Suddenly his eyes beheld his daughter — his precious Judith, and he arose and tottered toward her, falling at her feet, and calling her his beloved daughter.

But Judith, with harsh looks and angry gestures, ordered him away. She knew him not, and recommended that such an impostor be bound with strong cords, and kept securely until his fate could be determined. Poor Zachariah! He could not understand his daughter's hidden motive in thus denying him to his face; and so he solemnly gave her a father's curse.

All this was played with a quaint earnestness, a deliberate emphasis, and an unction not at all modern in spirit, and seeming to have been borrowed from the mystery plays of the Middle Age.

There were naïve touches of humor, of grotesque clown-

ing on the part of the Assyrians, which seemed to have
been taken bodily from those rude plays which the Russian
serfs were wont to produce before their masters at certain
festivities. Tradition, indeed, tells us that as late as the
seventeenth century a Russian Czar allowed a version
of "Judith and Holofernus" to be represented before him
by some newly arrived Germans, and laughed so heartily
at some of the jokes that the players were emboldened to
ask his favor. "Ask what you wish, and you shall have
it!" cried the delighted Czar. "Well, then, Majesty,"
said the head player, "we are Lutherans, and we would
like permission to open a Lutheran chapel in Moscow."
The Czar frowned, but kept his word. "You shall have
your chapel," he cried, "but on condition that you keep on
playing these plays to amuse me." And so it came to pass
that the pious Lutherans were unmolested in the practice
of their religion in Russia, and that they gave these
religious comedies on an extemporized stage behind the
altar rails of his chapel, for the delectation of the Czar.
Rescued from oblivion by some Jew with a taste for ferreting among the provincial archives, and carried into Rou-
mania, where the Jews were relatively free, this play of
"Judith and Holofernus" had fallen into the hands of
David's master; and after many shrewd touches by David
himself, who possessed the same talent for furbishing up
an old play that clever restorers shown in rejuvenating an
ancient painting, it was brought forth before the exiles,
thousands of miles from their native land.

And how heartily the exiles received the ensuing scenes
of the romantic story! How they roared over the humor
of Mufti, who suddenly transformed himself into an able
ally of Judith; who enabled her to visit her father's prison
in secret, to receive his forgiveness, and to free him from
his bonds! How they cheered when Mufti found time to

step out of the past into the present, and to sing them a
topical song in which there were ironical allusions to the
"sweaters"! And how eagerly, and with what awestruck
mien, they gazed at the grand closing scene in the tent of
"Holofernus."

The tyrant was prone on his luxurious couch, with his
head upon Judith's knees. His long hair and beard were
in disorder, and his gestures showed that he was inflamed
with wine. Judith lulled him to sleep with song. Then,
drawing the invader's sword from his belt, she burst into a
furious invective against him, and smote him with realistic
downward sweeping blow, while the light of the lamp went
out, and gusts of wind shook the draperies of the tent.

From the gallery of the cloakmakers came sighs and
groans and sonorous blowing of noses — expressions of
intense emotion in theatres the world over.

Another moment, and Judith's white face peered out
from the curtains, as Salvini peers after Desdemona is done
to death. Then forth she stole, with a ghastly head in
her hands, and sped away through the darkness without
uttering a word. Here the highest theatrical effect was
reached by the simplest process, and by unerring artistic
intuition.

Malcha's cheeks were aflame now. In her obscure and
muddy village in Russia she had seen nothing like this.
The lights, the music, the costumes, all were intoxicating
for her.

"Was not Miryam sweet as the little boy?" she cried to
her husband.

"Sweet enough to eat," answered Joseph, awakening
from a kind of dream, which, to his surprise, was filled with
the magnetic presence of Bathsheba.

And after the concluding scenes, in which dozens of
Hebrews in flowing robes chased scores of armor-clad

Assyrians, and smote them hip and thigh, and in which
Judith was seen enthroned near the High Priest, and
acclaimed as the deliverer of her people; when the lights
were turned down, and the quavering music died away,
Joseph went out from the theatre in a dread lest he should
meet Bathsheba in the passage-way. Curiously enough,
his heart rebelled against the woman; yet she seemed to
have established a certain influence over him. But he did
not meet her.

He was so silent on the way home, that Malcha feared
some new trouble, and questioned him, but in vain.

As they neared their humble lodgings in East Broadway
they heard a murmur of many voices, and although it was
very late they saw a throng gathered at the house's steps.

When Joseph was among them, and they had recognized
him, the murmur grew louder and louder, and swelled into
a shout, then into a series of plaints and supplications.

An old woman, bareheaded, her thin, scrawny arms bare,
threw herself at Joseph's feet, and grasped his knees.

"Help us — now, to-night!" she cried. "We are
starving."

"Yes, now, to-night," came the doleful refrain from the
crowd. "We are starving!"

Joseph gave little Zipporah to her mother, and bade her
go in at once. Then disengaging the old woman's grasp,
he leaned against the railing of the stone steps, and held
up a hand.

"Friends, neighbors," he said faintly. "Let me think a
moment!"

"No, no!" cried the old woman, clutching his knees
again; "don't think! Act! act! We are starving!"

And again the refrain came hoarsely — this time almost
menacingly — from the crowd: "We are starving!"

CHAPTER VI

THE NIGHT—MARCH

MALCHA hastened in, and placed little Zipporah in bed.
Then she came out again, and, locking the door, went into
the passage-way's entrance, from which she could watch
the movements of Joseph and of the mob.

It was indeed a mob, and it seemed to her that it was
hostile to her husband. An old hag with blackened teeth
and bleared eyes stood near her on the steps, and from time
to time stretched out her skinny arms, as if hurling a malediction upon the pale but impassive Joseph.

Although it was now almost midnight, the quarter was
as animated as at mid-day. A splendid summer moonlight
threw an enchantment over the scene, which by day might
have seemed sordid and repulsive.

The throng extended across the street, parting now and
then, with menaces and clamor, to let the horse-cars through.
It was increased every moment by delegations from the
side streets. Men and women and children came screaming, imploring, cursing, and quarrelling — all moved by the
mainspring of hunger; all concentrated on one aim, — on
Joseph the helper, the rescuer.

Pale toilers, who had not been under the open sky for
weeks before, rushed forward, brandishing their shears, and
crying for bread. Stalwart men, who shuffled along as if
crushed by the burden of work heaped upon them, came

leading their children, and listening anxiously for Joseph's words. Old women, half-nude, with thin gray hair streaming in disorder, and their withered cheeks aflame with anger, ran hither and yon, making wild gestures and uttering strange cries. And hundreds of half-starved girls, with their thin frames prematurely bowed and broken by sixteen hours of daily toil, were walking to and fro, also listening, as if awaiting the word of command to dart forth on a mission of vengeance and fury and spoliation.

The victims of hunger were ripe for any mischief.

A word, and they would light the torch of the incendiary.

A gesture, and they would sack the shops of the sweaters, and tear the contractors in pieces.

A cry, and they would fill the palaces of the great city with desolation !

Joseph noted all this, as his keen gaze wandered over the throng. He also observed that, on the outer edges of the gathering, Socialist emissaries, the adroit representatives of the compact little party which had given him much trouble, were freely scattered ; and that they were actively engaged in stirring up the people against him. The old woman at his knees was right. He must act, not think.

He raised his hand to enjoin silence. As he did so, a carrot whizzed past it, and at the same time one of the Socialists darted back into the crowd. Joseph flushed with anger, but he knew the folly of losing his temper just then.

"Friends," he said in his clear, resonant voice, which always imposed attention, " you tell me that you are starving ; and yet you can afford to throw away food ! How is this ? "

And stooping, he picked up the offending carrot, and held it high above his head, and close to the lamp, where all could see it.

"Shame! Shame!" cried a loud voice, which Joseph instantly recognized as Ben Zion's. "They are throwing things at Joseph, at our Joseph — without whom the sweaters would have drunk our blood long ago! Shame!"

A responsive roar from the crowd showed that Ben Zion had struck the popular chord. "Yes, yes, down with the Socialists!" cried hundreds of voices. "They can give us nothing but advice; Joseph, our Joseph, will give us bread!"

"Let the dogs of Socialists throw anything else, and we will fry them in their own grease!" shouted Ben Zion.

"Yes, yes; in their own grease!" answered the mob.

Tears coursed slowly down Joseph's pale cheeks, as he gazed at the rows of upturned faces in front of him — faces filled with serene confidence that he could conjure the demon of starvation. Getting free with no little difficulty from the suppliants who hung about him, he mounted the steps and prepared to address the throng.

A hand touched him lightly on the shoulder. Without looking he knew that it was Malcha's hand.

His courage grew.

"My dear friends," he said, "you tell me that you are hungry. So am I. You are poor and wretched. So am I. Each one of you is a victim of the miserable sweaters. So am I. You have only bread to eat, and not much of that. Come and look in my cupboard, and you will find nothing but bread there, and precious little of that."

"Yes, yes, we know, Joseph," cried the plaintive voice of a woman; "we are not blaming you: we know you are poor. But something must be done about the lock-out, or we shall all perish like cats in a deserted town. And you are the one to do it."

"That's right; stir him to action!" cried a mellow voice which sent the blood leaping through Joseph's veins, and made him clench his teeth. "Joseph is too soft: he needs stirring up; then he will be a great leader. Tell him the truth! Force against force! That is the only doctrine!"

It was the voice of Baumeister.

"It would be an imbecile doctrine for us!" cried Joseph. "And only an imbecile can utter such sentiments now and here."

A mocking laugh, which had a Mephistophelian ring to it, came back from the crowd. Baumeister had played his card, and he hastened to get out of the throng and into a comfortable shadow.

"Yes, Joseph, you are too soft, too yielding!" cried the old hag who had fallen at his knees. "If you would lead this company in front of Freier and Monach's place to-morrow morning, the damnable sweaters would sing a different song about their lock-out. Why did they take our work away from us? To make us more humble afterwards? God! were we not slaves already? Must we crawl? I say, demand that they give our men their work back again, and threaten to knock them on the head if they don't!"

"That's right, Mother Petwosky! You Poles understand how to make the dogs yield. 'Joseph is too soft!'" shouted half a dozen voices.

"We formed the Union to get our rights, but not to fight manufacturers!" said Joseph in a firm voice. "It is you who are too soft! You are soft-headed to talk such nonsense!"

A little ripple of laughter came and went; then the angry roar rose again.

"Bah! what do they care for the Union?" cried the old hag, wagging her grizzled head, and waving her skinny arms. "Much they are afraid of your Union! Come and see for yourself, Joseph, how much the landlords and contractors are afraid of you! Come and take a look at Mother Levitsky — the woman whom you tried to help! Poor soul! you made her landlord promise that he would not turn her out until you could raise the money to pay her rent, didn't you ? "

" Well," said Joseph, feeling a sudden wave of anger mounting to his brain, " and did he dare ? "

" Did he dare ? Oh, no ! Very good ! Did he dare ? Did he dread your mighty Union ? Come and see ! You will find that he has put Mother Levitsky and all her brood out into the street ! That's what you will find ! " And the beldame, raising her voice to a shriek, executed a kind of furious war-dance, snapping her fingers and brandishing her arms ; and finally screaming, " Yes, Joseph ! you are too soft ! " she fell down exhausted, and was dragged away by two compassionate girls.

Joseph could not stem the wave of anger. It was resistless now. It seemed to fill his eyes with blood. For a minute or two he saw everything red. At last he managed to stammer, —

" Is this true ? "

" Ha, ha ! " said a dozen shrill voices, " he asks if it is true ! Let him come with us, and see the old woman most likely lying in the dirt of the street. Much they care for his Union ! Ho, ho ! "

Joseph turned suddenly to Malcha, and urged her to go to the child. " Do not fear for me ! " he said ; " these people will do as I say. I shall come back presently." Then he stepped briskly down to the head of the throng.

" Come on ! " he said, " let us get at the rights of this ! " And the hungry leader, with fifteen hundred hungry and enraged men and women behind him, set out for Ludlow Street, where the rumored eviction of Mother Levitsky, for whom Joseph had so recently interceded with her landlord, was to be proved true or false.

Now that the throng had Joseph at its head, it became silent. Its movements were no longer disorderly, but in concert, as in obedience to one will. The Socialists followed at a distance. They knew that Joseph's sharp eyes would detect them, and order them out of his ranks.

Baumeister, in his cosily shadowed corner, chuckled as he saw the departure of the angry and resolute company.

At the angle of every street fifty or a hundred pale, gaunt men and women joined the procession. When they arrived in front of the tenement house in Ludlow Street where Mother Levitsky had made her home, there were at least twenty-five hundred men and women — starving cloakmakers and their wives and sons and daughters — in this company.

They went quickly. Hunger and anger are swift movers of human feet.

At last they stood before the double tenement house where the dilapidated Lares and Penates of the Levitskys had been set up. The landlord — himself a Russian Jew, and a dealer in strong waters and cheap politics, as well as patron of one or two of the worst sweating-shops in the quarter — lived on the premises.

Many windows were still alight, and in the upper stories the click-clack of sewing-machines was heard. From the narrow and darkened hallway came the nauseous odor of stale fish and fried onions and cabbage. Two little children were asleep on the doorstep, one mite leaning its curly head upon the shoulder of the other. A slight push would have sent the diminutive twain into the gutter.

"Where is the old fox?" said Joseph in a voice vibrating with passion. "Let us know why he does not keep his promises to me!"

"Yes, let us know, and let us knock him on the head!" said hoarse voices in the crowd.

"Silence there!" commanded Joseph. "No threats. We are going to try a case, not to execute anybody. Let me hear no more talk about violence."

"You hear what Joseph says, you ferocious demons!" said the mellow voice of Ben Zion. The pedler had crept to the front, and now fancied himself one of Joseph's lieutenants.

"Let a dozen of you come with me up to the third floor, where the Levitskys lived," said Joseph. "If they are not there we shall then know what to do."

Ben Zion, whose newly acquired authority none seemed to dispute, selected six men and six women, and they followed Joseph into the hallway, carefully stepping over the sleeping children.

The stairs were of the rudest description; they were unlighted, save by one wan gas-jet, shedding a mournful flicker upon the cheap ungarnished walls, which exhaled unhealthy odors.

The noise made by the hundreds of shuffling feet outside, and the clamor of tongues, had awakened the landlord, who was badly frightened, but who had summoned all his cunning for an event which he knew must be disagreeable.

His flat was on the second floor in front, and he stumbled out of his door into the passage just as Joseph and his escort appeared on the landing. The landlord was but half dressed, but he carried a thick stick in his right hand. He was a small man, of powerful build, with a capacious head, well set on stalwart shoulders. He would have shown fight to ten or twenty of the underfed and overworked cloakmakers, but he knew how dangerous it was to trifle with a mob.

"Be careful, Simon," whispered his wife over his shoulder; "there are hundreds of them in the street, and they mean mischief."

"Who are you, and what do you want at this time of the night ? " said the landlord, as Joseph stepped forward and faced him under the gas-jet.

"Simon," said Joseph, "what have you done with Mother Levitsky ? I hear strange stories about you — that you have broken your promise to me. Say that it is not true, and I will believe you and go home at once, and take all these good people with me."

Simon retreated a step or two, and gripped his stick hard. "What business is it of yours ? " he said with a sneer. "A pretty fool I was to listen to you — one beggar giving a guaranty for another beggar." He retreated another pace or two. "Go and find out for yourself what has become of the old woman. And no more meddling with my affairs, do you understand ? I have a telephone. In ten minutes I can have a dozen policemen here. Then you would all run for your lives. You, Joseph, would get into prison perhaps. Now go home, or I will use the telephone."

He was backing into the door when the strong arm of Ben Zion caught him and hauled him forth as if he had been a man of straw.

"In ten minutes, hey ? " said Ben Zion, grimly contemplating the trembling Simon. "Yes, and in ten minutes, if I were to throw you into the crowd down there, where would you be ? "

"You would not dare to murder me ! " said Simon, whose teeth chattered. "You would be hanged."

"Nonsense ! what is one sweater more or less ? 'When a horse falls down, they take another in his place.' "

This cruel application to Simon's case of the brutal saying of the sweaters, when an exhausted workman begged for mercy, used the landlord's courage up. He became limp and pale. "What do you want me to do ? " he stammered.

"Must I lose all my money because old women and girls come here to live without paying rent?"

Ben Zion took a fresh hold of Simon, and drew him after him up the staircase to the third floor. "You have as good as confessed," he said, "that you have thrown the old woman out to die! Come with us; and woe to you if you have done wrong!"

Joseph had already sprung up the stairs, and knocked at the door of the Levitsky flat. He heard the whir of a sewing-machine in an inner room, although it was now nearly one o'clock. There was delay in opening; and for several minutes nothing was heard but the feverish breathing of the little company, and the whine of Simon as Ben Zion shook him.

Presently the door was opened by a pale, fluffy-faced man with a black beard, and the company rushed in without apology. A gawky girl of ten, much frightened, came forward with a kerosene lamp.

Joseph gazed about him in astonishment. Every vestige of occupation by the Levitskys had vanished. These were new lodgers; this was different furniture, if two old boxes, one broken chair, and some very unsavory-looking mattresses could be called furniture.

He strode into the inner room. It was faintly lighted. Three pallid girls were sewing with sleepy gestures, near an old stove not yet set up. A pile of finished knee-pants, and of cloth for making others, stood in the centre of the apartment. A sickening odor, as from a hospital ward, arose, and seemed to flee in affright before the fresh air which had entered when the door was opened.

On the pile of cloth lay a girl six or seven years old, breathing heavily. Her face was flushed. As Joseph approached her an old woman stepped in front of him, as if to hide the child.

Joseph pushed the woman aside, and took a keen look at the girl. Then he drew back in fright. "That child has either scarlet-fever or small-pox," he said. "Can't you see it for yourselves? Get her out of here at once, or the Health Board will be here in the morning."

He rubbed his eyes. The Levitskys, infirm old mother and two grandchildren, weak and unable to support themselves, had been banished, and in their place a typical "sweater's shop" had been established. And here, enthroned on the piles of cloth to be made into garments, which would soon be scattered through the country, was the foul contagion which might be the means of slaying scores of innocent people.

Joseph shuddered. The woman, reassured by the sound of her native jargon, and thinking him some kind of inspector, caught up the child, hid its face with her apron, and retreated to a dark corner.

"Mother Levitsky has been put out, with her grandchildren, and Simon has got another sweat-shop established here, with greenhorns to work for him for nothing and board themselves," cried Ben Zion.

At this juncture Simon with a desperate effort wrenched himself free, and sprang out of the room and down the stairs. "He is going to call the police," said one. "He dares not," said Joseph.

The new tenants knew nothing of Mother Levitsky. Never had heard of her. They had come to the house that day; had been in the country but ten days. With a fresh warning about the child, Joseph and his band withdrew.

On the stairs a feeble hand plucked at Joseph's coat. He looked down, and in the dimness discerned the hunger-pinched face of one of the Levitsky grandchildren — a thin slip of a girl.

"I did not dare to come sooner," she whispered. "But

Simon has gone in now, and shut his door. Grandmother lies out in the yard at the back of the houses and " — here the little voice quivered — "you must come quick, for she's been taken very bad."

"Yes, yes, we are coming! Run ahead and show us the way!" cried Joseph, feeling ashamed that he had not believed the cloakmakers at once. They had shrewdly allowed him to make the search, hoping that it would arouse him to rage. "It is true, then!" he said to Ben Zion; "the dog has thrown her into the street."

"Then let us do the same to him!" said Ben Zion; but Joseph held him back, and they all went silently down to the ground-floor, and through the narrow passage to the little courtyard at the back, overlooked by a forbidding rear tenement, filled with sweaters' dens. Here, with no light but that of the moon to shine on the thin and wretched pallet which could not keep her wasted form from the dampness of the foul yard, lay Mother Levitsky — dying. At the head of the miserable couch were piled the few articles left this starving family, — a forlorn bureau with but one sound leg, a broken chair, and a shabby trunk filled with rags.

"Bring lights!" cried Joseph, "lights here on Simon's work! See how Simon the sweater treats his victims!"

The throng began to surge in. Lights were produced, and Joseph, bending tenderly over the dying woman, tried to comfort her. "You shall be moved at once, to my own house!" he said. Then he thought of his own terrible situation, — nearly penniless, without proper food, and with two or three thousand people clamoring at his back. It almost crushed him.

"*Armes kind!*" sighed the poor creature; "you cannot help me. I am gone; but do something for the girls, if you can!"

The last words were exhaled like a long sigh. Joseph was holding the woman's head on his arm. Suddenly he uttered a cry and drew back.

Mother Levitsky was dead. She was already in her last agony when the small grandchild had sought for Joseph, and he had arrived only in time to receive her final sigh.

" It was the shock that killed her," said one of the wailing girls. "This morning, when he put us out, he would not wait for you to help us, Joseph. He said that we were beggars — and that you were a beggar too."

And then arose through the night the weird Jewish wail for the dead, while pious hands covered the dead woman's face.

"Here!" cried Joseph in a furious voice. "Bring Simon here! Burning would be too good for such a wretch, but we must use no violence!"

There was a crash as the landlord's door was burst open; and in a minute or two Simon, still only half dressed, and followed by his screaming wife, was dragged down to the courtyard, and placed before his victim. Ben Zion stood guard over him with his own stick, which he had wrested from him.

"Simon, this is your work!" said Joseph solemnly. "The woman is dead. You killed her. Now listen to me. No bodily harm shall be done you." Here a roar of dissent from the mob made Simon wince. "But look me in the face, and listen. Here am I, a starving man, with two thousand starving people at my back. We have formed a Union to combat such creatures as you, and we will fight you to the death! We swear eternal enmity to you, and all such as you!"

And from the throng in the courtyard, the passage, and the street outside, came the echo, hoarse and terrible, " Eternal enmity to you, and all such as you!"

"I can't help it," said Simon sullenly. "What have I to lo with your bread and meat? Am I to blame because this old soul couldn't pay her rent? Must I keep hospital?"

"Liar!" said Joseph. "You steal the bread out of the mouths of old and young alike. Now go! Ben Zion, see him safely to his door!"

The people shrank away from him as he passed, white and shaking. Joseph's solemn manner awed them all.

"Take up the body!" said Joseph, "and let us bear it away with us! We will find a decent asylum for it, and for these poor waifs."

The body was borne tenderly into the street, and the bearers took their position at the head of the column.

"And now!" said Joseph, "here is my plan. In the treasury of your Union there is still forty dollars. You may come with me there at once, take that money, and buy bread for all. With bread we can live, and we will begin the active fight against the sweaters, and fight them to the death!"

"To the death!" responded the crowd hoarsely.

Joseph omitted to tell them that these forty dollars were his own, the salary which he had declined to draw as officer of the Union, when its poor treasury was so nearly impoverished. His heart was light at the thought of the temporary relief which he could offer.

The throng took up its march again, with the dead woman borne at its head.

A faint light in Simon's window indicated that he was watching them.

CHAPTER VII

THE PANORAMA OF SUFFERING

No officer crossed the path of the angry cloakmakers
that night. The soft May moonlight shed a mysterious
splendor over the hungry throng, as it went silently, with
Joseph and the bearers of the dead woman at its head,
through highways and byways, now disappearing in the
shadows cast from the old-fashioned brick houses with
their Doric columns and ornamental entrances, now showing, a black and winding ribbon, against the silver of the
moon's rays.

Joseph hardly knew whether he were really leading this
throng of melancholy refugees to the office of the Union,
to give them the promised money, or marshalling them
to a grand attack upon their enemies the sweaters. His
veins seemed filled with fire; his hands were clinched; all
the world about him swam in a red mist.

Had a luckless contractor, manufacturer, or landlord of
the type of Simon, appeared in the path at that time,
Joseph would no longer have tried to keep his followers
from violence.

As he trudged along he felt a hand on his arm. The
old woman who had tried, earlier in the night, to excite
him to violence, was beside him.

"Let me take *her* home," she said in a weird whisper.
"I live near by. I will give her all the shelter she wants

— until the last one. We will see to the burial. My man
don't object. And he will go and pick up the grandchildren's things to-morrow. We have the little ones with
us now."

Joseph rubbed his eyes. "True," he said; "I had forgotten the small folk. And neither you nor they have a
cent, I suppose. Well, we will send you some money from
the Union. And as for this poor woman," he said, pointing to the rude bier, "do as you think best."

The old hag stooped and kissed his hand.

Presently they came to the tenement in which she lived.
The whole rattle-trap, from top to bottom, was tenanted by
Russian-Jewish cloakmakers, so there was none to object
to the repose of Mother Levitsky under the roof, on the
way to her final resting-place.

The procession halted; the body was carried in; and
then the great company set off at a quicker pace for the
Union, where they were to receive the money which meant
bread — bread, and momentary relief from the gnawing
torture of hunger.

"Suppose that he should be deceiving us, and that he
has no money?" suggested one. "Joseph always was such
a dreamer!"

"There's a bakery over there," sighed another. "See!
the beast is just taking down his shutters! Yott! how fat
and comfortable he looks! Suppose we took his whole
stock? He would not dare to say anything. And we could
pay him afterwards — if Joseph really has any" —

"Yes, that would be better than waiting," snarled an old
man in a greasy hat, with corkscrew curls dangling in
front of his ears. "Come on; let's rush the baker! I've
seen it done in Poland. And there was only a few of us
who got three months. I don't mind leading!"

There was a shout and a rush, from which the more intelligent men and women held back. But suddenly the would-be rioters found themselves confronted by Ben Zion and Joseph.

The former was armed with the stick which he had wrested from Simon, and he laid it over the heads of the mob without mercy. This energetic action, seconded by Joseph's entreaties, brought the sacking expedition to an ignoble close, and Joseph succeeded in getting the whole company to the door of the Union's office without any breach of the law.

The Union's headquarters was a small basement in Cherry Street, equipped with a desk, an ancient safe, and a few broken stools.

Dawn was just flushing the east with daintiest pink as Joseph unlocked the door and let the leaders in. The women seated themselves on the steps and sidewalks, and the half-grown boys pressed in and began to jump and gambol about the broken stools.

Here two policemen were drowsily killing time, and they strolled up, swinging their clubs, and listening to the babble of the women. "What's going on here?" said one.

The women clamored for Joseph, and he came out, bareheaded, with his hands full of small money. "What is that you want?" he asked, turning his plaintive gaze on the officers.

"Nothing. Thought it was a fire," said one, eying Joseph curiously.

"It's worse than that," said Joseph, in his best English. "These people are starving. Their employers lock them out because they will not accept the very meanest wages and the very longest hours. So they are starving, and I am giving them what is left of the funds of their Union — to keep up the fight a little longer. When that is gone " — His voice faltered. He was not speaking to the policemen. He was communing with himself.

And still the red mist swam before his eyes.

"Well, it's pretty hard annyway," said the policeman. "Get your money and go home, and don't be blockin' up the way, you people. And maybe," he added, turning to Joseph, "if ye'd get a note in the papers, ye might get some kind people to help ye for a while."

"Help!" repeated Joseph despairingly, "who would help three thousand people — like us? How can we ask?"

"Well, maybe there's manny a one would help ye now. How do ye know till ye thry? Sure, the rich people never know you're alive unless ye make yourselves heard. If they was fifty thousand av ye here, now, instead of two or three thousand, how much would they know about it in Fifth Avenyer? I'm thinkin' that if ye'd ask help for your Union, ye might get it."

"I will try," said Joseph simply. He caught at this faint hope as the drowning man grasps at the straw, or the bubbles made by his own struggles.

Half an hour later the throng had vanished, after renewing its oath to fight the sweaters to the death. Money enough had been distributed to buy sixteen or seventeen hundred loaves of the poor bread which is sold so cheaply in the cloakmakers' district.

Ben Zion and the officers of the Union had departed, leaving Joseph seated before the old desk, with the sunshine stealing through a hole in the ragged curtain to light up his pale, tired face.

It was only after much entreaty that they had prevailed upon him to keep two dollars of the money (his own) for pressing personal needs. If they had not insisted, he would have gone home to Malcha without a penny in his pocket.

When Joseph was quite alone, he fell to reviewing his

recent past, and it arose before him in a series of dramatic tableaux, as if he had been witnessing it on the stage of a theatre.   He saw himself crossing the bridge between Germany and Russia, on that cold, dark night in 1887, when he had turned his back forever upon the petty and provoking tyranny of Russian officialism.

In the distance a sonorous bell was striking the midnight hour.   The sentry, whom Joseph had bribed, stared straight at him when he passed, but made no effort to stop him. He hurried on over the bridge, stumbling against a loosened plank, holding his breath and looking back in fear, while his heart-beats sounded like trip-hammer blows in his frightened ears.

No one came ; he was free — free from the hell of the "Pale !"   And he took off his fur cap and waved it above his head, and shouted as he ran swiftly toward Germany. Once well out of gun-shot of Russia he shook his fist at the Czar and all his people, and went forward, dreaming of the America of which he had read in the works of Zimmerman — the land of no passports, no police spies, no dungeons for political offences ; a land where liberty and work for all was to be found.

How many incoherent ideas went spinning through his head in that midnight hour !   He would achieve fame and fortune in America !   He had a good voice ; he could write for Hebrew papers; he could teach ; and soon good little Malcha, who had connived at his flight, could rejoin him.

And why had he fled ?   Then arose before him the mental picture of the friend coming to warn him that he had been "badly noted" by the authorities for reading Karl Marx's "Kapital."

Badly noted ! that meant that unless he were circumspect in the highest degree in word and deed, he would one day be seized and sent hundreds of miles away from home, and thrown into prison at the caprice of some quarrelsome official.

It meant that he must become the slave of the police spy if he remained at home; that his liberty would depend on the bribes which he was able to pay.

No, he would go away; he would drift with the current of exiles crowding all the channels of exit from the "Pale." But if he disclosed his projects of departure to any save his wife he might be detained. And then came before him the picture of his departure from his father's door, the lingering looks which he cast behind him, and the darkness which seemed to settle over the winter landscape when his old home was left behind.

Now the scene changed to America, whither he had come by Hamburg and Liverpool. He saw himself wandering in Brooklyn in search of work, and finally toiling day after day at unloading sugar from steamships, under the lee of a vast refinery. He saw the boss of the gang one morning approaching him, and saying, with a thinly disguised sneer, "You ain't a laboring man. You can't stand dis work. Say, why don't you go and write for de papers?" Joseph dimly understood, and left.

Then followed fleeting pictures of days and nights of misery, on which Joseph little cared to look. His knowledge of English was increasing; his stock of money was daily slipping away. And now he was himself in "Misery Market," with only a small sum and his gold watch in his pocket. He must have work, and he went to a fellow-exile, who had settled in Eldridge Street, to see how he was getting on, and to ask his advice. Ah! how clearly and with what deadly sharpness now arose before him the pictures of the next few months of his life, — the sickening search for work, the wretched lodgings, the repulsive food, the failure to find anything to do.

At last, when he had sold his two fur coats, his fur cap, and was beginning to despair, he was told "to become an operator." What was that? Ah! he must be introduced to a boss! Quick! Into Ludlow Street, to the top floor of a wretched house, and there he was presented to a "boss."

The face was familiar. Joseph looked at the man; the man inspected him. The "boss" used to be a servant of Joseph's uncle in Russia. Now he was in the noble industry of manufacturing knee-pants for the million. Joseph should have the privilege of learning this inestimable trade. It would cost him fifteen dollars to learn, and in four weeks he would be an accomplished operator. And he must have a machine, on which he must pay three dollars.

Joseph accepted, and sold his few remaining treasures for money to instal himself in what he dimly began to perceive was nothing more nor less than a "sweater's hell."

The boss obligingly set Joseph at work stitching pockets. At the end of four weeks Joseph knew nothing of this great, this ¦magnificent industry which the generosity of the boss had permitted him to learn, except stitching of pockets and bands.

Then the boss grandiloquently remarked, "I will pay you a dollar and a half a week, until you learn a little better;" and Joseph, crushed in spirit, accepted.

Ah! how terrible were the remembrances which now arose before him — the remembrances of that sweater's den, with the sweater, his wife, his three children, and four boarders, living there day and night, in an inexpressible and abominable atmosphere, and crowding in there by day, from long before dawn until ten at night, eight operators on machines, and seven finishers and a presser!

How the spectacle of this horrible life of rending and grinding toil, in which he and all the others were treated like machines, made him groan in spirit! He asked a question of the sweater, and learned by the response that he was no longer a man, with an identity, a name, but that he had a number, like a prisoner; that he was "number six." And as he contemplated this picture, it seemed to him that he could feel his fingers tightening around the boss's throat.

It was "dull season" for three weeks after Joseph entered the sweater's hell. The sweater did not volunteer to raise his wages. That never happened in sweaterdom! Oh, no! A kick, a scuffle, and a lowering of wages — that was the rule.

By and by the busy season came. Joseph watered the cloth over which he bent with his tears every day. The tyrannies which he saw all around him froze his blood. They alarmed him for his own safety. He felt that he was losing his manliness.

There he sat, in his corner, near the dirt-begrimed window, toiling to make a dozen knee-pants for thirty-five cents. He was on piece-work now, and he lived on bread and apples.

Joseph was a slow operator, and the first day of his piece-work he made seventeen cents. Hour after hour he toiled without rest, until the humming of his machine seemed to eat into his brain.

One day he cried out, "This is not a life for men; we are animals here!"

The boss grew angry, and said that he allowed no speech-making on his premises. He told Joseph to "get out."

"Give me my pay," said Joseph.

"A man who is discharged must wait a week for his money," answered the boss with his evil smile. And Joseph had to starve for a while as penance for his independence.

When he came for the money at the end of seven days he was so weak with hunger that he could scarcely stand.

The boss threw his miserable pittance in his face, and told him to begone.

Joseph had had a touch of starvation, and he did not like it. So in a day or two he was in the den of another "sweater," still in Ludlow Street. And this was the picture of the life in that second hell which now arose before him.

Four grimy and unventilated rooms, in which lived, ate, and slept the sweater, his wife, and four children, his brother-in-law, his wife, and two children, and three boarders. These boarders were poor wretches who were kept in practical slavery. The sweater would not let them out of his sight, lest they should learn of better things and desert him. Once a week they took the air, walking, pale phantoms, in some of the side streets in the quarter, but never getting beyond the sweater's tether.

They slept in dusty recesses in the kitchen, and arose long before dawn, and went into the hall while the women and children washed and dressed, and prepared the abject apology for breakfast which was set before them on the edges of their machines. How the passage of all these scenes before Joseph's inner vision tormented his soul!

It was like the reopening of an old wound.

Here Joseph was told that he would receive " forty cents a dozen for knee-pants." He went courageously to work, with a partner; Joseph preparing, the partner stitching.

His associate was a pale young Hebrew from Wilnau in Russia — a youth of nineteen, with high brow and handsome eyes.

But the cruel toil had, in less than a year, so bent and broken him that he looked like an old man. He spoke but little; now and then he sighed deeply. He would never stop for dinner, which was usually brought in from a neighboring restaurant — a miserable mess of poorly cooked food.

"I am not hungry," he would say, and he would go on stitching, stitching, and guiding with trembling hands the stuffs on which his tears often fell. It was in his behalf that Joseph cried out one day against the long hours — from five in the morning until ten at night — exacted by the sweaters. But the boss laughed in his face.

"I can get five hundred to take your place by shaking my shears out of the front window." And Joseph knew that it was true.

One day, when the heat was stifling in the den, Joseph was startled to see his "partner" lying with his head on his work, and his poor toil-scarred hands resting helplessly on the cloth.

He ran to him and raised him up, and the eyes opened for a moment, and the lips babbled of Wilnau, and of green fields, and of the good mother, and the quaint little village far away; then they closed again.

"He's done for," said the boss. "Take him to a hospital."

And it was in a hospital that the wretched youth died the next day. In his dream Joseph saw the vision of this death-bed, beside which he had knelt, and he shuddered in his sleep. The man had fallen under the lash, as slaves fell, and he had not had the strength to rally.

"Driven to death," was the epitaph which Joseph would have liked to place upon his humble headstone.

The dead youth's cousin came and claimed his wages — eight dollars and forty cents. That was his estate.

When Joseph arose from his long revery beside the bed of this martyr to the tyranny of brutal employers, his brain boiled with indignation. He wanted vengeance for the dead, for himself, for his insulted manhood, for the women and children perishing in the cesspools of civilization.

He went back to work. But he now began boldly to agitate for reform among the sweaters. A Hebrew "labor paper" had been started, and at its office meetings were held at which the victims of the Russian persecution met to compare notes. There Joseph found others, galled like himself by the sweater's yoke, and he began to talk of organizing for mutual protection.

The others looked at him. Then they began to talk of the "social revolution."

It did not take Joseph long to discover that they were not ripe for unions and the legal methods of strikes, but that they had been seduced by glittering descriptions of some mysterious social cataclysm, at the close of which they would be called upon the scene to divide up the vast riches of the millionaires of America.

Their imaginations were inflamed, and their ignorance of the new conditions of life in America, and of any language save their own, as well as the unnatural nervous state in which their excessive toil constantly kept them, rendered them peculiarly susceptible to belief even in the most absurd theories.

Joseph turned from these unhappy creatures in sorrow, and for a long time sought in vain for a way to check the tyranny from which he suffered. One day he strayed into a meeting held by the Hebrew branch of the Socialistic Labor Union in East Broadway.

The first speaker whom he heard was a well-educated man, who advocated the principles of trades' unionism. He said, "The only hope for labor lies in organization."

These were Joseph's sentiments exactly. He took the floor and said, "Are there any knee-pants makers here?"

A few men came forward timidly. But Joseph inspired

them with his own courage. They formed a Union then and there. Their first meeting was held on the following Saturday, with fifteen members, and Joseph was its secretary and treasurer.

The initiation fee was seventy-five cents; weekly dues were five cents. The men liked these conditions, and the Union kept growing.

Victims of sweaters in other branches of the trade started Unions. So Joseph welded all these together, forming the United Hebrew Trades. Now he began to feel strong, for he had a compact body at his back.

Meantime he worked steadily at his trade. One day the boss bestowed an evil smile on him, and said, "You'd better go to the United Hebrew Trades, and ask for employment there."

Joseph said, "I will take your advice." He left the sweater's hell, and devoted himself for a time exclusively to the union, working without salary. When he could starve no longer, he would go back to work — now as operator at cloakmaking, now as maker of jerseys, suffering petty vexations and tyrannies, and sometimes earning eight dollars per week by toiling from dawn until ten P.M.

Presently the bosses knew him as an agitator, and then they insulted and imposed upon him. One day, at a factory in Ludlow Street, his soul revolted against the boss, who was always drunk, and whose favorite pastime was kicking men out of the line on Saturdays, and then refusing to pay them until the following week because they had not kept in line.

Joseph thrashed this monster within an inch of his life, and left without claiming his own wages.

And so he went on for weeks, rebelling against the abominable tyrants, and receiving his discharge from places as soon as he was known as an agitator. Once,

after seeing an old man deprived of his work under circum-
stances of great cruelty, he went around to the Monday
evening labor meeting, and there found a delegation of
cloakmakers asking to be admitted to the United Hebrew
Trades.

Joseph interested himself in the lot of these poor people,
much more grievously oppressed than any of the others.
He organized them, and hurled them against their employers in strike after strike. He received no money for
these services to the starving workers; he had no time to
ask for it.

And now arose before him in dream the picture of the
old office in Hester Street, where he lived alone for eleven
weeks, organizing these strikes. He slept on a little broken-
legged sofa; he rarely ate more than once a day. From
dawn till midnight he fought the battles of the poor, and
more than one rich manufacturer had to avow that at last
the refugees were learning the worth of their services.

The cloakmakers started with thirty men in their Union,
but Joseph soon brought two or three thousand men into
the ranks. To do this he had so completely effaced his
own interest that he had few clothes, no money, and no
home, when, in sinister interference with the emancipation
toward which he seemed leading the starving thousands,
the great lock-out came.

The lock-out! The vision of the wan men standing
about, unemployed and starving, was so dolorous to Joseph
that he awoke from the uneasy slumber into which he had
fallen.

He looked quickly around. The door of the office was
open, and Miryam was standing near him, her charming
face radiant with smiles.

CHAPTER VIII

WHEN THE OX IS DOWN

"I MUST have been asleep," said Joseph, who felt a sharp pain in his side, and around whose forehead an iron circlet seemed slowly tightening.

"And dreaming," said the little maid. "And, Joseph, you talked in your sleep! Oh! you said such dreadful things against the sweaters! Well, it is lucky that no one but little Miryam heard you! How imprudent of you to go to sleep with the door wide open! Isn't it strange that no one has been here to wake you? And the clerk?"

Joseph explained that the clerk had been mercifully sent away some days ago, because there was no longer any money to pay him. "And as for speaking ill of the sweaters," he added briskly, "why, who speaks well of them?"

"But the door, Joseph, the door! Promise me that you will never go to sleep with the place wide open to robbers, and " —

"And Socialists," said Joseph, smiling.

"Yes, and Socialists. And, by the way, Joseph," said the pretty maiden, speaking lower, and glancing hastily around, "that is exactly what I have come to speak with you about. You know that some of the Socialists have terribly hot heads, and they are very angry with you. They say that you stand in their way."

"So I do," said Joseph grimly, and the fire flashed from his tired eyes.

"Yes, but — they might kill you, Joseph. They do not care what they do. They are men without hearts."

"We can die but once," remarked Joseph in philosophic tone. "But if you have heard any threats, Miryam, it is your duty to tell me what they are. Forewarned is forearmed."

"David heard," said Miryam, almost in a whisper. "He heard two Socialists saying something awful about you. It was, he said, enough to make the blood run cold."

"And yet he told it to little Miryam ? "

"N-o," answered the child-woman, flushing faintly.

"Then who did he tell ? "

"Bathsheba. You know, the wife of the dark-faced fiddler. Yes. He told her. And he said she must not tell me, because I am a little gossip. But she thought it was her duty to tell me at once."

"Bathsheba!" Joseph's heart gave a great jump, and the color leaped into his face. He could have struck himself for this. "Why — I thought her sympathies were with Socialists, and all such cattle."

"Perhaps they are. But she said you ought to know. She said that you were too earnest a leader to be lost in a street row. She said " —

Miryam paused suddenly, and cast down her eyes. Then, as if moved by an irresistible impulse, she raised them again, and as she looked Joseph in the face, he saw that they were swimming in tears. She held out both hands to the young leader. "Oh, do be careful, Joseph!" she said. "Think of Malcha and the little one ! "

"I do! I will!" cried Joseph, seizing the small hands, and giving them a brotherly caress. "But Bathsheba — I do not see how " —

"It is this way, Joseph," said Miryam. "Her husband sees a great many of these people, and gets into their way of talking. And sometimes she repeats what she hears him say. Then they say she is a revolutionist. But I know better. She hates them — only she is afraid of them. She says so." The girl seemed confused. But Joseph listened with an interest he could scarcely conceal.

"Listen," said Miryam. "They will not tell me all. They say I am too young. Even Bathsheba would not give me any details. But she will tell you — she says it is her duty to do so."

"She will tell me? How — when — where?"

"Do you know Mordecai Menzer?" said Miryam.

"The people's poet? No. I have heard of him, but I have never seen him. What should he have in common with a poor knee-pants maker like me?"

"O Joseph!" cried Miryam, with a sparkle of indignation in her eyes at the young leader's self-depreciation. "Mordecai worships the very ground that you walk on! You do not know how famous you are!"

"This is indeed news!" said Joseph, laughing in spite of his fatigue, and of the strange melancholy and languor taking possession of his heart.

"It is true. At this moment he is composing a poem about the sweaters and the poor work-people. And he asked me if I could not bring you to his house to-morrow. He wants to talk with you about the movement. And if you could come," continued the girl, very glibly, as if she were reciting a lesson, "Bathsheba could be there, and then she could tell you all. To-morrow, in the afternoon. If you could come for me at the theatre after rehearsal, I could take you there."

Joseph reflected. Waves of light came and went over his face, as if two spirits were battling above him, and

the sheen of their wings fell upon him. Presently he
said, —

"I will go with you to see Mordecai to-morrow. I will
meet you as you wish."

"And Bathsheba?" asked Miryam timidly.

"If Bathsheba is there, and has anything to tell which I
ought to know, I shall be glad to hear it, and grateful to
her," he said in a dry, cold tone. "And now let us go
to poor Malcha."

And as they went rapidly along the street, he told her
the story of the previous night. Miryam opened her great
eyes widely, but said little, until they were approaching
the house, when she remarked that perhaps he would like
to have Malcha accompany them on the morrow.

"No — not to-morrow," said Joseph. "And it would be
best not to say anything to her at present about the visit
or the threats."

"It would only frighten her. And she could do no good
even if she knew," said Miryam.

The streets were quiet in the cloakmakers' quarter.
Joseph and Miryam found Malcha and the child sitting on
the front steps. The little wife looked wan and worried,
but at sight of Joseph she rose up joyously, and ran to
embrace him.

She had heard the whole story of the night's work from
a dozen sympathizing souls, and was ready to adore Joseph
as a hero.

There was a touch of jealousy in the way in which she
drew him away from Miryam, placed little Zipporah in his
arms, and told him of the breakfast awaiting him — "just
like those he used to have in Russia." But she kept the
small actress to share their meal, and complimented her
on her personation of Jochanan in "Judith and Holofernus."

"Breakfast!" said the bewildered Joseph. "And I have been sleeping like a pig, and forgot to bring you this money," and he held out the two dollars which remained from the morning's distribution.

"Never mind," said Malcha with a twinkle in her eyes. "I still have ten roubles left, and that is riches in this quarter, I think."

"Yes; if a sweater knows you have got it, he will soon get it away from you," said Joseph, watching Malcha with admiration as she poured the tea from the homely little samovar, which recalled the old days at home.

Yet, in the burnished samovar he seemed to see Bathsheba's beautiful face dancing, as the will-o'-the-wisp danced over the green pools in the far Russian land when he was a boy wandering on the edge of the forest.

He put his hands to his eyes to shut out the sight.

"Poor Joseph," said Malcha, stealing an arm about his neck. "He is worn out with these doings. One thing I have sworn, and that is that no one shall disturb us until this tired man is refreshed, and has had a good nap."

"Yes, Joseph," said Miryam, "you look as if you had seen a spirit."

Joseph stared again at the samovar, but he took the cup of tea which his wife handed him, and drank it eagerly.

Just as they were laughing at some quaint remark by little Zipporah, and as Joseph was beginning to feel reposed and tranquil, there came a tremendous clatter at the door, and in rushed Ben Zion, his flaming hair and beard in disorder, and behind him were half a dozen cloakmakers, gesticulating wildly, and shouting in jargon.

At sight of this embassy, the fourth or fifth she had seen that morning from the perturbed laborers, Malcha's ire rose, and she sprang to her feet.

"Get outside of that door, every one of you!" she cried,

brandishing her knife and fork as if she meant to assault
the intruders, "and don't let me hear a word from you
until Joseph has finished his breakfast. Do you want to
worry him to death ? "

" My faith, missus ! " said one of the men, an ill-natured
fellow, " if he had no more breakfast to eat than we have
at our house he would have finished it long ago."

"Now, Malcha," said Joseph, rising and preparing to
attend to the men.

" Now nothing ! " cried the resolute wife, forcing him
down into his seat. " Are we slaves ? Isn't your breath
your own ? What are these folks to us ? Let them air
their troubles on the doorstep, and wait until you have had
a cup of tea."

Then catching up some dried fish and bits of bread from
the table, she distributed them among the men, saying, —

" Munch that outside, and wait ! Do you think we are
your servants ? "

" I'll attend to 'em, Malcha ! I'll keep them in order,"
cried Ben Zion ; and he hurried the men out.

" I see you don't understand, small wife," said Joseph,
" that a labor leader is the servant of his people. But you
will come to realize it after a while."

" Stuff and nonsense ! If another of those whining
needle-pushers sets his foot in here without permission, I'll
pour the tea down his back ! " she said. And she would
have done it.

But in a quarter of an hour Joseph summoned the delegation, and his heart leaped up with hope when he heard
the news that they had brought.

Freier and Monach, who were the originators of the
lock-out, and who had always been the most obstinate
and rebellious of the manufacturers, had at last consented
to receive a committee from the starving cloakmakers.

The truth was that they had heard of the doings of the previous night, and were alarmed. They had been told that some of the Socialists had proposed to sack their stores, but that Joseph had restrained them.

So they felt curious to hear what Joseph might have to say.

It was a recent action of Freier and Monach's which had brought the agony of the famished refugees to a crisis. The firm had suddenly and brutally ordered thirty of its men, one morning, to go home. The poor men, to whom going home in the dull season meant starvation, protested that they had an agreement with the firm to employ them until the busy season came round again.

Freier and Monach snapped their fingers at the agreement, and said, " You can do what you like. We are not afraid of you. Go and loaf with the thirty thousand others who are locked out."

" We must have a ' shop meeting,' " said the men, who hoped to tide over the difficulty. As a result of this meeting, which was promptly held, Freier and Monach made a price-list, which priced every garment by number. " Everything is now set down in black and white," they said. " There can be no dispute, and you can come back to work if you wish to do so."

The men fell into the trap, and it was not until Freier and Monach began to juggle with these new prices, that they saw through the trick, and understood why they had been dismissed and recalled.

They remonstrated against the new tyrannies which the firm now imposed, but in vain. Their wages were cut and pared, and all the conditions as to prices for " piece-work " were violated.

Then the men stopped work of their own accord, leaving Freier and Monach with a very large number of unfinished contracts upon their hands. The employers roared, but in vain. No one would come to work for them.

The toilers in many sweating-shops in relation with Freier and Monach stopped work also, out of sympathy for their oppressed brethren.

Freier and Monach roared again, and determined to strike back. They started an organization of manufacturers — and all the cutters were locked out. Then thirty manufacturers of cloaks simultaneously discharged their men.

Thus the industry was paralyzed, the necessary preparations for the brisk season were checked. The employers were anxious, and the locked-out workmen were starving.

And now, alarmed at the wild manifestations of the hungry men and women, Freier and Monach asked for a committee.

" Let us form it at once," said the men who were awaiting Joseph on the doorsteps, " and you shall head it."

" Very well," said Joseph. He picked out two or three resolute men, who represented the different departments of the cloakmaking industry, and placed himself at their head. Ben Zion remained to comfort Malcha and Miryam with his quaint sayings, and Joseph set out on his mission at once.

" You will let me deal with these people," he said to his fellow committee-men. "Forget that you are hungry! Remember that we are at war for our rights ! "

They strode into Canal Street, to the stuffy office where it was understood that Freier and Monach awaited them.

When they reached the place they found a greasy looking personage dressed in black, with a huge diamond in his shirt front, sitting on a pile of unfinished cloaks.

Joseph went in and faced this individual, who said gruffly, —

" What is it you want ? "

"We don't want anything," said Joseph. "It is you who want."

The personage with the diamond looked at Joseph as if he were some curious beast, or a bird of extraordinary plumage. Then he cried at him again, in a harsh, domineering voice, —

"Well, what is it that you want ? "

As Joseph felt that the question was already answered, he made no response, but stood to his guns.

"Oh, I suppose you are the committee from the Union," sneered the personage, talking in English, and appearing to look down on Joseph.

"We are," said Joseph; "and we have no time to waste."

"Well, you can wait until we are ready, I suppose."

"We will wait one minute — no longer," said Joseph. "And if we go away now you may find it more difficult to fetch us a second time."

At this there was a roar, like that of a wild bull, behind a thin partition at one end of the room, and Freier, the redoubtable sweater and oppressor, bounced out from his concealment, and came rapidly towards them.

Freier was a huge, brawny man, elaborately dressed, with a rolling shirt-collar and a profusion of jewellery, which gave him the air of a travelling theatrical manager.

He was renowned as a knocker-down and dragger-out of workmen who rebelled against his tyrannies. Tradition said, too, that he did not scruple to raise his hand against the hapless women whom he employed.

He knew Joseph, who had once been into his factory to claim justice for an old man whom he had abused. But it did not suit his present purpose to recognize him. He puffed up his cheeks, took out a cigar, lighted it, smoked in Joseph's face, and finally said, —

"Where do you come from ? "

Joseph smiled. "From Russia," he said; "and you?"

Freier scowled. "What is your purpose here?" he said menacingly.

"To confer with you as member of a committee on the subject of the lock-out."

"Yes, yes," said Freier. "All the men on the pavement, with empty bellies — and all because of your cursed interference."

Joseph's eyes flashed. "I will always interfere to see that my fellow-workmen are not oppressed," he said. "This is a free country. It might be well for you to remember that."

"All the manufacturers are acting with us," snarled Freier. "We know what we are about."

"'When the ox is down, many are the butchers,'" said Joseph, quoting the cynical Hebrew proverb.

"You will come to be hanged yet for stirring up the people," said Freier, coming close to Joseph and puffing clouds of smoke in his face.

"I have nothing to lose but my neck. You, too, have one that would fit a rope."

Freier raised his hand, but he saw Joseph's resolute, pale face, and he observed that Joseph's companions were closing around him. He dashed his cigar to the floor, —

"I will give you as much money as you want to go back to Russia and to stay there," he said. He disdained even to lower his voice. He fancied he could buy the whole committee.

"I would advise you not to say anything of that kind to me again," said Joseph, clenching his fist. The conversation had been in English, but he spoke the familiar jargon now.

"Well," said Freier, a little abashed, "if you wish to

be saucy, you can go home again as fast as you came. First of all, we are not going to pay any different prices, and we will make no different arrangements."

"If you will come to the office of our Union, you will talk in a different tone," said Joseph.

"I don't want to see a lot of pasty-faced Russian refugees," said Freier scornfully.

"They are not to be married to you, and they don't care for your opinion."

"I didn't lock them out," said Freier.

As this was a lie, Joseph did not think it worth while to contradict it.

"Then all our trouble in coming here is for nothing!" said one of Joseph's companions. "Leave the old fox in his den. He will get smoked out some day."

"If you talk that way," said Freier, "I will have you thrown out."

"And if you do," said the cloakmaker, "I will bring ten thousand women here to pull you to pieces. It wouldn't take long."

Freier stooped and picked up his cigar.

"Well," he said, "if I did make the lock-out, what do you suppose I did it for?"

His face was quite white now, and he showed his teeth like a wolf.

"It was because of men like *him*," he snarled, pointing at Joseph. "It was because I am tired of the meddling and interfering of such men, with their Unions and their committees! Do you think I am afraid of him, or anybody like him?"

He lighted a match slowly with his thick white fingers, applied it to the cigar, and blew great rings of smoke slowly into the air.

"You have come here, and you have threatened me," he

said. "You," shaking his hand at Joseph, "you — who
ought to be in prison. You threaten me. But I will show
you that we are not to be bullied. If your men want to
come back to work without any concessions, let them come.
If not, right about face, and get out of here! The police
of New York know how to put down labor riots. Get one
up, and see!"

And once more he puffed the smoke of his cigar insolently
in Joseph's face.

CHAPTER IX

THE PIG MARKET

IT was a hot and airless afternoon. The sun beat down with terrific force on the push-carts piled high with unripe or half-decayed fruit — with strawberries which had lingered too long in transit, and melons which had not seen enough of the sun. Sickening exhalations arose. The voices of the men chanting the attractions of their wares sank to a sickly wail. The old women squatted on the pavement, drooped their scrawny necks, and seemed ready to faint.

Round the corner, into the most crowded section of the "Pig Market," probably so called because everything but pig is sold there, came Ben Zion, languidly pushing his cart, which was heaped high with mottled strawberries. Behind him was a bevy of young girls, dark-haired and graceful, but with the fatal pallor of the sweaters' dens upon their faces.

"If you go a step farther, Ben Zion," cried the tallest of the girls, "you lose our patronage. Do you think we want to walk all the way to Jerusalem just to accommodate you?"

Ben Zion halted and backed his cart against the curb. The girls crowded around him. But he did not seem inclined to begin trading at once. He held up one hand, and bent his head in the attitude of listening.

"This is the place," he said. "Now hark, and you will

hear something curious. Open your ears, you silly girls,
and tell me what you hear."

The girls listened, and presently perceived, above the
clatter and hum of the street, the clicking of thousands of
sewing-machines, over which, in front and back garrets,
men and women were bending and working furiously, without thought or hope of rest.

Click-click-click-click-click ! went the machines, until
the brain was possessed with the burden of their chorus,
and seemed to dance to the rude and lilting rhythm into
which they gradually swung.

There was something almost sinister in the energy and
tirelessness with which the click-click went on, as if behind
it were a tireless and unbending will, disdaining fatigue,
scorning unhappiness, and toiling forward to some obscure
vengeance in the future.

" You hear it ! " said Ben Zion, shaking his hand impres-
sively. " Well, if the Czar who kicked us out of the Pale
could hear it, he would tremble and feel faint. Why ?
because every one of those clicks means that one of his
enemies — you know — one of those enemies that never
pardon, is moving on to independence, and to a position
where he or she can strike back ! I like to listen to the
merry chant ! It does my heart good."

" It sounds more to me," said one of the girls, across
whose pallid face a heavy shadow swept, " like infernal
music, to which the sweaters love to dance on our graves,
when we are used up, and can work no more, and they throw
us out ! "

" What a horrid fancy ! " said a little brunette. " And
what do you think such cattle as we are could ever do to
the Czar, Ben Zion ?   One wag of his beard, and you would
run all the way to Siberia ! "

" Do you think that I would run ? " said the little ped-

ler angrily. " If you had seen me and Joseph when we
took landlord Simon by the beard " —

" What did you do, Ben Zion ? " said one of the girls
breathlessly.

" I marshalled the army," said the pedler, brandishing
the three-cornered horn of coarse paper into which he was
presently to pour three cents' worth of damaged strawberries. " I was the grand marshal! If you had seen me
then, you would not dare to accuse Ben Zion of running
away ! "

At this moment there was a hubbub at the street corner
a short distance above them. The shuffling and the patter
of hundreds of feet were heard. Then there were angry
discussions, oaths, plaintive protests, shrieks, and maledictions.

A huge lumber wagon, drawn by smart horses, stood in
the middle of the street. Several resolute men were advancing beside it, peering at the contents of each push-cart,
and if the inspection disappointed them, they ordered the
suspected articles to be thrown into the wagon. Policemen
at front and back were ready to enforce the order.

Ben Zion understood the situation at a glance. He
whirled his little cart around, and was off, at the top of his
speed, down the street, and away from the Health Board's
Inspectors, without stopping to consider the total contra-
diction afforded by his act to the brave words which had
just left his lips.

As he sped along, his decaying merchandise strewing the
pavement on either side of the cart, the inspectors bawled
after him, but no one ventured to stop him, for Ben Zion
had a ready hand and a still more ready tongue.

The three girls laughed the hoarse, ghastly laugh of their
overworked class as they saw the pedler so belying his
courageous declaration, and they followed him as fast as

they could, around a corner and into a narrow alley beyond
the precincts of the " Pig Market."

" There, my lambs ! " said Ben Zion, puffing and blowing
and fanning himself with a red bandanna pocket-handker-
chief.   " I ought to have told you that the only thing I am
bound to run from is the nasty, prying American Health
Board.   We poor pedlers never have a minute's rest when
those fellows have a working fit on.   Down they pounce on
us, like eagles ; and if there is a fish in the neighborhood
that smells as if it had outlived its usefulness, bang ! they
seize up all the fish within a square mile around !   It is
the same with fruit !   What is an honest fellow to do in the
midst of such persecutions ?   And that reminds me, Esther,
that you are waiting for your lunch.   Did you say three
cents' worth of these very nice berries, my little dear ? "

Esther, the brunette, had been ferreting among the berries while the pedler was talking.   " Why, Ben Zion, this
fruit is not good," she said.   " It has been kept too long.
You were right to run away from the Health Board."

Ben Zion threw down the horn of paper, and, raising his
hands, shook them furiously in the air.   Then he folded his
arms across his breast, stood back, and gazed at Esther with
an air of deep disdain.

"Not good, you say, not good, my berries !   The little
witch has the courage to say that to me — to me, Ben Zion ! "
Then suddenly taking a " five-cent paper," he filled it to the
brim with mouldy fruit, and, pushing it into Esther's
hands, said, —

" There's double measure for you !   Give me the three
cents.   Now run home, and don't try to cheapen my fruit
any more ! "

This master-stroke of impudence had precisely the effect
contemplated by Ben Zion.   It brought the other two girls
to terms. They each left three cents in Ben Zion's coffers,

and carried away an invitation to cholera. But they were
wise enough not to eat the fruit when they saw how bad it
was. The commercial instinct was strong in them, and in a
few minutes they had exchanged the berries for a small
loaf of the wretched bread for sale on every corner of the
Pig Market.

The baker dressed up the berries in a little basket, and
shortly afterwards avenged himself on the tribe of sweaters
by selling them to a contractor for twenty-five cents. And
thus was the transaction ended.

"The girls are right!" said Ben Zion when left alone.
"There's too much richness and ripeness in this cargo ever
to pass the Health Board. So here goes!" And he emptied
the mass of fruit into the gutter, after which, producing
from an inner pocket a worn leather cigarette case, he
lighted a fragrant roll of tobacco, and, lazily propelling the
cart before him, he returned into the market.

The tumult was now greater than ever. Choosing a spot
directly in the path of the advancing inspectors, Ben Zion
tilted up his cart, stretched himself luxuriously in it, and
began to sing in a high falsetto voice one of the comic
folk-songs which he had learned in David's theatre.

"We shall have rare sport now, as the bear said when he
hugged the hunter," remarked Ben Zion, looking up with
eager interest as the sound of a fresh scuffle and a woman's
piercing cries greeted his ears.

The scene was as un-American as possible. There was
nothing but a fat policeman to remind one that he was in
the largest city of the United States. Even the narrow
brick houses, belettered as they were with signs in Hebrew
characters, had a strangely foreign air. But more foreign
of aspect than anything else was an old man in a long caf-
tan and a skull-cap much frayed at the edges, who sat on
the curbstone with both his wrinkled and knotted hands

folded over his knees, and with an air of saddened resignation upon his yellow face, on either side of which hung a
small curl of iron-gray hair.

"Why, how goes it, Father Manasseh?" said Ben Zion,
as his gaze fell upon this pitiable figure. "You don't look
over gay, because you don't feel so, as the fox said when
they were skinning him, I suppose. Any new trouble?"

"Ho! I can't complain," said the old man. "The society gave me three dollars a week when I was ill, and I
saved something out of that. So that I still have the crust,
you know, and might die happy if I could only get Shiphrah back."

He sighed deeply, and a tear rolled down his withered
cheek, and took refuge in his whitening beard, as if it
knew itself to be a luxury of which the old man would be
ashamed.

"Oh, yes! Shiphrah!" said Ben Zion reflectively. "She
ran away, didn't she? Or what was it?"

"Worse than that — worse!" said the old man, unfolding
his hands and rising painfully. "But don't ask me the
story now. It makes my heart bleed. I sit here every
day, hoping that I may see her again before I die; but she
seems to keep clear of the market. I shall find her yet;
but I won't ask the police; no, I won't ask the police!"

Suddenly the old man looked up at the pedler, with a
gleam of hope in his countenance. "Ah, I remember!" he
said, "you know Joseph — young Zalmonah — who is at the
head of the Cloakmakers' Union, don't you?"

Ben Zion arose, and assumed an air of quiet dignity.

"I perceive," he said, "that you have heard how Joseph
and I led the cloakmakers the other night. Do I know
him? It is a vain question, old man. We are hand and
glove. Well, and if I do know him, what then?"

"Why, then I would ask you to tell me the way to his

house. I would like to see his wife. I hear she has just
come over. She knew Shiphrah. They were from the
same town. Perhaps she may have been to see her. Will
you not tell me where I can find Joseph's wife?" he said in
querulous, piping tones, and laying hold of the frayed and
soiled skirt of Ben Zion's coat.

Ben Zion gave the lachrymose patriarch the desired
information, and looked after him thoughtfully, as he
hobbled away. "Well, well," he said, "that will be a
search. It is hard work looking for acorns after snow
falls, as the bear with the frozen paw said."

Some hundreds of "push-carts" like Ben Zion's were
ranged within the narrow limits of Hester Street, and were
laden with every conceivable kind of merchandise. Behind
the carts stood the black brigade of misery, the great un-
washed and saucy pedler's company, ready to starve, fight,
or suffer tortures in order to turn the nimble penny.

There were no ragged or crippled people in this company
of hucksters, and yet they produced upon the spectator the
impression of profound poverty. Old women in disordered
wigs and tarnished caps, and in petticoats which seemed
to have come from the junk man, squeaked out, in cracked
voices, the value of their wares.

Cunning-faced boys, already bent and faded like men of
fifty, laughed and told jokes, as they dispensed infinitesimal
portions of rancid fish and huge pieces of half-baked bread
to the pale-faced operatives from some adjacent garret.

At a street corner a shaky and greasy flight of steps led
down to a basement in which an old Jew in a green coat
sold mouldy-looking meat, while the steps were occupied
by a starving book-worm, who had a meagre array of Hebrew
literature displayed on a dirty shelf. In a little recess half
a dozen old men, leaning on their carts, furiously discussed
some knotty point, making the air vibrate with their sonor-

ous jargon. Small slips of girls, barefoot and haggard, went by like rays of moonshine, seeming as noiseless and unreal. They were the messengers despatched by the toiling employees in adjacent sweating-shops to procure them a little food for keeping soul and body in company. There were bands of dirty-faced men who recklessly sold green fruit, all the time shouting at the top of their voices, 'Sweet! Oh, sweet!'" And here and there was a pale, proud face with genteel lines in it — a face which spoke of refined life and comfortable position in the past — bent over the merchandise on a cart, as if afraid or ashamed to look the world in the eye.

Such a face Ben Zion now saw close to him, and he studied it with his quick eye, making up his mind meantime how he should address its owner. It was the face of a scholar, a thinker, who was reduced to the extreme of misery.

The man halted at Ben Zion's side, and, spreading a clean white handkerchief, sat down and leaned his handsome head against the little cart's side. For stock-in-trade he had only a few yellow bound pamphlets containing popular ballads written in jargon. And from the goodly number of them it was pretty evident that he had done but small business that morning.

"Well, comrade," said Ben Zion good-naturedly, "you haven't sold more than a thousand volumes this morning, I'll be bound. People don't want to read when they can't eat."

"I have sold nothing," said the man in a husky voice, and with an accent of profound despair. He spoke in the jargon, yet there was refinement in his speech. "Nothing. And I have eaten nothing since yesterday. If this existence is to go on day after day, in this terrible heat and in this turmoil, I will throw myself in the river over yonder, rather than endure it! This the land of plenty, indeed! Why, I am starving!"

"Yes," said Ben Zion, getting out of his cart briskly, and beginning to examine the new-comer's books, "that's all very fine; but drinking too much river water will not cure you of starvation, nor give you back the fine position and the money which the Russians robbed you of. We must work our brains, man! Work our brains! Stand up here by me a minute, and see how I will drag you out of the bog into which you have floundered."

The man obeyed feebly, doubtless feeling that anything, no matter how grotesque or humiliating it might prove, would be better than his own lack of success.

Ben Zion was bent on killing two birds with one stone. He saw the inspectors rapidly approaching (the Health Board cart was but two blocks away now), and he wished to appear before them as a seller of something besides fruit. At the same time he was sincerely anxious to rescue the poor man — a scholarly refugee who had been expelled from Moscow at four days' notice, losing property worth forty thousand roubles — from his peril of starvation.

So without any explanation he snatched two or three dozen of the little volumes from the other cart, and with them completely covered the floor of his own. Then he set up a shrill yell, "Books! books! cheaper than dirt! Wiser than Solomon, more venerable than Moses, because of the wisdom that is in 'em! Books — books! at — (How much do you sell 'em for?)

"Ten cents."

"At ten cents apiece — here they are — the wonderful songs and ballads of Mordecai, the poet of the people! Just the things to sing now, my friends, now that the day of reckoning with the sweaters is at hand! Ten cents apiece! Who'll buy?"

A silver coin fell into Ben Zion's ready palm. One of the little books vanished into the capacious pocket of a greasy-looking contractor, who was anxious to see what the "poet of the people" had said of his class. Then came a rabbi in a huge silk hat and a stained linen coat, who also purchased. He was followed by an asthmatic tailor, and next by a landlord.

"Take these coins and run and get your breakfast," said Ben Zion, thrusting the money into his pale companion's hand. "If you want to sell, you must shout! If you keep still in your corner, you will starve! Run! Trust me to make money while you are gone. I will look after your cart."

The man obeyed; and so it happened that when the inspectors came up with Ben Zion, whom they had plainly discerned running away a few minutes before, he thrust a book under their noses, and urged them to buy.

"Surely this is the man," said one of the inspectors. "He is one of the worst sinners in the business. He would peddle decayed vegetables by the ton, if we came around less often."

"Shall I run him in?" said a policeman.

Ben Zion flourished one of the books under the officer's nose. "Have a book?" he said. "Only ten cents."

"Yes, he's peddling books now," said the inspector; "but there are the stains of the fruit on the sides of his barrow. This fellow will poison the city some day. Can't you talk United States?" he said angrily to Ben Zion.

The pedler only flourished his books more lustily, and proclaimed its virtues more loudly in his copious jargon vocabulary; but, finally, placing the book again close to the officer's face, he said dryly, —

"Zehn cents. You better buy von."

"I'll pound your red head off, if you say that again,"

cried the exasperated officer; and the inspection procession rolled along. Before it swept a wave of lamentation from the old women, who saw their stock-in-trade seized and thrown into the hated wagon. An aged hag, sorting buttons in a heap on a push-cart, assailed one of the officers tooth and nail, and was carried off screaming, her whole family following her to rescue her if possible from the grip of the law.

"That was a narrow escape!" said Ben Zion. "I think I will stick to the side streets hereafter. Unless I sell pants again! People must have pants, even when they can't get bread."

And he was lost in thought on this important matter when the grateful man returned to thank him for intervening to preserve him from the pangs of hunger.

"Let me sell you a few more books," said Ben Zion. And he addressed himself so deftly to his task, that in half an hour the refugee was insured against want for several days. He at first refused to accept any commission for his labors; but when pressed he accepted a quarter. "It'll come handy to buy shoe-laces with," he thought. "But ought I to sell shoe-laces and suspenders now that I am a leader of revolutions?"

While meditating on this momentous problem, Ben Zion found the three girls to whom he had sold the berries standing near him again.

It suddenly occurred to him that they might have heard something about the lost Shiphrah. He began questioning them, and in a few minutes he was in possession of the information which old Manasseh had so long sought in vain.

CHAPTER X

"Come, Joseph," said Miryam, with a faint trace of petulance in her sweet voice, "if you drag along behind that way we shall be too late. When Mordecai has a singing fit upon him, he wouldn't wait for King Solomon."

"King Solomon has been dead for thousands of years," answered Joseph wearily, as he quickened his pace. "You live so much among those old historical personages in your theatrical world, that you get to think they are real."

"Ah! Joseph, Joseph!" said the girl-woman, turning her head and looking archly at him, "I know you well enough to feel sure that when you try the comical vein, you are worried about something. And why shouldn't you be worried, after all?" she mused with a sudden change of manner.

"There's nothing very humorous in my situation," sighed Joseph. "Thirty to forty thousand starving people ready to break into riot, if I can't invent some pretence for keeping them still! What would you do in my place, Miryam?"

The pair stopped in the shadow of a tall tenement house, as if the weight of Joseph's responsibility were pressing upon them both.

"I don't know," said Miryam simply, raising her beautiful eyes, and looking at Joseph with an expression of perfect trustfulness. "But I always feel sure that you will succeed — that you will do the right thing. It is as if — as if something were leading you on."

Joseph winced. There were times when he felt the unseen guidance, and when he would gladly have acknowledged it. But for the moment he seemed to have lost the touch of the guiding hand.

Since his stormy interview with Freier he had felt half stunned and helpless. The slave-drivers had shown a firm front against the revolt of the slaves. It was even evident that they coveted open riot, that they might have an excuse for harsher measures.

Surrounded by snares and pitfalls, friendless in a foreign land, with the laws and the very Constitution of which he was unfamiliar, and with a great army of desperate men and women urging him to lead it on to reckless and lawless deeds, unless he could find bread and work for it, he began to feel appalled at the immensity of his task.

His senses swam when he tried to think steadily upon the dangers and trials close at hand.

They were standing in Henry Street, that comfortable old region of quaint Dutch-looking houses which was once a fashionable promenade for New Yorkers, in those faraway days when a cow-pound stood on the site of the Fifth Avenue Hotel, and when a journey to Harlem was an event. Henry Street has still kept much of its ancient trimness and neatness, although tall tenement houses have thrust their ugly and angular forms in among the little mansions and have brought with them troops of dark-visaged folk, who seem as alien to America as if they had never heard of it.

"I wish I could help you, Joseph," said Miryam ; "I do with all my heart! I — I never saw you look as if you needed help before."

The mists arose, quite unbidden, in Joseph's eyes. His helplessness was, then, apparent even to this unworldly little waif ? He must make an effort, and he did, taking Miryam's hands, and saying kindly —

"It will all come out right. Let us go on."

A few steps more brought them to the entrance of a gray brick tenement house, which towered dizzily into air, as if it were not at all certain of its footing, and might at any time topple over. Miryam made her way among the sprawling groups of olive-faced babies, tended by little damsels with very womanly heads of hair, and with eyes which sparkled with curiosity and good-humor.

"This is it. Come up," said the girl, pointing to the annunciator, on which a small tablet bore the name in Germanic script : —

MORDECAI MENZER

A little pang of envy shot through Joseph's breast, but was gone in an instant. He wondered if he could ever attain to the dignity of a plate with his name upon it, as Mordecai, "the poet of the people," had done. At present, in his shabby lodgings in a frowzy quarter, he was far enough from any such style.

They climbed flight after flight of poorly lighted stairs hearing the click of sewing-machines and the droning voices of actors and actresses rehearsing their *rôles* in jargon, and a woman singing shrilly to the music of a cracked piano.

Through an open door they had a glimpse of a veritable "sweater's hell," where girls were toiling at the needle in the immediate vicinity of a red-hot stove, on which the pressing irons were heating.

The blast of fetid air which came from the room as a

pallid employee hastened to shut the door, was what one might imagine a puff from the cavernous mouth of hell to be.

On the fourth floor Mordecai Menzer's name again confronted them on a soiled and splintered door. Miryam rang, and a moment later she and her companion were standing in the presence of " the poet of the people."

He was a small man, on the borders of fifty, with a thin, sharp face, and a bushy beard which he had evidently dyed to conceal the snows of time upon it. He had a curious way of gazing out from under his brows which at first was rather startling ; but one soon discovered that it was only a manner. Mordecai Menzer was a man of intense nature, and he showed it even in his ordinary speeches and gestures.

His greeting of Joseph was so deferential that it confused the young leader, who was prepared to compliment the poet on his wonderful power over the hearts of the Jewish people. But Mordecai at first would hear little about himself ; his talk was of Joseph and his plans, — the lock-out, the labor revolution in progress.

The poet's domicile consisted of three diminutive rooms and a rather dark kitchen. In the tiny dining-room his rotund little wife and two modest and pretty daughters were busy with household cares. Here the poet had received his visitors. He now conducted them into the next room, a Liliputian *salon* in which some old faded tapestry-backed chairs looked as if they felt crowded and out of place. In one of these chairs sat a little nervous man with a dark face, holding a violin in his lap. And on a low stool behind one of the chairs, intently looking out of the window, was the beautiful Bathsheba.

Joseph's heart gave a curious throb as he saw her, and he could not refrain from gazing at her, until she slowly

turned her queenly head, and seemed to take possession of
him with her eyes. He looked confused; and although
Miryam rushed to Bathsheba, and engaged in a lively conversation with her, he thought of nothing but Bathsheba and
her eyes, while the poet Mordecai finally intoned his history, bestowing various picturesque maledictions upon the
government which had expelled him from his native Russia,
and had compelled him to begin his career anew in a far-
away land.

Mordecai had much to tell, and in an ordinary frame of
mind it all would have been intensely interesting to Joseph.
The poet told how, when a child at the carpenter's bench in
his father's shop, he had begun to compose ballads telling
the story of his people's joys and sorrows. As he grew up
he found that his singing was nearly all sorrowful, and he
learned that his people were oppressed and down-trodden.

Then came the magic and never-to-be-forgotten moment
when the spirit of revolt and the spirit of poesy moved within
him, and in a few tremendous verses, into which he had con-
densed the anguish of a whole race, he had struck out at
white heat the ballads which had won for him the name
of the "Poet of the people."

As a youth, and finally as a man, he had wandered up
and down the Russian land, wherever those of his race
were to be found, and he had sung to them the songs which
gave them life and hope, and also the spirit of vengeance.

He created the cradle-songs to which Jewish mothers
have for more than thirty years rocked their babes to
sleep, and in each and all of these songs there is a plaint or
a wail.

In the villages and at the country fairs the women and
children flocked to hear him sing his own songs; and, when
the Russian officials found that they often went away weeping, they began to spy upon Mordecai. Sometimes they

sent stenographers to take down his words; at another
time they gave him twenty-four hours in which to leave
the locality. And at last they became so threatening that
Mordecai, who supported his family by singing in public
and by selling reprints of his own songs, felt constrained
to give up his little home and to migrate over seas to " the
golden land " which he had already celebrated in his verse
— the golden sunset land of free and untrammelled
America.

Arriving here in the thick of the labor troubles, and finding his hapless countrymen and women starving by regiments, victimized in brigades, slave-driven in armies, his
sensitive nature had received a severe shock.

He no longer believed in "the golden land," and had
written, since his arrival, a bitterly satirical ballad tinged
with socialism, in which he ridiculed the United States as
a land of promise, but not one of performance.

Without being himself what the masses call a Socialist,
he had leanings in that direction, and was easily persuaded
to enter into friendly relations with Baumeister, and with
others who professed to believe in what they called " the policy of force."

And it so happened that Mordecai, although he had been
but a few months in America, had sung at several socialistic gatherings, and had composed one or two rhymed
invectives against " capitalistic legislatures " and other institutions of the present order of society, which quite
delighted Baumeister and his colleagues.

Therefore, when he was urged to bring his influence to
bear upon Joseph, he resolved to do it as a kind of duty,
and was readily persuaded by Baumeister to give the
young leader a rendezvous in his humble abode.

Baumeister, meantime, took excellent care not to appear
in the matter. He was acting by deputy, and, in this case,

he had chosen with great adroitness, and had decided confidence in the result.

For Bathsheba was his deputy.

Baumeister was a man of talent, of comprehensive vision, and great audacity. Bathsheba was a new convert, and converts are always more zealous than those born in the faith.

If she had remained in her native province of Russia, and had never been moved from the calm conventionality of middle-class life, she would have been the most exemplary of matrons, the coldest and most statuesque of beauties. It is doubtful if she would even have descended to the commonplace level of a flirtation with a provincial landowner, or a passing officer in some crack regiment.

But destiny had thrust her forth upon the world by filling her head with a caprice for this dark-faced fiddler, who had won her heart by playing gypsy melodies at a festival in her father's house one summer moonlight night. She had run away to marry him, leaving home and fortune behind her; and when she had come to the end of the few thousand roubles which her mother had sent her, out of sheer pity for the daughter whose erratic conduct she condemned, she saw that there was no new fortune to replace the old one.

She had married a man who, in the cold sunlight of every-day life, turned out to be nothing but an ordinary musician. In America he found crushing competition awaiting him in the very specialties in which he had hoped to succeed.

If this had not soured his happy-go-lucky temper, not so much could be said of Bathsheba. With the loss of her illusions had come an immense and overpowering disgust, which gradually transformed itself into a fixed hatred for Society and all its institutions.

The transfer of her existence from Russia to America, the keen shock of disappointment experienced on finding that the conditions of life, especially for the refugees, — victims of the labor-glut which they themselves created, — were so hard and forbidding, and the contrast — so appalling in New York — between the extreme of want and abject misery and the topmost height of luxury and abounding prosperity, gave the finishing stroke to the slender framework of piety and tradition which at home would have sufficed to keep her from Socialism.

A few words from Baumeister at the opportune moment, and Bathsheba was an active worker in the cause of the "force party," which she and her companions called "Socialistic" when they wished to be mild, and which they glorified by its real and more repulsive name when they were determined to speak out. The exalted, almost frenzied fervor of Bathsheba's work in "the cause" had led Baumeister to believe that he could trust her to do anything. Himself firmly convinced that a "campaign of force" was near at hand, he rejoiced at having within call a woman who would recoil at nothing, who would even undertake the mission of the assassin should he confide it to her.

She found in the keen intellectual delights of this conspiracy, hopeless and foolish as its aims and undertakings in reality were, a charming relief from the deadly monotony of life in a dreary street in an obscure quarter, surrounded by her inferiors, and sometimes in doubt where the next day's food was to come from.

She had early acquired an ascendency over her husband; and she made liberal use of it, converting him to the new doctrine, and persuading him that by means of it they might both yet attain to consideration and worldly success. Her beauty and strength of mind argued more for her doctrine than her rather wild words could have done; and the husband seemed, under Bathsheba's direction, as clay in the hands of the potter.

It was Bathsheba whom Baumeister had chosen as the instrument for the conversion of Joseph to his doctrine. When the leader of revolt against society in the metropolis had first had Joseph pointed out to him as one who worked steadily against the inroads of Socialism in the ranks of the oppressed people, he had fancied that he could sweep him out of the way by some adroit manœuvre.

But when he discovered that Joseph was his equal in sagacity and prudence, and his superior as a popular leader, he made up his mind that Bathsheba alone could operate the conversion. He proposed to her the mission of bringing the young leader over to the "school of force," and after some hesitation she consented.

At that time she had never seen Joseph, and supposed him to be some greasy cloakmaker, the very odor of whose garments would offend her nostrils. When she learned that he was a man of rare power, and that he impressed all who saw him with the idea that he had a mission, she found means frequently to see him without being herself observed. This careful espionage had begun weeks before the lockout was started. At first she found it a task, then, suddenly, it became a pleasure, and she discovered that the pale face of Joseph, with its patient weariness, had left its impress on her heart.

Thenceforward she watched him with keen and unflagging interest. She had not seemed to notice the young leader that evening when with David he had seen her in the lodge-room in Grand Street. But her eyes had followed his every movement, and it was with a rapturous joy which thrilled her that she noticed the profound impression made upon him by her beauty.

The next day she found herself possessed of a strange,

almost uncontrollable desire to see Joseph at once. If she had been tardy before in approaching her mission, she now sped to it with a willing foot.

She had gone to the theatre because she had felt the mad wish to see him that very night. Amazed at this new manifestation in her nature, which she had supposed to be no longer susceptible to romance, she began to analyze her emotions.

At the end of a few hours she had made up her mind that her position was singular and embarrassing, even for a disciple of Baumeister, and a revolutionist who believed but little in the sacredness of the marriage-tie, or any other of the social conventions.

Had she loved Joseph at first sight ? Certainly she had felt the dawning of a passionate devotion to the leader whom she had sworn to seduce from his allegiance to order.

Bathsheba knew that she was well watched, and she concealed her new secret with all the skill of an accomplished conspirator. She wished to see Joseph face to face again, to hear him talk, to touch his hand, before she decided on her future course.

She was a woman of more than ordinary courage and resources. She realized fully what this new love, if indeed it were love, was likely to mean for her — all the possibilities of tragedy, humiliation, suffering, contained in it ; and she felt that she must bring the fate closer to her, where she could inspect it narrowly, without delay.

So she had profited by her acquaintance with David and Miryam, and with Mordecai, the people's poet, to lead Joseph to her side. After she had heard his voice, had looked into his eyes, she would decide — she would decide.

But as she looked languidly out at the window, while Joseph listened to Mordecai's monologue, she betrayed by no sign the anxiety and commotion which reigned within her breast.

It seemed to her that she feared to hear Joseph speak, lest something which he might say should force her to overturn the idol which she had erected in the innermost sanctuary of her heart.

Miryam rattled on about the expedition of the night before, unconsciously throwing into it, with her theatrical training, a certain dramatic force, especially when she spoke of Joseph. To her surprise Bathsheba seemed to know many of the details, but scrutinized her with wild, widely opened, almost tearful eyes every time she alluded to Joseph's part in the night-drama. As yet it did not enter Miryam's innocent heart that Bathsheba might dare to love him, nor did she dream that the beautiful woman in whose lap she laid her head was a conspirator commissioned to convert or ruin Joseph.

Suddenly the girl caught her breath, and said, "Oh, I am so afraid that something will happen to Joseph! Do remember your promise to warn him!"

A wave of ashy pallor swept into Bathsheba's face and out again in an instant. "You may be sure that I shall do my very best," she said, and her voice had a curious tremor in it.

At this juncture Mordecai's round little wife appeared in the doorway with one of her husband's presentation silver salvers laden with peaches, grapes, and a dark-looking wine which they had brought over seas with them.

"May I join the worthy company?" she said in her quaint jargon; and Joseph was glad to get free from Mordecai's monologue, and to see a little movement in the room.

The company collected about the wine. The dark-faced fiddler smiled pleasantly at Joseph, smacked his lips, and said, —

"You don't get that every day, hey — you other cloakmakers — do you ? "

"Ho ! " said Joseph, "wine to drink ! That would be
luxury indeed ! Why, we are happy when we can get water
enough. I know a sweater who allowed the company to
cut off the water in his place. He declared that he wasn't
going to be taxed to furnish water for a crowd of thirsty
workers ! 'Let each man bring his own drinking-water,'
he said. 'And if he can't do that, let him choke.' "

"Good subject for a little ballad," said the dark-faced
fiddler to the poet.

"There are so many that father doesn't know which to
chose first, does one, father ? " said the small wife, holding
her wineglass with both hands, and looking up at her husband with a proud and pleased expression.

And now Joseph became conscious that Bathsheba was
near him, and the little fiddler was introducing him in a few
well-chosen words, and with an air which showed that he
was very proud of her.

"It was so kind of you to spare a few moments from
your poor people ! " said a melodious voice, and Joseph
looked up in surprise.

Could it be the voice of Bathsheba, the "Socialist," which
had spoken thus considerately of his mission ? He was prepared to hear her sneer at his down-trodden cloakmakers,
but not to sympathize with them.

He gazed at Bathsheba, as if waiting for her to explain
herself. The sincerity in his questioning eyes both pleased
and startled Bathsheba. She lowered her gaze.

"So good of you," she continued, "to give us a chance of
seeing you. Mordecai has been inspired by what he has
heard — and seen — of your work, to write a little song about
the sweaters. He was good enough to sing it to me — and
I thought — I thought," here she raised her eyes and flashed

their light upon Joseph's face for a moment, then swiftly lowered them again, "that you ought to hear it. Certainly it will be an engine to help you in your work."

Joseph was surprised that he did not readily find words to thank Bathsheba for what seemed such purely disinterested kindness. He was usually ready enough with his tongue, but now he dreaded to open his lips, lest he should say something foolish.

He felt deliciously flattered by Bathsheba's interest in him. It seemed to make his work larger, finer in his own estimation. At last he realized that he must speak, so he stammered, —

"I have heard it said that songs often make revolutions. Why, then, shouldn't they aid strikes? And Heaven knows that we have bitter need of aid! I am sure that if the poor cloakmakers now starving in Hester Street could see the impression their misery has made on you, they would be more courageous than ever."

But while he was speaking he felt like crying out to Bathsheba, "Woman! Woman! these are not the words I want to say to you. I want to ask you why your eyes burn so strangely into my being; why the touch of your hand on mine thrills me with a strange delight; why the little room seems full of a glory which emanates from you!"

Did his eyes ask these questions? He did not mean that they should do so. He meant to conceal the delirious disturbance which Bathsheba had wrought in his soul, and the purport of which he but vaguely understood.

They talked for some minutes, while Miryam aided the housewife and her daughters in cleaning the room, so that Mordecai might have a little stage for action.

"When he is excited in singing," said the small wife, "he walks up and down; and if he should happen to knock his shin against a chair, it would spoil the whole effect of his song."

"Not because he has a bad temper, I hope, Frau Menzer," said a cheerful voice at the door, "because you know the proverb, 'The sins of the bad-tempered are greater than his merits.'"

"Here is Reb David!" cried Miryam, "with his mouth full of wisdom, as usual. May he come in?"

"He must," said the little wife with effusive hospitality. "And as proverbs are dry eating, and leave a bitter taste in the mouth, he shall have a glass of wine."

David accepted the proffered glass, and went with it in his hand to join Bathsheba and Joseph, who were conversing in low tones.

"Now," said Mordecai, springing into the middle of the floor and addressing the dark-faced fiddler, "get your violin. I feel the inspiration bubbling up! Come! I will sing you the song which I have put into the mouths of the victims of the sweaters."

The fiddler gently refused the written music which the little wife handed to him. "I know the song by heart," he said, "and so will every cloakmaker and operator in New York before we have done with them."

Bathsheba and Joseph sat down, and listened.

CHAPTER XI

THE OBJECT—LESSON

A HUSH fell on the little company. The sacramental touch of art was upon it. Mordecai began to sing.

He stood in the middle of the floor, holding his verses, written in fine Hebrew script upon note-paper, in one hand, and nervously beating the air with the other, as if he were trying to catch flying words and phrases, and fit them to his song. Thus he seemed for a few moments irresolute, and a trifle ridiculous.

But most of his auditors knew that Mordecai was awaiting the exact moment when the inspiration would reach its height, and that, when it came, he would startle them with the wild beauty and eloquence of his rhymed composition.

Joseph studied him with all his might. He could hear, close beside him, the rustling of Bathsheba's dress, and her short, sharp breathing, as if she were painfully excited.

Suddenly the dark-faced fiddler struck a wailing chord on his violin, and instantly ceased to play. It was like the cry of a woman in distress and despair — a heart-broken wail which made the flesh creep.

Then came Mordecai's voice, and Joseph felt his heart hot within him, as, in a stern recitative, rhymed, yet roughly carven (such as an ancient Hebrew prophet might have sung before an erring king), the poet of the people told of the cloakmakers' torture.

And now the music of the violin accompanied the singer. At first it was in a soft and brooding undertone, like the sobbing of hungry children in the dark.

Presently it became stronger — less plaintive — fiercer — menacing — as the poet, in the homely jargon which was his native tongue, catalogued the sorrows and sufferings of his oppressed countrymen and countrywomen.

At last it burst out into a tone of triumphant irony — like that of a prophet who, despairing of remedy for a hopeless situation, calls on those who created it to look on their wretched work. This ironical vein was maddening. It made Joseph long to arise, to go down into the street, and, taking the first capitalist whom he might meet by the throat, to knock out his brains with a stone.

It made Miryam weep; and as she wept, the image of her dead mother lying on the trestles in the little room, with the flies buzzing curiously about her peaceful and worn face, arose before her.

It recalled to Joseph the day when he saw his young "partner" falling face downward on his machine, with his mouth distorted, and his poor lean cheeks withered with hunger. And with his brow aflame, Joseph started up, making wild and convulsive movements with his hands, and crying, —

"Stop ! Stop ! I can't bear it !"

But Mordecai motioned him imperiously to his seat, and went on, with a proud smile for a moment wreathing his thin lips, as a ray of sunshine sometimes plays about the crater of a volcano. "The fit was on him," as Miryam had aptly phrased it, and nothing but death could stay the current of his splenetic and vindictive singing.

There was a curious refrain to the eight-line verses, containing a passionate appeal to the workers, so terribly oppressed, to arise and strike down the tyrants. Into this refrain Baumeister and his band had wrought all the venom of their cunning; and, as delivered by Mordecai, it was a startling incentive to violence.

The last verse, which compared the young girls, fading so quickly in the noisome atmosphere of the sweaters' dens, to the flowers cut down by the mowers, and withering speedily in the harsh, sharp sunlight, was irresistibly moving. Bathsheba veiled her face, and great sobs shook her broad bosom. Then came anew the ironical refrain, with the mournful undertone of music. Mordecai's intense, vibrating tones died away.

He sank down into a chair, looking white and old.

The dark-faced fiddler hugged his violin, and gazed out at window, as if he saw there all the horrors mentioned in the song.

A new Marseillaise of the poor had been born in that humble apartment; and now that the singing was over, it seemed almost as if the palpitating listeners could hear the beating of the wings of the great angels of War and Revolution, as they receded to the spaces from which they had come down to infuse their spirit into this group of mortals.

David was the first to speak. He knew that the tension could be relieved only by a practical remark. So he said, —

"I will give you twenty dollars to sing that song as well as that on the stage of our theatre next Saturday afternoon, Herr Mordecai."

"Oh, father sings just as well one time as another," said the rotund little wife, who was jealous of her husband's reputation. "That is, you know, after the first inspiration has come to him. For he gets a fresh inspiration with every new song; don't you, father ? "

Mordecai ignored his wife's loving, although clumsy, efforts to aid him, and after one or two weak protests he closed with David's offer. "Such chances are not to be neglected," he said. "And if the cloakmakers were there to hear they might be influenced."

"They shall be there," said David, "for I will invite them. I can't feed the poor creatures, but I can point out the way" —

"For them to help themselves," said Bathsheba, arising with her cheeks aglow. "That is it! That is what your song will do, Mordecai. It will teach the starving people to ask in such a way that they cannot be refused. Do you not think so?" she asked Joseph, turning suddenly to him.

Joseph hesitated. It seemed to him that he was in a boat which had drifted loose from its moorings, and was at the mercy of tide and wind. For weeks he had fought the Socialists; had rebelled against the doctrine of Force; had stigmatized it as silly and criminal. And now here, after a breath of song, and under the influence of this woman Bathsheba's eyes, he was almost ready to admit that the true way to solve the cloakmakers' situation was to strike up Mordecai's song, and to march upon Freier and Monach and all the other tyrants, at the head of a legion or two of the starving people.

"I think that the poet of the people has sung us a great song," he answered, trying to cast off the influence which seemed mastering him. "And I am glad the men in our Union are to have a chance to hear it at the theatre. But I should not like to see them aroused to any deeds of violence, because I am afraid that — well, I feel certain that it would ruin the cause."

"Oh, yes, yes," said Mordecai in a bitter tone; "yield, yield, always yield, in the hope of concessions which never come! It is the story of our people" —

"Well, as to that," said Joseph, beginning to rally, "I

don't think I can quite agree with you. We have already secured a good many concessions from the sweaters — and who says that we shall not win the final battle? It seems to me that it is not so very far off, and sometimes I feel confident of victory. But what has the party of force ever done? I certainly never heard of its doing anything practical."

"There I think you misjudge it," said Mordecai uneasily, and looking at Bathsheba, as if he read his lesson in her eyes. "The party of force is preparing the grand revolution. If it were not for the partial revolutions of leaders like yourself — men whom everybody respects, and whose courage nobody doubts, but who are unwilling to admit that Society is rotten, and must be swept away by complete revolution — we, that is, the force party, would be much further advanced than at present."

Joseph listened attentively, but with the air of one far from convinced.

"And are those your sentiments also?" he said to Bathsheba, turning round to her so sharply that she started and lowered her eyes.

"They are," she said almost humbly. "Not that I would presume to criticise you or your work, which is so grand, so self-sacrificing" (the blood stole into Joseph's cheeks), "but because I feel that nothing can be done without a complete social revolution. I should like — be glad to see you associated in such work."

"How long have you been in America?" said Joseph, keeping his gaze steadfastly on Bathsheba.

"Long enough to learn that poverty is as bitter and terrible here as anywhere else," she answered hotly.

She began to rebel at Joseph's catechising mood. She had fancied that she would be able more quickly to establish her influence over him.

But the man seemed to have two natures, quite different, yet each in some respects completing the other. One was sensuous, passionate, sympathetic, yielding; the other, cool, practical, unyielding as steel, and capable of leading him straight to martyrdom.

With woman's unerring intuition she made sure of these things, and decided to accommodate her campaign to the newly acquired knowledge of his traits.

But Joseph was gaining ground every instant now.

"Poverty is hard enough to bear anywhere," he said; "but the remedy for it is not revolution in this country, I am sure. It would be poor policy to undermine and blow up a magnificent mansion because one could afford to live nowhere in it except in the basement."

Bathsheba's eyes flashed. She liked Joseph all the better for standing to his guns.

"Perhaps it is as you think," she said sweetly. "But I believe that you are mistaken; that here in this big city there are tens — yes hundreds of thousands who long for the Social Revolution — for the *régime* under which every one will do just as he or she pleases, and when there will be no inequalities of fortunes."

"Oh, dear, dear!" sighed Mordecai's round little wife, "what a blessed day that would be! No more click-clack of sewing-machines night and day, I should think, in those times!" And she took a huge pinch of snuff as fiercely as if she had been strangling a millionaire, or helping to hang a manufacturer.

"It may come to-day, to-morrow, in a week, in a month — this Social Revolution," said Bathsheba, lowering her voice, and looking around, for she had not yet learned that America is a free country, where one may speak without danger of spies. "How did you know that you were not in the van of the Social Revolution when you were leading the cloakmakers to Simon's house the other night?"

Joseph was startled. How little, indeed, it would have taken to send the mad mob of hungry men and women into the rich quarters, burning and sacking and ravaging!

He had thought that often enough since.

"But it could only have ended in disaster and despair," he said. A sudden vertigo seized him; he staggered and would have fallen, had not Bathsheba stepped forward, caught him in her strong arms, and gently lowered him into a chair.

The little wife came bustling with a glass of wine. But the touch of Bathsheba's arms had electrified Joseph; he sat up, feeling a little ashamed, and holding one hand to his head.

"You must excuse me," he said, looking around. "I have been up so much nights lately that I am a little top-heavy." He took the glass of wine, drank sparingly, and professed himself as well as ever. But the mortal pallor on his brow belied him.

"Fresh air is what Joseph needs," said David. "Instead of bothering him with your socialistic notions, all of which, I believe, will come to naught" (here Bathsheba flashed a keenly reproachful glance upon David), "if you would take him up to Central Park, or out on the river, you would be doing the cause of united labor a real service. And you, Joseph, be more careful of your health. Remember the proverb, 'Our days pass quickly over us, even as the shadow of a flying bird.'"

"I should be glad, for one!" said Bathsheba quickly, addressing Joseph, "if you would take David's advice, and if we might all go together into the upper quarters of New York. It would give us a chance to teach the labor leader an object-lesson."

"Yes," said Mordecai; "he would certainly feel the bitterness of poverty more keenly when we came back."

"Then why go?" queried Joseph. "No, I must go home to my wife and little one. I have left them too much alone since they arrived."

A shadow so imperceptible that no one save Miryam, who was opening her eyes now, observed it, passed over Bathsheba's face.

"Oh, it was only in the hope of justifying ourselves in your eyes," she said coquettishly.

"I have just come from your house, Joseph," said David, coming up and putting his hand on the young labor leader's shoulder, "and I met Malcha going out with the child. I told her I should see you this afternoon, and she wished me to tell you that she had found Shiphrah, and was going to stop with her until evening." He lowered his voice. "You know the poor Shiphrah whom you pitied so much. It seems that she is from the same village as Malcha, and Malcha asked me to implore you not to be angry."

"No," said Joseph, his brow clearing, "it is an errand of mercy. It is like Malcha."

"She told me to tell you another thing," said David in a whisper. "A letter has come from her mother, and in it were a hundred roubles, which the good woman sent just about the right time, didn't she? Now, don't be proud because of this good news. Remember what Rabbi Ashi said: 'He who hardens his heart with pride softens his brains with the same.'"

"There really is nothing to be proud of, unless it is Malcha's good sense," answered Joseph. But he felt immensely relieved even at this momentary cessation from grinding want. A sudden hunger for rest and fresh air, for the odor of trees and flowers, for contemplation of the calm of nature and the beauty of summer, seized upon him, and would not be appeased. The battle in his nature, caused by the intoxicating song, by the presence of Bathsheba, by the knowledge that he was treading on dangerous ground, had aroused new desires, new passions, of the existence of which he had never before dreamed. The spirit of resignation was dying away in him, and in its stead arose an intense longing for the riches and luxury of the world. To his inward shame and sorrow, he found that he was forgetting the poor cloakmakers, and thinking only of himself.

They lingered some time in conversation, while the little wife pressed the simple refreshments upon all. Then Mordecai sang once more — one or two comic folk-songs, which yet had in them the rebellious and menacing spirit ; and it was almost six o'clock before they started on their stroll up-town. David and Miryam, rejoicing that there was no theatre for them that evening, led the way, and it seemed natural that Joseph should escort Bathsheba down the narrow and ill-lighted stairs, Mordecai and his wife, very quaint in their provincial Russian Sunday best hats and cloaks, bringing up the rear.

As they were descending the last flight of stairs, Bathsheba turned to Joseph, with her hand gracefully raised, and said with an arch smile, —

"Will you promise to confess if the object-lesson convinces you ? "

"I hope I shall be frank," he said, his heart leaping as he gazed down into the beautiful face, with its deep mysterious eyes, from which Will-o'-the-wisp fires seemed to dart into the air.

At David's suggestion they went down to the East River, and there, at a pier below the bridge, they embarked on a diminutive white steamer, which went coughing and wheezing and blowing in and out among the statelier craft, and carried them rapidly up stream.

The sunlight lay in great gleaming masses on the water ;

it seemed as if one might cut out pieces of it, and take them home.

In the west there was a great bank of golden haze, which would have delighted the soul of Turner, could he have seen it, and which might have interested some of our American painters, had they not all been too busy interpreting the misty blues and pearly grays of England and Northern France.

Against this sumptuous background arose the lines of graceful masts and spars ; and now and then across it moved the symmetrical mass of a huge Sound steamer, its white sides glistening and its bows throwing up fountain jets of diamond foam.   Here fluttered gently down a group of white sails, capriciously hovering at the black sides of a battered ocean liner, drawn by two quarrelsome and aggressive tugs.   The sunshine cast its glory over the long lines of red brick warehouses, on the tottering and dirty docks, and on the hundreds of bare-headed mothers with children in their arms, seated at the dock's ends, in the hope of securing a few breaths of fresh air.   The vast current, swirling around the piers and boiling and eddying about the great vessels at anchor, caught the thousand points of darting light, and reflected them in a million ways and in infinitesimal variations.

A cool breeze fanned the heated brows of the poor refugees, and lent a sudden animation to their spirits, which for a time had suffered relapse from the tension caused by Mordecai's song.

Now the steamer began to dart along the upper reaches of the immense tidal stream : past sugar refineries, with little fleets of steamships lying at their wharves ; past the low shores crowded with evidences of abundant wealth and of the tremendous inland commerce of the nation ; past the " Island," with its pretty lawns and grim penal

institutions and asylums; and presently it skirted the
wooded shore of a smaller island, dashed in and out
among a multitude of yachts lying peacefully at anchor,
shot through a drawbridge which opened obediently
at its approach, and pushed up to the entrance of the
Harlem.

Here, at a rambling and crazy old dock (like all the
docks in the metropolis) the friends disembarked.

Miryam was in an ecstatic mood. She ran and gam-
bolled like a child of six, and rallied "Reb Joseph" and
Bathsheba on their solemn and careworn look. It was all
that David could do to subdue her gayety so that it should
not attract the notice of the passers by.

"Well," said Joseph, who had never seen so much of
New York before, "thus far we have set eyes on nothing
but the activity of people working hard for their daily
bread. And I must say that it would seem very hard to
upset all this energy and industry by a revolution, just
because there is trouble in a few trades like ours, and one
or two hundred rascals refuse to pay decent wages for
honest labor."

Bathsheba did not answer, and her silence impressed
Joseph more than any voluble defence of her doctrines
could have done. Gradually she assumed guidance of the
party, and, just as the soft summer darkness was stealing
over earth and sky, they came out upon Fifth Avenue, in
front of the Vanderbilt mansions. They had been walking for a long distance, having taken the elevated road at
One Hundred and Twenty-Fifth Street, and then left the
train at the wrong station and got lost; and Joseph's thin
cheeks were aglow with fatigue, and with the unwonted
fresh air, when they halted, and stood in mute contemplation of the line of palaces, churches, and hotels stretching
away on either side, as David expressed it, "like the

Devil's wheat-field, which was bounded on one side by the North Pole and on the other by the South Pole."

Now that they were beyond the familiar neighborhood of the East Side, the little company began to feel strangely out of place, and each gazed at the other as if challenging criticism on their respective shabbiness. Bathsheba glanced down at her worn and frayed dress, which was not in the prevailing fashion. She caught at the edges of her jacket, much too heavy for the season, and the collar of which was of decidedly antiquated design. She glanced from time to time at Joseph, and was ill at ease.

Joseph tugged at his frayed wristbands, and silently regretted that he had not been allowed to go home and don his one good coat. He took off his hat and gave it a surreptitious look. The band was stained, and the sunlight of two seasons had taken much of the color out of it. Even Mordecai, usually draped with effective majesty in his own dignity, seemed dimly conscious that his attire was not in harmony with that of the trim ladies and gentlemen who sauntered lazily by with the apologetic air of well-to-do New Yorkers detained in town in summer.

But they walked on, trying to be gay, and gazing at mansion after mansion without the remotest idea who inhabited any of them. Joseph had never been in Fifth Avenue before, nor had he ever set foot in the Park. Like tens of thousands of the inhabitants of the East Side of the narrow and crowded island, he had rarely been very far west of the Bowery, or north of Twenty-Third Street.

Up-town was unknown land to him. He now gazed at the acres of palaces, the majestic entrances, the noble basements well protected with railings of wrought iron, the exquisite windows overlooking vast expanses of ornate architecture, with astonishment.

He had never been in a large city in Russia; and nowhere before had he seen so much splendor. "Why are the houses all so quiet? many of them seem deserted," he ventured to say.

"O Reb Joseph!" said Miryam, "haven't you heard that all the rich people leave New York in the summer, and go to beautiful places in the woods and at the seaside, and only come back when there is no more hot weather?"

"While we sweat sixteen hours over our flat-irons and our sewing-machines, even when the thermometer is at ninety," said Bathsheba in a low voice in which concentrated passion seethed like lava at a volcano's mouth. "God! God! How can it be right that some should be so happy and fortunate through life, while others toil and struggle in torment, and die without leaving enough to bury themselves decently?"

The intensity of Bathsheba's utterance, and the bitterness of her words, seemed to touch a hidden chord in Joseph's heart.

He turned to her with the tears standing in his eyes, and murmured brokenly, —

"That is a terrible question. Don't ask it again; it stings me — here," and he touched his breast.

A baleful fire flashed from Bathsheba's splendid eyes. With a tragic gesture she pointed to the scene on the broad stone steps of a great mansion a little beyond where they were standing.

Two beautiful girls, in elegant dinner costume, had ventured out upon the steps in the warm darkness, and around them were gathered three or four young gentlemen, in evening dress, who paid assiduous court to the beauties.

In the doorway a majestic mamma was enthroned in an easy-chair, and two liveried servants were just bringing out a tiny Turkish table, beautifully inlaid with ivory and precious woods, and with a costly coffee service and *liqueur* cellaret arrayed upon it. One of the young girls was stripping flowers from her corsage, and distributing them with playful gestures to the courtiers at her feet.

Here were evidently some New Yorkers who had lingered in town in defiance of the conventionalities, and who were enjoying an after-dinner chat under cover of the friendly dusk without any fear of scrutiny.

Bathsheba clutched Joseph by the arm, and pointed to the comfortable group, the members of which had little idea that Misery at that moment had her envious eyes upon them.

"Do you see that, Joseph Zalmonah?" she hissed. "What more convincing than that do you want for an object-lesson? What do you think of the society that can permit such insolent luxury as that, and at the same time insist on such humble slavery as that of your poor cloakmakers? Do you think that you can ever reason with those people there?" pointing to the steps of the mansion. "Not much. And if you beg of them, they will put you in prison, or in an asylum." Her voice sank to a husky whisper. "Why, what is left, then, but to rise up and compel them — by force — to be just — to give a reasonable share of the world's joys and abundance to those who are starving for them? Why don't you answer me, Joseph Zalmonah?" and she shook his arm furiously.

"What is Bathsheba doing and saying?" cried little Miryam, running up with a protecting air to Joseph, who was staring at the group on the mansion's steps as if he meant that the memory of it should be graven on his heart.

CHAPTER XII

THE STORY OF SHIPHRAH

As they came away, the little dark-faced fiddler said timidly, —
"I don't see that those people were doing any harm. They were just enjoying themselves. They did not ask us to come to America and get into trouble."

Bathsheba gave him such a vicious pinch that he cried aloud, and was tempted to resent her reproof. But something in his spouse's look daunted him. He felt that she was in some mysterious way to derive profit from the incident.

The poet Mordecai was meditative. He was already composing a ballad on the episode in the manner of Nekrassof, most caustic of Russian popular poets, and was thinking out lines full of bitter irony. Presently David and Miryam turned the little party homeward, and Joseph found himself side by side with Bathsheba, and some distance behind all the others.

She laid her hand on his arm. Instinctively he stopped.

"Pardon me, Joseph Zalmonah," she said, speaking in Russian, a language which Joseph understood perfectly, but toward which he felt a kind of grim resentment, as if it were intimately associated with the misfortunes of his people. "I had something to say to you in private — something which I ought to say."

Joseph looked down into Bathsheba's eyes, and his head swam. He fancied that she must hear the beating of his heart.

"I am listening," he at last found courage to say. "But why should it be a secret? I don't like secrets. I have none from my family, my friends — my " — he hesitated an instant — " my wife."

Bathsheba understood. She had gone too far. She felt a strange delight that Joseph should instinctively repel the advance which she had made. It wounded her, but raised him immensely in her esteem. When she spoke again she was more timid.

"I just wanted to tell you that you are in danger. From what I have seen of you to-day, I believe that you are too valuable to yourself, and to others, to be sacrificed in a street brawl or a riot. Some of the men whom you meet daily are determined to do you a mischief. Don't ask me how I know."

"But why should they wish to hurt me?" said the young leader, studying Bathsheba's face intently. "I have never done anything to make enemies."

Bathsheba gazed at him in genuine wonder now. It was evident that this frank and guileless youth did not know that by the very sincerity and straightforwardness of his action he was creating enemies at every turn.

"I see that you do not appreciate the risks you are running," she said somewhat coldly, and moving away from him as she saw her husband looking round. "Well, I felt it a duty — as well as a pleasure," she turned her gaze full upon him, "to warn you against the Socialists. And now I will say nothing more about the matter."

"The Socialists! Why, they told me that you are a Socialist."

"And you think it strange that I should warn you

against myself, then ? " she said, with an odd little laugh, and catching up her faded draperies around her, with a swift and deft movement of her white hand.   " Come, the others are leaving us."

They went slowly onward, down the great avenue, a trifle abashed by its magnificence, and by the air of ease and comfort which characterized all the passers by. Through the soft summer darkness the huge and bold outlines of the mansions towered dimly.   Here and there a church, with pointed spire and sculptured portal, relieved the monotony of the brown-stone fronts.

From the open windows of clubs came the sound of laughter and gay discussions; and within they could see walls rich with gilding, and lined with costly paintings. Alcoves filled with palms and other exotics, and stairways richly carpeted, met their gaze.

Comfortable-looking elderly gentlemen, in cool yet prim garb, sat in arm-chairs at the broad windows, and discussed with sober and discreet gestures.   Servants in evening dress went leisurely to and fro, bearing seductive-looking drinks in crystal goblets on silver salvers.

Mordecai stopped now and then to look in upon one of these scenes of splendor, and as he stood with his gaunt face ravaged by the passion of anger, his eyes sparkling with resentment against the rich as a class, and his lips open, displaying his teeth, as if he would like to pounce upon the " idlers," as he called them in one of his poems, he was not a pleasant spectacle to contemplate.

While they gazed and walked and felt a growing new consciousness of the miserable nature of their own poor quarter to which they were returning, a sudden thirst for riches, an almost uncontrollable desire to participate in the luxury and ease before him, sprang into Joseph's heart, and behind it followed all kinds of mad and black ideas —

so that for the moment he was literally possessed of a demon in the old Biblical sense.

Did Bathsheba, by a magnetism so subtle that he could not perceive it, infuse her own ideas and longings into his spirit ? He never knew and never dreamed of asking himself the question.

But he did know that for a full half-hour, on that summer evening, sheltered by the darkness, he walked abroad the very incarnation of destruction, ready to hack, burn, and destroy, in order to gain entrance to the terrestrial paradises, glimpses of which were so new and so tormenting to him.

This savage mood passed away long before East Broadway was reached. Joseph left his companions in an elevated road train, and trudged home with a curious collection of hopes and fears crowding each other in his mind. As he arrived at his house he was surprised to see Ben Zion seated on the front steps, and Malcha haranguing him in a wild, passionate way.

Malcha's eyes were red, and it was plain that she had been weeping.

The husband bounded up the steps, and took the little wife in his arms. " Nothing has happened to Zipporah, I hope ? " he said anxiously, as the small mother laid her head trustfully against his thin and worn breast.

Malcha looked up, smiling through her tears. " Nothing. It is about Shiphrah. They have hidden her away, and won't let me see her."

Ben Zion arose, stretched himself, and came forward as if desirous of being called into action.

" Shiphrah ? " queried Joseph ; " but I thought that you had been with her all the afternoon. I am sure that David told me so."

" Ah ! we were to have been with her, but they have put her away where we can't " —

"Who?"

"The sweaters! Listen, Joseph. Shiphrah's father came to find me, hoping that I might have some news of the poor girl. But I had no comfort for the dear old soul, and while he sits here moaning and pulling his hair, and whining for his child, in rushes Ben Zion, all out of breath " —

Here Ben Zion came directly into Joseph's range of vision, and made a bow so full of dignity and whimsical self-importance, that Joseph's thin lips were wreathed with a smile.

" — and Ben Zion says, 'I have found out where Shiphrah is. She is hidden away in old Grunberg's, the sweater's, and he swears that she shall not go into the street until she has worked out her debt to him.' Then I asked her father to call the police and have them interfere, but he is an old fool, and won't do that. O Joseph, can't the police compel that beast to let Shiphrah go? They say she is dying by inches!"

"Who says so?" inquired Joseph calmly, but looking admiringly on his little wife, to whom the indignation which she felt over Shiphrah's fate had given a piquant and animated beauty.

Ben Zion recited to Joseph the story which the girls had told him in the "Pig Market." Joseph was thoughtful for a moment; then his fine face lighted up with intense resolution.

He brought one hand down upon the shoulder of Ben Zion with a force which made the pedler jump. "This is not a case for the police!" he said; "I will attend to it myself. Grunberg must give up Shiphrah at an instant's notice, or he must reckon with me!"

"O Joseph, do be careful, for Grunberg is a desperate man," wailed little Malcha. "Remember what they say of him, that he threw an old man down-stairs because he complained that he was getting blind in such a den! And they say that he strikes the work-girls!"

"He calls it ironing them," said Ben Zion in his unctuous voice. "When a girl doesn't work fast enough to please him, he takes one of the pressing-irons off from the red-hot stove and threatens to apply it to her back. A Polish girl threw the shears at him one day for threatening her, and he ironed her so that she couldn't get out of bed for a week. Her mother went to the police court about it; but there! they don't understand one-half that you say, and they never interfere unless there is an actual fight. What can you do?" Ben Zion held the palms of his hands up, and shook them with as much force as if he had been apostrophizing Grunberg himself.

"I will give him a lesson! He shall reckon with me and with the Union!" said Joseph, raising his right arm, and making a peculiar downward sweeping gesture, which he was wont to make when addressing large throngs, and when greatly excited.

On viewing this gesture, Ben Zion felt that the "whole business," as he afterwards expressed it in conversation with a neighbor, "was bitten off and chewed," and that he had nothing to do but to wait. So he agreed to meet Joseph at Grunberg's the next morning at ten o'clock, and then went away to engage in some one of his many occupations.

The story of Shiphrah was sad and exceptional. She had come with her father, Manasseh Rosenstein, from Russia three years ago. When the lonely Manasseh, with his shy and lily-faced little daughter, had left the town in which Malcha lived, they had a small capital, represented by the sale of their effects at half-price to the Russian offi-

cials who expelled them. Manasseh, who was the most
harmless of men, and whose only fault was an intense devotion to the tenets of orthodox Judaism, was boldly
accused by the officials of "attempting to conspire." It
was a meaningless charge, and without foundation; but it
served to secure his expulsion from the "Pale," with a
horde of common wretches, who were marched from
"*étape*" to "*étape*" under the cruel guardianship of gen-
darmes, and with fetters on their limbs.

Manasseh trudged uncomplainingly to the frontier with
his willowy, graceful sixteen-year-old daughter at his side,
and he quitted Russia without regret. In fact, he bestowed
upon it, beholding it while he was safe on German soil, a
malediction worthy the eloquence and the inspiration of an
ancient Hebrew prophet.

When the couple reached the promised land of America,
Manasseh accepted with meekness the humiliating disappointment which awaited him here. He shrank into a little
basement in Hester Street, filled a mouldy window with
mouldier Hebrew books, mostly of a pious nature, and went
through the forms of earning a livelihood.

A bit of bread and a black sausage satisfied his wants;
and he slept among his books, with his head pillowed on an
ancient Talmud, for which he might have got a handsome
sum, had such a sacrilegious thought as selling it ever
entered his head.

But Shiphrah could not participate in his contentment.
Although nurtured in the sternest orthodoxy, she gave evidence of a desire to rebel against the many observances
which make of the Jews a peculiar people. The damp little
room in the rear of her father's shop, where she made her
bed on two packing-boxes covered with time-worn furs
brought from Russia, and the occasional invasion of this
singular domicile by inquisitive and predatory rats, filled

her with disgust. The old man saw with horror that she was daily slipping away from him, and that all the barriers of the historic faith no longer existed between her and the outer modern world, with its dangers, its heresies, and its abominations. At first he was disposed to correct Shiphrah with sternness; but a conviction stole through him that it would be useless to try. He mourned in silence, and was more rigid than ever in his own observances of religious form.

In all that concerned the common life Shiphrah was compelled to conform. Manasseh was such a Sabbatarian as no New England farmer ever dreamed of being. On Friday night he began to prepare for the Saturday of prayer and repose.

His window remained open, and the books were exhibited, but he never made the smallest effort to sell them. A "reformed" Jewess was hired to cook the food which Shiphrah ate on Saturday; her father would not allow her to do any work on that day. He himself ate only food cooked the night before. He would not light the cigarette which on week-days was his main consolation.

He looked upon men and women who amused themselves by visits to theatre or social club on the sacred day as criminals. Dressed in a faded brown coat which hung down to his heels, in voluminous trousers which ended just above his boot-tops, and in a fur cap to which he clung even in the fierce heats of August; with long locks of hair combed in front of his ears, and with a pious book in his hands, he walked up and down Hester Street on Saturdays, with eye and brain oblivious to the secular world, the waves of which beat noisily around him.

He was a devout worshipper in one of the many synagogues scattered through the quarter.

It was reached by a perilous journey up dark and rickety flights of stairs, on which so many tiny children were always poking their way about that it was almost impossible to make a step without planting a foot on one of their squirming little bodies.

The synagogue, with its long rows of benches, divided into sections for the men and the women; with its central praying-desk, its dingy walls, and its schoolrooms, where children were taught the wisdom of the Talmud — this spiritual refuge amid the boisterous misery of the exiles' quarter, was Manasseh's favorite retreat. When he entered, a smile lighted up his usually dark and severe features; when he left it, and made his way back to the street, something of the spiritual glow still lingered, and he placed his hands benignantly on the heads of the children crowding about his door, with a patriarchal gentleness and protecting air, as of old his ancestors had done at the entrances of the tents of Israel.

One day Manasseh was troubled, and his hands trembled when he went into the synagogue in Ludlow Street, for he did not find Shiphrah there. Until then she had preserved all the outward signs of adherence to the strictest orthodoxy, and this backsliding was a great blow to the father. It hurt him all the worse because among the orthodox Jews the women are usually more fanatical than the men; and Shiphrah speedily had at her heels a score of feminine critics, ready to accuse her of all the sins in the calendar of wickedness, simply because she had fallen away from orthodoxy.

About this time old Manasseh fell ill, which was not wonderful, considering that he lived in a basement unfit for a dog-kennel; and Shiphrah, seeing the last few coins of their tiny hoard vanishing, and the father's trifling commerce at a standstill, quietly stepped into a sweater's shop and offered her services. After the preliminary purgatory of payments to learn the trade, Shiphrah was at last admitted to the sisterhood of misery, and began to earn four dollars weekly. And on this pittance old Manasseh and the girl had lived for two years, when the tempter came.

Shiphrah was pretty, of a voluptuous yet refined beauty rather uncommon in women of her class, and her privations and incessant toil had added a pensive grace to her naturally interesting features. While she was in despair at her hard lot, she attracted the notice of a small manufacturer, a Russian Hebrew like herself.

This man had set aside his wife because of some fancied or real grievance, and besought Shiphrah to give him her love, in return for emancipation from the horrible drudgery which was consuming her youth, and which weekly sent some poor man to die in the hospital.

The young manufacturer was handsome and pressing. Shiphrah yielded to his solicitations, but dared leave neither her work nor the wretched domicile of her father without an explanation which she feared might result in a tragedy.

But at last the chance came, and Shiphrah was quick to grasp it.

It was during the feast of the Passover, the eight days of which were for Manasseh a long spiritual relaxation. He left the cares of the vulgar world behind him, and revelled in the antique ceremonials which meant so much to him. The lowering April weather caused him torments of rheumatism; but Manasseh insisted on enacting each ceremonial as he had done in the old days when his wife and large family of sons and daughters, now all gone but Shiphrah, were gathered about him.

It was on the night when Manasseh observed "Seder" that Shiphrah saw her chance. A warm rain was falling. Manasseh closed his windows, drew the old curtains, and lighted the candles. Then he placed the half-worn pillow from Shiphrah's rude couch on two chairs, arranged a spread over it, and, as the head of the family, sat in solemn state beside it.

Shiphrah had arrayed on the extemporized table the plate with unleavened bread — the three flat cakes on a cracked bit of crockery; the bit of lamb, the cooked egg, the grated horse-radish, and the crushed walnut with wine. And now she sat in her corner, white and mute.

Manasseh had put on the white robe over his ordinary clothing, and his lugubrious appearance added to Shiphrah's steadily growing fear.

First he took one of the flat cakes from the centre, broke it in half, and placed the larger half under the pillow. Next, as the head of the family, he passed the unleavened bread.

Then, reclining as best he could in the narrow quarters, he partook of the lamb and the egg seasoned with the grated horse-radish, and Shiphrah also ate in silence. After this Manasseh began a long reading from the " Haggadah," and when bitter things were mentioned he placed his hand upon the crushed walnut as a reminder. On and on he read, in droning tone, while the candle sputtered, until at last, from very weariness, he ceased, and glanced over his great iron-bowed spectacles at Shiphrah, white and mournful in her corner. As he gazed at her a sudden compassion seized upon him, and he stretched out his hand to the poor over-worked girl.

She arose, tottered to his chair, and fell on her knees before him, crying, " Father, father, read no more to-night! O father, I have sinned, and am unworthy to remain in your sight. And now I must go away and leave you! But my care will always be over you — my love will be about you !"

Manasseh let the Haggadah fall from his hands, and sat

listening, with terrible grimness, while Shiphrah told her story. Then he arose quietly, and seizing the new plates bought expressly for the ceremony of that evening, he raised them high above his head, and dashed them with fury upon the floor.

This was his only sign of rage. Then he took the kneeling Shiphrah by the hand, raised her up, led her to the door, which was ajar, and threw it wide open. " Go !" he said hoarsely; " do not desecrate our home any longer ! "

The rain was still falling. Shiphrah was thinly clad and bareheaded : she made an imploring gesture, but the old man was implacable. He closed the door in her face, and in a minute the light in his window went out.

Shiphrah was alone. She walked through the rain to the sweater's house, and sat on his stairs until his doors opened. An hour later all her little household belongings were delivered there. The sweater knew of her adventure with the manufacturer, and understood. And that night the girl was installed in a comfortable home.

But the orthodox women averted their faces when she passed them in the street, and said that after her departure Manasseh had wailed long and loudly for her, as for one dead.

This was the beginning of the life romance of Shiphrah.

Manasseh did not wither away, as all his fellow-worshippers at the synagogue predicted. He grew gloomier and more fanatical than ever. But one day, a year after her departure from his door, there came news to him that Shiphrah had narrowly escaped death in premature childbirth; that she had been abused, and at last openly deserted by her cowardly lover, and finally that she had drifted back into the sweating-shop.

Then his heart longed for Shiphrah, and he sought her everywhere. But never had he been able to find her until, through Ben Zion's aid, he had learned that she was held in veritable slavery in Grunberg's den.

And now Joseph was to liberate her, as he had already liberated so many white slaves, from a bondage far worse than any ever suffered by the unhappy African.

CHAPTER XIII

GOD COUNTS WOMAN'S TEARS

A LONG ray of golden sunshine came in through the dusty window of the sweater's dingy and malodorous rooms, and, for an instant only, touched and glorified Shiphrah's face.

The girl sat in a corner, surrounded by half a dozen dark-haired, slovenly Polish Jewesses, one of whom was weeping as she toiled. Her tears fell on the garment in her hands; but that was so common a spectacle as to attract no special attention.

Shiphrah gave her fellow-slave a sympathetic look now and then; but she was the only one who ventured to glance up from labor and to bestow a little compassion. For the sweater was near by, standing at a table facing the girls, and he had a heavy hand.

He was a short, stout man, with a round head covered with bristling hair, with thick lips, and a nose conspicuously flattened at the nostrils. His hairy arms were naked to the shoulder, and when he flourished them every one in the two rooms trembled. Even his wife was afraid of him, and kept one eye on his movements, observing symptoms of rising storm, and sometimes giving warning of them to the girls by mysterious feminine signals, too acute for the apprehension of man.

The sweater had been " sweated " himself, and he knew

his trade perfectly. He understood the art of reducing the human body to a machine-like regularity of action, every atom of energy in which should be concentrated upon the production of salable articles.

He understood how to crush out every playful instinct, to repress each attempt at friendly conversation, and to menace when there was a tendency to unruliness. If a girl stopped to eat an apple, he had been known to take it from her and to throw it out of the window.

"You will have nothing to buy apples with at the end of the week, if you waste your time like that!" he would cry; and the poor slave would tremblingly resume her sewing, without daring to look up.

It was this sweater's boast that none of his cloakmakers belonged to Joseph's Union. "None of their nonsense for me!" he was wont to say. "If they meddle with my business, I will soon show them that I am independent. If they take my operators away, I can get a hundred more by whistling at my door." But he secretly feared Joseph; and on this very morning, as he counted, sorted, and piled the garments, he was plotting to propitiate him.

"I would like to knock off work at seven to-night," said a thin, pasty-faced operator, shuffling up to the "boss," and holding his hands clasped together in the supplicating and timid way which showed the strain of Orientalism in his nature. "We expect a new baby at our house, and my wife, she " —

"Expect and have are not twins, you know," said the sweater brutally. "Stay where you are, and without loafing, too, until half-past ten to-night! Don't try to play 'doctor' here. You can do that when you get home."

The man flushed deeply, then paled, and two great tears rolled down his cheek. He understood the allusion. In the sweater's lingo, a workman who is too particular, in their opinion, about the number of hours he works, is called "doctor;" and after he has been called so a few times, the sweater kicks him out of the shop, claiming that he is demoralizing all the others. He gazed sharply at the boss for a few seconds, then turned despairingly away, and hobbled back to his sewing-machine, which was in a dark corner.

It was a day of intense heat, and the sweat rolled from the brows of the swarthy men as they sat at the machines. It plashed on their arms, and left long marks on the woodwork, as the deft fingers guided the cloaks to the music of the needle. No one seemed to think of the heat; and in the centre of the smaller of the two rooms stood a round stove, with flat-irons upon it. This stove was red hot, and gave out a sickening odor, which made the girls seated nearest to it gasp for breath.

What tremendous activity pervaded the little company of twenty-five men, women, and children! Gazing on it with his merciless eyes, the sweater felt a pride in the talent for organization which it manifested. In this Inferno he made his fortune; every click of the machines meant profit to him. In the earnestness of his desire for gain, the hours did not seem long enough; and if his wretched toilers, after leaving at ten at night, were not back again before dawn, he cursed them, and often flew at them like a wild beast.

The operators began with sewing the seams, the sleeves, and fastening the "foundations" on to the cloaks. Then they sewed on the face-cloths, and raced the needles round the bodies of the coats, and sewed up to the slits.

After this they took the points out, and stitched all round. Then came the under-collar, which was stitched upon a piece of stiffening, and next the over-collar, after which the needles took another run round, to make all things firm.

Meantime the attendant girls were catching up cloak after cloak, as they came hot from the machines, and basting in the sleeves. Then the garments went back to the operators, to have the sleeves fitted and the bindings sewed on.

And now the pressman's work began, or, more correctly, never ended; for as fast as he had one pile of cloaks in shape, another loomed up before him; and when he dragged his weary legs away at night, mountains of cloaks cast a frowning shadow behind him.

Each cloak passed in review before the sweater, who with skilful fingers marked with chalk the places for the buttons. Then he distributed them to the button-sewers, throwing down a certain number of cloaks before each girl with a savage energy, which seemed to say, " If you do not hurry, I will apply the lash."

Every one of the girls shrank each time the sweater approached them, as if he actually had a whip in his hand. No matter if the fingers bled, no matter if the poor heads ached, no matter if a woman were faint from starvation, imposed upon herself that her children might have a little more to eat, there was no mercy, nor even the semblance of compassion. To see men and women worn to exhaustion by grinding toil was so common a sight for the sweater, that he no longer appreciated the horrible indignity, the immense pathos of it.

And so it is that a glut in the labor market can make brutes of men, and slaves of the weaklings whom they have the cunning to employ.

This sweater manufacturer paid the most wretched of wages, because he had no contracts. He bought cloth at bankrupt sales, and got great bargains. He paid workers thirty-five cents per piece when other sweaters gave seventy-five; and when his goods were finished he had them peddled from door to door among the large dealers, until some one would take the lot.

When trade was slack, or he had a considerable stock of unsold goods on hand, he became a veritable demon. At the least infringement of his beggarly regulations, he frothed at the mouth with rage. He spat in the faces of the old men who protested that they could not do their tasks. He threw one poor old fellow down-stairs for coming to bring his daughter a few apples and a cracked pot full of coffee at noontide. He drove a dozen operators from the place in one day, because they had arranged with an ancient dame to bring them a warm dinner, which they were to eat in their places at their machines. In vain did they remonstrate and protest that they must eat or die. "They could take their own time over their suppers," he said, "but they should not waste his." This to the wage-workers; and to piece-workers he was almost equally tyrannical. "Let them know what comfort is, and they will desert me in a body," he said to himself, and he was right.

There was an ominous silence in the sweater's rooms on this hot and stifling day; and it made the sweater's nerves tingle just a little with fear. His treatment of Shiphrah had aroused a dangerous desire for revolt—a feeling which as yet none of the poor over-worked creatures dared openly to manifest, but which was as full of perilous possibilities as the lava fire when it froths up to the rim of a volcano's crater.

Shiphrah was heavily in the sweater's debt: he alone had supplied the money without which she would have died after her heart-breaking experience with her cowardly lover; and when he found that there was no way of getting it back from that lover himself, he had turned in fury upon the girl, and had cried: —

"You shall never leave this place until you have worked

out every penny that you owe. And if any one who sews
here ventures to tell old Manasseh where his daughter is,
before she has paid her debt to me, I will throw the tale-
teller into the street."

This would have been an idle injunction if given to a
company of independent American workmen and women.
But to the shrinking and affrighted group of refugees and
exiles, who had scarcely recovered from the shock of their
summary expulsion from Russia, and who felt completely
helpless in this strange and new land, the command and
the menace were very effective indeed.

Not one of the slaving and starving cloakmakers employed in this horrible den had dared to hint outside that
Shiphrah was held in bondage worse than their own. For
that matter, many of them had never heard Shiphrah's
whole story, and were little likely to see or hear of old
Manasseh.

But at last the three girls who had known Shiphrah in
happier days had strayed into the establishment; had told
the story to Ben Zion in the " Pig Market; " and the
secret which the sweater fancied safely kept had gone
straight to the hearing of the man whom he really dreaded
most of all, — the redoubtable Joseph.

It happened that as the hot forenoon wore away one of
the Polish girls, who was so faint that she could scarcely
ply her needle, took from a little bundle a tiny earthen coffee
pot, in which there remained a cupful of bitter liquid unworthy the name of the famous Arabian beverage.

Glancing around with fear in her eye, the girl advanced
her thin arm, and placed the little pot on the stove.

At that time the sweater was in the inner room, cursing
an operator whose work was not done to his satisfaction.
The girl had managed to get the coffee warmed before the
monster's return, and holding the coffee-pot in her lap, was

exploring her bundle in search of a cup, when she heard
the tyrant's voice angrily raised.

In her nervousness she sprang up, overturning the coffee
upon the cloak in her lap, scalding her limbs, and uttering
a shriek, which brought the sweater to her side with an
ugly glare in his eyes.

When he saw what had occurred, he snatched the garment from the girl and struck her twice, brutally, over the
head with it.

One of the buttons raised a livid scar on the poor creature's cheek.

She stood panting, mute, chilled to the heart by this
insolent cruelty, but with a desire for vengeance growing
in her heart, and filling her with a fury almost too great for
expression.

Yet at last she clasped her hands and wept and cried
aloud. The earthen coffee-pot fell to the floor, was shat-
tered, and the poor girls near by set up a sympathetic
wail.

The sweater's face grew white, but his eyes blazed with
passion. He advanced toward the girl again, flourishing
the heavy cloak, as if he meant to strike her down to the
earth with it.

Shiphrah could not endure this spectacle. She sprang
forward and implored the sweater not to strike.

But the brute in the man was now thoroughly aroused.
He pushed Shiphrah aside, and, roaring with fury, struck
the culprit again.

"I'll teach you," he cried, "to come breaking up all the
discipline of my place with your swineries."

This time the girl stood quite still, with the pallor of
death upon her gaunt face. A thin stream of blood trickled
from one of her nostrils, and the tears coursed slowly down
her cheeks.

She raised her brow slightly, as if inviting and expecting the next blow, which should finish her martyrdom.

" Stop, neighbor ! " suddenly cried a loud, clear voice which made the sweater lower his hand and look confusedly around him.   " Have you forgotten the good old Jewish proverb, 'God counts woman's tears ' ? "

Then arose a humming and whispering and tittering, interspersed with cries of indignation, and one or two threats.   The sweater instinctively felt that unless he made some authoritative move instantly he would find himself face to face with a revolt.

He turned angrily to see who had ventured to intrude.

The new-comer was Ben Zion, with whom the sweater had a slight acquaintance.   The pedler held in one hand a long pole garnished with two or three hoops, from which hung "pretzels" in various stages of staleness.   In the other he carried a huge jug; over his shoulder was a pack, from which came a not unmusical clinking of tinware.

At sight of the sweater's inflamed features, and his eyes in which murder was written, Ben Zion grinned, and made a mock obeisance, remarking, —

" Sorry to interfere in a family difficulty, as the bear said when he ate the moujik who was beating his wife, but I thought the good people up here might like a few mouthfuls of lunch.   Now, these pretzels " —

And he extended the pole, so that its point almost touched the irate sweater in the face, and effectually prevented him from striking another blow.

" Get out with your miserable trash !   Do you want to poison my people ? " yelled the sweater.   " Haven't I given strict orders that no begging pedlers were to come into my place ?   Out with you !"

" Oh !   A little minute ! " said Ben Zion caressingly. " Why, I've only just come in !   And really, when it comes

to choose between being poisoned, and beaten to death, I
don't suppose that your cherished employes "—

The maddened sweater hurled the cloak from his hand at
Ben Zion. But the garment fell upon the red-hot stove,
where it was scorched crisp, at which a yell of triumph at
the sweater's discomfiture arose from the seven or eight
operators watching the scene.

Ben Zion had raised his pole, but he brought it down
again so adroitly that it served as a barrier to keep the
sweater from the corner in which Shiphrah and the poor
Polish girl were cowering and expecting to be cast out of
the workshop by the sweater's brutal hands.

"Why, there's the pretty Shiphrah, after whom her old
father has been hunting so long!" said Ben Zion, assuming
an air of intense surprise, and at the same time winking and
grimacing in his endeavor to convey to Shiphrah that he was
a friend.

"O my father!" cried the girl, springing forward. "Is
he alive? Does he hate my very name? I wish I might
go to him, and pray him to forgive me!"

"So you shall, pretty one! so you shall!" said Ben Zion,
cautiously setting down his jug, and slipping his pack from
his back. And as the sweater tried to rush forward to
Shiphrah, Ben Zion suddenly gripped the pole with both
hands, and tapped the sweater's head pretty smartly
with it.

"Excuse the accident!" said Ben Zion, smiling serenely,
"but I really must speak with this young lady a minute.
And as she and her companion there seem positively faint,
I must offer them a cup of this excellent coffee and a pretzel. Won't you have a pretzel too?" he added, shoving
the pole into the sweater's face again. Then, in answer to
Shiphrah, he said, —

"You shall see your father to-day. His daughter shall
not be a slave any longer. Deliverance is at hand!"

Ben Zion spoke these last words with a fine melodramatic air; then, stooping down, he brought forth from his pack some tin cups, filled them with coffee from the jug, and plucking some pretzels from the hoops, he passed this frugal luncheon to the two girls, who were too amazed to refuse.

"By your leave!" said Ben Zion, grinning at the sweater, whose face was purple with rage. The operators and seamstresses were now all crowding into the front room, laughing, whispering, shaking their heads ominously. Never before had so much time been lost in a sweater's den on the East Side. The revolt was complete.

"Now, friends," said Ben Zion, "who says coffee and pretzels? Only three cents for each person! You'll work all the better afterwards. Oh, never mind him! He'll come round to our way of thinking after he has joined our Union! Come! who buys?"

"I'll discharge the first man or woman who touches any of that trash!" shouted the sweater. "And as for you," shaking his fist at Ben Zion, "get out of this room, or I will send for the police!"

"Do; and I'll give you in charge for kidnapping Shiphrah!" said Ben Zion, pouring coffee for an operator who had mustered up courage to brave the sweater. "Ah! you are more quiet now! We live and learn, as the bear said when he was hunting for honey, and the bees stung him."

"My father!" moaned Shiphrah, suddenly awakened to new hopes. "If I could see him once more!"

"He will be here in a few minutes," said Ben Zion calmly.

"Here!" screamed the sweater; "I'll break every bone in his sanctimonious old body if he dares to come here. And Shiphrah shall not leave this house until I have been paid my money, all my money — do you understand?"

His voice rose to a shriek — the shriek of the miser fearing to be deprived of his treasure.

".How is that, man ? " said a voice which made the sweater more frantic than before.   " Is this a debtors' prison, or a workshop ?   Do I hear that you are keeping women here against their will ? "

Everybody gazed at the entrance, where stood Joseph, with Malcha leaning on his arm, and old Manasseh bending over his staff, and looking like a prophet of doom.

" Who are you, and what do you want ? " snarled the sweater, his eyes dilating like those of a wild beast at bay.

" I am the representative of the Cloakmakers' Union," answered Joseph calmly, but drawing himself up, and making the downward sweeping gesture which always compelled attention to his speeches.   "And I want to know how it is that when we are engaged in a life-and-death struggle with the manufacturers, your place is open, and you are driving your employes harder than ever ?   Perhaps you can answer me that."

The sweater felt shivers of rage sweep over him.   The dreaded Joseph was here, and had doubtless brought revolt in his train.   He must act quickly against him.

"I know nothing about your Union, or you either," he said rudely.   "And I give you notice that if you come a step farther into my shop you'll rue it ! "

As he spoke he advanced hastily to the stove, the sides of which were ruddy with intense heat, and seized a huge flat-iron from its top, shouting, —

"Out with you, or I'll mark you for life ! "

Joseph looked at the maddened man sternly as he answered, —

" We shall see who will go out first ! "

At that moment a lithe form brushed past the sweater, and sprang into the arms of old Manasseh.   Shiphrah had found her father again. Malcha withdrew with the girl and her father into a corner of the darkened landing, and the three quietly awaited the victory which they knew would be Joseph's.

"Out, I say, or I'll brand you!" howled the sweater.

The operators and the women were huddled together, gazing almost reverently at Joseph, of whose prowess as a popular leader they had heard. Some of the women were muttering prayers.

Joseph's face shone with excitement. "Coward!" he said to the sweater. "It is men like you who make it so hard for our people to rise! But you shall tyrannize over these poor men and women no longer."

The sweater concentrated all his malice, and hurled the hot iron with tremendous force straight at Joseph's head. But at the next moment he received such a thrust from Ben Zion's pole that he nearly lost his senses, and when he could breathe and see again, he noticed that his missile had done no harm, and that Joseph was standing over him, white and stern.

"Listen to me," said Joseph. "Shiphrah shall go to her father, and in time what she owes you shall be paid. But don't try to keep her now, or you may be torn in pieces. And now, brethren and sisters," he cried, turning to the astonished workers, "the Cloakmakers' Union will march to Freier and Monach's at four o'clock. Will you join us? Will you strike for freedom? or will you let this ruffian bully you?"

"We will march — we will go with you!" shouted the operators, and the women also feebly assented. Then they poured out of the shop, leaving the sweater and Joseph face to face.

"Follow them!" commanded Joseph, "and let me see you in the line of march at four o'clock, or it will be the worse for you!"

"Never!" snarled the sweater, foaming with rage.

"Follow them!" cried Joseph in a deeper voice, and pointing to the door.

This time the sweater yielded, and he slunk out of his own shop, and went timidly past Ben Zion, who stood on guard with the pretzel pole at the door, and crawled timidly down the dark stairways.

Meantime, Shiphrah was sobbing upon old Manasseh's breast.

CHAPTER XIV

THE HUNGER PROMENADE

Shiphrah would have knelt at Joseph's feet and kissed the hem of his coat with veritable biblical fervor. But the young leader would not permit it.

Malcha took the girl away to her house, old Manasseh hobbling after, and muttering many pious phrases expressive of his joy.

Joseph and Ben Zion remained upon the field of battle.

" Are you aware," said Ben Zion, flourishing the pretzel pole as if it bore a triumphal banner at its summit, "that this is the Fourth of July, the anniversary of the great day when the Americans dictated a peace, on the shores of England, to the king who was trying to enslave them? They sailed over there, I'm told, and scattered the fleets of England and France, and then made a proclamation of Independence, which they still repeat after their prayers. When was it? Many hundreds of years ago, I'll be bound!"

"Not so very many," answered Joseph, with a quiet smile at Ben Zion's distortion of the historical facts, which he himself could not have stated with absolute accuracy; "not so very long ago but that they are still much in love with their own independence, and care precious little about anybody else's. Fourth of July, indeed! And our six or seven thousand hungry devils are going to parade, just to show these well-fed, independent citizens how wretched we are! It makes my heart ache."

"Don't grumble, Joseph Zalmonah," said Ben Zion. "Think of the nice lump of money that the newspapers raised for the Union! Where should we have been without that, for the last day or two, I should like to know?"

"True," said Joseph, "I don't mean to complain; but if anything is galling, it is to be poor in the midst of plenty. But come, we have no longer any right here — hark! what was that yell?"

"It sounded like the cry that Levi Obermann gave the day they threw him out of the synagogue — you remember; the contractor! They nearly tore the poor fellow in pieces! Halt there!" he cried, lowering his pretzel pole like a lance at rest.

The sweater rushed across the darkened landing, dodged Ben Zion, and threw himself at Joseph's feet, cowering like a whipped dog. "They will kill me!" he whimpered. "Don't make me go out there alone! Go with me, or they will tear me in pieces!"

"And they would not be far wrong!" growled Ben Zion, prodding the sweater with the pole. "Get up, you lump of a needle-shifter, and try to be a man! Are our fellows ready to march?"

"They are," said the sweater, his teeth chattering. "What dreadful thing are they going to do?"

"Get up!" repeated Ben Zion, seizing the sweater by the collar, "or, by the bones of Abraham! I'll iron you with your own flat-irons! Join the procession, and ask no questions, as the ant said to the elephant when they went into the ark. Your life is safe enough under the protection of our Union. And yet, only an hour ago you were fighting against it!"

"'Our Union,'" said the reassured sweater, with a twin-

kle in his eye ; "I thought you were a pedler. And what
are you doing in the Cloakmakers' Union ? "

"I — oh — I am just a deputy to keep the fools in order," stammered Ben Zion, who had found the question a
little confusing; "so get along with you, and don't so much
as dare to look at Herr Joseph, here, or he may not let you
join us. And then your goose certainly would be cooked."

It was at least a quarter of an hour before Ben Zion's
arguments, kicks, and proddings with the pretzel pole
could persuade the sweater to accompany him to the street.
When at last they came into the little square in front of
the house, they found Joseph, who had preceded them, trying to reason with a mob of women who had heard the
story of Shiphrah's detention, and wanted to lynch the
sweater before starting on this "hunger parade."

Public sympathy, as the kind-hearted policeman had told
Joseph, needed but to be aroused to yield goodly fruit; and
little sums had found their way to the Union's treasury,
and made the cloakmakers more resolved than ever to fight
the lock-out to the bitter end.

The manufacturers had set non-Union men at work in
some of their establishments, and boasted that all the
power of New York's authority would be on their side if
these men were attacked. Therefore it had been deemed
expedient that the starving cloakmakers, who had been
thrust from their places because they dared to protest
against an infamous scale of wages, and as substitutes for
whom the non-Union men had been employed, should
promenade in a body, and still further enlist the pity of the
citizens of the metropolis.

Joseph did not approve of this; it jarred upon his sense
of independence. And yet, in his heart, he admitted that
it was adroit and practical; and at the last moment he had
placed himself at the head of the procession. He had

halted the motley company before the sweater's, that he
might do justice in the case of Shiphrah; and now he was
ready to march.

"On to Freier and Monach's! to Freier and Monach's!"
screamed the women. "Let them see how starved we
look."

"Yes," snarled an old crone; "and if they laugh at us
we'll tear them limb from limb, won't we, darlings?"

"Limb from limb!" came back the answer in a shrill
chorus, which made Joseph turn pale. He knew that the
women would fulfil their threat, if they had even slight
provocation.

A tootling band, lent for the occasion by a friendly labor
organization, struck up the "Marseillaise," which the throng
did not recognize; but when it played one or two German
airs, the starving people showed some little animation, and
stepped out as if they were going to take a new Bastile.

The sweater marched unmolested, and a dozen of the
workers who had just rebelled against his tyranny were
close behind him.

The day was intensely hot and airless. The ill-kept
streets steamed with rank odors. The tall gaunt buildings
seemed to sweat like the populace.

The throng was much smaller than that which had accompanied Joseph to the landlord to demand justice for
Mother Levitsky. But in the glaring light of the summer
day it seemed more hideous, gaunt, and dreadful than the
company of the night march.

A thousand women, hundreds of them with puny, wailing
infants in their arms, headed the line. The misery of
these poor creatures was appalling. They were walking
skeletons. Their almost fleshless yellow faces; their fierce,
staring eyes; their matted locks; their ragged garments,
which scarcely covered them decently; the way in which

they clutched their starving infants; the strident laughter with which they hailed appeals for moderation and compromise in case they visited the manufacturers' premises — all were terrible.

There were women who had nursing children at the breast, and who had tasted nothing but a little coffee for two days. They flourished their lean arms; they wagged their swollen tongues; they danced hysterically, and proffered dreadful threats of vengeance.

The streets rang with the uncouth echoes of the "jargon."

Meantime the men, less talkative, but equally angry and inflamed, dragged their weak limbs along. Some shivered in spite of the intense heat; others were sunstruck, and had to be revived in the friendly shade of doorways; all clamored for water. Old men trudged on, munching bits of black bread between their toothless jaws. The younger operators had dressed themselves neatly for the occasion, but the fierce heat had prompted them to take off coats and waistcoats; and long before they reached Freier and Monach's, they were reeking with perspiration, and as dishevelled as the women.

They came at last to the hated manufacturers, the head and front of the lock-out, the arch enemy of their Union, and they set up a fierce yell. Most of them were ignorant that the Fourth of July is a national holiday; but those who knew it felt certain that the tyrants would have some one on hand to represent them and protect their property.

Joseph halted his starving company, with strict injunctions to make no attack on Freier and Monach's, and to await his return. "There will be no 'scabs' at work there to-day," he said. "Besides, we must hear what the firm has to say."

"Tear them limb from limb," shrieked the women; but it was evident that they would respect Joseph's admonition.

So he assembled his committee — the identical one which Freier and Monach had so badly treated on the previous visit, and applied for admission.

They got in without difficulty. Freier and Monach were both there, writing busily, and smoking huge black cigars. Joseph was a little astonished to see Freier jump up and come forward with much cordiality of demeanor. "Look here, Zalmonah!" he said in German, "call off your fellows out there. We don't want any disturbance, and things may all come round right yet. Come with your committee and see us to-morrow about this hour. There's a good fellow. Say to your cloakmakers that it will all be right — to-morrow — arrange, you understand?"

"No, I can't say I do," said Joseph. "Your last message was one of war. Now you are as peaceful as moonlight. What assurance can I give" —

"Your army out there?" said Freier, laughing uneasily. "Oh, tell them that you are arranging the matter."

While he was talking he had edged away from the gaping members of the committee, holding Joseph by the arm, and had managed to get him into a little recess behind a table. Here he said to Joseph in a hurried whisper, —

"And, say, Zalmonah, you are a man of sense, and I've heard that you wish to perfect your education. Now, if you will drop all this labor business, I'll be your banker as long as you like, and will write you a check for five thousand dollars any time you ask for it. Come! Choose between that out there" (indicating the waiting cloakmakers) "and this good offer. Accept, and you will find plenty of friends."

Joseph put out his hands quickly, and thrust the tempter violently away from him.

Thinking that he was about to be attacked, the members of the committee rushed forward.

But Joseph stayed them with an imperious gesture.

Then he gave Freier a look of blazing indignation, which turned the man white with apprehension.

"We will not come here to-morrow," he said; "you need not expect us. When we are ready we will come back for our final answer about the close of the lock-out. And I would advise you not to renew then the proposition which you have just made to me. If you should do so, I would hand you over to that crowd there yonder, and it would tear you into shoe-strings!"

"You are an insolent beast, and I will have you put where you can't talk so much!" said Freier through his clenched teeth. "You think you can come here and dictate to us Americans!"

Joseph snapped his fingers in Freier's face. "That for your threats!" he said. "Perhaps we shall soon find out who is master in this business. Good-day."

"I defy you!" said Freier. "We Americans" —

"Oh, come," cried Joseph, "your American citizenship is too new to brag about. There are men in the procession out there who are better American citizens than you are."

He stalked out with the committee at his heels, and thus the second meeting with Freier ended like the first, in anger and unfruitfulness.

"He tried to bribe me!" said Joseph in a choking voice, as he returned to the head of the hungry company. "Let him alone to-day! Come along to Broadway!"

And to Broadway they went. Thousands of promenading citizens were startled by the passage of this melancholy throng of tottering men, and tattered women with skinny children in their arms. They looked with astonishment on this sudden apparition of Misery in the very centre of prosperity. It alarmed and enlightened them. When the cloakmakers tottered home that night, almost despairing, they had won a host of supporters.

At the office of the Union Joseph found two hundred
dollars in crisp bills, "the product of a collection down
town," awaiting his arrival.

He sent out trusty messengers to distribute this far and
wide among the starving ones, and then went home and
threw himself down on his bed, feeling strangely hopeful
that the lock-out would soon end. Malcha and the
child, as he learned from a note, were at old Manasseh's
with Shiphrah.

Joseph was just falling into an uneasy slumber in the
hot and ill-ventilated room, when there came a timid knock
at the door. At first he was disinclined to answer it; but
finally, fearing lest it might be the news of some new disturbance among the cloakmakers, he arose and groped his
way wearily to the door, threw it open, and found himself face to face with Rudolf Baumeister.

At sight of the nervous features of that energetic conspirator, Joseph could not repress a frown. But Baumeister saluted him so politely, and seemed so anxious to enter
into conversation, that Joseph rubbed his eyes and muttered,—

"Well, Herr Baumeister, what is it? Has your revolution begun? Is Society turned inside out, and have you
come to call me to see the remains?"

"Zalmonah," said the man in a tremulous tone, "we are
on the eve of great things. The time is ripe for revolt.
The harvest awaits the reapers. I have come to ask you
to thrust in your sickle with the rest of us. Don't send me
away as you did before. Join us, and work with us at
the grand overturning!"

Joseph felt inclined to shut the door in Baumeister's
face. But weary as he himself was, and in deadly earnest
though Baumeister certainly was, he could not help ap-
preciating the humor of the occasion.

"Come in," he said; "and before I make any decision about joining, I should like to know what you propose to overturn, and how many of you there are to overturn it."

"Always satirical, Herr Joseph," said Baumeister, entering slowly, and leaning against the blackened wall of the kitchen chimney and breathing hard. "Let me sit down, please; my head feels heavy."

"You look white and faint," said Joseph kindly. "Let me give you a glass of tea, if we have any left."

"Yes," said Baumeister, with an odd little laugh, "I am as weak as one of your poor locked-out creatures. The fact is that I have not tasted solid food for two days. I haven't felt like eating; and it makes my head turn round — you know the feeling."

Joseph looked at him attentively. He gave Baumeister a chair at the little kitchen table. Then he placed on it a wooden platter on which was a small loaf of bread and a fried fish.

"When you have eaten we can talk," he said gravely.

Baumeister thanked him faintly, and began eating with an apparently voracious appetite, saying between the mouthfuls,—

"I often get out of money, you see, when I am following an idea; and I won't beg. I wait. Sometimes it is hard work this waiting, when you are hungry " —

"Yes, I think I know something about that," said Joseph dryly.

He was watching Baumeister narrowly, for he suspected some conspiracy. His first thought was that the Socialist had been drinking. But presently he saw that the unsteady flame in his eyes, the slight tremor in his muscles, the curious inflections in his speech, were all the result of some recent profound excitement. Was his hunger real? Or was it a trick assumed to enlist Joseph's sympathies?

Joseph suspected him, but pity arose to dull his suspicions as he saw the would-be overthrower of Society seated on the old wooden chair, munching the hard bread.

"You were speaking of overturning," he said gently, when Baumeister showed signs of relenting his attacks on the bread and fish.

"Ah! Overturn — burn — destroy — and plant again; but not the old seed — no — no — none of that!" said Baumeister in a loud voice, rising hurriedly and coming quickly to Joseph's side. "The hour is at hand, Zalmonah. That procession of the hungry was a great thought, worthy, my young friend, of your masterly mind. It has made a tremendous sensation. The public is alarmed. The newspapers are talking about labor riots on a grand scale, close at hand. The capitalists are quaking in their palaces! What a grand chance for the 'party of force'! What a moment for a demonstration! One push, and we might topple the whole wall down! Ha, ha, ha! Topple it down, and bury the fat carcasses of the capitalists under it. Ho, ho, ho! Ha, ha, ha!"

Joseph stood listening to this tirade with a contemptuous smile on his lips. But there was something so strangely exalted in Baumeister's manner, that it almost frightened him. The voice had an unsteady ring; the gestures were almost grotesque.

"The last time you came here, Herr Baumeister," he said, "I declined to believe that we cannot win our cause by legitimate methods. Everything that I have seen since your visit tends to confirm my belief. So that I am as little disposed as before to go into the overturning business, which does not seem to be giving you a very good living."

"Never mind me — my living," stammered Baumeister; "the cause, the cause is all! We must have you to help

us : you are a tower of strength. We are losing chances
daily ! A few hours ago, at Washington Square, we might
have started the great Social Revolution ! Your procession was a splendid pretext for beginning. Make another
procession — to-morrow — dear Herr Zalmonah — another —
and we can in a few hours be trampling capital under our
feet. The masses will rise with us ! and the victory will
be easy ! You must — you shall help us to start the Social
Rev " —

Baumeister glared suddenly at Joseph. The word " revolution " died away on his lips. He uttered a loud yell,
and fell forward, foaming at the mouth, and breathing
stertorously, in an epileptic fit.

Joseph felt a slight touch on his arm. He turned and
saw Ben Zion. " I saw him coming here, and I followed
him," said the pedler, " thinking he might be up to some
mischief. I'll bring him out of that fit — I know how.
My father's brother used to have 'em regular." And seat-
ing himself astride the fallen Socialist, he began to bang
his insensible head against the floor.

" You will kill him," cried Joseph.

" See ! He's already coming round !" said Ben Zion ; and
in another minute Baumeister opened his eyes, his heavy
breathing ceased, and he murmured as if he had never
ceased speaking, —

" —olution — yes, the Revolution. You shall help us
to start it to-morrow." Ben Zion helped him to a chair,
and Joseph bathed his head with water. " You must have
got a touch of the sun," said Joseph; " you went down as
if you had been shot."

But Baumeister seemed to have no knowledge of the fit.
" Tell me," he said, almost pleadingly, " that I may count
you among the members of the party of force from this
moment henceforth ! Tell me that you will co-operate
with us to-morrow !"

"You have already had my answer on that point," said Joseph firmly. "Neither to-morrow nor at any time. I think your Revolution is a dream — or a madness!"

"Ah!" said Baumeister, looking up quickly, with a startled smile, "you wish to get rid of me, and so you call me crazy. It is a poor argument."

He seized the tumbler in which some tea was standing, and drank the liquid greedily. Then he arose slowly, gripping the glass so fiercely that it cracked to pieces. He gave Joseph a long, weird look, then dashed the fragments of glass madly to the floor, and shouted with great force, —

"You will not make the Revolution with us? Very well; then we will make it without you! And look well to yourselves if you get in our way!"

He extended his hand, and shook it menacingly in Joseph's face. Then he picked up his hat and went out, staggering like a drunken man.

"I'm afraid the heat has made him mad," said Joseph.

"The work was well begun before the heat finished it," remarked Ben Zion. Then he thrust his hand into the breast-pocket of his faded coat. "Here's a message. I forgot it when I saw that lunatic in his fit. A little boy brought it to me in the market, and asked me to get it to you post-haste."

Joseph tore open the unaddressed white envelope, and took from it a slip of paper, on which was written in delicate Hebrew script: —

"I warned you once, but I am afraid that you did not take it enough to heart. You are in great danger. If you do not join Baumeister and his party you must be vigilant and wary. Those men are desperate. I know what they mean to do if you fail them. They think your martyrdom would bring on the flurry that would turn into revolution. You must take a decision, and act. B."

A second warning from Bathsheba! It was lucky that

Ben Zion's attention was diverted to the safety of his push-cart outside; for otherwise he would have seen Joseph, moved by a sudden passion which he himself could not have explained, press the little missive to his lips, and then hide it carefully in an inner pocket.

Ben Zion presently went away, and Joseph opened the window of the front room and sat down, looking out over the wretched world of East Broadway, where his people were making their starveling preparations for their Sabbath. There was an ominous stillness. People spoke in low tones, and seemed preoccupied, as when a pestilence is abroad, or war or famine is at hand. And when Malcha came home an hour later, leading tired little Zipporah, who could scarcely prop her sleepy eyes open, she found Joseph seated, staring straight into space, as if he saw signs and wonders there.

CHAPTER XV

JOSEPH AND BATHSHEBA

A WEEK passed, and Joseph thought for the first time in his life that the hours had leaden feet. One hot, malodorous day followed another, each bringing nothing to distinguish it from its predecessor save an increasing number of deaths among the famishing cloakmakers.

From time to time Joseph received contributions from charitable persons, societies, and churches. He trudged about in the heat, refusing even to take horse-cars or " L " trains, in his anxiety to save every penny.

" Each five cents may mean a baby's life — a poor mother's rescue from starvation," he said.

Of the money he took only his share. " Malcha and the child were not to suffer," he said. " As for myself, I like suffering. It adds a kind of savor to life."

" Those who have not suffered have not truly lived," he would sometimes say to Malcha, when he started out in the hot mornings to distribute his succor.

The cloakmakers stood valiantly to their colors; but, as yet, the manufacturers, headed by Freier and Monach, gave no sign of weakness.

One morning Joseph went out very early, to carry a few dollars to a family whose chief had shown him the night before a " dispossess " notice. " If we haven't the money at nine o'clock to-morrow forenoon," he had said, " out we

go on to the pavement. My wife is already sick with the
hunger-fever. You know what putting us out would mean."

As Joseph hastened on his errand of mercy, at the angle
of two streets he met Freier face to face.

He would have avoided him. But Freier smiled, and
spread out his arms in most engaging fashion.

"Oh! Ah! Here is my good friend, the enemy!" he
said, with an effusive politeness which was maddening to
the poor labor-leader. "I am sure that he will forgive me
for getting into a temper every time we have a conference."
He spoke in jargon, but suddenly changed to English,
saying, —

"Now, look here, Herr Zalmonah, don't pull away from
me in that angry fashion ! I am anxious to have the differ-
ences between us settled ; but your obstinacy blocks everything. Say, there's nothing in it for you, if you do win the
fight, don't you know ? Why not give up your share in
the matter, and let the greasy devils take care of themselves ? "

The veins in Joseph's temples stood out in bold relief.

A strong color came into his face. He raised a warning
hand. But Freier was determined to be heard.

" Come, now, Zalmonah," and his voice sank to a whisper, "you didn't like my proposition the other day. What
do you say to a trip to London, and then to the old country, to Russia, to see your folks, and make them a few useful presents ? You need not be gone more than four months,
and by that time all this difficulty will have blown over.
Say the word, and I'll make the check the same that I
offered before, and sign it to-day. What does a thinker
like you want with all these labor brawls ? "

Joseph's voice trembled as he said, " So you would like
to send me to Russia, and have me stopped at the frontier
by the paternal police, on the ground that I am a suspi-

cious and revolutionary person, eh, Herr Freier? I see that you persist in taking me for a simpleton. Once for all," he said, raising his voice suddenly almost to a cry, "take notice that I do not accept bribes! I scorn and spit upon them, and upon you! And I warn you not to stand an instant longer in my path!"

The interview was in the shadow of the roaring "L." An Italian bootblack, polishing a somewhat decayed pair of shoes on the capacious feet of a Spanish negro, and another Italian, busily engaged in brushing imaginary flies from an already too thoroughly fly-specked stock of fruit, were the only witnesses to the colloquy. The passers-by did not even turn their heads to observe what the shouting was about.

Freier moved aside. His face was livid for an instant; then it became ghastly white. But he smiled an evil smile.

"Oh! very well, Herr Saint Joseph!" he said. "If you refuse all the assistance which your friends offer you, you must not expect any sympathy when you come to grief!"

Joseph made a contemptuous gesture, pushed on, and in a minute was lost to view in the hurrying throngs.

"And you will come to grief, my fine fellow!" continued Freier, shaking his clenched fist in the direction which Joseph had taken. "You will come to grief much sooner than you imagine. You are rushing upon your fate now, without knowing it. But a trip to London! And a chance to talk to the labor-leaders there! Who would have thought him strong enough to decline those things? I see: we must try heroic measures with him."

Joseph, when the errand of mercy was finished, found himself not very far from David's theatre, and felt that a little conversation with the purveyor of plays and proverbs would refresh him.

So he presently made his way into a sort of loft at the right of the stage, where David had assembled the members of his company around a property throne, turned on its side, and serving as the table on which was spread a substantial lunch of bread and cheese and sausages, and a jug of weak beer.

The company had been rehearsing a new historical drama in costume; and kings and prophets, shepherds and warriors, dancing-girls and angels, were seated on piles of canvas scenery, munching contentedly before returning to work.

David was fluttering about, helping each one to his portion, and teaching a young girl how to sing her *rôle* in Hebrew as he cut bread and carved cheese.

" Why do you not sit down with the others ? " said Joseph, as he entered.

David gave him a quizzical look. " Don't you remember what Rabbi Juda said ? " he queried. " It was good advice. 'No one should sit down to his own meals until all the animals are cared for.' "

Upon this the girls fell upon David, and with laughing protests, and with a bombardment of bread-crumbs, drove him almost breathless into a corner, whither he beckoned Joseph to follow him.

" I have been wanting to see you," said David, suddenly becoming very grave, " to thank you for the gallant way in which you acted about poor Shiphrah. I know the girl," a shadow passed over David's face, " and I was sorry to learn of the way in which she was going. Miryam has gone to her to-day to give her some work — some sewing for our theatre. I — I just wanted to thank you."

As they clasped hands, Joseph saw that David's eyes were filled with tears.

He turned away hastily. " It was nothing — nothing

but duty," he said. "I thought I would run in to inquire
why you had postponed the production of Mordecai's
'Hymn,' and to get away from my sad thoughts for a time."

"The hymn? Oh, I am waiting for Mordecai. At the
last moment he backed out — said the time was not yet
favorable, and that when the condition of the cloakmakers
was a little worse he would give me the word. I believe
he thinks that the song would start a revolution."

"Such things have happened," said Joseph. "But perhaps the lock-out will be ended sooner than Mordecai
imagines."

"Let us hope so. And, by the way, I was thinking of
you and of Mordecai when you came in. For the fair
Bathsheba has just paid me a visit, and left me an important bit of news."

A tiny spot of color showed in one of Joseph's cheeks,
but he said nothing. David continued, —

"She was looking bewitchingly cool and stately in a
brand-new gown of some soft texture, and she told me that
her husband has had a stroke of luck. He has been engaged for some garden in Chicago, where he will play gypsy
melodies at a very good salary, all the rest of the summer.
As for Bathsheba, she is going to remain here and to study
for the Hebrew stage ! What do you think of that ? "

"It does not surprise me, " said Joseph. "Women like
that must have a public career. They can't live without it."

"She was so calm and self-satisfied, " David remarked,
"that I tried to provoke her about the Socialists — the
'Party of Force' — or whatever they call it — to which she
is said to belong. I could get no information from her on
that point. She pretended not to know what I was talking
about. But all the time, so little Gershom, here, says, that
arch-revolutionist, Baumeister, was waiting for her outside."

"Is he much with her ? " asked Joseph sharply.

"I don't know, but I think she follows his doctrines. You know the proverb: 'Beat the gods, and their priests will tremble.' I abused him roundly, and I don't think she liked it. She inquired very symoathetically after you."

Joseph had suddenly become thoughtfu.. He smoked the fragrant Russian cigarette which David offered him, and listened to an old Hebrew melody which the children who were to appear in the historical drama were singing.

Their fresh and pure voices followed each quaver and roulade of the ancient music, as David's skilled baton indicated the way.

"Ah! your life is the happy one!" said Joseph. "You are safe in the ideal world, dealing with shadows; and you really have all the bread and cheese you want. But we poor folk who deal in realities can get neither bread nor cheese. What is this mystery?"

"Yes, I am very much at home here among my pupils," said David cheerfully; "but I am really nobody outside of these surroundings. 'A small coin in a large jar makes a great noise;' but in the street it would soon be lost. And as for feeding on the fat of the land, why should we? 'He who increaseth his flesh but multiplieth food for the worms.'"

With this rather cynical proverb ringing in his ears, Joseph went away, and was plunged into sloughs of work all day.

Late in the evening he perceived an unusual beauty in sky and air. The intense heat still lingered, and down in Hester and Ludlow Streets the poor people were stretched in rows on their gaunt mattresses on the steaming pavements, gasping for fresh air.

But the moonlight was strangely weird and tender; and when by chance a wandering breeze from the East River penetrated the baking quarter, it seemed to have in it some of the inspiring salty smell of the sea.

The poor little babies, with their drawn faces, puny bodies, and thin legs, sprawled beside their mothers, wailing and beating the air.

Now and then a mother, nursing her hungry child at her hungrier breast, had a vision of cool, delicious fields in some far corner of the Russian " Pale " — a corner where wild grasses, waving rhythmically, sent forth a sweet savor, which seemed to kindle a delirium in the blood.

She saw the peasants reclining in the shade of great trees, plucking flowers, and laughing as they pelted each other with blossoms tinged with all the colors of the rainbow.

Then she gnashed her teeth, as she looked around her at the squalor of Ludlow Street, and felt the pestilential vapors arising from the pavement to stifle her and her child.

The yelling of the children, which all the afternoon had been fierce and menacing, as if even the little ones were about to revolt against the tyranny of hunger, gradually died away. Now and then the shrill wail of a baby persisted; but finally the slumberous darkness imposed its tranquillity.

Babes and mothers forgot their troubles; the starving fathers had a little peace, and lay beside their families, glaring up at the cloudless blue sky, as if reproaching it for its answerless and indifferent calm.

The old men, who could not sleep, moaned and groaned, disturbing the others, who petulantly rebuked them. Pedlers slept in their clothes, struck down by fatigue, like soldiers by shell or bullet on a battle-field.

And so by hundreds, by thousands, the hungry refugees lay in the street, on the housetops, on the steps of old-fashioned brick mansions, even in the middle of certain

streets, their heads thrown back, their arms tossed about
fantastically, their pinched faces distorted and ghastly
under the moonlight which swept in measureless and
magnificent waves down on and over them, bestowing upon
them silent benediction.

As Joseph threaded his way among these unconscious
sleepers, three-fourths of whom were now dependent upon
his efforts for security from absolute starvation, he felt
as if he were walking through the streets of a city where
the plague had just run riot, leaving the dead in every nook
and corner.

Here were two thin, consumptive girls, fast asleep in
each other's arms. As Joseph stepped over them on his
way to Ludlow Street, it seemed to him that they were
dead, so pallid and motionless were they. But a second
glance showed him that they were faintly breathing.

An old man caught him by the skirt of his coat, and
asked him for a cigarette. Joseph found him one in a side
pocket, gave him a light from his match-box, and went on.

At this moment a dark figure left the angle of a house,
and went swiftly past him. Joseph caught a momentary
glimpse of the face. It was that of one of the Socialists
who, on the night of Mother Levitsky's funeral march, had
tried to incite the cloakmakers to riot.

A shudder swept through the young labor-leader's frame.
He remembered Bathsheba's latest warning.

Joseph was on his way to the same house from which
Mother Levitsky had been evicted, and in which he and his
followers had so peremptorily taken to task the landlord
Simon.

He had been summoned thither by an urgent call from a
consumptive cloakmaker, who was to be sent to the
hospital the next morning, after having sacrificed his
existence to the Dagon of the sewing-machine; and who

wished to have some provision made for his infant child. As a member of the Union he solicited Joseph's good offices.

It was nearly midnight when he reached the door of this house. Stepping over the recumbent forms in the open passage-way, he went swiftly up four flights of stairs to the sick man's room, arranged for the removal of the child (whose mother had been buried only a fortnight ago) on the following morning, and had reached the third floor on his downward journey, when he was stopped by a sight which sent the blood coursing like quicksilver through his veins, and set his knees to trembling violently.

All was darkness on the landing, but a door directly in front of him was open, disclosing to him a small room flooded with soft light; and, standing in the centre of it, a beautiful vision, so fantastic, so ethereal that he could hardly believe it real, stood Bathsheba!

She was robed in a white gown of ancient pattern, which left her stately shoulders bare, and the soft and clinging folds of which outlined her noble form in all its ravishing perfection.

One shapely arm was raised in graceful gesture, as if she were a queen or a goddess beckoning an adorer to approach. In the other she held a necklace of pearls, which gave out soft glints under the mild radiance, and which she was evidently about to don.

The room was profusely and picturesquely littered with costumes and stuffs, some of which were evidently very costly. On a little table at the right lay a tinsel crown and a quaint antique sceptre. A large willow trunk, the lid of which was raised, was filled to overflowing with dresses, girdles, Oriental embroideries, slippers, flasks; and a cimeter with sparkling stones in its hilt reposed where it had been carelessly thrown, upon a fur-bordered cloak such as rich Polish matrons wore half a century ago.

In a corner a tall manikin such as milliners use was draped with an exquisite silver-gray costume ; and at Bathsheba's feet was a mantle which she had apparently just tried on, and rejected as an unworthy accessory to her charms.

Joseph rubbed his eyes. "It is curious," he said to himself, in an undertone, "how I see that woman everywhere. Of course that is not Bathsheba. It is some actress taking stock among her stage dresses, and my eyes have simply played me one more trick! Heigh ho !"

He was continuing his way, with his gaze still fixed on the beautiful figure bathed in the floods of chastened light, when the woman started forward, and stretched out one hand to shut the door.

Afraid that he might be mistaken for a robber, Joseph darted forward to get past the door, and descend the stairs, when the woman saw him.

It *was* Bathsheba, and they were face to face. He felt her warm breath upon his hand, which he had raised as he turned.

She looked at him for a moment with a vague fright in her eyes, then turned half around, and sank to the floor in a swoon.

In an instant Joseph was kneeling beside her, and, raising her splendid head, he laid it, superb with its magnificent masses of dishevelled hair, from which came a strange perfume to trouble his senses, upon his shoulder.

Then he gazed earnestly into her face.

Yes, it was Bathsheba; but a transformation had been wrought upon her features since he had last seen her. The sternness was gone ; it had given place to a tender sensuousness, almost childlike, as she lay there unconscious and helpless.

The wrinkle between her brows had disappeared. There

was a faint impression of rapture about the lips. This was not the destroying angel of the "party of force," but a siren and a charmer whose influence might be illimitable.

"She is an enchantress!" thought Joseph. "Am I bewitched? Perhaps this is only her image, and her real self is far away, plotting with Baumeister, or listening to Mordecai's hymns of revolution."

Bathsheba opened her eyes. She did not move her head, nor for a full minute did she try to speak. It was a minute of mingled rapture and torture for Joseph. He was in truth under the influence of an enchantment, the same mysterious charm which has lured men to destruction in every age since time was born.

The woman at last lifted up her eyes. As her gaze rested upon Joseph's perplexed and anxious face, a red flush sprang into her cheeks, and the glow of her naked shoulders so startled Joseph that he tried to withdraw his arms.

But Bathsheba swayed, and would have fallen.

A moment more, and he raised her gently to her feet, where she stood unsteadily, looking at him as if she were about to order him to withdraw.

Then she moved to the trunk, and caught up a fleecy wrap.

One twirl of her deft arms, and her shoulders were draped.

Another twirl, and the disarranged tresses were brought into subjection, and attractively knotted at the back of her Juno-like neck.

And now she spoke, in a voice so tremulous that she seemed to be suffering from fear.

"How came you here? How did I happen to swoon? It was very silly of me. I — I — am confused — Herr Zalmonah, will you give me that little scent-bottle on the

dressing-table ? Thank you. How can you ever forgive
me for being such a child ? But — you — frightened me
so — and just at that instant, too, when I was thinking of
you."

"Of me," said Joseph in a faint voice, which did not
seem like his own. "You were too kind. I suppose that
you were thinking how the poor cloakmaker's delegate
came to be staring at you at such an hour — in this house ;
but I will explain."

And in a few words he told her of his mission to the
invalid, and of his surprise at finding her in such a place,
among the sweated drudges.

"And masquerading in such rich attire," said Bathsheba,
who was all at once quite well again. "It is I who owe
my friend an explanation. We have — that is my husband
has had a great stroke of luck. He has got an engagement
in Chicago, which pays him very well indeed ; and, thanks
to that good fortune, I am able to gratify my wish to study
for the stage while he is absent. All these pretty things
with which you see me surrounded were the property of
that unlucky actress at Reise's theatre. I think our people
liked her better than any one else who had come here from
Europe to play the historical dramas. The poor thing had
drifted from one abode to another, until she was stranded
here in this odd rookery of Simon's — you know Simon ? "

"I ought to know him. This is the very house from
which he evicted poor old Mother Levitsky — the house
which we came so near to pulling down about his ears."

Bathsheba looked troubled. "So it is," she stammered.
"And I never thought of it until this moment. I should
not have come here. I see it now — but I was carried
away by the splendid chance to get all these lovely things ;
and for that debt and a hundred dollars, which my husband was able to advance out of his contract, they are

all mine! Are they not beautiful? And do you think
that I ever could be worthy to wear such charming costumes on the stage? You perhaps know that I can sing,
but I feel that I am frightfully wooden as an actress. Give
me a frank opinion, Herr Zalmonah. You know how much
I respect your judgment."

"I don't know. It is all too sudden. I — I — am glad
you are so fortunate. I — am sure that it must be delight-
ful to act."

The woman looked at him through her half-closed eyes
with the faintest suggestion of a smile on her face. She
saw that Joseph was confused, and she triumphed in his
confusion.

"If it had been any one but you, Herr Zalmonah," she
said, adroitly combining eye and lip flattery as woman alone
can do, "who had come upon me while I was trying on
these pretty things, I should have been ready to die of
vexation. But I know that you understand that it was not
vanity that impelled this masquerade. It was simply the
desire to test my capabilities — to see if I had confidence in
myself." She cast down her eyes.

"And what do you propose to play first?" inquired
Joseph, who could not take his eyes from Bathsheba's face,
although he felt her gaze burning his forehead.

"I don't know. Something strange and original. What
a pity, Herr Zalmonah, that you are not an author. Then
you might write me a play."

"And what will become of your special work while you
are acting?" said Joseph. "I thought you were very
much devoted to that."

Bathsheba looked up at him with languorous half-closed
eyes. She sighed deeply, and opened and closed her hands
nervously.

"So I was," she at last said, "until — I met you."

The scent-bottle, which she had carelessly replaced on the little table, fell to the floor and was shivered to atoms. A faint and sensuous odor filled the whole room, and seemed to take possession of Joseph, as some subtle philter might have done. His temples throbbed, and lights danced before his vision. Finally he seemed to push a great weight from his chest and to say, —

"And how could I interfere with your plans — your desires to reform society — the world?"

Bathsheba appeared to move toward him, and yet he saw her but dimly, as though she were surrounded by a golden mist. Some irresistible force was impelling him to stretch out his arms and to welcome her to them. But now she was answering him.

"Can — you — ask — me — that?" she said, almost breathlessly.

She threw aside the wrap, as if it oppressed her, and stood palpitating with lovely life and with her strong emotion, as if soliciting from him a word, a caress, a look.

There was something so exquisitely appealing in the humility of her tacit confession, which expressed so much more than her words, that Joseph was carried away by it.

He stretched forth his arms, and in an instant she was beside him, and her head was upon his breast.

For a moment — then they stood apart, gazing around them with a vague fright in their eyes.

From one of the floors below came a piercing cry, uttered in the jargon, a cry of terror and anguish: —

"Fire! Fire! Fire! Save yourselves: the old shell is burning!"

Joseph listened intently, then turned and ran down one flight of stairs, and listened again in the darkness. Suddenly a puff of acrid smoke came full in his face, and he saw the red glare of the flames.

He rushed up the stairs again, and found Bathsheba, pale as a marble goddess, seated in a chair, and listening intently to the concert of voices in the street, which every moment grew louder and more frantic.

CHAPTER XVI

THE TRIAL BY FIRE

BATHSHEBA was the first to speak. "What is it?" she queried in a husky voice.

At the same time her woman's instinct prompted her to catch up the costumes, the tinsel jewellery, the handsome wraps, and to thrust them into the trunk.

With feverish energy she pressed them down, unmindful of the confusion in which they lay. Suddenly she turned her whitening face quickly around, looking first at Joseph, then bending forward in the attitude of one listening intently.

At last she sprang up with a muffled cry, and placed her hand over her heart.

Meantime Joseph said nothing. He stood like one deprived of speech and motion.

It seemed to him that he had been walking in his sleep on the edge of a precipice, and had suddenly awakened to see the awful gulf yawning before him.

And now the abyss sent forth a column of smoke and the bitter savor of fire; and from it sprang a flame which threw its red glow on the sides of the chasm, and thrilled him with awe and horror.

Had Bathsheba dreamed the same dream? Had she awakened to the same terrifying reality? Why did she start forward thus and glare at the smoke, and clasp her hands and raise them in supplication, then fall upon her knees, and tremble as if she expected instant death ?

" Fire ! Fire ! "

Joseph heard the words faintly, as if they were shouted at him from an immense height, and it did not strike him as strange that the words were spoken in the jargon of his people.

Then, suddenly, he awoke to reality, and became conscious of the miserable Bathsheba cowering before him, praying him to save her, and lamenting because her newly purchased treasures were in danger.

Fire ! The house was on fire ! Joseph knew very well what that meant. Unless he set at work instantly to get the unhappy woman and her treasures to a place of safety, a falling wall, or a stairway transformed into a fiery furnace, might cut off all chance for life.

Joseph would be burned with Bathsheba, in the house of Simon, and his work would be at an end.

His precious cloakmakers would starve, and he himself would soon be forgotten, like all the unfortunate ones who fail, no matter how heroic their struggles !

The lion in his soul bounded into action.

" Don't speak to me again until I find out what has happened," he said imperiously to Bathsheba, who shrank back and cowered before him. " I think we are in danger, but there is no use in wailing about it."

Bathsheba ran to the window and looked out. She returned shuddering and shaking her head, and wringing her hands like one demented. " My beautiful dresses ! " she murmured ; " they will all be lost ! And I have never yet worn them once in public. What a pity of pities ! "

She sat down helplessly on the floor, and began making feeble efforts to close the trunk. But as she had thrust all the costumes into it, the lid would not shut down, and Bathsheba merely bruised and cut her fingers.

Bathsheba's rooms were at the front of the house, at the angle overlooking two streets. Joseph looked from the corner window, down to the surging throng of women and children, each of whom was yelling, " Simon's house is on fire ! " but he saw no smoke or flame.

From the front he could see nothing but a muttering company of cloakmakers, driven away from the house by a policeman.

Where, then, was the fire ?

Was it at the back of the house ?　And — all important question — on which floor was it ?

The New York tenement house is a shell. Its mean walls of poorly laid brick go down like paper before a brisk flame. Its ladder-like staircases of coarse planking, and its narrow air-shafts, act as funnels to fan the flames, and to send them, roaring and crackling, to cut off the escape of any wretched people caught in the upper stories.

Such a house will serve to shelter a hundred, or sometimes a hundred and fifty persons, and it can be burned to the ground in half an hour.

The firemen know that it is as dangerous to enter one of these houses when the flames are raging in it, as to charge against a well-intrenched enemy in time of war. Yet they do their duty unhesitatingly, and with a chivalrous disregard of self rarely rewarded as it should be.

The nerve which can take a man through a sheet of flame, or make him crawl on hands and knees in a room filled with suffocating smoke, until he finds some aged woman or tiny child left behind by a family in its mad rush for safety, is the nerve of heroes. It merits as high recognition as the bravery of the soldier.

But it does not get it.

Joseph ran into the passage, and swiftly down the stairs. On the landing he stopped and listened: nothing.　The doors were open, and the occupants were probably in the street already. Few of them had any belongings which they could not have carried on their backs.

Joseph went down the next flight, and was instantly surrounded by wailing women, each of whom besought him to save her. "There's no danger yet — none that I can see, good women!" he shouted; and shaking himself free he went to the ground-floor.

He stopped on the last stair, and his heart stood still for a moment; for now he realized what a mistake he had made in not seizing Bathsheba, and bringing her along with him.

With characteristic greed Simon had leased a large room on the ground-floor to a dealer in chemicals willing to pay a huge rental for the privilege of not being disturbed.

Although the man himself admitted that frequent explosions, the result of his experiments, created a standing danger of fire, Simon had been willing to take him, and had threatened with expulsion any of the wretched "sweated" tenants who dared to complain of, or even to mention, the fact.

And now the end had come! It looked as if an explosion in this den of chemicals had not only cost the experimenter his life, but had sent out the roaring column of flame which was licking at the wood-work and the heated bricks, and would soon crumble them like tinder.

Joseph saw this column of fire and the half a dozen men flitting in the glare of it, trying to appease it with a few puny buckets full of water.

He gazed as if fascinated by it, until it suddenly leaped straight at him. as though actuated by some mad impulse to destroy him, and he could feel its hot breath upon the walls of the staircase.

If he chose to go forth alone now he would be safe.

No one had recognized him. He could walk out at the door and mingle in the throng of rescuers.

He looked at the flame once more, and, while his attention was so occupied, a tall, lithe figure glided up the stairs, and disappeared in the darkness.

Yes — he could go away. But he could not thus desert Bathsheba. His conscience forbade him to do it.

Yet was she not a disturbing and dangerous element in his life ? Had he not been shaken to the very foundations of his being by the subtle and sinister power which she seemed able at all times to summon ?

What was Bathsheba to him ?

And now the great flame-monster leaped angrily and menacingly again, and one of its tongues licked the wall, and seemed loath to withdraw. Joseph felt as if some invisible force were drawing him to the street.

But he resisted it valiantly, and went swiftly back up the darkened stairway. As he reached the first landing there was a yell below, and he saw the tongues of flame lapping greedily at the planking of the stairs. Then came a grand rush of red flame, and a cloud of smoke.

Joseph flourished his hands wildly, and ran like a maniac up the second and third flight of stairs. It was now evident to him that escape by the stairways was impossible ; and that he must persuade Bathsheba to descend by the fire-escape.

Meditating on the best way of doing this, he arrived at her door, and to his great surprise he found it partially closed. He was about to throw it open, when he heard the sound of voices in angry colloquy.

He stood still, and could not help hearing all that was said.

Bathsheba was crying. "You may say what you like of him — if it is true that he is a coward," she sobbed. "I could have believed anything but that."

· "A coward!" said the other voice; Joseph smiled bitterly as he recognized it as that of Baumeister. "That's a hard word. But confess that your admiration — shall I say love ? — for the heroic cloakmaker has had a severe shock ? And come! let me save you while there is time. How do we know that he did not set the house on fire, just to spite his old enemy, Simon ?"

Joseph threw open the door.

"Who is the coward ?" he said in a deep voice, and making a gesture which brought Baumeister almost to his feet, so tremendously energetic and commanding it was. "Who is the coward ? — the man who tries to kill another's reputation, or the man who seeks for an avenue of escape for his enemies, even while they are plotting against him ?"

"His enemies ?" cried Bathsheba, who appeared to have recovered her senses. "Surely you do not count me as an enemy, Joseph! You could not — you cannot do that!"

"Yes, both of you!" said Joseph, springing into the room and shaking his closed hand in Baumeister's face. "As for you, woman, I see you in the true light now! If I needed any proof that you were preparing to play me false, I could find it in the presence of this man here. I know you for a fine pair of conspirators! But that shall not hinder me from saving your lives."

A cracking and rending sound was heard below. Baumeister ran to the door, looked down the stairs, and uttered a loud cry.

"The passage below is already filled with smoke!" he said, returning to the room. "We must hurry down. Come! we can finish our disputes in the street."

He smiled maliciously at Joseph, and tried to seize Bathsheba by the arm, and to drag her forward.

"Not that way!" shouted Joseph. "Are you mad ? The staircase nearest the street has already fallen in; and

the flames are rushing up here. We must get out by the
window ! You are standing over a raging volcano at this
moment !"

Bathsheba turned to Joseph, her beautiful face transfigured by a smile. "I knew he was no coward !" she
cried, and before he could stop her she had thrown herself
passionately upon his breast.

Joseph made a supreme effort, and unwound her arms
from his neck. This struggle seemed to take all his
strength, and he staggered back against the wall, and
placed one hand over his heart, as if Bathsheba had just
dealt him a blow there.

"Repulse me if you will !" she said; "I don't care, now
that I am certain of myself ! My heart — yes, my soul
— has spoken. The rest is of small consequence. As for
you, Baumeister, you see that you can no longer expect an
ally in me ! Ah ! Heaven be thanked that Fate sent you
here to-night to see this and to know the truth ! I would
not care — if all the world — knew it now !"

She spoke with melodramatic force — desperately, defiantly, as woman speaks when she knows that she has out-
raged all conventions, and has no mercy to expect from
vindictive judges.

As she repaired the disorder of her hair, displaying her
beautiful round arms while she tremblingly bound up her
tresses, Baumeister, who seemed to have forgotten all about
the fire, gazed at her with undisguised admiration.

"I think you will make an actress !" he said; "I do,
indeed ! And your husband would think so too — if he
were here ! I am not so sure about your capacity for
conspiracy. But come ! where is the fire-escape ? Herr
Joseph has admitted that he has no intention of burning
us alive, much as he dislikes us ! So let us get down to
solid ground ! These tenement houses have an ugly way
of falling in without warning !"

"There is no fire-escape!" said Joseph calmly, returning from an investigation of the front and side windows.

"At the back of the house then! There must be one," cried Baumeister, beginning to rock to and fro, and giving signs of an approaching epileptic fit.

"None there," answered Joseph curtly; "I looked before I went down-stairs. And the stairways are now a mass of seething fire. Hark! Do you hear the timbers crack?"

"I shall jump down," said Baumeister doggedly, approaching the window. "I prefer broken legs to being roasted alive."

Joseph seized and held him back. "You will do nothing of the sort," he said. "Strip up those dresses into narrow pieces; make a rope: I will make another. We will knot them together, tie them to the window, and slide down on them. Quick!"

He sprang upon Baumeister with uplifted hand. The man cowered before him, and in an instant he was at the work.

"My beautiful costumes!" screamed Bathsheba. "Ah! what a punishment! To own them but a few hours, and then to see them destroyed by fire!"

The men worked with desperate energy, goaded by the fierce heat now close upon them, and by the smoke creeping upon the landing, and sending light ashen blue and greenish wreaths and puffs into the room, to float above their heads.

"Now take a part of your rope," said Joseph to Baumeister, "and fasten this woman to me so that she cannot slip or fall. Stand here!" he said curtly to Bathsheba.

She obeyed meekly and without question.

"Bind us together," commanded Joseph; "and see that you do it well, or I will keep you here until the floor falls in. You know I am a man of my word."

At the same moment his fingers closed over Bathsheba's scissors, lying on the little dressing-table.

"Bind!" he cried to Baumeister.

It was done; and Joseph could feel Bathsheba's heart beating fiercely against his own.

She was bound to him so that she could not fall when he clambered down the rope, but so that his limbs were free.

Entreating Bathsheba to be mute, and to remain perfectly quiet, he strode with her to the window, and fastened his line, knotted with what remained of Baumeister's, to a stout old-fashioned hook in the sill, evidently once used for fastening a rope for lowering bundles.

"If this gives way," he said, "some of us will learn how broken legs feel." Then turning to Baumeister, he said, —

"Down the rope! hand over hand! Down with you!"

Baumeister trembled and hesitated. Joseph gripped him by the collar. "Do you want me to throw you out?" he cried.

The terrified Baumeister swung over the window-sill, and began the descent.

Joseph had calculated well. The rope made of Bathsheba's ruined costumes served. It touched the ground. In a minute Baumeister was out of danger.

Just as he was descending there was a great cry from the crowd, and all ran around the corner to the front of the house.

Joseph examined the hook in the sill. "It may hold us both," he said; "I hope it will. Don't be frightened. Hang as quietly as if you were dead, while I go down hand over hand. If you struggle we are lost!"

Bathsheba bent forward and kissed him passionately on the forehead.

"Shall I cut the bonds?" he said in a terrible voice,

"and leave you to perish alone ? Another caress like that, and I swear to you that I will do it ! "

Bathsheba's lips paled. Joseph felt her weight heavy on his arms. She had swooned.

"It is better so !" he said.

It needed almost superhuman care to get out at the window with his unconscious burden without falling. But he did it.

He slipped the scissors into a side pocket, grasped the frail rope, closed his eyes, and swung down by one-hand.

He felt as if his shoulder were unjointed, and fancied that the house was falling in, as he brought up his other arm and caught hold. The next change was still harder. Suddenly fire flashed out from a window at him. Again and again he steadily lowered himself and his burden. It seemed ages.' His brain was in a whirl. He fancied that they were flying through the air pursued by a fiery demon. Then they were hurled against a mountain and fell down.

Joseph's strength had given out as he was raising one hand to relieve the other for the last time. His grasp gave way, and he fell. But, as they were within five feet of the street, no bones were broken.

The shock revived them both. Joseph seized the scissors and hastily severed Bathsheba's bonds. A stout fireman was approaching them.

"Don't stand there," he said; "the wall may come down any minute. We just cleared all the people out o' this street. Where t' 'ell 'd you two come from ? "

Baumeister was nowhere to be found. Joseph and Bathsheba turned and hastened away in the direction opposite to that indicated by the fireman. That functionary was about to call them back, when the crash of falling walls interrupted him.

Simon's house was falling into shapeless ruins.

"Oh, my beautiful costumes!" sobbed Bathsheba, as she heard the noise.

Joseph was angry, and was about to reprove Bathsheba for thinking of her small loss, when so many greater ones were to be mourned, when they came upon Baumeister, limping and gesticulating like a madman.

When he saw them he ran up to Joseph, and, grasping his hands, he cried out, —

"If it had not been for you I should have been roasting up there now. Yes, you have saved my life; and you shall see that I am not ungrateful. Let all that took place up there to-night be forgotten. You must not suppose that I shall ever mention it to a living soul!"

Joseph, who withdrew his bleeding hands with impatient haste, looked grimly at Baumeister.

"I have nothing to conceal," he said. "But for this woman's sake it is better so. Remember your promise; and now let us see what we can do for the poor people who have been driven out. What can we do for her?" pointing to Bathsheba.

"Let her come with me," said Baumeister, drawing the trembling woman to him. "I will find shelter for her."

"Shall we not see you again soon?" said Bathsheba. "You who have saved us?"

"I shall go on with my work," said Joseph incoherently, "and when it is finished I am going away — I don't know where! I am tired of all this roar and turmoil and misery! I don't think it would be of any use to see me again."

Bathsheba looked almost imploringly at him; but he turned and walked away briskly, and the twain watched him as he parleyed with two or three angry firemen, then leaped over some hose, and pushed his way to the front of the burning house.

A moment later the flames burst through the wall down which they had recently lowered themselves, and the sky was lighted up by the leaping fire.

The wall swayed and trembled, and then fell in with a tremendous crash. Immense volumes of black smoke arose, sending abroad noxious odors. The hum and beating of the fire-engines in the adjacent streets went on with rhythmic fierceness.

And now a vast clamor of shouting and wailing arose, and was steadily maintained for some minutes, rising to the acuteness of shrieks and groans each time that some fresh disaster was announced.

"Ha, ha!" shouted Baumeister, shaking his blackened hand in the direction which Joseph had taken. "I think we shall see the young labor-leader again. Sacrament! I am decidedly of the opinion that he has not seen the last of us. And we have him in our power now, Bathsheba — in our power — do you hear? Let him run his race; he will find us at the end of it. It has been a fine night's work — yes, a brave night's work!"

Bathsheba stood gazing at him as if she had but little idea of what he meant. And when he suddenly screamed and fell face downward in the middle of the street, she was so alarmed that she could do nothing but stand staring at him and wringing her hands.

Just then a clumsy figure appeared among the smoking ruins at the back of the house. It was carrying a small child tenderly in its arms. Cleverly dodging a mass of red-hot brick which came toppling down, the figure went toward Bathsheba.

It was Ben Zion.

CHAPTER XVII

"That was a narrow escape, as the pig said when he slipped out of the bear's mouth," quoth Ben Zion, addressing Bathsheba as if meeting her at that moment were the most natural thing in the world, and as if he had known her since they both were children. "And see what I have picked up while I was skirting the ruins of the house! By the bones of my ancestors! I believe some woman must have thrown the child out of a third-story window."

He held up the bundle, and exhibited a wretched little crippled child, at least twenty months old, but so starved and woe-begone with a hundred miseries, that it did not look half its age. Its arms and legs were so thin and bony, its face was so drawn and pinched, that Bathsheba shuddered with disgust and horror as the glare of the conflagration lighted up the puny waif.

"Take it away," she said; "it is horrible!"

"Come, this is hospitable," croaked the pedler, "hospitable beyond belief, as the fox said when the trap took him in. I am just about to put the baby in your arms, and to ask you to care for it, and you turn your nose up as if it were a changeling. Come, a little courage!"

As he extended his arms once more, with the bundle in them, toward Bathsheba, he tumbled against the prostrate figure of Baumeister.

"Come! now, you must take the little foundling!" he cried, "for here is some one trying to dig his own grave, and I must see who and what he is."

He unceremoniously placed the child in Bathsheba's arms, at which she shuddered again, and cried out, —

"I don't want the little monster! How do I know that it hasn't come straight from some room reeking with typhus?"

"Ah, bah! we are typhus proof, you and I," answered Ben Zion, who was gradually assuming a very familiar tone. "Now, whom have we here? Baumeister! Of course! Another epileptic fit. I begin to understand. And his hands are bleeding." He looked up sharply at Bathsheba. "How happened you to be here to-night, and in company with this man? I wonder if his conspiracy has anything to do with the burning of that house? You haven't told me why you are here — and why you look as if you had seen the Devil himself!"

While he talked he bumped Baumeister's head against the hard bed of the street, and did it with such seemingly ferocious energy, that Bathsheba begged him to desist.

"Leave him to me," he said. "He doesn't mind love-pats like that. I'll bring him to his senses, if I have to smash his skull. Only to think that if I should give one pat a little harder than the others, one of the worst of Joseph's enemies would be out of the way! But fair means are the best!"

Baumeister suddenly revived, sat up with a bewildered air, and looked first at Bathsheba, then at Ben Zion, and last at the flaming ruined walls near at hand. Then he put his hand to his head, and drew a long sigh.

After all this he began in the most natural tone in the world to tell them of some youthful adventure in Russia. The fact that Bathsheba was holding a child in her arms did not seem to him worthy of attention.

Presently he got upon his feet, and walking unsteadily
to where part of the rope which they had used for descending had fallen, he said as if communing with himself, —
" This must be burned at once. It is lucky that I found
it. Bathsheba, let me whisper to you."

He came up to her so swiftly that he almost frightened
her, and hissed into her ear in German, a language which
Ben Zion but imperfectly understood, —

" Not a word to this peddling fool about having seen
Joseph in the building just burned! As you value our
work and your life, remember!"

Then he turned and walked away without a word of
thanks to Ben Zion, or seeming to be aware that he had
just been grovelling in the street.

" That's the second time I've driven the black devils out
of him," said Ben Zion. " They have called me a sorcerer
before now for less than that in Russia. Our friend yonder
don't seem to me quite strong enough for a conspirator.
And — you haven't told me why you and he were watching
the moon from this particular angle when the fire broke
out."

" I was in danger of being burned alive in the house, and
he saved me," said Bathsheba, determined if possible to
throw him off the track. A wave of crimson swept into
her cheeks as she uttered the falsehood, the utterance of
which she regretted a moment later.

" So," said Ben Zion, " you were one of Simon's lodgers?
Well, he will never persecute you for rent again. They
say that he was one of the first to be baked. And the
firemen tell us that at least ten others are in there with
him. Quite a lively evening, as the wolf said when he
carried off the moujik's baby!"

At that moment a sense of her utterly helpless and forlorn condition flashed through Bathsheba's mind, and pre-

vented her from dismissing the sententious pedler with a stinging exhortation as to the virtue of minding one's own business.

She thrust one hand into a fold of her dress, where she had been thoughtful enough to put her purse, which contained a few dollars and two or three bits of plain jewellery. But everything else was gone! "All my beautiful costumes!" she said once more, and began to weep bitterly.

Ben Zion looked at her with much curiosity. But he did not question her further. "We shall gain nothing by standing here, except a hot brick or two on our heads," he said.

"I must find a new lodging," said Bathsheba.

"Come with me," said the little man. "I will give you shelter until morning, and then you can look about you. And where is your husband?"

Bathsheba told him, at the same time holding out the baby, and imploring him to take it again. So without more ado the little pedler clapped the mite under one arm, and crying, "Come on!" set off at a rapid pace through the fire-illumined streets.

They were soon away from the smoke and flame and shouting; and at the corner of two dirty streets Ben Zion halted before an uninviting basement.

"This is my palace," he said. "Don't stumble on the steps, and if you see a rat, don't scream. The rats are good little folk, and they won't bite unless you try to take away their privileges. I wish we had as much courage as they have!"

While he rattled on in the quaint jargon which at any other time would have brought a smile to Bathsheba's lips, he was pushing open a creaking door; and, striking a match and lighting a rusty lamp which he had brought with him from Russia, he ushered the faint and trembling woman into a little cellar almost bare of furniture, and in one cor-

ner of which stood the push-cart, the faithful companion
of his laborious days.

Presently Bathsheba discovered a three-legged stool and
a rudimentary table dimly outlined in the obscurity. Sinking down on the seat, she hid her face in her hands, and
wept silently.

"Ah! you have found the arm-chair!" said Ben Zion,
now assuming a cheerier tone. "I am sure that you will
be at ease there! And now to put the child in the cradle!"

He laid the human mite in the push-cart, saying, "Don't
squall, or the wolves will get you! You shall be fed soon,
and that will be a novelty in your life! But first let me
get breakfast for the grown-folks."

He groped beneath the table, and Bathsheba sprang up
in terror as she heard much angry squeaking, and knew
that the rats had been disturbed.

"Ungrateful little demons!" said the pedler. "I feed
them every night, and yet they break into my larder and
steal my provisions when I am out leading the cloakmakers,
or rescuing poor children. Let me see what their teeth have
left!"

He drew from his hidden storehouse a small piece of
bread and one or two apples, and placed them gently before Bathsheba on the primitive table. Then he set the
candle so that its feeble rays would fall upon this meagre
repast.

From a mouldy cupboard in the corner he took a small
bottle and a glass, and added them to the feast. "And now,"
he said, "if you would only condescend to eat something!"

Bathsheba opened her eyes and dried her tears as best
she could.

The small pedler's face shone with the graciousness of
heartfelt hospitality. The poor woman gained courage,
and, with an attempt at a smile, she took up one of the

apples, and began to eat it. "You are very kind to me," she said; "but we must not forget the child."

"Not I. In a minute or two I am going to get it some hot milk at an all-night place on East Broadway. You will not be afraid to sit here without me for a little while? I shall not be long. Or — that would be better — look here!"

Ben Zion raised the candle and showed Bathsheba that she was seated close to a pine partition, which had evidently been put in by the enterprising landlord for the purpose of renting to two tenants a wretched cellar barely large enough for one.

He threw open a small door in this partition, and, beckoning to Bathsheba, he said, "Come and look in."

Bathsheba obeyed, and was astonished to see on the other side of the partition a little old man, with a face seamed and forehead garnished with wrinkles, seated on a bench before a small sewing-machine, and working with astonishing rapidity.

The tiny room or hole in which this valiant toiler was lodged had but one small window, through which in the daytime only a few rays of light struggled feebly and timidly, as if they knew that they were intruders, and expected to be expelled as soon as discovered.

As he guided the garment on which he was toiling round and round, submitting it to the strokes of the needle, he was crooning to himself an "Alleluia" which Bathsheba had often heard sung in her childhood, and which David had incorporated in one of the history plays of his theatre.

The old man had a thin, highly pitched falsetto voice, which rose triumphant above the click-clack of the machine, and seemed to give to the needle's work a kind of rhythmic grace.

There was little else in the room save a hard bench covered with a few rags, on which the old man evidently re-

posed when he could no longer sit at the machine. An
ancient hair-cloth trunk, sprawling open, displayed a book
or two, a soiled cravat, a few bits of Oriental-looking dra-
pery, a pair of Russian top-boots, and a flat cap such as all
"greenhorns" wear on their arrival.

"Well, Father Israel," cried Ben Zion, "I see you are
hard at it. And no more idea than usual, I suppose, of
what is going on in the outside world ?   I thought I would
give you a little air, and ask you to keep watch on my place
for five minutes, while I run out on an errand. I have
picked up a foundling, Father Israel, and I don't want any
one to carry it off."

"Good ! " said the little old man, without looking up.
"Nursing foundlings is pious work, but 'tis wearing. You
didn't happen to hear, did you, what the play is at David's
theatre to-morrow night ? "

"Yes ; it's ' Ahasuerus.' "

"Good !"   The old man arose, and showed a face sparkling with enthusiasm. "That is the play of all plays that
I wanted to see."   And he resumed his "Alleluia" in a
louder key, took a few turns up and down the narrow
cellar, then drank a little water from an earthen pitcher,
and sat down at the machine again.

Click-clack went the needles. He seemed to have completely forgotten the existence of his neighbor, Ben Zion.

"That old dreamer thinks of nothing but his work and
his theatre," said Ben Zion, as they turned away from the
opening in the partition.   "He works sixteen or seventeen
hours a day for six dollars a week, and he spends at least
four on visits to the theatre. He goes to see the history-
plays which tell the story of the Jews when they were a
great united people, and he has got so that he lives in the
past. He knows more about Pharaoh and Joseph, the
Shulamite and Judith, and Mordecai and Esther, than

about Harrison and Cleveland, or the Czar and the Pope of
Rome. Well, there now! I suppose the old fellow finds
his present so disagreeable, that he likes to take refuge in
the past. Some call him cracked, but I don't think he is."

He took up a tin pail and went out, leaving Bathsheba
alone to watch the shadows, and to fancy, every time the
flicker of the candle changed them, that they were huge
rats coming to besiege her.

The "Alleluia" of Father Israel continued, without interruption, to bring into its grave and impressive rhythm
the semi-staccato of the sewing-machine needle.

Ben Zion's steps were turned toward the all-night restaurant, where the announcement of complete meals for thirteen
cents, including two glasses of beer, had often attracted
the attention of the Health Board, when he heard a tremendous noise of confused shouting in the direction of the
fire.

He listened attentively, and a grin of satisfaction hovered
about his lips. "It sounds like a battle," he said. "The
big words certainly are flying about as thick as bombshells.
Let's see what they mean."

And, forgetting the probably urgent needs of the foundling awaiting him in the push-cart at home, he ran swiftly
to the scene of the fire.

The whole side of the house near which he had met
Bathsheba had fallen in, but the other was still standing,
with portions of the roof clinging to it. Ben Zion hastened
to the front, and found himself in a throng which the firemen
and policemen were pushing back with ungentle hand,
because the clamorous men and women threatened to interfere with the work of isolating the fire.

The low buildings in the rear of the yard in which
Mother Levitsky had breathed her last were now burning,

and jagged streaks of flame were shooting from them to others. With axes and hammers the firemen fought desperately to hurl down the blazing beams, so that their flames could be smothered in the mud and wet ashes below.

As Ben Zion arose, after having been carried off his feet by a lurch in the excited throng, he observed that the men, women, and children were all yelling at and execrating one person, — the miserable landlord, whom he had supposed to be burned in his own apartment. He raised his hands and clapped them with glee, and danced as well as he could in such a dense crowd.

Of two or three thousand persons who saw the plight of Simon at that moment, there were not three who would have extended to him a helping hand, so acute was the hatred of the class which he represented; so lively were the remembrances of the injustices and cruelties which he had committed in the name of his property; so terrible was the animosity against him since the eviction of Mother Levitsky.

Simon had been awakened in time to escape from his own rooms, and had hastened to the rear house, in which two flourishing sweaters were established. In the cellar of this house he had long ago buried a little stock of money and valuables, declining, with the cunning and suspicion of his class, to trust to safes or safe deposit companies.

The process of unearthing this was almost as laborious as that of old Pepys when he dug up his concealed money after the "great fire" in London. Time fled faster than Simon fancied, and, when he came to the first floor and was going into the yard, he found the terrible flames raging directly in his path.

Above him toppled the wall of the other house, obstinately refusing to share the fate of its twin, as though it had been reserved for some peculiar purpose.

The hot breath of the monster came full into Simon's face, and singed his unkempt black beard, and sent a horrible pang through his eyeballs. He ran up to the second floor of the low-studded, rudely built house, which was filled with clothing, and would burn in twenty minutes when the flames got a good hold on it.

Simon intended to climb from a back window of this second floor on to the roof of an outhouse, whence he could reach the street in the rear. But as he threw up the window there was a horrible rush of hot and hissing masses past his face ; then came clouds of blinding steam, produced by the torrents of water falling from the hose of the engines upon the fiery fragments of the wall.

At last he could look up, and to his horror he saw the wall above him beginning to tremble and topple. Another two or three minutes and it would come down with a crash, and bury him in this fragile house beneath the ruins.

He shrieked wildly in the extremity of his terror. Then he extended his hands and prayed aloud. Finally he staggered back to the front of the house, to find that its stairs were burned away, and that long fiery tentacles had seized upon the walls.

The roar of the flames was louder than the pulsations of the engines or the shouting of the motley throng gathered on the sides of the now open courtyard.

He rushed up to the roof of the house, and stood glaring wildly about, tossing his hands aloft, and praying. Standing thus, his cowering figure was brought in bold relief, and the crowd saw it, and saluted it with a shout of execration.

Despite Simon's fiery situation, this cry sent a deathly chill to his heart. He looked down at the yelling people, and extended his hands to them. They answered with a burst of derisive laughter.

"Stay there and roast, Simon !" shouted an old woman.

"It will make you think of the many times you roasted us in your sweater's den, before you got to be a rich landlord!"

"Say good-by to your wife and children, Simon!" yelled a bent and withered man, with bloodshot eyes and palsied gait. "They are saved — but you are damned!"

Tears of rage and despair dimmed Simon's vision. His knees were weak now, and it was an effort to hold up his hands. At last he managed to cry feebly, —

"I won't be singed alive here! I shall come down and run through the flames."

"Do, Simon! Do!" screamed the old hag, "and we will throw you back again! You must burn, Simon! You must burn!"

At that moment the wretched landlord saw Joseph remonstrating with the vindictive old woman, and he heard him shouting, —

"After all, he is a human being like the rest of us! I will go up and bring him down!"

And he turned to rush into the smoke and flame.

"I am saved," thought Simon. "Joseph will save me. But perhaps he will let them kill me afterwards."

"No! No! Joseph; you shall not go!" howled half a dozen of Simon's tenants, and they threw themselves in his way. "Let the villain burn; let the sweater sweat for once, and see how he likes it."

Joseph struggled in vain with the furious people.

Suddenly there arose a vast yell of triumph and exultation. The wall overhanging Simon, and towering at least fifty feet above the roof on which he stood, was falling.

Simon threw up his arms in despair. He heard the voices of firemen calling from the rear of the building to "come and jump into their arms," and telling him it was "his only chance."

Then there was a shock which seemed to rend him limb from limb, a horrible sense of burning and suffocation, the acute lingering in his ears of the yells of vengeance from the thousands in the street below — and the mortal part of Simon was of no further use in this world.

The wall had crushed in the smaller building, which was now obscured from view by the dense smoke arising from the smouldering piles of clothing.

Joseph turned away, sick at heart and trembling, and would have fallen if Ben Zion's faithful hands had not just then supported him.

"It is horrible!" he said, after he had recovered a little. "What could be gained for our cause by letting that poor fellow be burned to death?"

"Ho, ho!" shouted a harsh voice, "Herr Joseph has become very mild, all of a sudden!"

Joseph looked up and saw one of the men who belonged to Baumeister's group, a loud-mouthed Hebrew who had made him great trouble while he was organizing the Union, by constantly trying to incite the cloakmakers to violence.

"I don't think we require your opinions on the matter," he said curtly, and turned away.

"Oh, indeed!" cried the fellow, pushing his way up to Joseph, and eying him rudely. "Why, you change about like a weathercock! Look here, all of you!" he continued, flourishing his arms and apostrophizing the crowd. "This is the same Joseph who counselled burning Simon alive once — on the night that old Mother Levitsky died — who doesn't remember that? And now he pretends that he doesn't want his own counsels to be followed! Ho, ho!"

He would have said more, but Ben Zion suddenly brought his tin pail with metallic twang upon his head, causing him to jump and roar with pain; and at the same moment the prancing horses of the fire-engines coming up put the

whole crowd into a scamper, and Ben Zion lost sight of
both Joseph and his violent critic.

Then the little pedler was smitten with remorse that
he had forgotten his errand of mercy for the foundling, and
he started off at a brisk trot to get the battered tin pail
full of hot milk.

When he reached the cellar again he found Bathsheba
seated where he had left her, with the child upon her lap.
She was vainly endeavoring to still its moaning, and at the
same time was intently studying its face.

Ben Zion's torrent of explanation, and the feverish haste
with which he presented the hot milk in a cracked glass,
did not seem to attract Bathsheba's notice.   She was
absorbed.

"Is the brat good-looking?" said the pedler; "I suppose
I must find some one to adopt it to-day."

"I was thinking," said Bathsheba dreamily, "how wonderfully this child resembles Baumeister. Look! There is
his identical expression when he is excited! It is very
curious!"

"Hum!" said Ben Zion.   He took a careful look. "You
are right. The child is a second edition of Baumeister,
wicked smile and all! Now, how shall we account for
that?"

"We will not try, just now," said Bathsheba, and she fed
the hungry child.

Old Father Israel was still singing and sewing in the
next room, and his "Alleluia" arose sweet and clear.

CHAPTER XVIII

THE MARSEILLAISE OF THE POOR

" Hush ! " said a deep resonant voice which every one in the theatre recognized as Joseph's. " Mordecai Menzer is going to sing."

The play that night was " Ezra, " a romantic drama which dealt with the persecutions of the Jews in Russian Poland. It was played with intense earnestness, although the heat was stifling, and it was a night to be in the open air, rather than at a theatre.

There was a wicked noble in it, who wished to carry off an old Jew's daughter, and who, by the aid of a cunning priest, fastened upon the venerable Hebrew and his pretty Rebecca the dread accusation — still as terrible in some parts of Europe as it was in the Middle Ages — that they had slain a young Christian child, to use the blood in their mystical sacrifices.

The old man and his child were dragged to prison ; and then came Ezra, the deliverer, a banished patriot returned to his native land to organize insurrection.

There was a striking scene in which Ezra assembled the young men and maidens in a desolate field covered with snow, and there made them swear vengeance against the oppressor. This scene closed with the singing of religious melodies, and there was a chorus ending with " Alleluia," sung by a dozen maidens, who looked not unlike the old pictures of angels, as they knelt with folded hands and eyes raised heavenward.

This chorus thrilled Joseph to his very soul, as he sat in the darkened corner of the same box in which he had witnessed the performance of " Judith and Holofernus ; " and the whole drama, with its strange and bitter savor of patriotism, seemed to invite him to action.

There were phrases in Ezra's speech which stirred his soul like a trumpet.

Now the curtain had fallen on the third act, and Joseph came forward to announce that Mordecai, the " poet of the people," was to sing the great song which might awaken the cloakmakers to instant action.

As for Baumeister, cowering in a humble place in the gallery, his eyes glistened with the hope that the poet's song might influence the hunger-tortured throng to fall upon their employers, or upon any one else who came in their way, and to hack, burn, and destroy.

After Joseph's announcement there was a great clapping of hands and waving of handkerchiefs ; and presently Mordecai came in front of the curtain, and stood, rather timidly, awaiting the arrival of his " inspiration."

The sight of this little man, worn by sorrow, and with his lean, angular face furrowed by thought, was inexpressibly pathetic to Joseph, who recognized in him one of the leaders of the people.

But to the rank and file of the audience it was a trifle disappointing, and whispers and suppressed laughter were heard while the poet shuffled about, looking at the footlights.

At last he held up his hand, and the orchestra struck into the singular air which Joseph at once recognized as that which he had heard the small fiddler play at the rehearsal of the song.

Then Mordecai began to sing. He threw his head back, raised his arms, and waved them violently, as if he were hurling upon the audience the ringing ironical sentences in which he denounced the sweaters, and expressed compassion for their prey.

Before the first verse was finished one or two of the " sweaters " who had been skulking in boxes arose, and tried to make their exits without attracting attention.

But they were observed, and one of them was caught and buffeted. His hat was smashed over his eyes, his clothes were torn, and, expostulating and cursing by turns, he was pushed headlong out of the theatre.

Others, following, escaped with nothing worse than execration. One man shook his fist in the sweater's face and shouted, " Ah, we feel very uncomfortable just now, don't we ? as the devil said when he was crossing the river on the ice and broke through ! "

It was Ben Zion.

Mordecai had warmed to his task when the third verse was reached, and he delivered it with terrible emphasis. An old white-haired man in the orchestra laid down his violin and sobbed aloud.

His sobs were contagious. The poor overworked girls in the side seats burst into weeping when the lines alluding to their dreadful fate were recited, rather than sung, in a kind of frenzy.

Presently sighs and groans were heard from all parts of the house, and from the gallery came the sound of curses. Then all at once a sharp voice cried in jargon, with the unctuous gutturals and languorous drawling of the unlearned man, —

" That's song enough ! We know exactly what we have to do now. Come on, comrades, and let's end this business ! Those who remain slaves any longer deserve to be kept in slavery forever ! Come on ! "

Joseph thought that the voice sounded like Baumeister's, but he was too excited to be certain, and he had no chance to investigate. For suddenly the whole audience, almost entirely composed of the starving cloakmakers and their families, arose, as actuated by a common impulse, and poured into the street, leaving Mordecai panting and gasping in front of the curtain, and the actors half crazy with curiosity in their nooks in the wings.

Mordecai had done more than he expected to do. The cloakmakers had made the most extraordinary sacrifices to be present on this occasion. It was out of season for theatres, but they had determined to make the affair imposing by a full attendance.

They were in an exalted and dangerous frame of mind, and the few incendiary words which Baumeister scattered among them as they ran to and fro in the Bowery were like coals of fire applied to tow ; or, as Ben Zion afterwards described them, " like upsetting a kerosene stove in a tenement house."

The sparks flew and the flame grew.

A small number of the spectators returned, but the interest of both audience and actors was now diminished in the fictitious drama. All had concentrated their attention upon the real drama, which they knew to be near at hand.

Joseph went out into the Bowery, and found himself confronted by a tall policeman, who scowled at him and stood in his way.

Joseph's blood was hot, and he returned the scowl with interest. " Look here, young feller," said the majestic man of buttons, " your people's gettin' excited. Why don't you call them off home ? We can't be lettin' them block up the street like this."

" Well, unblock it then — that's what you are paid to do!" said Joseph.

"Maybe so," remarked the policeman, grinning. "But it's just as well to let you know that if there's any chance of a riot, the broken heads'll be mostly on your side. Tell 'em to run along home now, like a good feller."

Joseph was too wild with rage to reply. But he went out and wandered away from the crowd, thinking of what he had heard Freier say about the very poor chances of a labor riot in New York City.

He never could exactly remember where he spent the rest of that night. It was as much a blank to him as if he had been intoxicated, so absorbed was he in his many bitter reflections, so turbulent were his emotions.

He only knew that when morning came, bringing the sickening heat of a brazen July day, he was tottering, faint and sick, along one of the side streets in the cloakmakers' quarter, and heard that great crowds were gathering in Ludlow Street, in Hester Street, in East Broadway, in all the avenues where hunger had for weeks been spreading its reckless counsels.

"They are going to make a rush for Freier and Monach's to-day," said the man who informed him about the crowds; "and they say that if you don't lead them they will go without you."

Joseph raised his drooping head. "I will lead them," he said, "if only to keep them out of mischief. And it is right that this matter should be settled once for all. We can starve no longer."

He went home to find committee-men seated on his door-step and sullenly awaiting him. Malcha wrung her hands in despair at his forlorn condition, and at the exciting rumors every few minutes brought in. "Where have you been all night, Joseph?" she said as she brought him a cup of tea.

"I don't know," he replied with such frankness that she

stared and peered curiously at him. "I have been wandering — getting ready — ready for the storm."

Malcha began to cry, and this aroused Joseph to comfort and reassure her.

He had not been at home an hour when a man came running in, breathless with excitement, crying, —

"They are all going to march, and they want you, Herr Zalmonah. They mean to pull Freier out of his den " —

"Tell them not to make a move — on their peril — until they have seen me!" said Joseph, resuming his leadership.

A little later he was in a small restaurant in a side street not far from Broadway, talking with an intelligent cloak-maker who had volunteered to help him hold the crowds in check, when he heard a tumult outside.

The old women began to run to and fro, and hurl their skinny fists aloft — as certain a symbol of coming mischief among the Russo-Jewish refugees of to-day in New York as it was in ancient Israel.

Suddenly there was a blood-curdling chorus of yells, and a dozen men came running up, and dragging along, and beating as they went, a poor fellow whose clothes were torn to rags, and whose cheeks were livid with fear of death.

For he read murder in the eyes of his captors.

"He's a scab!" yelled one of the men, hopping around him like a bird of prey. "A scab, a loafer of a scab! We caught him as he was on his way to Freier and Monach's! What shall we do with him?" And he shook his lean fingers in the victim's face.

"Kill him! Kill him!" was the fierce response, roared by a hundred voices. And away down the street, where the people did not know what was going on, they took up the refrain, and shouted, "Kill him! Kill him!"

The unhappy man fell on his knees and grovelled in the

dust. "Don't let them kill me!" he cried, wringing his hands and crawling to the right and left. "I have a wife and children in Russia."

"Kill him!" cried a captor, aiming a terrible blow at his head.

At this moment the ranks parted, and Joseph appeared on the scene. He pushed the aggressive man rudely away.

"Why are you fighting among yourselves?" he said. "Have we not trouble enough already?"

"He is a scab, a wretched scab!" said the man sullenly, pointing to the kneeling figure. "He said to me, 'I get twenty-five dollars a week, and you are living on cabbages and boiled shoe-strings because you are a fool.' Do you think I will let him talk that way? I say kill him!"

He raised his arm again, and his fellows prepared to join him in a mad rush upon the unfortunate "scab."

"And I say *not!*" cried Joseph loudly, and advancing on the men. "Do you wish to ruin your own cause?"

"I don't understand you, Herr Zalmonah," said the man, falling back again. "I think you are foolish!"

And now there were fresh tumults in all directions, as other "scabs" were captured and were surrounded by the locked-out cloakmakers.

Joseph rushed to and fro, trying to save the men from being beaten. But he felt sick at heart when he saw them laying about with broken heads, and noticed that one of them was kicked into the gutter, as if he had been a dog.

Then there was a rush and a chorus of imprecations from the men and wailing from the women as a compact body of roughly dressed fellows came sweeping down the narrow street.

One or two of them carried drawn revolvers; others were equipped with stout cudgels; and although they bore no insignia of authority, they acted, as Ben Zion remarked, as

" if they had just bought the town, and wanted all the room
in it for themselves."

A few of the cloakmakers tried to stop their onward
movement, whereupon the new-comers charged with their
clubs, and a dozen of the locked-out men fell into the dust.
Then the assailants began to gather up the wounded and
frightened " scab " workmen and protect their retreat.

"The Pinkertons!" cried Joseph bitterly. "So *that* is
Freier and Monach's little game!"

He looked around him and saw that in all directions
there were dense throngs of his own people. This little
handful of Pinkertons, these modern swash-bucklers, whose
services had been secured by a manufacturer who did not
wish to be coerced to do right, would be swallowed up in a
twinkling of an eye if he were to give the signal.

Crack! That was the sound of a revolver! Joseph saw
one of his own men fall, and the man's wife throw herself,
shrieking and weeping, upon his body.

The man was shot through the arm; he sat up after a
little, and began to curse loudly.

While Joseph was looking on at the fight, and was still
irresolute as to his own conduct, a sharp voice full of hate
cried, close beside him, —

" A nice leader you are, helping the Pinkertons to rescue
scabs! Yes! a nice leader! I am more than half inclined
to think you are a Pinkerton yourself."

Joseph looked up in astonishment. He found himself
confronted by a group of low-browed and sinister fellows,
whom he at once recognized as Socialistic malcontents.

He thought he caught a glimpse of Baumeister's face just
behind them. But when he took a second and sharper look
the face was gone.

Some of these men had at one time belonged to his
Union, and had dropped out of it — this one for non-

payment of dues, another because he found the atmosphere uncongenial, a third because Joseph would not set a day for the Grand Revolution. He had reason to believe that they were all active, malevolent enemies, who would not hesitate to put him in a false position if they could.

He stepped back a little and gazed contemptuously at his accuser. "What have you done," he said, "which gives you any right to criticise?"

"You are a false leader!" shouted another. "You want to sell out the cause!"

"Yes; you are in league with the Pinkertons!" yelled a little man with iron-bowed spectacles and a long beard.

"You were seen talking to Freier not long ago. You are a spy! You ought to be crushed!" howled a hunchback, whose only garments were a pair of summer trousers and an old winter overcoat with a moth-eaten fur collar.

Just then Joseph felt a gentle touch on his arm. He looked down, and saw the sweet girl-figure of Miryam at his side. Instinctively he moved forward so as to place himself in front of her, and to shelter her in case the missiles began to fly.

Miryam looked up at him, and he saw that she was violently agitated. "Come away," she whispered; "these are the very people about whom I told you. They mean to do you a mischief. Don't expose yourself to be killed, Reb Joseph; *please* don't."

There was such a tremor in Miryam's voice, that Joseph looked down in surprise into the pure little face, and was startled at the depth of tenderness and emotion which he noted there. "Come away, Miryam!" he said. "These men are mad, I think! Surely nobody will believe their ravings."

"Ah! he's backing out! He's running away!" yelled the conspirators, in chorus. "Look at brave Reb Joseph run-

ning for his life !   Watch the deliverer of scabs as he makes
his retreat !" and a fragment of a broken chair, which one
of the men had picked up in the street, whizzed past
Joseph's ear.

"Cowards !" said the young leader, trembling with righteous wrath, "do you want to tempt me ?   You know that
if I say the word, there are within call twenty thousand
hands to tear you in pieces !   Be off, or it will be the worse
for you !"

"Ha, ha, ha !" laughed the little hunchback hoarsely,
"Reb Joseph thinks that he still has an army at his
back !   He will change his mind when the cloakmakers have
all been told that he is the defender of scabs !"   And the
misshapen man seized an old bottle and hurled it with mad
force at Joseph !

But just then Ben Zion came running up, and leaped like
a tiger cat upon the hunchback, and rolled him in the dirt.
"Run, Joseph !" he cried, as he came uppermost for the
second time, pounding his man all the time ; "run to the
head of the column !   They are waiting for you, and they
are not afraid of the Pinkertons !"

"Ho, ho !" laughed another of the conspirators, "Joseph
won't lead any column to-day."   And he and his fellows
picked up some loose brickbats and stones at a corner, and
hastened forward.

"Fly, Joseph !" shrieked Miryam.

"Never !   I will rout all these dogs single-handed;" and
he sprang forward to fulfil his threat.   At that instant there
was a shower of heavy missiles, and he saw Miryam placing
herself directly in front of him.   A moment later her fair
young head sank heavily.

A stone had struck her as she stood thus shielding her
beloved leader.

She fell, face downward.

Joseph felt himself pulled violently backward, and in a minute or two he had lost sight of the angry conspirators, and was surrounded by his own men.

"Miryam! Miryam! save her!" he gasped.

But the men and women did not seem to hear him. The names of Freier and Monach were the only ones which he heard, and they were repeated over and over, in hoarse and savage refrain.

"You are bleeding, Herr Zalmonah," said one of the men, pointing to his forehead. "Something has hit you on the head. Was it a Pinkerton who did it?"

Joseph felt faint and half stunned, now that the excitement of the encounter with the Socialists was beginning to subside. He took out his handkerchief and mopped his brow. In so doing he discovered that he had received a severe flesh wound.

An old woman bandaged his head, and another ran out of a tenement house with a little pot of hot coffee, and gave Joseph a drink, after which he felt better.

But the sun was now beating down with terrific force, and he saw that it would soon melt and subdue the courage of the half-starved people whose rights he was about to assert; so he staggered forward, saying, —

"Get all the officers of the Union together, and we will go to Freier and Monach's."

A tremendous shout rent the air.

The women screamed and flocked around Joseph, and laid caressing hands upon his arm, as if they wished to acquire courage by touching the garments of the prophet and leader.

In a few minutes all the men had assembled, and Ben Zion had joined the group, without asking leave or license.

"You cannot have the fun without me, as the fox said to the hounds," he remarked in a whisper, as the great crowd began to press forward to the den of the oppressors.

It was eight o'clock, and Freier and Monach's shop above
their counting-house had been humming with industry for
hours, when the advance guard of the locked-out cloakmakers arrived in front of their doors.

The manufacturers had been warned of the uprising, and
a line of policemen stood quietly ready to guard their
property if need arose.

Freier had heard that Joseph was disabled, if not killed,
in the Socialistic riot, about the origin and purposes of
which his spies had brought him reports; and he was
amazed when he learned from a burly guardian of the peace
that a committee " of them Jews was waiting to talk to
him."

He flushed angrily, then grew white, and lighted one of
his huge black cigars.   " Mind that your fellows stand firm
if they try to rush the place," he said to the policeman.
" You don't know them when they get excited.   They are
devils ! "

" Most of them look this mornin' as if a breath would
blow them away," remarked the policeman, with a contemptuous glance at Freier.

" Let those fellows in," snarled Freier, showing his teeth,
and looking so very like a wolf that the officer retreated
precipitately.

Joseph and his men were soon before Freier.   " I
thought," said the latter with a grin, " that you were not
coming again to see me."

" My people changed their minds," said Joseph, " and I
am only their agent.   They say that unless you do them
justice this morning, — now, within the hour, — they will
come in here and see you for themselves.   You know exactly what we want !   Are you ready to let us have it ?
No ?   Then I have nothing to do but to turn my mission
over to them."

" Hold on a minute! " said Freier, in a voice hoarse with passion. "Before you begin to dictate, let me tell you one thing. If you raise your voice to me, I will have you arrested and run in for attempted assault! Look at that line of blue coats out there!"

"Fool!" exclaimed Joseph, snapping his fingers in Freier's face. " Do you know what would happen if you should so much as lay a finger on me? Here! step upstairs and look down on the crowd from the front window. Up! We will accompany you, and you can tell us what you think."

He pushed the hesitating Freier to the stairs. In a few moments they stood overlooking the great assemblage of starving men and women.

It was a piteous spectacle, and touched even Freier's hard heart.

There were long rows of old men sweltering in the hot felt caps and coats in which they had left Russia, and looking ready to drop down into their graves. There were hundreds of bent and shrivelled old women, shaking their heads menacingly. There were whole regiments of thin, black-whiskered, pallid-faced men of middle age, with children clinging at their coat skirts, and with slattern and woe-begone wives, pinched with hunger and tormented by despair, crouching behind them.

And all these forlorn creatures were pushed forward resistlessly by the bony hand of Hunger.

They were ready for the assault.

Freier felt this, and was afraid. He shivered.

" Open the window," said Joseph calmly.

Freier obeyed, cursing inwardly. He did not dare to refuse.

The moment he showed his face there was a yell of execration which made him feel cold about his heart. His knees trembled.

Joseph pushed him aside, as if he were a child, and, calling his committee-men, he said, —

"Take out the window-sash, top and bottom!"

"In God's name!" said Freier.

"Silence!" shouted Joseph. In a few seconds the window was removed. "Now," said Joseph to his men, "Freier and I will stand together in the open space, and you may stand behind us."

"I will see that Freier does not get away!" whispered Ben Zion.

The young leader was saluted by a ringing shout, instantly followed by a second outburst of execrations for Freier.

The "scabs" who had been at work within crowded up to see this curious spectacle, and the policemen below listened eagerly.

The vast throng of the cloakmakers stood, open-mouthed, awaiting developments.

"Now, Freier," said Joseph, "justice must be done. I am going to announce it in your name. If you contradict and belie me, you must take the consequences."

Freier said nothing, but his knees continued to tremble.

"Fellow-workers," said Joseph, lifting up his voice. "Freier and Monach are anxious to come to an understanding with you, and to stop all the misery and misfortune which the lock-out has caused."

A murmur of incredulity ran through the throng.

"And now, Herr Freier" — at this point Ben Zion pushed him violently forward, eliciting from him an audible groan of terror — "desires to inform you that the lock-out is at an end."

Freier groaned again, whereupon Ben Zion thumped him terribly in the back.

"At an end — the lock-out! And he is ready to sign an

agreement with us to secure you in your rights hereafter. He, and the association which he represents, will accept nine hours as a day's work — and you shall have one full hour for dinner. In the three summer months there shall be a Saturday half-holiday ; wages shall be increased from twenty-five to forty per cent ; there shall be no over-time without pay ; and Herr Freier and his association pledge themselves to do everything in their power to abolish the sweating-system ! And this new condition of affairs shall begin at once ! Do I quote you correctly ? " said Joseph, turning politely to Freier.

" Yes — yes," answered the frightened man, on whose back Ben Zion had just given another powerful blow ; "anything, everything ! You are the masters, and if you ruin us, we can close up, I suppose ! "

" Then tell the people that we are agreed," said Joseph.

Freier managed to stammer forth a few words, announcing the "end of the lock-out — brisk season coming soon," and then would have fallen back, had not Ben Zion propped him up.

" You can all go home now," said Joseph to the throng. " The agreement will be signed to-day ; you can go back to work to-morrow. Do you hear ? Move off at once — to your homes. I say the Union has won the fight ! You shall starve no more ! "

There went up a scream, rather than a shout of triumph, and the upturned faces beamed with joy and with gratitude.

Hundreds of voices cried thanks and praises to Joseph, and prayed him to come out, that the crowd might bear him in triumph to the office of the Union.

" No — no ; go home and get ready for to-morrow's work ! " said Joseph ; and at last the people moved slowly and reluctantly away.

Joseph stood, white and calm, watching their departure. Nor would he stir from the window, or allow Freier to go down, until the last of the cloakmakers was disappearing round a corner.

"Now let me see you keep your promise, sir!" he said, turning almost fiercely to Freier.

CHAPTER XIX

LIGHTNING IN CLEAR SKY

THEY were about to sign the agreement.

Freier had summoned all the manufacturers interested with him in the matter, and, with a cynical smile on his sensuous lips, had conceded the points insisted upon by Joseph and his committee.

"And now," said Joseph, "let these men and women get to work, for they are starving. How would you like to sew for a week, with nothing to eat, in such weather as this?"

Freier did not answer. He shuffled his papers, and seemed anxious to complete the business.

Joseph wiped the dripping moisture from his brow, and turned away. To his momentary exaltation had now succeeded a profound depression. His triumph did not seem worth much, after all. But he felt that he had prevented a riot and an assault on Freier, and surely that was worth something.

Just then one of his men spoke, sharply and decidedly, and continuing the train of thought which Joseph had started —

"Yes, that's the hardest of all. Going back to work and having nothing to eat. That isn't right. Reb Joseph, you must make him do as the Germans do when the manufacturers have to give in. He must pay a contribution to the Union, to compensate us for the time we have lost."

Freier turned quickly on this man, with his hand raised
as if he would strike him. His teeth snapped like those of
a wolf. The cloakmaker retreated a little, but looked very
surly.

"Come, Reb Joseph," he said, "make him pay five
hundred dollars to the Union. It is the custom, and he
owes it."

"But the agreement is all ready to be signed," objected
Joseph, fearing a new delay.

"Never mind! Make him do it!"

The manufacturers said that they would leave the matter
in Freier's hands, and departed. Freier accompanied them
to the outer door. When he came back he said loudly, —

"Well, men, be off! I have my work to attend to, and
you ought to be about yours."

"These men," said Joseph, "insist upon having five
hundred dollars paid by you as damages."

"It will teach you not to lock us out again, perhaps,"
added the cloakmaker.

"I will give you no money," said Freier.· "You have had
concessions enough. I want you to get out of my place."

"Not until you promise to give the money," said the
cloakmaker, folding his arms.

"Never!" shouted Freier; but an instant later a new idea
seemed to strike him. He turned away, apparently to pore
over some accounts, then whirled back.

"Look here!" he cried, sitting down on the edge of his
desk. "I will give you a check for one hundred dollars
just to save time. If I do that, will you promise to leave
me in peace?"

"No, five hundred," insisted the cloakmaker.

"Five hundred devils! If you want the one hundred
you can have it; you will get nothing else."

"Very well," said Joseph, thinking of the starving ones,

and anxious to help them. He motioned to the cloakmaker
to be quiet. "Give the check and we will go."

A smile crept along the features of Freier, and seemed to
give them a peculiar glow.

"Shall I make the check payable to your order, Herr
Zalmonah?" he said, turning to Joseph. "Mind you, I
yield to force, and am doing this because you compel me —
to your order."

Joseph scarcely heard him. He was thinking of something else — of that moment when Bathsheba had clung to
him at the window, with the fire raging below them. The
memory of her caress seemed to sting him with a wild,
sweet pain. A minute later the remembrance had faded
away.

Freier was handing him the check. He took it, and the
others crowded around to see it, and that it was made to his
order.

Then the agreement was signed, and Freier opened the
door, and bowed them out with an ironical politeness which
so angered Ben Zion that he could scarcely refrain from
leaving the manufacturer a memorial of his visit in the
shape of a black eye.

"Leave me alone for a few hours," said Joseph to his
men as they returned to the cloakmakers' quarter. "I have
much need of rest."

But they would not listen to him, and, catching him up,
bore him along on their shoulders, dancing and shouting as
best they could in their famished condition.

Gradually a long procession formed behind them; and
although Joseph watched a trifle anxiously for the Socialists, none of them appeared in it. And so Joseph arrived
in triumph at his own door, and was received with open
arms by Malcha, almost beside herself with joy at the news
of the victory.

She thrust a cup of tea into his hand, and made him sit down in the bedroom, where he found David and old Manasseh conversing in low tones.

At sight of David, poor overworked Joseph let his cup fall, and clasped his hands to his forehead. "And Miryam! coward that I am! what has become of Miryam, who saved my life when the Socialists were throwing stones at me? I saw her lying half dead on the ground as I was whirled away in the crowd this morning. Where is she?"

"Miryam is safe," said David quietly, approaching and giving Joseph his hand. "She was struck down by the blow meant for you, and she was badly hurt; but she has regained her cheerfulness now that she is laid away snugly in bed at the theatre."

"What a noble child!" said Joseph with tears in his eyes.

"She is like a delicate plant among weeds, when she is with us," said David modestly. "Miryam is a little saint. Her nature is like the myrtle. You know the proverb, 'A myrtle in the desert is a myrtle still.'"

David was in excellent humor. His eyes sparkled; a little color came and went in his face. "To think," he said, "that old Mordecai's hymn against the sweaters should have resulted in this! You prepared the way, Joseph, and Mordecai gave the final impulse. Ah! you remember Bathsheba's warning, do you not? Well, you see that it was necessary enough. And, by the way, if we call Miryam a myrtle, what should we call Bathsheba? Did you hear that she had taken a room in Simon's house on the very day when his house was burned, and that she lost all her precious costumes? It will be some time before she can play the Shulamite, I fear."

Joseph turned mortally pale, and looked earnestly at David. But evidently the latter knew nothing of the manner in which Bathsheba had escaped from the burning house.

"I must go to little Miryam," he said, turning to Malcha. "Will you not go with me?"

"We are all going presently," replied Malcha. "But if you don't eat your breakfast and hold your tongue, you will be put to bed with your feet tied to the bed-posts."

This playful threat recalled Joseph to reason, for an hour or two. But at the end of that time business once more invaded his mind. His committee was summoned from the front steps, where it had been sitting patiently, to go with Joseph to the bank, and get the Freier check cashed, and then to see the money duly deposited in the safe of the Union.

After this was done in the presence of many witnesses, appeals for succor began to flow in freely; and they did not stop until Joseph had paid out all but the last twenty-dollar bill in small sums for the purchase of bread.

"Take some of the money yourself, Joseph," said one of the committee-men. "You need it at home. You are as poor as we are."

"I am poorer," said Joseph with a weary smile. "Poorer, because I have no time to work and earn my living. But I will not touch a cent of the money."

The men shook their heads and looked at each other gravely after Joseph had gone. "He will not last long," said one; "he is too willing. Bending the bow too much makes it crack."

"But it sends the arrow to the right spot," said Ben Zion, who was angrily listening. "So what are you grumbling about? as the cat said to the fish when she was eating it."

"I suppose if some of the money was offered to you, it wouldn't be necessary to ask you twice," said a committee-man, who considered Ben Zion an interloper.

"To me? What do I want with your money?" cried Ben Zion disdainfully. "I am a merchant."

The half-starved throng laughed in derision.

"Very well," said Ben Zion, "the next time that one of you wants something out of my push-cart, I will show you whether I am a merchant or not."

Joseph returned home slowly and painfully. There was an ominous buzzing in his head, and his limbs were heavy. As he turned into East Broadway he was compelled to stop and rest.

Once he looked up hurriedly, for he thought the clouds were gathering in the fiery sky. But presently he saw that mists were rising in his eyes. He tried to raise one hand, and a sharp pain shot through his arm.

Alarmed, he hobbled the rest of the way as fast as he could, and gasped for water when the frightened Malcha received him in her arms. Then he began to babble in a disjointed and incoherent way about fire and danger.

"I believe he has got a touch of the sun," thought Malcha. But after a little he revived, and, looking around him like one just come out of a dream, he saw an old woman sitting on a stool in a dark corner.

"What does *she* want?" he asked Malcha.

"I don't know. She will talk to nobody but you, she says."

The woman came forward with a grin. "I have brought you something from the landlord, Herr Zalmonah," she mumbled in English. "Something that won't wait!"

A shiver ran through Joseph's frame as he took the folded paper which the crone handed to him. It suddenly flashed through his mind that, in the rush and hurry of his work for the cloakmakers, he had totally forgotten to make provision for his rent.

At first the landlord had been lenient, observing that Joseph was powerful among his own people, and not wishing to offend him. But by and by he became surly.

Joseph now remembered that a few mornings before the landlord had met him, and asked him for the month's rent, overdue, and that he had scarcely answered him.

He opened the paper, and smiled bitterly as he saw the familiar word " Dispossess," which he had seen so many times in papers served upon unfortunate members of his Union. A sharp pain smote him at the heart. Turned into the street! That was all very well when he was alone; but now Malcha and little Zipporah were here, and it was not only humiliating, but appalling.

He sent Malcha out of the room on some feeble pretext, and then said to the old woman, "I am sick to-day, and don't want to move before next Monday. I suppose we can stay until then? Perhaps by that time " —

" No," said the old woman brutally; "the landlord says he's had enough of labor-leaders, and he won't have ye no longer at no price. So you want to git out before to-morrow night! We need tenants that can tend to their own business, and not be meddling with other folks."

" Very well," said Joseph, turning his back on this abuse; "you needn't stay any longer."

" Oh, no, I suppose not," shrieked the woman, suddenly becoming aggressive. " Just remember that you will be fired if you are found here to-morrow night!" and she stalked away.

Joseph let the paper fall on the floor; an idle tear or two dropped on it. This, then, was his reward! No roof over his head, and no money in his pocket!

He thought of the meagre twenty dollars in the Union's treasury. "No!" he said resolutely; "that will be needed to-morrow to buy bread for starving children."

Malcha did not return; and Joseph sat looking into the black future until fiery specks danced before his eyes, and his head felt as if it were made of melting lead. Pres-

ently he heard a light footstep, and looking up he saw
David standing near him. His heart yearned for a bit of
sympathy.

"Friend David," he said, "I am humbled to the very dust."

"'He who offers humility to God and man,'" answered
David in his oracular fashion, "'shall receive as great a reward as though he had offered all the sacrifices in the world.'"

"True, true, David; but I am afraid that proverbs will
not help my case."

"Then we will find something more substantial!" cried
David. "I know the cause of your sadness, Joseph. Do
you fancy that I will let that old skinflint, that landlord
without mercy, drive you out-of-doors just when you have
saved so many of our people from starvation? He is
boasting that he will land you on the pavement; but he
won't," and he dropped on Joseph's knee four crisp five-
dollar bills. "Send that to the old fiend," he said, "and so
you will be safe for a while."

"No, no, David! I deserve to suffer: I have been too
negligent. I must begin to care more for my wife, and less
for the woes of other people."

"You must take the money. And now come with me to
see poor little Miryam. She has been calling for you at
intervals ever since she was hurt. Your presence will help
to make her better."

Joseph was finally prevailed upon to accept enough of
the money to satisfy the landlord's claim, and he had
brightened up and looked refreshed when Malcha returned.
She was loth to let him go out into the sun once more, but
he insisted; and keeping in the shadow of the houses, and
stopping now and then to rest in a cool cellar, they finally
came to the theatre.

A simple couch had been arranged in the little loft where
Joseph had seen the company at lunch; and upon it, cov-

ered with fantastic Oriental draperies, and with her dainty head propped up by the cushion on which Judith had executed "Holofernus," Miryam was lying, her eyes wide open, and staring at the bare beams of the roof, and her thin girlish hands crossed on her breast. She was so strangely still that Joseph's heart beat tumultuously at the thought that she might be dead.

He was about to whisper to David, when the child-woman turned her face, which was suddenly transfigured with a heavenly smile, toward Joseph, and, as if moved by an irresistible impulse which she herself did not understand, stretched out her arms to him.

He hastened forward and knelt beside her.

"O Herr Joseph!" she said, "it was very sweet of you to come — in your hour of victory! I have heard — I know — I told everybody that you would win!"

A divine tenderness stole into her eyes; and a strange look, which made her seem older, and gave to her gaze a womanly warmth and grace, thrilled Joseph deeply.

He took her hands almost timidly, looking round at David, who encouraged him with a smile.

"Dear Miryam!" he said, "did those brutal villains harm you this morning? If they did I shall have them punished!"

"They meant to take your life, Joseph!" sighed the girl, clinging to Joseph's hand with a yearning caress which touched him beyond the power of expression.

"I know — I know, Miryam! But I was mad — I was foolish to let you remain there an instant! And to feel that the stone aimed at me should have struck you down!"

"It does not hurt now, Reb Joseph," said the girl bravely. "It burned a good deal at first, but it is calmer now, and it will soon be nothing. Ah, Reb Joseph! my spirit would have been happy if I had been stretched dead at your feet, and you had walked over me to victory!"

She touched Joseph's hand reverently with her thin lips; then sank back as if exhausted with emotion and pain.

"Dear little Miryam!" whispered Joseph; "she is like an angel of light. She is out of place in this rude life of starvation and struggle. Heaven forgive me for bringing a single pang to the poor child!"

"'The rose grows among thorns!'" said David sententiously, stooping over Miryam to listen to her breathing, which was labored and hoarse. "She must sleep now. The doctor is coming soon. She could not rest without seeing you. Now it is our duty to make her well and strong."

"How I wish I could do something to help her!" sighed poor Joseph, who had been growing more and more impatient of his poverty ever since the victory over Freier. "But what can I do?" he cried, clasping his hands. "I have nothing, I am nothing! Tell me, is Miryam seriously bruised?"

"She has youth and courage on her side," said David evasively. But his face darkened, and his eyes looked troubled as he spoke. Then he drew Joseph softly aside, and they sat down together on a pile of costumes in which a Hebrew army was that evening to vanquish an oppressor in one of David's biblical dramas.

"Now that your battle is over, Joseph," said David, "I wish to give you a bit of advice. You are not strong enough to carry on this struggle, as it may be necessary to do again and again. You have done your part; your duty now is to your wife and child."

"I know, I know," said Joseph humbly; "I am going back to the machine at once."

"You can do better than that. Up in the Connecticut hills I hear that there is a colony, made up of our people, who have been helped by generous people abroad, and who

are doing well.   You might go there, and found yourself a
home, and live with them.   They would be glad of your
counsel and assistance.   Our people are foolish to settle
in these city slums.   But it is useless to reason with these
mobs.   With you, Joseph, I can reason, and I entreat you
to found a home, an independence, a refuge."

"If it could only be!" sighed the weary Joseph.   "But
who would take care of my poor folk here?"

"Others will spring up to continue your good work.
Promise me that you will think of the colony, Joseph."

"I will."   Joseph grasped David's arm, breathing hard,
and looking as perturbed as if he had seen a spectre.   He
drew David back with him behind a high pile of "proper-
ties," and stood trembling and apparently angry.

Bathsheba had stolen in, and, moving lightly to the couch,
had knelt beside Miryam, and taken the girl's thin hands
in hers.   Joseph could hear her speaking caressingly to
Miryam, and the girl was answering in a whisper.   He
looked at Bathsheba curiously.   She was as coldly, statu-
esquely beautiful as ever: there was nothing to indicate
that her nature was capable of the mighty passion manifested when she had thrown herself upon his breast, or when
they stood lashed together, ready to descend from the
window of the burning building.

"Come away!" whispered Joseph; and by crawling over
a beam or two they managed to regain the exit without
being seen by Bathsheba.

David placed both hands on Joseph's shoulders and
looked him squarely in the face as he bade him good-by.
"Think about the colony, friend Joseph," he said.   "Up
there you would not be troubled by any more glimpses of
Bathsheba"—Joseph flushed, but did not appear to be
angry—"and perhaps that would be as well.   'Trust not
thyself until the day of thy death,'" added David, conclud-

ing with a proverb, as usual, and turning away with a mistiness in his eyes.

Joseph went home perplexed in spirit.

There was a great meeting at the Union that night, at which the young labor-leader was fairly worshipped by the mothers and wives who recognized in him the deliverer, leading their sons and husbands up out of the land of Egypt, and it was long past midnight before his weary head rested on his humble pillow.

Toward six o'clock he awoke, with a delicious sense of relief from the furnace heat which for the few days past had made life almost intolerable.

A cool wind, laden with the aroma of the sea, was blowing through the open casements. Large raindrops were plashing upon the window-sills; and presently there came a deep, magnificent thunder roll, which seemed to shake the city to its foundations.

Malcha and the child were sleeping peacefully. Joseph arose and dressed himself slowly, meditating on his many escapes from trouble. His landlord was pacified: his victory over Freier was decisive. Now he would go to work!

He went out to the front steps, and sat down, enjoying the brisk air and the cool rain breaths. Life began to seem large and fine to him once more. Vague ambitions slowly took shape in his mind. David's advice drifted through his memory. He had a momentary vision of a charming country home, where he and his were snugly ensconced, free from cares and jealousies and impressions.

"Does Mr. Joseph Zalmonah live here?" said a sharp, but not unkindly, voice close beside him.

He started, and found a keen-faced, gray-eyed man, dressed in a blue flannel suit, a derby hat, and a pair of untanned leather shoes, stepping briskly around so as to face him.

"I am the man," answered Joseph politely.   "What can I do for you?"

"Mr. Joseph Zalmonah, the labor-leader?"

"Yes."

"Well, Mr. Zalmonah, I'm sorry to trouble ye, but I have a warrant for your arrest, and if you will come along with me, I'll explain it a little to ye, as we go along."

Joseph laughed.   Probably some trick of Baumeister's, some trivial accusation of assault, or — was it a blow struck out of the dark by some more powerful enemy?

"Come," said the man, "sorry to bother ye, but business is business.   And you might as well know the charge, because ye don't seem to think it's serious.   The charge is Arson."

The word fell heavily on Joseph's brain.   "Arson?" he repeated wonderingly.

"Yes — burning a house when they's folks in it — see? Come, now, Mr. Zalmonah, we don't want no crowd; git your hat, and we will trudge along before the storm ketches us."

CHAPTER XX

THE LIVING TOMB

WHEN Joseph went in to get his hat, he approached the bed, and saw Malcha and the child slumbering so peacefully that he at once decided not to wake them.

Little Zipporah had clambered high up, and laid her pretty head confidingly on her mother's arm, and she nestled there in the most charming of postures.

The mother's deep regular breathing showed that she could be awakened only with difficulty just then. Her face wore a pleased smile, as if she were dreaming of something very agreeable.

"She looks," thought Joseph, "as she did when she was a young bride, with no care on her brow."

He bent down and kissed her, and as his lips touched her face, flushed with sleep, a pang, as of a sudden stab, shot through his breast, and he thought that he would have fallen.

But he recovered in an instant, and, seizing his hat, he quickly rejoined his watchful captor at the door.

He did not dare to look backward. For he knew that if he did he should fly to Malcha's arms, and awaken her to all the wretchedness of a despairing good-by.

"Come on," he said; "I am ready for you now."

"You seem to speak English pretty well," said the man. "Ben in this country long?"

"Long enough to know that there is as much injustice
in it as in most countries," answered Joseph bitterly.
"What fool has trumped up a charge against me? I will
make him sweat for it before the day is over."

The man shot a keen glance at him. "A day ain't much,"
he said, not unkindly, "when a feller's in your fix. If I
was you, now, I wouldn't be too impatient. And when we
get over there," he made a gesture to the westward, which
might have meant anything this side of California, "I
recommend you to send home and let your folks know
where ye be. It'll save trouble."

"What do you call 'over there'?" said Joseph, looking
at the man fixedly.

"Wal, we're bound for Essex Market now," he answered,
"and then I suppose that if you don't get bail it'll be the
'Tombs.' And it's pretty hard getting bail on arson now,"
he added reflectively.

"Oh, the 'Tombs,'" reflected Joseph aloud. He had almost forgotten that he was to be put in prison. But now
the fact loomed up before him, large, grim, and terrible.

With the instinct of any live thing which finds itself in
a trap, he looked desperately and quickly to right and left,
and then shot a swift glance at his companion.

"Now, Zalmonah," said the officer, moving up to him with
astonishing quickness, "you look like a man of sense.
Just prove it. I know that this part of the town is full of
your folks. But it wouldn't do you the least good to break
away. I'd git ye again, if I had ter have the militia called
out. You bet I would."

He took from his hip pocket a package of "fine cut" and
selected a capacious chew. "I'm right, hey?" he queried.

"Yes," responded Joseph; "you are right."

At that moment he heard the click-click-click clack-clack
of a sewing-machine, and it sounded like music in his ear.

They had turned into a quarter where cloakmakers abounded, and the clack of the machine indicated that the poor people had gone to work again. They would have bread now, he thought, as the great tears stood in his eyes. What mattered it what became of him ?

Each moment he expected to see one of his followers recognize him, and ask him where he was going; but he encountered no one who knew him.

The fact was that every cloakmaker was at home or in the shops, working for dear life to make up for lost time, and no one thought of glancing into the street.

In a few minutes they were at the Essex Market prison, where Joseph had often been to intercede for an indiscreet workman or woman who had been illustrating her argument with scratches upon her neighbor's face.

Here he was interrogated and locked up; and after he had written a little scrawl to his wife, begging her not to be alarmed, and to come and see him at mid-day, he sat down on the bench in his cell, and in a few minutes fell fast asleep.

The relapse after the long strain had come. Joseph was as weak as a child.

Two days after his arrest Joseph stood, a little tremulous and disturbed, but still full of courage, at the entrance to the "Tombs."

He had seen Malcha; he had seen Ben Zion; he had seen kind friends who were indignant at his arrest. But the magistrate had placed his bail so high that no one in his humble circle — no, nor any ten of them combined — could raise it; and so he was going to the "Tombs" to await his trial.

Joseph vaguely noted the long, low wall, like that of an Egyptian burial-place ; the diminutive entrance, with the words "City Prison" in modest type, and a grating, just inside of which a fat policeman sat, with a cheerful smile upon his face, and an apparent willingness to let everybody and anybody in the world go in, although he might have totally different notions about allowing them to go out again.

A shadow seemed to rest upon everything. His captor pushed him forward a little as the grating swung back, as if he feared the sudden revolt of the flesh in favor of liberty.

Joseph stepped briskly in. The policeman swung the grating to position, popped the key into his pocket, and proceeded to stare with great earnestness at nothing at all.

Now that he was caged, Joseph took accurate note of everything. He observed the low, old-fashioned vaulting of the ceiling of the reception-room; the high desk out of which a clerk stared in a coldly unsympathetic way, as if bored by the new arrival; the wooden railings, behind which the prisoners were compelled to file, and the smooth polish which had been put upon them by the innumerable hands of thieves, murderers, drunken ruffians, and outcasts on their way to even less comfortable abodes.

He was ushered into a deep recess beneath the vaults, and seated at a table beside his companion. But no one else came near him; the shadows fell more deeply around him. He fancied that it was something like being dead. The silence and gloom of the living tomb had already taken hold upon his spirit.

He let his hands fall listlessly in his lap, and sat contemplating them with reproachful gaze, as who would say, "Now, what have you done wrong to bring me to such a place as this?"

By and by he heard a footstep, and an elderly man in a neatly fitting frock-coat of expensive material — Joseph remembered long afterward how he eyed that coat, and tried to discover whether or not it had been made by a sweater's bondman — entered and looked at him with a cold glance, but without greeting him at all.

"This is Zalmonah, Warden," said Joseph's captor. "You know. Case of arson in the first degree. No bail."

The warden looked at the man with a frigid stare.

Now came much writing down of Joseph's responses to questions asked by the clerk, who came out of a dark recess, and careful searching of pockets; and then warden and clerk seemed to fade away, and Joseph's captor arose and essayed a grin, at the same time holding out a huge knotted hand, and saying, —

"Well, so long, Zalmonah. I guess you'll be all right here. And if, as your friends say, you hadn't nothing to do with that case of arson, why, you won't be staying here a great while."

Joseph reached out one hand — he seemed gifted with extraordinary strength for a moment — and gripped the officer by the collar of his coat. Then he drew the man close to him, and looked sharply into his eyes.

"Do you mean to tell me," he said, "that you have ever for an instant supposed me guilty of arson?"

"Well — perhaps," stammered the man, who was the least bit daunted; "but now that I have seen you" —

"Then if you could believe that," said Joseph, spurning the fellow away, "you are a greater fool than I take you for. Now, what do they want to do with me?"

"This way," said a cracked voice, and Joseph saw at his elbow a small gray-headed man in a faded dark blue uniform, with a slouch cap on his head, and a bunch of keys in his hand. This elderly person led the way as if he were a hotel porter showing a guest the best rooms in the house, until they reached the railings, when he got Joseph in front of him, and said curtly, "Turn to the right."

A lock clicked, a grating swung open; an attendant seated in the obscurity peered out sharply at Joseph, as if determined to be sure of recognizing him again; and then Joseph and his guide rambled along under the archway. From point to point lanterns cast dubious rays, which seemed timid about affronting the general blackness.

"Pretty good weather to-day, ain't it?" said the guide, jingling his keys.

"Fairly good," answered Joseph. "But you would never know it here. This is like a tomb."

The man looked fixedly at him for a moment. "Wal, that's right, ain't it?" he said querulously. "They call it the 'Tombs,' don't they? What d'ye expect?"

"Nothing," answered Joseph with a sigh.

And indeed he had arrived at that point where he really expected nothing more. It seemed to him as if the end of his self-imposed martyrdom had come, in a universal blackness in which he should soon find oblivion. A host of confused and fleeting images — his wife, his child, Miryam, David, Ben Zion; Mordecai, with his songs; Bathsheba, with her sinuous grace and dangerous wiles; Baumeister in his epileptic fits — came around him, were luminous for a moment, and then were consumed by the shadows.

And now they were at another door, which was opened with a grating key, and which, swinging inwards, disclosed a consumptive-looking keeper sitting in a low chair, from which he arose to open one more creaking and heavy portal. This led into a narrow corridor, along which Joseph was hurried, without perceiving that the first turnkey had left him, and that he was between two others.

They passed through a gate, on one side of which, on a little perch, sat a harsh-featured man, and Joseph was ushered into a small cell on the lower tier of the section reserved for prisoners awaiting trial, and found himself

welcomed with a sort of fierce joy by a commonplace de-
faulter with an East Side drawl, who said he was lonesome,
and mighty glad to see company ; and he furthermore added
that if Joseph had any tobacco, he would be "much obliged
for some."

Joseph at first turned his back on this importunate fellow-
prisoner, because he felt an imperious need of retiring into
his own spirit, and compelling the world, with its prison-
walls, to vanish from his thoughts. He sat down on his
little bed, and held his head in his hands so long that his
companion said, "Huh! cracked, I guess!" and began
writing on a piece of foolscap, with a soap-box for a table.

Joseph did not look up from his revery until the preparations in the corridor told him that night had come. He
thought of Malcha lonely in a strange land, with a little
child to care for, and with no resource save manual labor,
and then the hot tears gushed from his eyes. He lay down
and turned his face to the wall, and that night the iron
entered into his soul.

But next morning he was more tranquil, for there was a
bustle around him, and an air of cheerfulness pervaded even
the living tomb. On the corridor above, reporters were
flocking about the cell of a financier who had fallen by the
way, and he heard them laughing and talking in a high key
with the wretched man.

Joseph was allowed to send for such things as he needed,
and was informed that a friend had opened a credit for him.
He was offered a newspaper, and permitted to smoke cigar-
ettes, and to write and send letters. But no matter how
absorbed he became in the petty occupations permissible,
he could not shake off the feeling that he was entombed
alive, and that for him the sentient, breathing world, with
its colors of sunrise and song of birds and kiss of wife and
children, was lost forever.

That day brought him a visitor. It was David, serene and quaint as usual, seeming to bring with him the fresh air of freedom, and some hope for the future.

"And Malcha?" gasped Joseph, clinging to the grating, and shaking it desperately in his anxiety.

"Malcha and the child will be provided for until your innocence is proved," said David. "The poor wife was going to work in a cloakmaker's (a groan escaped Joseph's lips), but I put a stop to that. I have a project, Joseph, and I have come to tell you about it. But first take these little things which Malcha and Miryam have sent you," and he handed in a little basket, which had been duly examined by the Cerberus at the entrance.

"Food and flowers!" said Joseph, glancing at the gifts. "They can wait. The scheme — the scheme!"

"You know," said David, hugging the bars of the grating, "that when the righteous dies ''tis earth which meets with loss.' You are too valuable to us to be lost in this battle that you are fighting against such fearful odds, Joseph; and as soon as you are free I mean to take you and yours into a new and a safer field of action. Joseph, I am going to found a colony myself."

"Well, there now," said Joseph, "if I heard Ben Zion say a thing like that, I could listen without a smile! But when I hear an intelligent and practical man like you — Since when were our poor people qualified for the rough work of colony life? They were not successful enough with farming at home to try it abroad."

"Yet we are going to try it, Joseph, and we want you to lead and encourage us. Up among the hills, a hundred and fifty miles from here, in a State they call Connecticut — do you remember my mentioning a colony already founded there? — we have found a half-deserted section where we can get homes cheaply, and where we can establish small industries. And now our first duty, Joseph, is to get you free, so that you may help us. In the fresh air of the country, and with land of your own, you will be a new man. We will draw the refugees away from the sweaters to us! We will leave them without slaves to tyrannize over! We will outwit them, Joseph, and they shall lose all their ill-gotten gains."

Transfigured by his enthusiasm, David shook the bars so, and talked so loudly, that a keeper came to peer curiously at him.

But Joseph shook his head sorrowfully. "I am afraid that it is all a dream, David. And how am I to be got out of here, even if your dream is realized? No, no; I must stay here in the darkness — my enemies have laid their hands on me; and 'Israel is smitten, as the reed is shaken in the waters.'"

He tried to smile.

"Come, now," said David, "'into the well which supplies thee with water cast no stones.' Why refuse the pleasing prospect of the colony? I shall keep an interest in my theatre, which pays me well; and we will have a home for Miryam and Malcha and the child, and for Manasseh and Shiphrah"—

He paused, and a wave of color came into his face. "I would like to have Shiphrah included in the scheme, if you do not object, Joseph," he said almost humbly.

Joseph did not answer at once. He was beginning to understand that David's interest in the unfortunate Shiphrah was more than a benevolent one; that the young play-wright and manager had learned to love the erring one. Presently he put out his hand, and David took it.

"Did I not deliver Shiphrah out of the hands of the sweaters?" Joseph said; "and was it in order to hinder her from receiving any gift of God which might come to her?"

The two friends understood, without further words.
When they parted Joseph felt a fresh breeze of hope on
his brow, although David had not been able to give him a
single iota of information about the real author of the fire
which had burned Simon's house, and with it many of the
unlucky tenants. David was confident that the real culprit
would be found; that meantime bail for Joseph would yet
be accepted ; but that was all.

Left alone, Joseph began to reflect seriously on his duty
to himself in the matter. The most serious evidence against
him seemed to be furnished by his presence in the house
at the time the conflagration was discovered, and the
fact that he had cried out to Simon, on the night when the
cloakmakers had gone to rescue poor Mother Levitsky,
something about having his houses burned. If two, three,
or a half dozen of the hostile seceders from his Union were
to swear in court to these things, Joseph felt convinced
that it might go hard with him. Was Baumeister at the
bottom of the intrigue ? and would he arise to swear away
Joseph's life and liberty, and to cause him to be forgotten
of men ? Was he capable of such baseness ?

When weeping Malcha came to see him that same day,
Joseph felt as if his heart would burst. How could he
answer the flood of questions which she poured into his dis-
tracted ears ? How tell her that he was with Bathsheba
in the burning building, and that he had rescued her from
it ? The blood arose to his cheek as he thought on these
things. But it faded away again when Malcha, who was
the very acme of goodness and patience, and whose belief
in him was absolute, told him that in a day or two she was
to begin work in a cloakmaker's.

Joseph besought her not to do it, and told her of David's
project of the colony. "Wait a few days," he said, with
an attempt at a smile, "and all will be well."

But Malcha would not hear of it, nor of any reliance upon David's friendly assistance. To the machine she would go, and earn her own living, until Joseph should be given back to her. And there was a fierce resolution in her pallid little face as she held up Zipporah above the railings to be kissed, and went away, looking back with a scared, hunted sort of glance which cut Joseph's pride severely.

When she was gone Joseph entered his cell, and fell into such a paroxysm of despair that his companion feared that he would attempt his own life. But little by little his courage came back, and he steeled his soul as all heroic natures have done since Society invented torture for those who reprove its crimes and follies.

By contact with the earth he got new strength, like Antæus. He was thrown down and trampled on; but he felt growing within him an infinite strength for resistance to suffering.

Days passed, each one hailed by Joseph as likely to produce an event, and each, like its predecessor, stealing away slowly amid the dull round of prison duties. Now and then came a "new boarder," who was curiously scanned by all the old pensioners, and at once rated. Joseph discovered that the tongue of scandal and slander wagged far more busily inside prison than outside.

Night came, with its awful stillness, its locked and double-locked gratings, its blackness, which seemed as if it must be denser than that of the tomb. And then came morning, with click and clatter of locks and with the hundred annoyances to which Joseph daily subjected his poor soul because he could not bring himself to think that he was a prisoner.

One day, after he had been in the "Tombs" three weeks, Joseph was seated in the door of his cell, gazing moodily into the glowing coals of the huge heater which, winter and summer, does duty in the damp and unhealthy corridor, when "the visit of a lady" was announced.

He hastened to the grating, thinking that it was of course Malcha with the child.

But it was not Malcha and Zipporah. It was Bathsheba; and before he could draw back from the grating her warm hands had touched his cold ones, and had sent a passionate thrill through his whole being.

"No — no," said Joseph faintly, like one who is slowly swooning; "I did not desire to see you. I cannot — talk with you now."

Bathsheba did not speak just then. She withdrew her hands; her cheeks grew ashy pale, and she stood looking at Joseph through the bars with an air of offended majesty.

"Go away," he said; "I cannot hear anything that you have come to say. If it affords you pleasure to look upon your work, gaze at it! But don't expect me to join in your joy at my ruin!"

The woman found her tongue now. Her eyes sparkled; she tossed her head saucily, and stamped her feet upon the stone floor.

"You call this my work!" she said. "And after I was the first to warn you!"

"A pretty warning indeed! You found me walking into the trap, and did not tell me I was in danger."

Bathsheba took no notice of this accusation. "What if I were to tell you that I could set you free — within a week?" she whispered. "Would you believe that?"

"No. I do not think that I shall ever be free again."

Bathsheba looked at him in unfeigned surprise.

"Go and do your worst!" said Joseph with a fierce energy. "You and Baumeister between you can easily make up a story that will send me up the river."

"His mind is wandering," said Bathsheba in a low tone, as if communing with herself. "I tell you, man, that I am going to set you free," she said, looking at him as if she were wondering why the words did not throw him into transports of joy. Then a great tear rolled down one cheek, and was speedily followed by another. "In a week. You will see."

"When I see it then I will believe it," said Joseph. "You will have to produce the person who set the house on fire. Can you do that?"

"Perhaps."

"Then it is your duty. Why not go and do it, instead of coming here to look at me?"

A great sigh caused Bathsheba's bosom to heave convulsively. Her eyes overflowed with tears. "You are cruel, very cruel, Joseph," she said; "but I will do my best to save you, even though you turn away from me forever as you do now. I wanted to see you, to tell you that I am once more at work studying for the theatre"—

"The theatre!" cried Joseph. "My God! she talks of theatre, as if we had not enough of tragedy in real life!"

"— for the theatre," continued Bathsheba, not heeding his interruption. "And I wanted to tell you of Miryam — she will recover."

"I am glad," said Joseph. "Do as you please; think as you please; act for me or against me, but leave me now. Do you not see that I am dead and buried? Then why hang about my tomb?"

"I came," concluded Bathsheba, "to tell you those things, and to bring you this." She threw a little package inside the grating, saying in very good, clear English to the keeper seated near by, "You needn't jump; the bundle has already been looked at." Then she turned around and went with a slow and stately step down the corridor.

"Gad! she's a hummer!" said the keeper coarsely. "Sister?" he asked of Joseph.

The vexed and worried labor-leader did not answer. Presently he picked up the parcel and retired with it to his cell.

It contained a few books, among them a little yellow-covered volume of Mordecai Menzer's "Songs for the People," with the famous verses which had awakened the cloakmakers to action printed on the first page. There were some bunches of grapes, and a flower or two. And on the top of all these poor offerings lay a picture of Bathsheba as she must have looked when a school-girl in that far-off Russia which now seemed separated from Joseph by an eternity of sorrow and suffering.

Her picture! He tore it into shreds with such fierceness that his cell companion smiled.

But next day, when he was seated at his grating, gazing again into the glowing coals through the open door of the heater, he saw the face of the picture there, looking mournfully and reproachfully at him.

CHAPTER XXI

THE WONDER-RABBI

BATHSHEBA hastened back to her humble lodgings, where she was living surrounded by misery so much greater than her own that she seemed rich by comparison. A kind of rage against Joseph, against fate, against the whole world, took possession of her.

So, then, there were no illusions left! She was face to face with the barren fact that Joseph despised and disdained her.

There was something in this so intolerably humiliating to Bathsheba's pride that it cut her to the heart. The exquisite torture of Joseph's rebuff seemed also to bring her thoughts down once more to the gloomy level whither they had descended when she had first joined the "party of force." She longed to wreak upon the world, upon Society, the vengeance which her love forbade her to undertake against him.

As she wound in and out of the dirty and narrow streets of the East Side, she often raised her hands and shook them at the sky, as if she were menacing the unseen powers which would not allow her to shape her life in harmony with her own conceptions of happiness.

Spurned! Very well! she would study, toil night and day, become a great actress, gain fabulous sums of money, and spend them in fighting this grim, unyielding social order which was inflicting such wretchedness upon Joseph and tens of thousands of the hapless refugees. She felt that she could attain greatness.

In the intensity of her preoccupation she made more gestures — fiercer ones ; and, pausing at a corner, she tapped her brow dramatically, asking herself aloud in Russian, —

" Have I not the power here with which to win ? "

A fat policeman lounging near by observed Bathsheba curiously. He crossed the street toward her, saying, " Loony, I guess," and was about to speak to her, when a little man with red hair and beard, dressed in a singularly variegated collection of clothes, came up, and, greeting Bathsheba, led her away.

"I have been looking for you everywhere," said Ben Zion, with a certain reproach in his tone. " Ah ! I see that you are admiring my new clothes. I got 'em at a bargain — three dollars for the lot. That was a great find."

He raised his hands, and, laying the palms open on the air, shook them up and down as if weighing imaginary money which he fancied that he had saved by his bargain. " Now," he said, " you will not be ashamed to be seen in public with me. And do you know — I have got a clew."

" Have you ? " cried Bathsheba delightedly. " What is it ? "

" Hum ! that is a long story. You must come with me at half-past five to the house of the Wonder-Rabbi, and if there we don't stumble upon something to prove Joseph's innocence, then may I never peddle more !"

" The Wonder-Rabbi ? What is that ? Some cabalistic nonsense, I suppose," said Bathsheba disdainfully. " Never mind, I will go, whatever it is ; for at the mere thought of seeing Herr Joseph free my heart leaps up like — like " —

" Ah ! it isn't every woman I'd ask to go with me into the Wonder-Rabbi's house," said Ben Zion, glancing around, as if he feared being overheard. "Not Malcha now. She'd spoil everything. Not even you, unless you were cool — as you have been lately. Will you meet me, then, at the Wonder-Rabbi's door at half-past five ? If you will promise, I will give you the address."

"Very well ; I will come."

Ben Zion handed Bathsheba a greasy slip of paper, on which was written the number of a house in an adjacent street — a neighborhood filled with the very poorest people.

"Your rabbi must be a 'wonder' if he can get a living in that neighborhood," said Bathsheba.

"Pooh! wise men can live where the foolish starve," responded the pedler. "Now I will run home and see if the rats have carried off that Baumeister brat — but I know they haven't, for he kicks at them like a little thorough-bred, he does ! "

And he ran away before Bathsheba could ask him why he still kept the child which he had saved on the night of the great fire.

She reflected that she had not seen Baumeister since then, and she resolved to ask Ben Zion what had become of him.

Neither Mordecai nor any of the apostles who had been grouped under Baumeister's teaching had seen him. Had he given up his task as hopeless, and vanished ?

At the appointed time Bathsheba met Ben Zion at the door of an old-fashioned house in a little corner near Rivington Street. Two generations ago this had been a new and handsome mansion, set in a pretty garden, with a charming outlook over the East River.

Now it was walled in at front and back by acres of ugly scrambling tenement houses, into many of which the sunshine crept only for an hour daily.

Near the door stood little groups of refugees, conversing

in whispers, and glancing over their shoulders at the door in awestruck fashion.

"He is certainly a great man, is Reb Moiser," said an old woman in a quavering voice. "They say he talks directly with Jehovah. Every Friday night, just before the services in the synagogues, he has ceremonies; and while he is talking with Jehovah, he turns white, and he groans like a man in great pain. You will hear him to-night. And I know that he can cure the blind and make the lame walk!"

"I must try him, then," said a red-eyed cloakmaker, "for working in a dark corner is ruining my eyesight. I can scarcely see Mother Abramovitch's face there, six feet away!"

"He's the man for your money, Reb Moiser is," croaked the old woman.

"Bah!" said Bathsheba to Ben Zion, as they went up the steps, "I thought you were above things like this, Ben Zion."

"Wait until you have seen Reb Moiser, and you will sing another tune," croaked the little pedler in his quaint guttural, as he pushed boldly into the grimy passage-way, and beckoned Bathsheba to follow him.

They climbed a greasy flight of stairs, picking their way with difficulty among the infirm old women seated on every other step, waiting in the hope of seeing the Wonder-Rabbi, and securing his precious advice.

Ben Zion turned into a little room at the right, where sat a tall, gawky youth, accoutred, in spite of the fact that the thermometer registered seventy, in a heavy long cloak, a pair of top-boots, and a pointed fur cap, which gave him a fantastic appearance, as if he had walked out of some mediæval chronicle, and suddenly come to life.

This youth peered sharply at Ben Zion and his companion; then taking his pen in hand, as if preparing to make an entry in the great book which lay open before him, he cried, —

"Approach, Jew!"

"Well, well, here we are, as the bear said to the moujik when he bit his head off," responded Ben Zion querulously.

"Silence!" said the youth, looking askance at the pedler; "this is no place for laughter."

"Yes, we know it isn't a theatre; but you needn't be so crusty about it," piped up Ben Zion.

"Who are you, what is your name, your age, and how many children have you?" said the youth glibly, at the same time motioning Bathsheba to step forward

Bathsheba was amazed to hear the little pedler answer with equal glibness, —

"I am a clothing dealer, named Rosenstein, forty years old, a widower with four children, and this is my poor sister who lives with me."

This astonishing statement almost took Bathsheba's breath away, and she was about to denounce Ben Zion, when she suddenly perceived that he was playing a game for some purpose, as yet hidden, and she decided to hold her peace.

"Good!" said the youth, flourishing his pen as if he were imparting a benediction. "And how do you know, Jew, that Rabbi Moiser will consent to see you?"

"Oh, I am sure," said Ben Zion, instantly assuming a cringing attitude, "that he would not have the heart to refuse us. We are in great trouble, and no one but the rabbi can help us."

"You must pay fifteen cents each," said the youth, extending a bulbous paw.

The money was paid by Ben Zion, who grumbled that it was "very dear," and the youth arose and lumbered into an inner room. Returning after a little, he ushered the visitors before the far-famed and redoubtable Wonder-Rabbi.

That personage proved to be a corpulent and mild-looking man, with a yellowish complexion, a fat face, with a beak-like nose, and an iron-gray beard which rippled down upon his breast, where it was neatly parted.

He wore a black silk gown, and his head was crowned with a conical fur cap, around which a few languid flies were buzzing, as if they felt certain that coolness must linger in such Arctic headgear.

The room was darkened, and on a little desk two long tapers were burning. By this dim light Bathsheba could see that the rabbi's eyes twinkled merrily, and that he was no whit austere of mien.

As Ben Zion moved forward the Wonder-Rabbi opened his lips, and in a solemn voice said, —

"You are a clothing dealer, named Rosenstein, forty years old, a widower with four children, and this is your sister who lives with you."

"O Rabbi," said Ben Zion, seemingly overwhelmed with this evidence of supernatural divination, "great and learned man! we know that you hold converse with Jehovah, and we have come to you for help."

"You are well and hearty, both of you," remarked the Wonder-Rabbi, rising and advancing toward them with measured pace. "Why do you come to me? Do you know that I can read your souls if I will?"

"We know, great and learned man," answered Ben Zion, affecting to tremble, "that you who can talk with Heaven can read our hearts. We know that there are no secrets from you, and so we have brought our troubles to you. Is it your will to advise us before we tell our story?" he added, with a malicious wink, which made Bathsheba bite her lip to refrain from laughing in the rabbi's face.

266 JOSEPH ZALMONAH

"I could advise you, son, but it is better to hear first what you have to say, that I may see in what temper your soul is. And if you intend to consult me, my fee is fifty cents each."

Ben Zion began puffing and blowing and protesting that it was ruinous. But he finally produced two discolored half-dollars, which were laid upon the little desk. And now the Wonder-Rabbi's eyes twinkled again.

"Speak, Jew," he said with solemn unction, folding his fat hands across his breast.

"It is this way, great and learned man," said Ben Zion, still affecting utmost humility. "We are poor folk, as I told your learned and worthy self just now, and 'tis a chance with us, as the bee said in the frost-bitten garden, if we manage to pick up a living in this land of refuge. Now, it happened that the other day a tenement house not far from where we live was burned, and, while I was rummaging round at the back of the burning house, seeing if I could not save something or somebody, bang! I felt a burden come down on my shoulders, and when I pulled myself together and looked at it, it was a little baby, three-fourths bones, with precious small life in 'em — a kind of living skeleton, dressed in rags, learned rabbi."

Ben Zion paused, caught his breath, and glanced warily out of the corner of one eye at Bathsheba, to see that she maintained her *rôle* accurately. Then he continued, —

"'Surely,' I said to myself, 'this small creature must have been thrown from the house by some half-crazy mother, who, poor thing, is most likely burned to a cinder by this time, so I'll take charge of it for a moment, and give it food and drink, as the ravens fed Elijah, because there seemed to be no one else to do it.' Yes; and I got away from the house lest the walls might fall upon me; and I opened the little bundle of rags, and took the small bag of bones by the hand, and I grinned at it, and said 'Scholem alaichem!' and I thought the brat's lips answered back, 'Alaichem scholem!' Then I fetched the creature away, and near by on the ground I found a man in a fit."

"Silence, Jew!" said the Wonder-Rabbi, arising and lifting one hand with a gesture intended to be majestic. "I shall now give you a proof of my power, so that you may never venture to doubt it hereafter."

The wild looks of Ben Zion and Bathsheba betrayed their astonishment.

"The name of the man whom you found lying on the ground in a fit is Baumeister. He is a Socialist, or something like that. And the child which you had rescued was his child, which he had wished to destroy and forget!"

"Great Rabbi!" stammered Ben Zion, "I was convinced that everything past and present and future is known to you."

The Wonder-Rabbi drew himself up to his full height, and looked at his visitors with a triumphant smile.

"There are those," he said, "who have presumed to doubt my power. I think, in future, you will not be of the number. And to convince you thoroughly of my wisdom, I will tell you something which until this moment has remained a secret with me."

Then, in a sort of mystical chant, he added this singular phrase : —

"The mother, deserted by the father and husband, came far across seas with her child to find him. And when she had come near to him, and had made her presence known to him, she perished in the flames, but the child was spared to confound the father."

Ben Zion began dancing and capering about the room until the tapers on the small desk rattled. "Prove me this, learned Rabbi," he said, halting suddenly in his mad career, "and I will see that a purse of five hundred dollars is made up for you, and that your reputation as a learned man who talks with Heaven is sounded to the four quarters of the refuge colony."

Now the Wonder-Rabbi's eyes sparkled again, but this time it was with avarice.

"Your chief rabbi, and your leaders in the synagogues, speak ill of me," he said. "But there is not one among them who could tell you what I have told you — that Baumeister is the father of the foundling which you picked up."

Bathsheba looked around her uneasily. It seemed to her that the place was bewitched. The dim light, the pompous manner of the Wonder-Rabbi, the musty odors exhaled from the tapers and from the rabbi's fur cap, all impressed her unpleasantly. She felt like running away, and was turning to do so, when the grave voice of the rabbi was heard again: —

"And now tell me your trouble, my children, for you have not come to that yet. But before you proceed further in this business we shall demand a new fee of two dollars each."

Without a grumble this time Ben Zion counted out the money. "Our trouble!" he cried in cheerful tones; "you know well enough what it is! We want to know what Baumeister was doing so near the fire that night, and why his child was in danger there?"

Bathsheba's heart stood still for an instant. Did the Wonder-Rabbi know that she had been in the house, and that both she and Baumeister had been rescued thence by Joseph? What would he say of her?

If he knew this he made no allusion to it.

"And what is the reason that you are so curious about Baumeister?" he said.

"Because an innocent man," shouted Ben Zion, "is lying in prison, accused of burning a house and the people in it; and because, if you can prove that Baumeister did the job, our friend will be free, and you will have the five hundred dollars! Do you understand that, old man?" shouted the pedler, entirely forgetting his reverence and his manners in the joy at the thought that he might serve as the instrument of Joseph's release.

The Wonder-Rabbi did not lose control of himself. He kept his *rôle* to perfection. "You shall hear more, my children," he said, advancing toward them, and smiling serenely as Bathsheba held up her arm to ward him off, as if she suspected him of casting a spell upon her.

He resumed his mystical tone, as if listening to revelations which came to him from an unseen world; and in a species of rhythmical chant he uttered these words: —

"Esther was her name. She was the wife of his youth, and he basely deserted her. From Podolia she came hither to find him. Then the husband and father was wroth with the wife, and sought to destroy her with fire."

"How do you know all this?" cried Bathsheba, springing forward. "Did Baumeister fire Simon's house so that his wife and child might be burned alive in it? Speak, man! Don't you know that Justice demands it?"

The Wonder-Rabbi concealed his fat hands in the folds of his sleeves, and smiled pleasantly on the excited woman. "I can tell no more now," he said softly.

"But the innocent man in the 'Tombs'!" cried Bathsheba.

"And the five hundred dollars!" shouted Ben Zion.

"When I have them in hand, Jew," said the Wonder-Rabbi, "we can proceed further."

Ben Zion hung his head. He was convinced that he had promised too much. "I am a poor man, learned Rabbi," he said, " but if a quarter of that sum would do, I could raise it by to-morrow night."

"It will do to begin with," said the Wonder-Rabbi, bringing out his fat hands, and rubbing them briskly. " But the witnesses against Baumeister are few and feeble. If the mother was burned in the fire " —

"And how did you know the mother ? " asked Bathsheba.

The Wonder-Rabbi did not notice her question. He was studying Ben Zion very carefully. At last he said, —

" Do you know where this Baumeister can be found ? "

"I can produce him," said Ben Zion.

" Then see that he is at the meeting in the lower rooms of this house to-morrow, which will be Friday evening, and if he is guilty, he shall confess then and there ! "

"Alleluia ! " cried Ben Zion. " The work is done. Joseph is free. The Devil is beaten ! And now I must not lose a minute in finding out Baumeister, and telling such a tale that he will be sure to come here to defend himself. Then, crack ! the trap shuts and the fox is taken. And I will see to your money, worthy man."

"No more to-day," said the Wonder-Rabbi sleepily. " Be sure to have Baumeister here before eight o'clock, and to be here yourselves. The rest — trust to me ! "

He gave them a piercing glance, and then retired and sank back upon his chair and closed his eyes. Bathsheba could almost have sworn that she saw him vanish in a cloud among flashes of flame, like Don Juan in the opera.

She went out like one walking in a dream, and when they were safely in the street, she burst upon Ben Zion with an impetuous flood of questions.

"How could that old humbug know all about Baumeister ? "

"I will tell you," answered Ben Zion. " 'T was easy. This was the way. One day an old woman came to my cellar to borrow a few apples, and she saw the child. 'Miracles of Moses!' she says, 'but I saw that baby in a woman's arms at the house of the Wonder-Rabbi not two weeks ago,' she says. 'And what's the Wonder-Rabbi?' says I. 'Why, the old man who knows everything, and talks with Heaven!' says she. Then I began to see a light, and I says, 'Ben Zion, here's your clew!' And I followed it up, as you see."

"How?" stammered Bathsheba.

"Why, the woman with this child, which is the living image of Baumeister, might be Baumeister's wife. She is hustled over to America with a lot of refugees, and landed here in this devil's Babel. She wants to find her husband. So the first man she makes for is the Wonder-Rabbi, like the poor ignorant thing that she is! He takes her money for his worthless advice. But he takes her address too, and he follows up her movements with his spies — these old fakirs all have their confederates. You can be sure that he knew as soon as we did that Baumeister wished to get rid of her, and that he was only waiting the right time to spring the whole thing on him."

"O Ben Zion! if this could all be true!" sighed Bathsheba.

"Ah, woman, if you had been gifted with a head as long as mine, you would have found out these things for yourself already!"

Ben Zion was an active enemy. Before dawn of the next day a rumor was spread through the whole cloak-makers' district that the Wonder-Rabbi, the mystical man who talked with Heaven, had, in a trance, declared that Baumeister was the author of the crime for which Joseph was suffering in prison.

As it spread rapidly from garret to garret, it grew in

proportions, and by the time it reached the ears of Baumeister, who had been lying sick of hunger and fever in
the lodgings of one of his Socialist disciples, since the conflagration, it was a terrible tale.

"You must go to the Wonder-Rabbi's house and give
him the lie in his teeth, or you are a lost man," said his
friends to Baumeister. "The cloakmakers will mob you
unless you speak out!"

And so Baumeister arose from his couch of unfinished
cloaks and coats, and, looking like a ghost, went swagger-
ing about, saying that he would be at the Wonder-Rabbi's
house, and would confound the liar in his teeth, that very
evening.

His fierce looks, his trembling limbs, his wild language,
convinced most of those who saw him that he was guilty.
But his followers clung around him, and said that he would
drive the rabbi out of town.

David had been communicated with, and after having
prudently looked the Wonder-Rabbi over, had privately
said to that strange personage, —

"I have no doubt that you are an old fakir, but you may
have secured knowledge of some facts which will help us."
Then he showed him one hundred and fifty dollars. "It is
yours," he said, "if Baumeister confesses publicly to-night."

"Have no fear," said the Wonder-Rabbi.

At eight o'clock Friday evening the crowd was dense in
front of the Wonder-Rabbi's house, and a yell of angry
disapproval was heard as Baumeister, pale, disordered, and
with his eyes staring before him as if he saw ghosts, pushed
past the throng, and, escorted by seven or eight of his followers, entered the house.

The front rooms below were filled with women conversing together in awestruck whispers. Some of them had

brought ailing children, for whom they intended to bespeak
the Wonder-Rabbi's advice, when he had finished his talk
with Heaven. A tall boy dressed in a shiny black Russian coat was placing fish, bread, and black wine upon a
table on which four tapers were burning.

Presently came a second boy, wearing a long black coat
and a fur cap, and little curls in front of his ears. He
covered the bread and fish with a white napkin, and then,
sitting down, seemed absorbed in silent prayer.

The excitement was now intense. Women climbed on
the benches, ranged at the ends of the packed room, and
craned their necks to see better.

Suddenly two folding doors leading to what had been in
old times the back parlor of the mansion were thrown open,
and the Wonder-Rabbi appeared. He wore a white fleecy
robe, dotted with stars cut in tinsel. This robe hung
loosely above a long black surplice of rabbinical cut. On
his head was perched his conical fur cap, and his flowing
beard was neatly combed.

He covered his face with his hands, and began to walk
with solemn pace towards his seat at the table.

At that instant Baumeister, at the head of his troop in
the passage, caught sight of the white robe and the fur
cap.

"That's the old fakir, there, is it?" he cried. "That's
the charlatan who tries to take away my good name! Let
me get at him, and I'll teach him to keep from slander in
future! Yes, and then I'll hand him over to the police for
swindling the poor people!"

An ominous roar behind Baumeister indicated that he
had some backers who were courageous enough to help him.

"Bring the old fox out!" shouted Baumeister, "and
I'll teach him to talk of honest men!"

David, Bathsheba, and Ben Zion, huddled in a corner,
watched the scene with eager curiosity.

The Wonder-Rabbi removed his hands from his face.

"Is that Baumeister?" he said in a deep voice. "Let him come and stand here before me!"

The crowd parted to right and left, the women and children falling over each other, and Baumeister strode defiantly in, and went up to the Wonder-Rabbi with menacing air.

But the Wonder-Rabbi advanced upon him, and, pointing at him with his long right forefinger, he said, employing the familiar "thou" of the jargon, —

"Baumeister, thou hast no secrets from me! Esther was thy wife's name. She was the wife of thy youth, and thou didst basely desert her. From Podolia she came hither with her child to find thee. Then thou wert wroth with her, thy wife, and thou didst destroy her with fire!"

At the last words he raised his voice to a high, sharp pitch, which so affected the overwrought nerves of the women that they screamed and wailed.

Baumeister staggered back as if he had received an arrow in the breast. "This man is a demon!" he said hoarsely. "He knows all things. Esther was her name. From Podolia she came. And I did it. It is true. I did it. I destroyed her with fire. All the world must know it now."

He uttered a loud cry, reeled, and fell down in a fit.

David felt Bathsheba's head heavy upon his shoulder. She had fainted.

The Wonder-Rabbi covered his face with his hands again, and, guided by his sons, moved slowly to his chair, and took his seat at the mystic table.

CHAPTER XXII

THE SWEATERS' TRIUMPH

DAVID was anxious to get through with the "little tragedy," as he called it, and to fly to Joseph with the news which established his innocence. But a moment's reflection convinced him that not all the cheering tales in the world could extricate the young labor-leader from his cell that night, and that it would be best to devote himself to others for the moment.

An old woman sprang to the relief of Bathsheba, who had sunk into a death-like swoon; and seeing her cared for, David and Ben Zion tried to make their way through the densely packed throng, and to see that measures were taken for the arrest of Baumeister.

But this duty was taken out of their hands, for the cloakmakers had clamorously besought a policeman's services; and presently a blue-coated guardian, as round as a barrel, and almost as unwieldy, came into the house, and laid about him so vigorously with his elbows and fists, that he reached Baumeister, had him aroused out of his fit, set upon his feet, and arrested in very short order. Baumeister's partisans made a terrible clamor, and threatened to tear the officer limb from limb; but secretly they were much alarmed for their own safety, and eager to get away.

The Wonder-Rabbi sat very quietly at his table, still keeping his face covered. But from time to time he groaned and struggled, and uttered fragmentary exclamations supposed to be ancient Hebrew ; and the old crones said that he was beginning to talk with Heaven.

This did not hinder the policeman from interrupting him long enough to tell him that he would probably be wanted as a witness, and that he must not attempt to decamp under pain of being sent to the House of Detention.

There was small danger of the Wonder-Rabbi's flight. He saw, with his usual cunning, that his mysterious unveiling of the real criminal in the now celebrated arson case would be attributed by the poor uneducated folk to supernatural power, and not to the simple fact that the deserted Esther's first visit on her arrival in New York had been to his house, where she hoped that she might by some sorcery gain tidings of Baumeister.

The *séance* was broken up by the incursion of the policeman, the arrest of Baumeister and one or two of his followers, and the catechising of the Wonder-Rabbi. When Baumeister, who since his fit seemed to have fallen into a semi-conscious state, had been dragged away, the throng diminished ; and presently no one was left save a very old Jew in a shiny black hat of exceedingly ancient fashion, with corkscrew curls dangling in front of his ears. He sat swaying back and forth, and wagging his head in a sort of religious ecstasy, long after even the most superstitious of the old women had vanished, and the Wonder-Rabbi had retired to an upper room to receive the reward, which David paid him gladly.

" Ouf ! " said David as he left the house, accompanied by the now restored Bathsheba and Ben Zion. " I am glad to be out of that atmosphere. 'He who mixes with unclean things becomes unclean himself,' " he said, almost unconsciously quoting the rabbinical proverb. " That old fakir laid his plans very nicely," he added. " Of course it is clear that Baumeister's wife, the minute she reached here from Podalia, went in search of the Wonder-Rabbi; and he and his spies found the man, and sent the wife to him to claim her rights. Then came the arson, which gave the old pretender a chance to turn a penny."

"A penny!" said Ben Zion scornfully; "a hundred and fifty dollars, you mean. Why, it is a fortune to him! And that is the reason that I mean to watch his house to-night, to make sure that he doesn't give us the slip. He may be afraid that his practices will come to light and get him into trouble. And you, Bathsheba, what will you do?" said Ben Zion kindly, noticing her worried and perturbed look.

"She is going with me now, to take Malcha the good news," said David.

Bathsheba gave him a lightning look out of the corners of her eyes; but David either did not see it, or pretended that he did not.

"And then," he said, "she can go to the theatre, and stay with poor Miryam, who will also be glad to learn such good news. Dear little soul! I should believe that she is half in love with Joseph if I did not know that she is overcome by her reverence for him."

"Ah," remarked Ben Zion, assuming a discouraged air. "I must have the Baumeister brat provided for somewhere; for if it is left alone in my cellar so much, the rats will be carrying it off."

"We will take it to the colony with us," said David quietly: "if the mother was really burned in that house"—

"And if she wasn't she would not be much good," interrupted Ben Zion.

— "It is our duty to care for the little creature. And you, too, will come with us to the colony, won't you, Bathsheba?"

David had never addressed her so familiarly before.

Something in his voice touched an emotional chord. Her eyes filled with tears as she answered, —

"You are forgetting, in your desire to be kind to me, that I am studying very hard for the stage, and that my husband is soon coming home."

"True," said David dryly ; "I had quite forgotten that. And then you will want to stay here to see Baumeister's trial. But if I am not much mistaken he will never be tried. He is as crazy as a bear when the bees are stinging him."

When Ben Zion had left them they tramped rather wearily to Joseph's domicile. Bathsheba talked freely to David, expressing gratitude for his offer to include her in his colony project, and protesting that her duty lay in New York.

When she learned that David intended to take the liberated Joseph and Malcha with him, she gave him another piercing look, which he seemed to feel to the very marrow of his bones, but she remarked simply, —

"I should hate the country. It is the whirl and turmoil of the city which stimulates me to life."

"I suppose," said David with the most innocent manner, "that the 'party of force' will expire, now that Baumeister has been taken in such a sin ? "

A spasm of pain passed over Bathsheba's beautiful face, and a moment later it was followed by a darker shadow.

"Don't put me on the rack to-night, please," she said with such a piteous appeal in her voice that David reproached himself for a brutality of which he was not really guilty.

When they reached Joseph's house they found lights dancing about, and heard little Zipporah shouting for joy, and Malcha sobbing hysterically. Then they felt that the good news had reached there before them.

Some of the cloakmakers had run all the way, and were now sitting, breathless and dust-stained, on the steps, talking loudly and excitedly. Half a dozen of them were volunteering to go to the "Tombs," and demand their leader's release; but when David had told them that they would probably succeed only in getting locked-up themselves, they renounced their wild scheme, and sat picking their nails and looking black.

They felt an imperious need of vengeance upon somebody; a desire to cut, burn, destroy, for the sake of showing that they could and would resent the manner in which their leader had been treated.

Old Manasseh and his daughter Shiphrah were there, seated humbly in a corner, amusing the small Zipporah, while Malcha "had her cry out."

"There, there!" said the old man arising at last, and hobbling over to Malcha, "'tears solace the heart, but beware lest they leave wrinkles,' the wise man said. Come, dry these drops, girl, and be patient until the morning."

"And if they should find some new excuse for keeping him longer than to-morrow," said Malcha. "Oh, I could not bear it any longer!"

As she said these words she turned, and saw David and Bathsheba facing her.

It was instinct rather than knowledge which made the little wife shiver and draw back a trifle from the beautiful woman on whose brows so heavy a shadow now lay. Had she known of the adventure of Joseph and Bathsheba in the burning house, she could not have shown a more sudden repulsion.

Bathsheba felt it to the very core of her heart, and it seemed to her unjust. She flushed angrily, in spite of a violent effort at self-control, and the greeting between the two was not cordial. Malcha held out her hand, nevertheless, and Bathsheba took it, saying, —

"We hurried here, hoping to be first with the good news, but some one was before us."

"You mean about my husband?" said Malcha, smiling faintly through her tears; and Bathsheba was surprised to note that the last word gave her a sudden start, and made her heart beat more rapidly than usual.

"Yes; and I hope that your troubles are over now, and that he will be able to work for himself, after all the pains he has taken for others."

Both women were speaking the familiar jargon, with its thees and thous, and the passion which was rising within their hearts was veiled under the friendly forms of speech.

"If he gets out, I suppose he will continue his work," said Malcha valiantly; "it will take something more than prison to frighten him."

"Oh, you quite misunderstand me!" cried Bathsheba; and at this point David interrupted with a proverb: "Come, come, 'there is no occasion to light the lamp at noontide;' nor to borrow trouble to-night about Joseph's course to-morrow. The great thing is to be ready for the unexpected, and to get some sleep to-night, so that if Joseph needs us in the morning he can have our services."

Bathsheba presently excused herself, and went away; and after David had had a long talk with Manasseh and Shiphrah, urging then to join in the project of the colony, he also departed, leaving them to console and encourage Malcha.

On the way down the street he saw two cloakmakers gesticulating furiously, and heard one say to the other, —

"They say that Freier was at his office late to-night, and one of his old employes — one of the old men who had been half killed with overwork in a sweater's shop — went in and said, 'Joseph will be out to-morrow, eh, Freier?' and laughed. Then Freier ran after him, and threw his cigar at him, and kicked him, and called him all sorts of names, and said, 'Joseph will be a jail-bird for many a long day yet!' Now, if Baumeister is the criminal, what does that mean?"

What, indeed, did it mean? David walked home musing on what he had heard, and dark with foreboding of the morrow.

He thought he knew what it meant at noon next day. Baumeister, trembling and abject, and seeming under the influence of some strange preoccupation, repeated before a magistrate the confession which he had made to the Wonder-Rabbi, and was installed in prison, while Joseph's innocence was recognized.

Not one word did Baumeister say about meeting Joseph inside the burning house; not one word concerning Bathsheba's presence there. He said that his wife had come from Russia without his consent; that he could not care for her and attend to his "great work" at the same time; and that when she had hunted him down he had conceived the idea of getting her burned in Simon's house, and had started a fire in the shop on the ground-floor, where the explosives were kept, hoping that the conflagration might be ascribed to an accident there.

His repentance was too lachrymose to be sincere, and there was a black look on his face when he spoke of Joseph which showed deep hatred.

Shortly after he was locked up he fell into a deep stupor, which lasted for hours, and which his guardians at first attributed to some drug. When he was aroused out of it he talked glibly, but without coherence. "This is a lunatic they have given us to keep," said one of the two men who examined him.

It was said that Joseph was to be liberated in the afternoon of that day, and there was a great crowd waiting to receive him within the gloomy walls of the "Tombs." Malcha, Zipporah, David, and Ben Zion stood anxiously awaiting the appearance of their hero.

At last he came forth, hollow-eyed and tremulous; and his smile when Malcha laid her head for a moment on his breast was wan and feeble. But the joy of regained freedom was gradually beginning to appear in his eyes, when suddenly Malcha and Zipporah were hustled to one side, and Joseph found himself again arrested, this time at the suits of various manufacturers, for "extortion."

When this misfortune was explained to Malcha, she fainted, and lay like one dead in the prison, and finally had to be borne away, followed by the wailing Zipporah, and by a screaming and gesticulating mob of women, who flourished their lean arms, and threatened to tear down the "Tombs" unless Joseph were soon released.

Joseph stood dry-eyed and almost smiling under the stroke. He was beginning to understand the depths of the hatred which he had aroused, and to feel that there was much suffering before him.

Ashy pale at the lips, and with his clear, frank eyes dilated by the excitement, he was marched back to his cell to await events.

Before leaving him, David said cheeringly, "Pooh! this is nothing! The bail will be small, and I will have you out and on the way to my new colony in a day or two."

So he ran off to see about giving bail.

Great was his consternation when he discovered, after forty-eight hours of wearisome labor, that no sums which he or his friends could assemble together would procure Joseph's deliverance. The bail was not only placed outrageously high, but bondsman after bondsman whom he brought up was rejected, and emissaries from the prosecutors kept a close watch upon his movements, and seemed to possess means for outwitting him at every turn.

The poverty-stricken Union made desperate efforts to get the requisite sureties, and also sent emissaries to the lawyers to learn what was the basis for the charge of "extortion" brought against the long-suffering and unselfish Joseph.

When they at last discovered that the charge of "extortion" rested largely on the fact that Joseph, for his Union, had accepted the check of Freier and Monach for the one hundred dollars, a practice general among the German Unions, the idea being to make the "boss" sorry that, by a "lock-out," he has caused his employes a vast amount of misery, they laughed the stupid accusation to scorn. Joseph, they explained, had done what the Union instructed him to do. He had taken the check for one hundred dollars, and, in company with other members of the Union, had gone to a bank and cashed it, after which he had placed the money in the treasury of the Union, not even accepting a penny for himself.

"But," said the sapient lawyers, "was not the fatal check made out to his order?" It was. "Very well, then he must bide where he is, and stand trial for extortion;" nor could so dangerous a personage, who very likely had repeated the same manœuvre with a dozen or perhaps a hundred manufacturers, be allowed to go at large until after his trial, unless he could summon most formidable sureties.

The days flowed solemnly and slowly away, with that supreme disregard for our unhappiness which becomes so striking to those who feel the hand of misfortune. When we are happy, all nature seems to rejoice with us. When we are in trouble, she appears calmly indifferent.

Malcha, white and frightened, came and went in the gloomy prison, bringing Joseph news and decent food, and sometimes a little money which some admirer had left for him.

One day she brought forty dollars, wrapped in a handkerchief, and told him that it had been left for him by a beneficent society which had approved of his moderate course during the lock-out.

Joseph suddenly became thoughtful. Here was money which he could accept without dishonor. He called to David, who had come in with Malcha and Miryam, and was now standing a little apart from them, with the child-woman at his side.

"Take Malcha and Zipporah with you to the colony, David," he said. "I foresee that my stay here will be long; perhaps, who knows? I may be convicted."

"But you will appeal," said David, who had been studying American law forms with great care.

"Of course, of course," responded Joseph impatiently, gripping the bars with his long, slender fingers; "but it will all take time. And while I am packed away here, they would starve or go into the sweaters' hells to look for bread. For the sweaters will triumph now, ha! ha! Have they not laid me by the heels? Take Malcha and the child with you and go, David."

And so it was agreed. A few days later the initial trip to the colony was made, and David's theatre had to conduct itself as best it could for a week, while the clever manager installed the melancholy Malcha and her little one, with Miryam, in an old farmhouse on the "abandoned farms" which he had bought for a song, in the Connecticut hills.

Miryam was pale and weak when she first reached the colony, but in a few days her strength returned, although her color seemed to have fled forever.

From time to time she would suddenly raise her hand to her heart, as if she felt a sudden spasm of pain there.

But she appeared to have regained her spirits; and while she labored with Malcha at the making of cheap porte-monnaies, suspenders, combs, and other simple articles which the colonists were trying to produce in large quantities, she sang the quaint old religious songs from "Ezra" and "Judith and Hólofernus," and "Queen Alexandria," from "Esther," and from a dozen other historical dramas of David's repertory.

David plied back and forth between the colony and New York, and often brought news of Joseph, who, stern philosopher in his prison, was endeavoring to dissuade the cloakmakers from clubbing together their little earnings to defend him.

One sorrow lay heavily on David's heart. He could not prevail on old Manasseh and Shiphrah to accompany him to the colony. David's heart still yearned toward the once erring, but now repentant, Shiphrah; and he was determined to save her before she fell back into the hell of misery out of which she had been raised by Joseph's bravery.

The month of August had worn itself out with sullen heat, and September had brought a little comfort with a cool dash of rain, when David, who had hastened down from his colony to respond to some of the innumerable demands made upon him by the lawyers conducting Joseph's case, found an hour at his disposition before returning to the train.

"I will spend it," he said, "in trying once more to persuade Manasseh and his daughter to join us."

But when he reached the cellar where Manasseh and Shiphrah made their humble abode, he found that they had gone away. An ancient dame who sold stale fish hard by thought that Manasseh had taken a cellar down near the river. "Better inquire of the United Hebrew Charities.

And the girl — she had gone back to work at her trade, and no one had seen her for a week."

A thrill of horror passed through David's breast. Had Shiphrah been caught once more in the sweaters' web ?

Every day he heard tales of the audacity of these cunning sweaters — the vampires who sucked the blood of the poor exile. Although the cloakmakers threatened to mob them, they were starting up again in a hundred places on the East Side.

The manufacturers encouraged them, pointing to the plight of Joseph as an indication that they need have no more fear.

Freier pretended that he was giving strict adherence to the compact which he had made with Joseph. But he was aiding more men to build up sweating-shops, and inventing new infamies for the persecution and plunder of the poor laboring men and women.

He told the fresh contractors, who timidly said "that the had heard that pushing the laborer was dangerous," how the law could be violated with impunity by pretending to make concessions, whenever public opinion or sentiment was aroused, and inspection, even of the very partial and incomplete nature thus far essayed in New York, was imminent. "And then," he said, "you can do your work on the quiet. Who will think of looking for a contractor [i.e. a sweater] in some out-of-the-way street ? Besides, your workmen and workwomen can be brought directly from the steamers to the workshops, and allowed to go out only after dark. A little sweating in New York will take the country roughness out of them."

Thus spoke Freier, as vile a slave-driver as ever lived, practising his infamous calling in the very teeth of the opposition of organized labor, and trampling down even such steadfast leaders as Joseph.

David heard of all this, and his heart sank when he pictured Shiphrah as once more in the hands of the villains. He dreaded Malcha's displeasure each time that he failed to bring Shiphrah home.

Now, it happened that the poor girl had really gone back to the very sweater from whose clutches Joseph had rescued her. This miscreant had set up in a new quarter under another name, and surreptitiously worked for Freier, winding his tentacles about his old victims whenever he could.

One day the great Freier paid a sly visit to the shop, and there Shiphrah was pointed out to him as Joseph's friend.

The sweater laughed coarsely in the girl's face as he said this, and placed his big hand familiarly on her shoulder.

"Oh, this is the wench, is it?" said Freier, approaching, and puffing a cloud of smoke from his huge black cigar in her face. "I say, she ought to be in jail along with Joseph, and we'll have her there yet if she says much, hey?"

The maddened girl struck Freier in the face, and then burst into tears.

With an oath he raised his hand, and returned the blow, like the coward that he was, and Shiphrah fell, with the blood gushing from her nostrils.

"Ah, pick her up, some of you," said Freier, retiring down the stairs, followed by the contractor. And when he was in the street he said, —

"They ain't people, them creatures up there, you know. They're only cattle."

But he felt uneasy when he thought of what might happen if Joseph were to be acquitted.

CHAPTER XXIII

THE WHITE FAST

OLD Manasseh sat on a broken bench in the crowded synagogue, listening rapturously to the wild recitative of the chazan, which had been kept up for hours, without seeming to weary the robust voice of the intoner, or the patience of the pious listeners.

The long room, on the second floor of what had once been a tenement house in Ludlow Street, was packed with the faithful, who were celebrating the "White Fast," Yom Kippur, the Day of Atonement, which comes ten days after Rash Hashshanah, the New Year, and is a recognition of God's grace in forgiving the transgressions of weak human creatures.

On each of the five floors of this narrow, ill-contrived firetrap of a tenement, a synagogue for a congregation of poor cloakmakers had been installed. The worshippers in Manasseh's company could hear the tramping and shuffling of feet above them, and the shrill notes of the chazan's voice, rivalling those of their own ministrant.

In the whole building ten or twelve hundred of the refugees had been gathered since dawn. The September day was now drawing to a close, but none of the people showed any inclination to go away.

Now and then a child stole in with a whispered message to the father or grandfather — message which provoked a faint smile, because it was understood to be a command to come home to supper, and not to imperil health by too long a fast. But generally the response was a negative shake of the head and a mystical closing of the eyes, which signified a stronger inclination to commune with the sacred mysteries than to attack the supper of dried fish, pickles, and coarse bread.

Manasseh's soul swam in seas of delight. He was penetrated with a vague consciousness that on these new shores to which he had come there was absolute freedom of worship; and it seemed to him that every minutest ceremonial of this day of days had a sweeter savor for him than ever before.

He mused on the three books of Rabbi Jochanon — those supreme registers of human action, and wondered in which the names of his neighbors had been inscribed. Had the long period of penitential days between Rash Hashshanah and Yom Kippur been duly improved by him?

He reviewed each one of his actions slowly and minutely, and shook his head, as if he could not decide for himself. Then he murmured a response or two to the musical cries of the chazan, and finally his head fell forward on his breast.

The fatigue of the long day's fast had worn old Manasseh's strength quite out.

The room was filled with rude benches, on which the young and old men sat together, dressed in their best clothes, and wearing their hats. At the end next the street was an altar, before which burned the lamp the light of which is kept aglow night and day.

Here stood the chazan, looking Oriental in his skull-cap, and with the striped prayer-shawl thrown about his shoulders; and here were grouped a few of the elders — those who had earlier in the day given the strange and impressive blessing of the "Cohanim."

At the other end, in an enclosure provided with windows, sat the women and girls apart. Through the yellow curtains at the windows of this enclosure they could see without being seen.

This touch of Orientalism added to the picturesqueness of the gathering. The sound of the feminine voices coming from this secluded apartment in response to the chazan produces a singular impression on the spectator who sees it for the first time.

Manasseh was old, hungry, and scarcely knew from whence his next crust of bread was to come, but he was happy. In this blessed period, which combined the memorial of the deliverance of Israel from Egypt with the days of Judgment and Forgiveness, what need was there to worry about earthly concerns?

Yom Kippur, the sacred time when the question of sin is settled for the year between God and man — what should interfere with it? The Lord had written in the book, but it would remain unsigned until eleven days after Yom Kippur. This thought was pleasant to Manasseh, and consoled him for exile and suffering, and for the new disappearance of his daughter.

Shiphrah had not left him to the pitiful fate of the helpless aged deserted in a great city. Every week she sent him by mail a tiny sum of money; but she would not let him know where she was. He was thinking of her as his head drooped and his eyes closed, and he finally fell into a deep sleep.

As evening approached, the yellow wax candles which had been set up in memory of the dead gave forth a sickly glare. The heated atmosphere, thick with dust and reeking with effluvia, became almost intolerable. The women, as they sat on the rudely cushioned benches in their little compartment, fairly gasped for breath.

The cloakmakers and their half-grown boys were huddled together in a submissive attitude. The peace of faith was upon their faces. It had been a hard struggle for many of the fathers to procure, in their half-starved and moneyless condition, the "scapegoat chicken" which an old custom requires them to kill at Yom Kippur, in order that their sins may be sworn upon it. The sacrifice of the chicken is held to wash away the sins which one may have committed during the year.

It was a strange scene. The intensity of the worship was heightened now and then by the prostration of some suppliant on the bare boards of the dirty floor. One aged man knocked his forehead against the planking, beat his breast, and cried aloud for help from God.

He called out one by one the list of his sins, most of them peccadilloes; and although there was something highly ludicrous in the circumstantial character of his catalogue, no one ventured to smile. The most minute details of the gathering were sanctified by The Presence.

The synagogue at this moment was something more than a place of worship. The dear familiar ceremonies, clung to with all the more passionate intensity because the people had been persecuted for their sake, seemed sweeter and tenderer than ever before, because they took the minds and hearts of the refugees back to their old homes, and brought up remembrances of their childhood and youth to men who were bent and broken with protracted toil.

While the weird melodious chant of the chazan resounded through the rude chamber, men and women saw arising before their closed eyes the vision of the cool Russian uplands, with their wealth of wild-flowers in summer, and their covering of dry, feathery snow in winter.

They saw the mud-begrimed villages, with their wooden houses, in front of which were tiny gardens, or piles of wood for fuel, or great wells around which the youths and maidens gathered to gossip in the still, mystical evenings in autumn, when the last warm hazes lay along the level lands. They saw, too, the oppressor in his fur cap and jack-boots, and the scurvy knaves who drove them from their homes, and divided their little possessions among themselves.

But all these things were in a kind of golden mist, and caused a delicate feeling of love and longing for the old home to arise in the heart, and to bring with it tears of vain regrets for the vanished fields and the forever-deserted graves of beloved ancestors.

Many a man and boy among the worshippers dreaded the moment when it should be announced that the three stars had appeared in the evening sky, and when they would be compelled to go out into the cold world with its sombre realities, its dreary sojourn in the bleak lanes of a foreign city, its climb to the desolate beds in the back kitchens or the stifling workrooms of the tenements, and its terrible toil during all the daylight hours, and far into the night.

The door creaked, and a woman, coarsely dressed, with a veil such as married women of the Orthodox faith wear, partially concealing her face, stole in, and hastened to find a dark corner in the woman's compartment.

It was Bathsheba.

Fortunately there was a vacant seat, and so far in the shadow that, had any one known her, it would have been hard to recognize her, once she was ensconced in it.

She had been studying all day in her lonely little room, working hard upon the *rôle* which she had chosen for her *début* at a small theatre lately sprung up as a rival to David's prosperous institution.

Her husband had sent her money, and the news that he approved the resolution to study for the stage, and would soon be at home to help her. She recognized that she ought to be contented, and yet she was overmastered by an immense and constantly growing discontent.

In her soul a strange revolution had been in progress for some time. So long as Joseph had been free, and at his work, she had been willing to admit that he was right, and that Baumeister and she herself were wrong, and that the " party of force " was a ridiculous illusion and a dangerous snare.

But now that she saw Baumeister fallen by the way, and recognized that he had never been anything save a vulgar self-seeker; now that she saw Joseph in prison, insulted and derided by his enemies, and apparently deserted by that society, the interest of which he had so valiantly labored to protect against the party of revenge and disorder — a kind of savage protest against Society in general awoke within her, and blossomed into a flower which might prove a poisoned bloom.

Besieged by emotions which she could not define to herself, tortured by Joseph's indifference to her, vexed and worn down by fatiguing study and by hopes and fears for the future, Bathsheba felt the need of the old familiar forms, which might bring consolation to her spirit. And so, although she had long been inattentive to her spiritual duties, and had been sneered at by some of the Orthodox, who knew her as a reformed Jewess, she threw on her cloak and veil, and hastened to the Ludlow Street nest of synagogues, which happened to be nearest her abode.

For a few minutes she sat very still, feeling a little abashed, and wondering how much of her history one or two women who eyed her curiously must know. But presently she discovered that they did not recognize her as one whom they had ever seen before; and she listened to the musical wail of the chazan, and to the muffled responses of the men, with a sense of delight at which she was surprised. She fell to thinking of the luxurious home of her childhood, and a deep wrinkle appeared between her brows, and for a moment gave a sinister and forbidding character to her face. Then it disappeared, and her face resumed its usual serene and impassive beauty.

Presently there was a vacant place next the little line of windows through which the occupants of the woman's section could see what was going on among the men.

Bathsheba went over to it, and by kneeling on the low divan, and looking through a broken pane of glass, she had a very good view of the singular proceedings.

A tall, gaunt figure, arrayed in a kind of white robe, which gave it the look, in the dim light, of a colossal spectre, was moving forward timidly, as if a little doubtful of the reception in store for it. But the men and boys made way slowly for it, as if recognizing that it needed more room than they did, and that it was about to engage in some important ceremonial.

At last the figure had room enough in front of it. Stretching out long arms and making wild gestures indicative of despair, it began slowly to sink on bended knees, all the time muttering to itself something which sounded like a confession of sin.

One family group, seated close to this singular penitent, seemed to overhear what it said, and arising suddenly, with alarmed and indignant looks, left the synagogue without a word.

Now the figure clasped its hands, and, bending forward, knocked its head violently against the floor, still muttering, but in a lower tone than before. Evidently it had some grievous sin upon its conscience, for over and over it repeated this contrite ceremony, never once raising its eyes to look at one of its neighbors.

There was something indefinably terrible in this figure, robed in garments which looked like grave-clothes, and bowed down in the anguish of supplication on the evening of this "settling-day" with God.

Bathsheba could not take her eyes off the figure. It fascinated and frightened her. When one of the yellow tapers, burning in memory of the dead, cast a sickly glow upon the white robes, as the gaunt figure arose, she uttered a stifled cry, and buried her face in her hands, as she had done when, a timid girl, she had been alarmed by some sudden sound.

Boys and men now began leaving in large numbers. The arrival of this, and one or two other apparitions like it, was a sign that the worship of the day was nearly over; for the desperate sinners who came to stand face to face with God in the synagogue, and to pour out in his holy place the confession of their guilt, usually chose the closing hours of the service, that they might be the less disturbed.

As the congregation thinned out the tall white figure became more demonstrative. It smote its breast with terrific force; it tossed its arms on high, and cried aloud the names of persons whom it had wronged. Bathsheba thought that she recognized one or two names spoken; but perhaps that was a mistake. If the figure would but turn!

At that moment it did turn, as if in obedience to her wish, and to her astonishment she saw the well-known features of a notorious "sweater," one of the meanest of the contractors who had been guilty of robbing the helpless poor — a man whose name was execrated by every one who had ever worked for him.

How came he there? Was he, then, a member of the synagogue? And could he come there among the very people whom he despoiled, and publicly confess to God his sins against them, and get them all marked off for the past year, and a new set of "soul books" opened with no more difficulty than this ?

The thought seemed so absurd that it brought a contemptuous smile to Bathsheba's lips, and a wild resolve instantly into her breast.

The sweater at his prayers ! The sweater imploring pardon in his grave-clothes on the day of the White Fast! Surely it was a cruel mockery !

Scarcely knowing whither she was going, Bathsheba leaped from the divan, and ran out into the men's section. Such an unheard-of act, at so sacred a moment, instantly provoked a profound commotion. Men arose, pointing at her; boys laughed confusedly, and the chazan turned to see what was the matter.

The tall figure scrambled to its feet, and stood swaying clumsily, looking so unearthly that the men and boys shrank away from it.

Bathsheba pointed directly at the sweater, and cried in a high, piercing voice, which rang like the blare of a silver trumpet : —

"The oppressor of the poor and helpless in the congregation of the Lord ! The sweater in the synagogue, to insult us with the catalogue of his sins against us ! Out with him ! Let him be spat upon and trampled in the dust ! Away with him ! "

Her voice died away into a wail, which had an electrical effect on the cloakmakers present. They rushed forward; and, although not many of them recognized the sweater, who had his den in an obscure street, and masked his occupation under another business carried on in the same building, this startling feminine accusation was enough to make them raise their hands to strike him.

"It is such villains as this man — this robber of the poor who insults us in our sacred worship — such men as these who have put your leader in prison, and who are driving you to the slaughter again. Down with the sweater!"

Rushing forward, she shook her closed hand in the sweater's face. He shrank back in terror, and, finding himself surrounded by the bent, broken, and prematurely aged workmen, whom he might presume to be his natural enemies, he uttered a hoarse roar, like that of a mad bull shut into an enclosure.

Then all at once rallying his courage, he swept back the aggressors, and called on the chazan to protect him. His face became as pale as his prayer-clothes, and he fully believed that his last moment had come.

The chazan, who was an old man, could not see well, and came forward with his hands outstretched, as if imploring peace. The men made way for him; and, as he complained of the darkness, one of them took a newspaper from his pocket, twisted it into an improvised torch, set it on fire at a candle, and held it above his head.

The sweater cowered at the chazan's feet, begging him to save his life, and to re-establish order.

"A sweater! A sweater!" cried Bathsheba. "His presence defiles the congregation of the Lord! Drive him out!"

"Peace, peace! my children!" said the old chazan, curiously scanning the sweater's features by the light of the burning paper. "God is ready at all times to acknowledge true penitence; and of repentance there are seven degrees."

"True!" cried Bathsheba, advancing, and looking like an inspired prophetess; "but listen! This, too, is from the Talmud: 'God is merciful, and pardons the sins of man against himself; but he who has wronged his neighbor must gain that neighbor's forgiveness before he can claim the mercy of the Lord!'"

The chazan stood confused. This strange woman who

long under the feet of hundreds, leaping, crawling, fighting, on the way down from the synagogues in the upper stories, in each of which the alarm had been given by shouts of " Fire ! " echoed from mouth to mouth.

In the dark stairway, with their steep, narrow stairs, men and women and children were wedged so tightly that they could scarcely breathe. They fought with each other. The strong trampled down the weak; the brutal jumped upon the heads of their fellows, and tried to walk on them.

The sweater and the poor chazan were pushed down the stairs together, just after Bathsheba's escape, and many of the blows aimed at the sweater were received by the venerable ministrant, who was in a half-dead condition when finally dragged out. The sweater avenged himself as best he could by savagely trampling on the faces of one or two of the cloakmakers, as he with almost superhuman strength got free of the press, with no worse accident than a dislocated shoulder. The groaning and imploring, the yells and imprecations, the wailings and snarlings, were like those which arise from a battle-field. And still the terrible pushing of the dense black masses coming down from above crushed out the breath and life of those weaker ones who, like sheep in an overcrowded pen, had fallen beneath the impetuous rush of the stronger.

Among the feeble ones who had been thrown, and now lay two deep, on the last flight of stairs leading to the street, was old Manasseh.

Hastily awakened from his slumber by his neighbor on the bench, he had succeeded in getting through the door, but had speedily been thrown off his feet, and so trodden on, that his faint hold on life was almost loosened forever.

He was dimly conscious that a great disaster had occurred, but his senile imagination was excited by the belief that he had been selected for a species of martyrdom. When the

cruel feet crushed in his ribs and tortured his chest, a smile
of angelic sweetness lighted up his severe but patient face.
He could not move his body, but he turned his eyes heavenward, and then eastward to the land of his fathers and his
fathers' God.

He seemed to see his daughter Shiphrah, radiant as she
had been in her innocent youth, before she had lost hope
in the sweaters' hell, coming swiftly toward him on a
starlight Friday evening, to announce that everything was
ready for the wonted ceremonial. And who was that
behind her ? Was it the image of his dead wife ?

He tried to rise, but the effort seemed to take all his
life from him. The violent shock of bodies falling upon
him caused fires to dance in his eyes. Then they died out
with strange suddenness. A cool calm was stealing over
him.

Manasseh shaped his aged lips to say the sublime words
which he had often said over a dying friend : —

" SHEMA, YISRAEL, ADONAI, ELOHENU ADONAI ECHAD ! "

And with this declaration of belief in the divine unity
comforting his soul, the patriarch passed from the land of
exile, swiftly and undismayed, into the Great Unknown.

CHAPTER XXIV

JOSEPH COMES FORTH

JOSEPH read, in the newspaper brought to him in his prison, of this dreadful panic, which resulted in the loss of a dozen lives, and the maiming of two-score poor creatures.

But it was not until Ben Zion arrived, with the radiance of his enthusiasm seeming to communicate an unusually fiery glow to his shock of red hair, that he heard the story of Bathsheba and the sweater. The journals had not secured this, or they had not chosen to print it.

"And to think," cried Ben Zion, "that the beast got away after all, while so many worthy men were trampled to death in their prayer-shawls! Well, well, we shall meet again, as the bees said to the bear when he stole their honey; and it will go badly with the sweater on that occasion."

"Now, don't be vindictive," said Joseph to his henchman.

"Reb Joseph!" cried the little pedler, getting into a highly agitated state, "you are too calm and too forgiving. You must have more spirit of vengeance in you, if you want to be a popular leader! Do you ever see me, now, pardoning the beasts of sweaters? I'd prick 'em to death with their own needles if I had my way. But you, Joseph, you would forgive everybody — even Freier — or — or Baumeister."

"What news of Baumeister?" inquired Joseph quickly.

"He's going crazy at a fast pace, they say. When he comes out of one fit he chatters about his work until he has another one, like the monkey that ate the green pepper. Some think he's shamming, but I call him a sure enough crazy man. Who else would have opposed you and tried to get you killed, Joseph ? "

"Who, indeed ? " said Joseph with a weary smile. "But if I am ever free of this place, I will go to visit Baumeister, and do all that I can for him, and for the child which you have told me of."

Ben Zion made a gesture which indicated his extreme willingness to perform one office — that of hangman — for the now disconsolate leader of the "party of force;" but he took care to say no more of his uncharitable sentiments to his leader, whose forgiving nature was a source of perpetual perplexity to him.

On one point Joseph's patience did not seem exhaustless. When Ben Zion told him that Freier was moving heaven and earth to undo all that the Union had succeeded in doing to promote the independence of the poor working-men, the imprisoned leader's eyes flashed, and he rattled the iron bars of the "dangerous offences" section so that a keeper hurried up to see what had happened.

Another month went by with such slowness that it seemed a year to Joseph. He lived in a kind of waking dream, from which he was aroused now and then only to hear of the burial of old Manasseh, and the fact that Shiphrah in her den of slavery had not heard of her bereavement until a few hours before the funeral ; or to be told that Baumeister would never be brought to trial, having already shown such violent insanity that he could not be produced in public ; or to consult with the counsel which the Union had furnished him, with reference to the conduct of his own case.

He had lost all hope, and had but one wish, — to know the worst, so that he might steel his spirit to endure it. His heart bled for his wife and child; he felt no anger toward any one, not even toward the prejudiced people who represented him as an enemy to Society and a corrupt demagogue.

On the day before his trial began in the court of Oyer and Terminer, Bathsheba made an attempt to see him; but he refused to receive her, and sent back word that "she must have courage for herself; he had none left to offer her."

This was so bitter a speech for Joseph to make, that he himself regretted it after it was made, and would have recalled it had it been possible.

Finally came the trial; the shock of removal from the prison world, with its tomb-like stillness and the half lights, to the glare and bustle of day, with the eagerly curious, unsympathetic, sneering faces in the street; the curt insolence of keepers and deputies, and the fierce attacks of the prosecutors upon him.

One thing alone kept him up. It was the almost reverential demeanor of his poor cloakmakers, who daily sent a delegation to watch the trial, and to offer him their feeble aid. The sturdy sympathy of David and Ben Zion, who were with him whenever it was permissible, was also encouraging.

"It was wise not to let the women come to court, Joseph," said Ben Zion. "They would have been making a scene. But we stoics know how to shut our teeth hard, and bear whatever mischief the Devil sends us."

And Joseph himself was glad that Malcha was not there, when, at the close of the trial, in which it seemed to him that all his motives and aims were misrepresented, he found that he was sentenced to twenty-one months imprisonment in Sing-Sing, as a common malefactor.

A gray mist seemed to arise before his eyes. His life appeared a useless garment, which he might now lay aside. He had been crippled in the battle; and what could it matter now where he was laid away to die?

While he sat stunned, vaguely wondering what they would do next, his counsel placed his hand on his shoulder, and said, "Cheer up, friend Joseph! the fight is not at an end yet — by any means. We shall appeal the case; and meantime we shall apply for a certificate of reasonable doubt of your moral guilt, which I think the judge is disposed to give. If we get that, we will have you out of the 'Tombs' on bail in less than a week! Then it might be a long time before the decision in Supreme Court General Term."

It took Joseph some minutes to grasp this idea. When he had mastered it, a little color came into his thin cheeks.

"And I could be free to pursue my work for six months, or perhaps a year, before the appeal is decided!" he cried, rising up. "Why, I ask nothing better! It would be a chance to give Freier another lesson!" And he closed his hands tightly, and drew a long breath.

Freier had been in court twice, with his sneering face and insolent manners; and had even nodded familiarly to Joseph, and grinned an evil grin. Joseph's blood boiled as he thought of the man's contemptuous air, and the way in which he displayed his fat fingers loaded with heavy gold rings.

Bathsheba, too, had appeared at the trial once only. Joseph had seen her face for a moment, and she had grown very pale, and turned to avoid his gaze. Now that there was some small prospect of at least temporary freedom, he was surprised to find himself asking, "Shall I ever see her again?"

After a few days of dreary waiting the lawyer's predictions were verified. Appeal had been taken from the decision, and the "certificate of reasonable doubt" was granted. Bail was reduced to a figure which the Union could meet, and Ben Zion and half a dozen others at once set off to make the necessary arrangements.

Malcha had insisted on coming to see Joseph as soon as his conviction was announced; but he had compelled her to return to the colony and await his liberation on bail.

David comforted the little woman with assurances that the Court of Appeals would never confirm such an infamy as the sentence; and this sentiment was making its way in the Union. But wherever the cloakmakers were beginning to hold up their heads again, the malignant influence of Freier appeared, and the hand of Freier came out of the darkness and struck the poor slaves to earth.

Early one morning Ben Zion came bounding into the section of the prison where Joseph was confined, with so aggressive an air that the keeper was at first inclined to lock him up for a few minutes, to "take the cheek out of him." But when he heard that the little pedler brought news of bail, and immediate freedom for Joseph, he forgave him.

Joseph's hands trembled, and he could scarcely pack the few small articles strewn about his cell. Now that the doors were to open, an immense responsibility seemed to settle down upon his shoulders, and he gasped as if it were crushing him.

Getting into harness again was not easy.

Two hours later the formalities were all fulfilled; the bail which long ago had been scornfully refused, was now accepted, and Joseph was soon in the office of his counsel.

He reeled like a drunken man, clutched at the back of a chair, and asked piteously for a glass of water. He caught sight of his face in a little mirror, and felt shocked to see how pale and wretched he looked.

"Let me give you a bit of advice, Zalmonah," said his counsel; "I hear that some of your friends have started a little enterprise up in the country somewhere. If I were you, I should join them. To go back to agitation at once might have a bad effect on your case, you know."

"Have I been brought out of the 'Tombs,' to be led away and made useless?" said Joseph, who spoke very precise English when aroused. "If I have, I am ready to go back at once."

"Oh, do as you please, my boy!" said the famous lawyer, who had had a good many hundred dollars, raked and scraped together by the cloakmakers and the friends of Joseph, since the case began, and who felt that he must do something for his money. "But I think a little prudent abstention, you know"—

"Good-day," said Joseph, and tottered out, followed by Ben Zion, who was muttering that lawyers ought all to be hanged on one tree, after which men could settle their grievances at one-half less than they now pay.

Once across the Bowery, and in the familiar world of the East Side tenement region, Joseph found a perpetual ovation awaiting him. The women held up their babies that he might touch them; the old men in caps and caftans muttered blessings on him; the poor pale girls smiled their languid thanks for his martyrdom in their behalf.

And now came Malcha and Zipporah rushing to cast themselves into his arms; and David, smiling and sowing proverbs in all directions; and Mordecai Menzer, "the people's poet," with his little wife, holding out hands, and uttering flowery welcomes; and one or two repentant members of the old "party of force," who had been warned by Baumeister's sad fate, and had decided to return to their primitive allegiance while there was yet time.

Together they went, tumultuously happy, to the offices of

the Union, where such a throng was gathered that the police hung anxiously on its outskirts.

In the little room with the broken-backed chairs and the lame writing-table, where the officers of the Union held their meetings, Joseph stood up to make a speech, with Malcha looking on proudly, and David and Mordecai applauding every other sentence.

He concluded with this phrase, " I will take up the work again, if you will agree that you will remain in rebellion against the cruel taskmasters who make your lives 'bitter with bondage.' "

The good old words from Exodus seemed to put force into his breast.

" Yes, yes, Joseph ! go away now and rest, and when you come back we will smite the sweaters and drive them out of the trade."

" And if you require a leader while Joseph is gone, you have only to apply to me," said Ben Zion in a loud voice, and smiting himself on the breast with an air of importance.

Everybody laughed, at which the little pedler bristled up and looked fierce, which provoked still more laughter.

And presently Joseph and his friends went away to the loft in David's theatre, where they had a simple meal, and sat listening to the members of the chorus rehearsing; and Joseph, dazed by the fresh air and the excitement, fell asleep on a pile of costumes, and enjoyed the first really refreshing slumber that he had known for weeks.

When the young labor-leader awoke it was late in the afternoon. Near him, and waiting patiently for him to open his eyes, two cloakmakers — a wretched operator, already half paralyzed by his terrible slavery on the machine, and a gawky boy, arrayed in nothing but a flannel shirt and a pair of much-worn trousers — were sitting.

David came bustling in. "Now, say your say to Reb Joseph," he cried, "and be off! Has not he done enough for you yet?"

The man assumed a whining tone, and, ignoring David, he said, "Reb Joseph, we heard that you got out this morning, and we hurried to find you, and ask you to interfere and save us."

"What can I do?" said Joseph, sitting up and looking around rather sleepily. "Am I not a fallen leader?"

"Reb Joseph," said the man, "since you were put in — there — we have been working for a contractor who got garments from Freier and Monach. Things went on bad from the start, but we did get some wages every week, until last Saturday, when the scoundrel of a contractor up and bolted. And he has carried off the wages of all the people in the shop. Two hundred and seventy dollars, it was. My share was fourteen, and we can't get anything. Even the machines had been mortgaged by the contractor weeks ago. We can't touch them. Oh, but he was a cunning rascal! And we are starving!"

Here the boy in the flannel shirt began to blubber sympathetically.

"We went to Freier," said the man; "he laughed at us, and said he had paid the contractor, and had nothing to do with us. And he told us to get out. He shut the door in our faces himself."

"When?" said Joseph, arising suddenly, and making his old gesture of command.

"Yesterday, Reb Joseph."

"Don't Reb me. Do you take me for a patriarch? Get up and stop that boy's howling; give me the address of your shop, and go home. I will see Freier, and tell him he must find you work in the old place until the scoundrel of a sweater can be caught and punished. Go to the Union and tell the secretary to give you a dollar each. That will last you a few days, won't it? I have lived on a dollar and a half a week. You can."

The man and boy arose, gave him the contractor's address and went away comforted.

"What time does the train leave for the colony?" inquired Joseph.

"At seven o'clock. Lie down and rest, for you will need all your strength for the journey," answered David.

"I will return here in two hours."

Malcha came running to him, and threw her arms around him.

"No work to-day, Joseph, I beg of you!"

"I am going to have a little talk with Freier before I leave town," he said calmly.

Malcha began to cry. "What new trouble, Joseph, will you bring upon us? That man will provoke you if he can, and have you put in prison again."

"Nothing of the sort will happen, and Herr Freier will be as obedient as possible. Come, Ben Zion, I shall want you as a witness."

The little pedler trotted out after Joseph, who seemed to have all his old strength again.

"Let them go," said David to the lamenting Malcha. "Joseph is right. Freier will remember that he still has a dangerous antagonist in Joseph." And when she would have reasoned further he closed her mouth with a proverb.

Meantime Joseph and his little henchman strode away to the office of Freier and Monach, which they reached in fifteen minutes, not without gathering in their wake quite a company of cloakmakers out of work, who were eager to see what Joseph would do.

Freier was in his private office, surrounded by contractors who had come to solicit the privilege of receiving from him the cloth, already cut, which they were to make their "slaves" transform into garments.

The contractors saw Joseph first, and scattered like frightened sheep. Most of them knew him by sight; the rest from description : all feared him.

"What's the matter?" said Freier, in jargon, laughing at the sweaters. "Have you seen a factory inspector coming around the corner?"

At this moment the door of the office swung open, and Joseph entered, with Ben Zion at his heels.

"Oh, I understand!" snarled Freier, turning very pale, and stepping back behind a board table, on which lay a formidable pair of shears. "No wonder the poor fellows were frightened. Here, men!" he shouted, "you needn't run away. We have a distinguished visitor — Mr. Joseph Zalmonah, fresh from the 'Tombs,' and he has something to communicate."

"Quite right," said Joseph; "but you need not fortify yourself. I wouldn't touch you any more than I would touch a snake. I have come here to tell you what you must do before nightfall, unless you wish to have me summon my beggar's army, as you once called it, and pull this house down over your head."

"Ah! you hear him?" snarled Freier, retreating gradually; "he gets bailed out of prison, and he comes straight to me, and he threatens me. Take notice, all! I'll have him arrested on a new charge."

Joseph strode forward so quickly that he had turned the corner of the table, and placed his hand on Freier's shoulder, before any one could stop him. "Don't let me hear any more of that sort of talk!" he said in a low tone. "You know who is master just now. I have but a few words to say."

And briefly he recited to Freier the complaint of the starving cloakmakers whose "sweater" had run away.

"You must go to that shop, furnish those people with work, and pay them for it at the end of the week. They cannot perish of hunger because your man has proved a scoundrel and has run away with their wages."

"I have nothing to do with them!" screamed Freier. "Let them starve and rot! They are no good anyway. I can get a thousand better workers by whistling out of the door."

Joseph looked Freier steadily in the face. "I understood your little game from the first," he said, "but I am not sorry to have heard you confess it. You have worn out that lot of men and women with overwork, and you and your hound of a sweater have arranged a conspiracy between you to get rid of them. You are an inhuman wretch. I have been released just in time to check you in this new trick. And now choose! Will you give those starving people work, until your confederate the contractor can be found, or shall I tell my Union what I think is the proper punishment for a man who has broken every contract that he has made with us?"

Freier's whole frame quivered with excitement, but he managed to control himself. At last he shook himself free from Joseph's hand, and said sullenly, —

"Well, I will give the poor devils one more chance, because I do not want trouble with you just now. I will furnish them work and wages until another contractor will take the job. But let me tell you, Herr Joseph, that your new reign will be very brief. You fool! Do you think that you will be allowed to meddle much longer with an industry which amounts to twenty-five millions of dollars a year in my branch alone? Haven't you already had a taste of what you may expect if you keep on? I hear that you are out on appeal now. That's all right. But the appeal will be decided against you, and you'll go up the river all the same by and by. And while you are up there for twenty-one months we can do as we please, hey?"

"Perhaps," said Joseph haughtily; "but you can't do so now."

Freier fairly foamed at the lips. He seized the huge shears and dashed them with terrible violence to the floor. The contractors gathered around him, but dared not interfere.

"Now," said Ben Zion, "no more theatrical business, Freier, or you might get a taste of the 'Tombs' yourself, and you wouldn't like it. Good-by. You don't look pretty when you are angry. Come, Herr Joseph."

"Remember," said Joseph, shaking his hand warningly at Freier, "if your promise to care for those people is not redeemed by six o'clock, I will take the case into my hands."

Freier bellowed with rage, and turned and ran to the rear of the office, and threw himself into a chair.

When Joseph had got into the open air again, Freier's menacing prophecy seemed to follow and torment him. Was it true then? Was he irretrievably ruined, and would the enemy triumph? He went back to the little theatre-loft and sat in a corner, gloomy and unwilling to talk, until Malcha summoned him to start for the train.

Just then Ben Zion, who had been detailed to report on Freier's movements, came in. "You can go in peace, Herr Joseph," he said. "Freier is still afraid of you. He has done as he promised."

"Come, then," said Joseph, with a flash of his old bright spirit, "let's be off to the colony!"

CHAPTER XXV

PURIM IN THE COLONY

It was a still, dreamy afternoon at the end of February — one of those days when, since the singular moderation of our coast climate, violets are sometimes found timidly unveiling their exquisite beauty in sheltered glades among the New England hills.

Long ago the children thought themselves fortunate if they could find beneath the crust of snow in the late days of April the dainty pink flush of the hardy arbutus. But all that is changed — at least for a cycle of years ; and as Joseph sat amid the fragrant newly sawn planks in the old-fashioned saw-mill down by the serviceable stream which supplied the colony with water, he could almost persuade himself that spring had arrived.

"Sixteen months and a half," thought Joseph. "All that time have I been here. It seems to separate me from the old life as if it were a period of ten years. Sixteen months and a half ! Am I the same man ? "

After nearly eight months of anxious waiting Joseph had been delighted to learn from his counsel that the Supreme Court, General Term, had reversed the decision of the Oyer and Terminer, which had sentenced him to twenty-one months in state prison. In this the upper court had probably been influenced by the "certificate of reasonable doubt" granted by the judge in the lower one ;

and by the fact that Joseph, as the agent of his Union, in
compelling Freier and Monach to pay a sum as compensa-
tion for the loss of the workmen's time during the lock-out,
had but followed the general practice of the foreign Unions
in New York City.

Joseph's counsel encouraged him to believe that this was
an end to the whole matter; but the event proved that he
was too sanguine. The District Attorney announced his
intention of carrying the case to the Court of Appeals,
and refused to quash the indictment until that court of last
resort had decided whether or not Joseph were guilty of
the crime of extortion.

This course was unusual, and was at once cited as persecution. But the prosecuting officer disclaimed any feeling
in the matter, and considered himself insulted by the mere
supposition that he could wish anything else than a clearing up of the points of law.

Joseph was at first profoundly discouraged by this new
complication, which left the sword still hanging over his
head; and his discouragement was increased by the news
brought to him by Ben Zion that Freier was wild with
delight at the new turn matters had taken.

He proclaimed everywhere among the sweaters that
Joseph would certainly be sent back to prison by the Court
of Appeals; and Joseph suspected that an anonymous
letter which reached him at the colony, containing these
words, "You will see Sing-Sing yet, so don't get proud,"
was the work of Freier's pen.

But Malcha and David and Ben Zion and the majority
of the cloakmakers believed the enthusiastic declarations of
his counsel that Joseph's troubles were over, and that he
would soon be able to return to his work among them,
untrammelled, justified, and triumphant.

Joseph arose from his seat on a log, and went over to the

primitive sink where he and his workmen made their rude toilet after work. A piece of broken mirror was tacked to the pine planking, just level with Joseph's eyes. He looked into it and started back in mock dismay.

"I have grown younger," he said, "not older; and those ugly wrinkles have covered themselves up. What a grand thing it is to have enough to eat, appetite to eat it, and fresh air to breathe!"

His features expressed content. Yet he sighed. And at that moment, as by some magic, he seemed to see arising, in the little square of glass, the beautiful, but sad and yearning, face of Bathsheba.

A shadow fell across everything for a moment.

But it went as swiftly as it had come, and Joseph returned to his work, murmuring, —

"Heigh ho! I wonder if the poor thing is happy at last?"

The memory of Bathsheba brought in its train a host of other remembrances, and he passed them in review. Baumeister, long ago transferred from the "Tombs" to a lunatic asylum, from which he was likely never to emerge; Freier, with his evil smile and menacing gestures; Shiphrah, with her heart-broken air, her pallid face and trembling limbs — these had been a part of his life. Would they ever interest him again? Was it not selfish of him to breathe fresh air, and eat wholesome food, while his people still struggled in the noisome dens of the East Side?

He felt guilty because of his own physical well-being. He seemed to hear a voice saying, "Joseph, hast thou forgotten thy brethren?"

A little door at the back of the mill flew open, and Zipporah bounded in, her olive-colored cheeks tinged with a wholesome red, her eyes sparkling, and her small frame, grown chubby since she had come to the colony, all quivering with excitement.

"O Tate !"¹ she cried, taking off her hood, and swinging it by the strings, "have you chosen your present to David for Purim? Don't you know that you should give it to-day?"

Joseph took Zipporah on his knees, and stroked her rumpled hair. "True," he said, "we must give David something nice. Here's a little money; run down to the store and buy it, and mind that you don't tell him before-hand what it is to be."

Zipporah took the coin and bounded away on her mission, leaping over the planks like a young fawn.

Joseph's memory went back to his boyhood's days in the Russian village, when presents were sent from one house to another, and when each recipient immediately sent one in exchange, wrapped in a handkerchief, and accompanied with good wishes.

Purim! The feast of gladness. The day when old and young rejoiced together, and when families were reunited around the festal board.

"Ah! that accounts for the noise last night, I suppose," he said. "The young folks were jumping on Haman. I thought that was it."

Purim is preceded by the feast of Esther, the clever beauty whose witchery helped to save the Jews. On that day the sacred story is read aloud; and whenever among the Russian Jews the name of Haman is mentioned, it is the subject of universal execration, and the children and youth go through the motions of "jumping upon him," and trampling him to death.

In some of the densely settled sections of the East Side this ceremony is attended with so much noise that the police come running to see where the riot is. "What is the disturbance about?" they anxiously ask.

"Jumping on Haman," is the quiet reply, and the salta-

¹ Papa.

interrupted the service and quoted the Talmud astonished and shocked him.

A cry of approval of Bathsheba's last words went up from the cloakmakers. "Ay !" cried one, "ask the sweater if he has been forgiven by all the poor people that he has just accused himself of sinning against !"

The sweater tried to pull off his white robe, and to escape. And now the improvised torch, the newspaper, went out, leaving an odor of acrid smoke, of which a cloud arose and hovered over the assembly densely packed in the front part of the room.

A timid voice in the woman's section was heard saying, " Fire ! What's burning ? I am not going to stay here. I smell fire !"

In vain did Bathsheba, who paled with sudden intuition of the danger, spring backward and explain to the women that the odor came from a paper which had been trampled underfoot, and that there was no flame visible. The alarm was taken, and there was a mad rush for the narrow door, the unique means of exit.

Six brawny women rushed to the door, shrieking, "Fire !" and, forgetting that it opened inward, threw their united strength against it, and, splintering the panels and carrying one hinge away, crawled out, dazed and hysterical.

With the instinct of self-preservation urging her on, Bathsheba sprang after them, and, after getting an ugly gash in the wrist, she reached the outer landing. There she felt herself pounced upon and hurled along by a maddened throng escaping from the floor above ; and, bruised, with her clothing torn and ruined, and her senses reeling in dismay, she was pushed into the street, and dragged off by strong arms. And then she fainted.

In less than a minute the panic had become general. The worshippers escaping from the second floor fell head-

tory exercises are kept up with increased vigor until morning.

And here they were celebrating Purim in that far-off New England colony, thousands of miles of stormy water and of vast plains intervening between them and their old Russian home in the "Pale," where they were at liberty to do almost nothing without a "declaration." Here they were free to celebrate as they chose, and no one interfered with or spied upon them. Surely this was a great gain. Joseph felt a wave of thankfulness arising in his heart.

He had been absent when the feast occurred on the previous year. This year he would participate in it.

David's colonial experiment was prospering. With sixteen hundred dollars which he had saved out of a prosperous season at his theatre, he had purchased three abandoned farms on the edge of a Connecticut village, and had placed a dozen families, taken out of the clutches of the sweaters, upon them.

The farms had been bought from a railroad company, which had purchased them from their migrating owners for the timber which their forests contained. This had been stripped away; but the rocky acres and the numerous buildings, most of them in very good repair, were a godsend to the poor refugees when they arrived.

David gave them everything rent free for the first year; and, installing themselves in the old-fashioned farmhouses and even in the deserted barns, they began the manufacture of cheap wallets, of suspenders, of silk hats such as the Bowery beau delights in. They got sewing-machines from a neighboring town, and then began a "race with labor for independence," as David expressed it.

Accustomed to the long hours of the sweaters' dens, they could not bring themselves to reasonable periods of toil, and the Yankee farmers round about, who thoroughly respect a talent for hard work, began to take a liking to the temperate, inoffensive new-comers, who worked from sunrise until eleven P.M., and spent their holidays in song and in picturesque ceremonials.

In the keen air of the New England hills the men and women whose faces had become deathly white under the horrible slavery in the sweaters' dens were getting a healthy color. Old patriarchs who had been tottering on the verge of the grave suddenly seemed to receive a new lease of life.

The women, who now and then had a chance to observe the prim neatness of the Connecticut farmers' wives, began to leave their slattern ways behind them. And the children romped all over the fields in all seasons, and laughed and rejoiced from sunrise to sunset, as if they had never known the horrors of Ludlow or Essex Streets.

Here and there a family worked at the making of clothing, and turned an old farmhouse kitchen into a reproduction of the crowded shops of the East Side. But the windows were open; air and light were abundant, and wholesome, although coarse, food was plenty. "The workers in our shops sing at their toil," said David one day to Freier, whom he had chanced to meet on the Bowery, and who had asked him, with a thinly-veiled sneer, for news of "that enthusiast," Joseph. "Our people sing at their work, but yours never do."

Freier had scowled and passed on, and that day he had been more than usually brutal to contractors, sub-contractors, poor people imploring "jobs," and all who came within the scope of his tyranny.

Having got this little social experiment well under way, David had returned into his old life at the theatre, where he continued to prosper and to quote proverbs. But Miryam remained behind, and abode with Joseph and Malcha.

Miryam was a child no longer; but with a precocious womanliness had come to her a mysterious languor and a strange pallor, which disquieted all who loved her. Her grave, sweet face, with its introspective eyes, was never more beautiful than when she was watching Joseph at the work which he had chosen, and which the physician, who had warned him that his lungs were in danger, had advised him to adopt.

As Joseph was destined to be a leader wherever he might be, he very soon found himself surcharged with the cares of the little colony, so that his own work sometimes suffered. But he prospered none the less; and the two or three visits which he had made to New York had convinced him that the Union was holding out fairly well under the guidance of those whom he had appointed to replace him.

The sweaters had been held in check for nearly a year after the termination of the great lock-out. But now they were beginning to raise their heads again. Joseph heard this from many sources; and he said daily to Malcha, "I must have another brush with those fellows yet."

A curiously misspelled letter from Ben Zion now and then confirmed this conviction. In one instance the wages had been reduced without the shadow of an excuse; in another, the sweaters were beginning their old trick of making cuts in wages on trifling pretexts; in yet another, they were insisting on a return to the long hours, and were paying women only three dollars weekly for sixteen hours' work daily.

" It will get better again soon, Joseph," pleaded Malcha; " why waste your life in fighting those wretched sweaters ? " and Joseph would stop talking about the subject, only to begin again on the first favorable occasion.

On this day of Purim his thoughts roved far from the colony, as he sat alone among the logs and planks in the mill. He had worked but little there during the winter, although the river had not been frozen; and on this beautiful February day, so like spring, he had been giving the old saw a trial. Now he was resting and thinking.

The image of Baumeister arose before him. He remembered the day when, shortly after his installation at the colony, he had returned to New York to see Baumeister at the insane asylum to which he had been transferred under a judge's order.

This visit had been a great shock to Joseph. As he stood facing poor crazed Baumeister in the narrow and crowded ward of the asylum, he had felt as if he were standing on the perilous brink of some black and bottomless abyss.

Out of this dread depth came up questionings and menaces and all kinds of incoherent prophecies, but nothing which could serve in any way as a guide to poor toiling exiles and refugees.

Joseph dimly felt, although perhaps he could not have expressed it so, as if Baumeister, with his wild and reckless aspirations, his passionate hate of society and desire for vengeance upon it, and his utter lack of conscience, were the product of the dull centuries of Russian oppression and savage cruelty. The soul had been stunted, and was not competent thereafter to arise to the full measure of a large liberty.

Baumeister did not seem to think Joseph's visit at all extraordinary. He greeted the young labor-leader in the most natural manner, and began pouring forth a torrent of complaints about his sufferings while he was in prison.

"Everybody went to see you, Herr Joseph," he said, "and carried you good things to eat, but nobody came near me. And they kept me in a very damp place. All this because that old fool of a Wonder-Rabbi swore my liberty away."

Joseph gazed at him in astonishment. Had Baumeister

forgotten the events which led to his imprisonment; or was he feigning forgetfulness?

" Tell me, Baumeister," he said, "did you really set fire to Simon's house, knowing that your wife and child were there and might be burned to death? And have you forgotten that you were seen in the house by Bathsheba, by me, and that I saved you from getting roasted yourself? Come, now, there's a good fellow, try and remember!"

Baumeister did not answer for a minute or two. He began rocking to and fro, staring at the keeper, who was listening rather jealously to their conversation in the jargon, of which he understood not a word.

Suddenly he jumped up and down, and a wild, fierce light came into his eyes. Joseph recoiled a few steps, but Baumeister came up to him with quick, stealthy step, like an animal about to seize its prey, and shouted, —

"Esther was her name! She haunted me! She hindered my work! And she went up in smoke, she and the child!"

"No, Baumeister, no," said Joseph with an expression of intense pity in his eyes; "the child was saved, and shall be cared for as long as I live. Ben Zion has it in his keeping, and you know he is a good little man."

Baumeister looked earnestly at Joseph for a long time. Then he began to laugh; his eyes burned with a curious light, and his breathing grew hoarse. Finally he spread out his arms, and fell face forward in a fit.

"It's no good talking to him any more to-day," said the keeper, edging Joseph away, as if he meant to push him out of the ward. "When he gets over one of those fits he is as crazy as a loon; wants to have a crown, and thinks he is the Czar of Russia, and a hundred things wuss than that."

And so it proved. When Baumeister recovered consciousness, his first act was to recoil from Joseph with an expression of horror, and to say, " Don't let him touch me! He

has claws and horns !   Bring me my crown and sceptre, and
I will command him to retire."

Joseph went out heart-sick and dazed.   "The poor creature gets crazier every day," said the keeper.   "He will
never be brought to trial.   Sometimes he thinks he is leading a party of rioters, and he dances up and down the ward,
shouting blood and thunder, burn, sack, and destroy, until
you'd think the universe was coming to an end.   Now and
then he gets some of the violent cases in the ward to follow
him when he makes a rush ; and on my soul, when you'd see
them lunatics a-charging, with Baumeister shouting out the
few English words he knows to 'em, you'd think we had an
assemblage of mad tigers in there, 'deed you would ! "

"Has the poor man no visitors ? " said Joseph.

"Once in a while a lady comes to see him — a mighty
fine-looking creature she is — an actress maybe ; and she
jabbers away to him for an hour, with him cryin' as if his
heart would break, and she weepin' too.   It 's quite heart-
breakin'.   But she hasn't been here for a long time now.
Sometimes she sends the poor fellow some flowers, or a book
in them funny characters, all black and three-legged —
a jargon book, they call it, and it's all jargon to me."

Bathsheba still had a kindly thought for Baumeister.
This seemed to please Joseph, he could not explain why.
Even now, as he sat in the old saw-mill, months after his
last visit to the asylum, musing on it, this remembrance of
Bathsheba's good-heartedness comforted him.

He wondered what she had done with all her fierce
dreams of social revolt and revolution, and whether she
would ever be contented in her new career as an actress.
She had made her *début* a few months after Joseph's liberation, and had achieved only a modest success.   But she had
shown great aptitude for the stage, and this and her beauty
had enabled her to rise rapidly.   At present she was the

central figure in a large company which purveyed romantic dramas and religious operas, the subjects of which were invariably taken from Jewish history, to the quarter of a million Hebrews of all classes and grades of prosperity who inhabit the metropolis. She was already a celebrity, and was gaining ground daily.

Twice only had Joseph seen Bathsheba since he had sent her away, sorrowing and humiliated, from the prison. He had met her once at the house of Mordecai Menzer, the poet, where, in company with her husband, who was now a prosperous *impresario*, she had come to consult with the poet about the recitation of a popular poem to be recited between the acts of a drama.

She had greeted Joseph quietly, coldly, and had made no allusion to the past. He fancied that to her, as to himself, it seemed as if a gate were closed between that past and the present with its new duties and trials. But when she gazed at him for a moment, mournfully, with those lustrous eyes, searching the depths of his being, he felt as strongly, as irresistibly drawn to her as of old.

He took his hat, mumbled some excuse, and got away out of Mordecai's house as quickly as he could.

The second time was at David's theatre, when he was making a flying visit to New York. She had come in to ask David for the loan of some historical costumes for a benefit performance. While David jested with her about thus aiding his rivals, she had kept her eyes fixed on Joseph. That day he was troubled as never before, and when he spoke with her he acted like a man in a dream.

David noticed his abstraction, and when the beautiful Bathsheba had gone he said, as if communing with himself, —

"Commit a sin twice and it will not seem a crime."

The wisdom of the old proverb sank deeply into Joseph's heart.

All these things passed in review before him as he worked and rested alternately in the saw-mill, his heart heavy despite his many reasons for content, despite the fact that the feast of gladness was at hand.

Presently one of the elders of the colony, an orthodox Jew who had prospered wonderfully, and had housed his large family in one of the old farmhouses, came to invite Joseph and his wife and little Zipporah to attend with him and his family the simple festivities which they had arranged for the evening.

Joseph accepted gladly. "I was but trying the saw, Jacob," he said; "I hope you don't think I was working seriously on this good day. We will be with you at dusk."

Miryam was unusually still and thoughtful at the little home festival of Purim, celebrated by the pious father with his numerous family around him, and to which she, with David, Joseph and Malcha and Zipporah, had been invited.

Supper was spread on a long table in the old-fashioned room; the wax tapers burned cheerfully, and in their light the red wine in the quaint decanters glowed.

At the head of this table stood the father of the flock, his gray hair crowned with a black skull-cap. Near him sat the wife; on the right and on his left was a favorite daughter. Farther down on either side were ranged the other daughters, and the family of a married son, with a flock of children. The men wore their hats and the striped prayer-garments, and the women the veil which covers the forehead and the hair of the orthodox Jewess.

There was reading of the story of Esther, and of the wreck of Haman's plot because of her beauty and address; there was much drinking of cups of wine; and the head of the family then distributed little presents to each member of the household.

So simple and patriarchal was this scene that no one could have beheld it without pleasure. Even Joseph, fond of saying that formalism and tradition were eating the heart out of the race, felt a thrill of happiness at the sound of the old familiar songs of gladness and the time-worn passages reciting the discomfiture of the evil Haman.

After the supper the hymns were sung with enthusiasm until a late hour, and David had improvised a quaint little play not unlike an old mystery of the fifteenth century, in which all present took part.

Miryam personated an angel, and as she passed by Joseph, who had been detailed to represent an Assyrian soldier on guard, and raised her soulful eyes to meet his, Joseph thought that he had never seen a more spiritual and lovely face.

The play ended, the grandparents led out the little children in the dance, and the wheezy extemporized orchestra acquitted itself wonderfully of its difficult task.

The moon was shining brightly when the party dispersed; and in the confusion of leave-taking Joseph whispered to Malcha, "Do not sit up for me; I am going to walk a little in the moonshine," and got away, as he thought, quite unnoticed by any one else.

He walked swiftly from the farmhouse, down the hill toward the river and the saw-mill.

Why he directed his steps thither he could not have told. He went as if pushed by fate.

All was dark and silent in the old mill, and the pungent odors of the sawed planks made the head heavy. Joseph lighted a bit of a candle which stood on the edge of the sink, and sat down to read a letter which had been shoved into his hand by the ancient Father Israel, once joint lodger with Ben Zion in the cellar where Bathsheba had taken refuge on the night of the fire, but now removed to the colony and promoted to the high office of its postman.

Father Israel, in giving Joseph the letter, had confessed in trembling tones that he had got it from the post-office, five miles away, with numerous others, ten days ago. "But it slipped into a hole in the lining of my coat, Joseph," quoth the old man, "and I clean forgot it until now. I hope it is nothing that can't wait."

Joseph had not looked at it then. But as he brought it under the light now a wave of color swept into his face. and then receded instantly, leaving him ashy pale.

He tore open the missive, and his hands shook as he read. It was a curt note from his counsel, saying that his case had suddenly been pushed forward, and was to be heard in three days. As the Union had no money, he must hasten to make a provision, so that they could send a man to argue against the District Attorney, or bad consequences might follow. "Five hundred would do," said the counsel.

"Five hundred devils!" said Joseph. "And how quietly he writes this to me, when I have not five hundred cents! And the letter is ten days old. And as no one has been to town from the colony, and no other letter has come to warn me, and the argument has been made, I am lost, I suppose! But perhaps the decision is not given yet. Surely we should have heard" —

At that moment Joseph's quick ear detected the sound of a light footfall outside. "Who can that be?" he murmured; and, opening the door, he stepped out into the moonlight, and found himself face to face with Bathsheba.

CHAPTER XXVI

THE GREAT TEMPTATION

SHE was very pale; her hair was dishevelled, and she seemed to be suffering from extreme fatigue. She did not look up at him, but kept her gaze fixed on the ground, and seemed abashed. As Joseph approached her, he fancied that he could hear the loud beating of her heart.

A sudden pang seized his own heart, and he felt that she had come to warn him of impending misfortune. His breath came quickly; the blood was hot in his veins; his legs seemed heavy as lead. He stretched out one hand with a gesture which was almost imploring.

"Speak!" he said huskily.

Bathsheba struggled to obey, but no sound came from her lips. The moonlight, falling full upon her lovely face, gave her an expression so weird, so unearthly, that for an instant Joseph thought that she was dying. In spite of his determination not to do so, he darted forward, and caught her in his arms.

She swayed heavily forward, and for a moment or two she leaned her head against his breast. Her splendid hair was damp with the night dews; and when she looked up Joseph saw that there were tears upon her face. They stood apart again, Joseph almost humbly awaiting the message of fate which he felt sure that she had brought to him. Espying a huge log, which had been hauled up the

day before to be ready for the sawyer, she went to it and
sank wearily down upon it, saying in a hoarse whisper, —

" Water ! "

Joseph dashed into the mill, and soon returned with a
tin pail filled with clear cold water, of which Bathsheba
drank a little. Then she wet her handkerchief, and held
it to her forehead and eyes. At last she said faintly, —

" I was burning up. The fever seemed to tear me to
pieces. It is the impatience. I have hurried so. And all
for — what ? "

She let the tin pail fall at her feet, the water trickling
down her dress, and sat for a minute with her hands folded
in her lap, and her eyes gazing into vacancy, like one
demented.

" How did you come here ? " said Joseph gently. " How
did you find your way to the colony, and in the night ? "

" I walked," she answered, gradually recovering her voice.
" At the depot I tried to hire a team, but the farmers wouldn't
let me have one. I suppose they thought it was too much
trouble, and yet I told them that I was in mortal haste !
But they laughed at me ! So I walked."

" And why ? " timidly asked Joseph. " What has happened
that you could not wait and come by day ? And will you
not let me take you to Miryam, or to — Malcha ? You
must be worn out. Do you know that it is eleven long
miles from here to the depot ? "

" And if it were eleven hundred," said Bathsheba, with a
rising exaltation of manner which alarmed Joseph, " I
should not have felt them or noticed them. It seemed to
me that I was buoyed up by celestial wings ; I felt like
soaring away over the woods and streams into the delicious
moonlight. But I remembered my purpose, and I bent my
course here. It is nothing. When I was a little girl, I
walked across twenty miles of snow-covered steppe, just

to say that I dared. The winds howled, and so did the wolves. But I did it."

She arose and arranged her falling tresses, and drew her loose veil over her head. "Joseph," she said, "hear me to-night without anger. What I have to say will not take long. But is that your house there? If it is, come farther away."

"No; it is an old saw-mill. My home is nearly a quarter of a mile off. There is no one stirring in the colony but us, I should think, unless David should happen to be making one of his night rounds. When he can't sleep he walks in the fields, and composes plays as he goes along."

"Is David here?" queried Bathsheba breathlessly.

"He is, and has been for some days."

"Ah! I wondered how it was that he had not sent you word about the "—

She paused and turned away, as if to conceal the emotion which was betrayed in her voice.

"About the what, Bathsheba? Something has happened, and you are afraid to tell me! Speak! I can bear the worst! Is it about the appeal?"

Bathsheba nodded, and at the same moment a convulsive sob shook her whole frame. Suddenly she felt Joseph's hand upon her shoulder, and looked up, tearful, but with a smile of such divine tenderness, that it awed him. He felt like one to whom a great treasure is offered, and who knows that he has no right to accept it. The angry revolt in his soul shook his whole frame, but he stood his ground.

"Listen, Bathsheba," he said: "tell me all, and at once. I know, I feel, that the case in the Court of Appeals has gone against me. Is it not so?"

"O Joseph," said the woman, turning and looking up into his face, "it is true, and I hurried with all my might to be here among the first. Fate has been kinder to me than

I had dared to hope. It has let me be the one to break the news to you, and it has brought us together, face to face, here in the still night, where no one can disturb us. This is reward enough."

She uttered these words in a deep voice, tremulous with passion, and Joseph looked at her in astonishment.

"Joseph," she said, "the appeal is decided against you. The court of last resort has agreed with the sentence in Oyer and Terminer, and your original sentence is reaffirmed. You must go to Sing Sing for twenty-one months, unless the governor pardons you."

"Very well," said Joseph. "That does not frighten me. I will give myself up, and not have any nonsense about extradition from another State. I would not have my enemies think that I am afraid of them."

He drew himself up, and paced to and fro in the moon-light, Bathsheba watching him with gleaming eyes.

"The decision was in the afternoon papers," she said. "Oh, I have been watching! It appears that the argument was made six or seven days ago. Everybody wondered when they heard about the argument that you and your friends in the colony gave no sign of life. Freier spread a rumor that you had run away. Some of the poor folk in the sweaters' hells believed it. Ah, Joseph, they are help-less! My heart bleeds for them! But no one man can save them. You have done your share."

Joseph stopped short in his walk, and looked sharply at Bathsheba.

"When I am buried underground, or at the bottom of some river, I shall have done my share for them — not before," he said..

"All vain — all vain!" cried Bathsheba, coming rapidly to him, and gesticulating madly. "The sweaters are vic-torious. Fresh thousands of exiles come in every week;

and the people who are starving must work on any terms.
Law is dead, — at least, no one enforces it, — and the men
and women are turned into miserable slaves! The greedy
manufacturers make the strong among the exiles drive the
weak! The ignorant are ground down in this land of
liberty as they never were ground in the Pale! And what
is your reward for all your efforts to bring order out of this
hideous chaos, to let the light in upon this festering slave-
market, to expel the oppressors and to protect the helpless?
What does a free land — a liberty-loving nation — give
you for all this? A prison, and the name of a common
malefactor!"

She was speaking in Russian now, and with a nervous
eloquence which grappled upon Joseph's soul. But he felt
that it was his duty to throw off this influence, and he
said, almost sadly, —

"Woman, would you tempt me again from the path of
duty? Why, if a hundred thousand prisons lay in my
road, I would face them all rather than give up because I
have been worsted once by the manufactures."

"No — no, Joseph," cried Bathsheba in strange, muffled tones, as if her emotion were stifling her; "don't say
that!" And, before he could stop her, she had fallen on
her knees and clasped her arms about his limbs. "Don't
say that! Don't throw away life and all that makes it
worth living, for the mad war for the working-man! Hear
me, Joseph. I have thrown everything to the winds, and
cast my whole life on the hazard of to-night, and I must
speak! Hear me, and kill me afterwards if you will."

Joseph struggled to free himself, but Bathsheba only
clung the tighter; and kneeling there in the moonlight,
magnificent and enticing in her imperial beauty, she poured
forth her impassioned soul, while the young labor-leader
listened and trembled.

"Come away out of this horrible mesh of constant toil and suffering," she cried. "I cannot have your young life broken and degraded by the slavery of the prison. I cannot bear to think of the humiliation which they will heap upon you. O Joseph! Man against whom I once thought to plot and conspire, you conquered me by the magic of your earnestness, and now I am pleading to draw you away from it. But it is for your good. Listen! I have renounced all for you! I have thrown my theatre engagements to the winds; I have sent away the few things that I possess; I will never return into that hell of misfortune and poverty. And let me plead with you, Joseph, to come away with me. See! I have prepared all — money — Come! by to-morrow night we can be in Canada, and take ship to London, where they will not think of hunting for us. Come! I will be your slave, and toil for you; but I cannot see you taken and thrust into prison, and ruined for life. See, Joseph! I implore you! Do not spurn me."

Bathsheba threw her head back, exposing the exquisite beauty of her superb throat; and her hair, falling in picturesque disorder around her face, lent a new charm to her powerful and seductive beauty.

Joseph trembled so violently that he thought he would have fallen. The woman's clinging arms seemed to burn into his flesh; his brow was hot, and his eyes ached, while strange flashes of light came and went before them.

The odors of the calm, silent night arose around the striving pair, — the penetrating aroma of the sawn wood, the fresh smell of the bark on the old log, the cool fragrance from the hillside covered with new forest growth; and they seemed momentarily to steady Joseph's dancing senses.

Yet he felt himself yielding, and it seemed to him that one more move of Bathsheba's arms, one more of those fiery caresses into which she had put the ardor of a nature long repressed, would force him to stoop and take her in his arms, and to fold her there forevermore, and to rush away madly with her into the future, leaving behind the cruel present with its dolorous prospect of prison and persecution, and dull round of prosaic duties in the service of the ignorant and the wronged.

One kiss, one mutual caress, and all the world would melt away, and they would live for each other alone.

He heard the sigh of the night breeze in a thicket near by; he felt the rapturous tugging of Bathsheba's appealing arms; his head swam, and an ineffable delight stole through his being. A long sigh shook his whole frame, and he was extending his hands to invite Bathsheba to rise, and to be clasped upon his heart, when a light footstep sounded near, and a moment later a lithe little figure sprang into the moonlight close beside him.

It was Miryam.

Bathsheba loosened her imploring hold upon Joseph's knees, and, crawling away a few paces, leaned her head against the old log, and began to cry passionately.

Joseph stood looking over Miryam's head into the moonlit space beyond, not knowing, not caring, what she might do or say, but feeling profoundly thankful that she had arrived in time to save him from what might have been a fatal step.

He was at first surprised to see that the girl did not hasten to Bathsheba, and raise her up and question her as to why she had come. Then it became apparent to him that Miryam had perhaps heard all; that Bathsheba was blameworthy because she had tempted him to desert the path of duty and honor, and that he himself had wavered strangely. Had he not almost yielded?

Miryam placed her hand over her heart, and coughed

slightly once or twice. A spasm of pain wrote its lines
upon her lovely face. She stood looking first at Joseph,
then at Bathsheba, as if she hardly dared ask what so
strange an interview, in so singular a fashion, could mean
at such an hour.

At last she put out one little hand, and took Joseph's
right hand in hers. It seemed to him that there was comfort
and safety in this brave, virginal clasp of the girl who had
so long revered him, and who had now been made the un-
witting instrument of saving him.

"Miryam," he said softly, as if he were afraid of the
sound of his own voice, "Bathsheba has brought me bad
news, and she has been begging me to take a course
which " —

"Bathsheba's a bold, wicked woman," said the girl, " to
say what I heard her say just now ; and why and how she
should come here at such an hour I don't know."

She paused and looked confused, as if even the contemplation of Bathsheba's boldness were contaminating. "And
why, Reb Joseph, has she been talking to you of prisons and
such dreadful things ? I thought all that was gone by.
Speak! Why don't you answer me ? What has Bathsheba
told you ? "

"She has brought me the first news of the fact that the
Court of Appeals has decided against me, and that my old
sentence is still in effect. And she is trying to persuade
me that it is not my duty " (here Joseph spoke a little
bitterly) "to go to State prison for twenty-one months ! But
I must go, and I will."

"O Reb Joseph ! How terrible ! "

Joseph looked up quickly, for there was a peculiar sound
in Miryam's voice which alarmed him.

The girl was standing with both hands now pressed
tightly over her heart. Suddenly, uttering a faint cry, and

as if struck down by the dread news which she had just heard, she fell as if she had been shot.

With a moan on his lips Joseph sprang forward to raise her up. As he turned her face to the moonlight he broke into a sob. Little Miryam was dead.

She had died instantly of heart-pang.

Then arose before Joseph the vision of the fateful day when he was attacked by the ignorant members of the " party of force," to which Bathsheba had herself belonged, and he saw the valiant maiden throwing herself in front of him to shield him from the missiles, one of which had struck her full in the breast. It was that cruel missile which had been the begetter of the heart-pang which had now stretched Miryam dead at his feet — between him and the woman to whose seductive wiles he had. almost yielded.

Miryam had died for him — to save him from Bathsheba — to preserve him for his duty, and, if need be, his martyrdom.

A great rage arose in his heart against Bathsheba.

He laid Miryam gently down upon the ground, and going to the sobbing woman he took her roughly by the wrist.

" Rise up," he said, " and look upon your work ! "

Tremblingly Bathsheba obeyed. She gazed at Miryam without asking a question. And she went on sobbing as if her heart would break.

" Good God ! woman, don't you care ? Have you no remorse ? " he cried.

Bathsheba bowed her head.

" Now go, and never let me see you again. Go back to your work, and forget all the foolish things which you have said. I shall be in New York soon to give myself up. But let none of your sort of people come across my path."

The woman stretched out her hands with a gesture of appeal or of regret. Joseph was too deeply stirred to distinguish which it was.

"Go!" he said in a terrible voice.

Bathsheba went to the log where her veil was lying, took it up, put it on, and departed with slow and measured steps, like one carrying a heavy burden.

And now Joseph remembered that the woman had travelled eleven miles on foot that evening in pursuit of her reckless and criminal mission, and that she was probably fainting for food. What if she should fall and perish by the way? His heart was all at once filled with great compassion for her; he was sorry that he had spoken so harshly.

He strode after her, and touched her gently. She turned, trembling, as if expecting him to strike her down.

"I was a brute!" said Joseph. "I drove you away hungry and exhausted. Forgive me! Come to my house, and Malcha will give you food and a place to sleep."

"Your wife?" said Bathsheba with a strange look. "No, really, it would be asking too much. I have bread and meat in my pocket."

She held up a little package. "Don't worry about me." And she turned and began walking off again in the same slow, heavy way.

"But it is not wise that you should go, now Miryam is dead," said Joseph, wringing his hands; "and you must remain here to testify as to the manner of her death."

"Dead! Miryam!" and Bathsheba uttered a shriek which rang through the still, cool night and seemed to go mounting up into the stars. "Dead! The beautiful child!"

She rushed back to the place where the girl was lying, white and calm, and, kneeling near her, burst into low, passionate wailing.

A minute or two later David came up from the river-bank by a little path which led around the mill. He was musing as he pursued his midnight walk, and it was not until he was within a few yards of the group that he heard Bathsheba's lamentations and saw the little group.

He sprang forward and seized Bathsheba's head in his hands, bent it back, and gazed into her face.

"You here!" he said. "What do you want?"

Bathsheba pointed to the body of Miryam, which lay a little in the shadow. David uttered a scream like that of a parent who sees his child struck dead before his eyes.

Then he beat his breast, and Bathsheba's head, released from his grasp, fell forward as if she were dead like Miryam.

"She is gone — she is dead!" murmured Bathsheba. "I came here to bring Joseph the dreadful news that the appeal is rejected, and that he must go to prison. Miryam came and heard, and she fell down — straight down. O Reb David! Can it be possible that she is dead?"

"The cruel news killed her, my pure, my sweet, my darling one!" said David, communing with himself. He put out one hand and brushed Bathsheba aside; a moment later he seemed to have forgotten her existence.

Then he took Miryam in his arms, and, rising slowly and painfully from the kneeling posture into which he had thrown himself to examine her features, he moved away toward his house, repeating brokenly the words of the old saying of the wise rabbi, which he had been heard to quote many times : —

"Life is a passing shadow. The shadow of a tower or a tree ; the shadow which prevails for a time? No ; even as the shadow of a bird in its flight, it passeth from our sight, and neither bird nor shadow remains."

"Come!" said Joseph to Bathsheba. "Here is tragedy

enough for one night. Are you going back to the depot,
or shall I find you a place to rest ? "

He spoke like one heavy with sleep, or dazed with
excitement.

Bathsheba sprang up with nervous energy.

" I am going," she said. " Perhaps you will think of
me when you are growing gray and old before your time
in that hell of a prison. Perhaps you will see my face in
your dreams. I feel almost certain that you will."

She paused, and looked intently at him. Joseph seemed
to feel the solid ground giving way beneath his feet.

" O God ! " he cried, suddenly raising his arms and turning his face upward, " judge Thou between this woman
and me. Set my feet in the right track, and hold them
there, or I am lost ! "

Bathsheba gazed still more sharply at him. At last she
burst into a shrill laugh ; then she snapped her fingers in
the air, and whirling around went off at a swift pace.

But when she was well out of sight of Joseph and the
mill she fell down in a swoon, from which she did not
awaken for a long time. After her senses came back she
sat by the roadside, ill and confused, until sunrise.

A passing farmer gave her a ride in his ox-cart, and she
reached the depot in time to climb into a slow train for
New York.

It was evening when she once more saw the lights of the
great city. As she set foot on its pavement she remembered that, in her mad departure, she had given up all her
engagements, and had written a letter to her husband, who
was in a neighboring city, to say that he need never expect to see her more.

Nevertheless she dragged her weary limbs back to her
old lodgings. To her surprise her husband was there, with
a smile on his lips.

"Been having the tantrums, I hear!" he said. "That's what comes of studying too hard for your stage business. Oh, come in and rest, and you'll be all right again. What have you done with your trunks?"

She did not dare to tell him that she had sent them to a city near by, there to await her orders after her flight.

"I suppose you had no real intention of running away," said the dark-faced fiddler, lighting a cigarette. "Just a tantrum, so old Frume, your dresser at the theatre, said. Running away wouldn't do with me, you know. I'd run after you and bring you back. You're too valuable to lose."

Bathsheba sat down. She shivered and closed her eyes.

"By the way, there's bad news about an acquaintance of ours — that Joseph — the labor-man, you know," continued her husband. "The cloakmakers are full of the news to-night. It seems that he's got to go up the river, after all. He'll be badly broken up, won't he? Mordecai will have to make up a new ballad about him, he, he, he! The sweaters are still ahead, aren't they, now?"

"He wasn't practical," said Bathsheba. "Such men always come to grief. Don't talk to me any more just now, there's a good fellow. I'm going to lie down. I feel chilly."

CHAPTER XXVII

CARRYING THE CROSS

It was morning, and the sun shone in a sky of crystal blue. Here and there fleecy clouds sailed swiftly forward, evanescent and exquisite as mist-wreaths around a mountain peak. The moist woodland exhaled fragrant odors; and in the edges of the thickets the squirrels frolicked with apprehensive air, as if certain that this mid-winter mildness would soon be followed by snow and cutting blasts.

Joseph came out upon a headland, and paused to enjoy the majestic spectacle of the blue and smooth waters of Long Island Sound spread far below. Never before had this serene and beautiful countryside, with its picturesque coast, with innumerous miniature bluffs, with caverns, with promontories, with islets in the softly moving water, seemed so beautiful as now.

A tiny sail was fluttering around a distant point, and the fleck of white awoke a sudden longing in Joseph's heart. O to tear himself now and forever from the dull and pestilential orbit of the existence in which his lot had been cast! .O to seek some unknown and slumberous land where life was poetry and the struggle for bread never intruded itself upon human attention!

The intensity of his longing at that moment, with the sordid and wretched mockery of his bounded life stinging

him, and the gray walls of the prison rising, a dismal
vision, in front of him, was so great that his eyeballs
were strained until his vision became indistinct, and his
finger-nails were imbedded in the flesh of his palms.

And with this longing came the vision of a lovely, even
a sensuous face, filled with the mysterious and indefinable
languor of the Russian type — touched with a tender
grace of Orientalism borrowed from Semitic origin. It
hovered before him in the luminous air; its bewitching
gaze seemed to lure him on to fields which he had not yet
trod.

Was it Bathsheba's face — etherealized, transfigured?
He dared not answer this question. When he closed his
eyes the vision came nearer, was more provoking, sweeter,
maddening.

Thus were the saints of old tortured by the visions born
of those longings which they were victoriously treading
underfoot.

Joseph was on his way to the office of his counsel in
New York, to deliver himself up. After the wild emotions
through which he had passed in the last two days, it
seemed to him that he was all at once many years older.
The colony life lay behind him in a kind of haze, as if it
were an experience of long ago.

He had agreed with David that nothing was to be said to
Malcha and the others of Bathsheba's mad visit and mad-
der proposal; but he had told David all, not even concealing any smallest detail which tended to inculpate himself.

The testimony of the two men as to Miryam's sudden
death from heart-pang, "while she was talking to Joseph,"
was unquestioningly accepted by the members of the little
colony, every person in which revered them both. All
night the Jewish wail of mourning was heard in the farmhouses, for Miryam had been dear to all.

Joseph thought it best to keep his bad news from all but Malcha, during the day following Bathsheba's visit and Miryam's death, and to go away quietly in the night. The colony would know soon enough, and at present he did not feel that he could support the anguish of a general leave-taking. David knew, and Malcha knew, and they could mourn in silence with him.

But in little Malcha's resolution Joseph found exceeding comfort. " We will work night and day to secure a pardon from the governor," she said; "and we shall have a home here when we need it. So why worry about us? "

" A pardon — for a man who has committed no crime!" said Joseph disdainfully; and his whole soul rebelled against this idea.

But David and Malcha persuaded him. And he did not suspect, as he kissed the sleeping Zipporah and parted with Malcha, to start upon his journey, that ere he was out of sight she would fall down in a swoon, from which David with all his arts could with difficulty arouse her.

When she recovered she was brave, and all day she went about superintending the preparations for Miryam's funeral, and carrying her sad secret locked within her breast. " Joseph had been called to the city on business about the Union." That was all that she could be induced to say, and fortunately no news came from the great city. What would have been her anguish had she known with what phantoms her heroic husband was struggling on the way, and how, at times, he seemed tempted out of the path of duty and honor!

Joseph left the headland, and walked briskly along the highway, which here and there ran beside the water. Once or twice the thought came to him: A plunge into the blue waters would end all your cares. Why prolong life in which there is so little to get and so much to suffer — in which the vain, the mediocre, and the mean prosper and grow fat, and the unselfish are plucked and tortured ? One cool plunge !

But presently he brushed away these suggestions as unmanly ; and, as he hastened on toward the depot, the visions left him. His spirit became calmer.

A farmer who knew him by sight met him on the road. "Fine day, Mist' Zalmonah. Goin' to taown ? " said the rustic cheerily, and nodding a hearty salute.

Joseph looked at the man in astonishment. Had he not heard ? did he not know ? And then there drifted in upon him the feeling that he was but a speck, a mote in the universe ; and that his small sorrows, his ridiculous anguish and sense of injustice, were of trifling consequence in the world. There was a kind of rude comfort in this feeling.

He answered the farmer with a hearty, " Yes ; a little visit to New York," and went on, and on, and on toward his prison.

When he reached the depot he learned that the train was an hour late. He sent off a despatch to his counsel, saying, " I will be in your office before dark : make such arrangements as you think proper." Spelling the words correctly in English occupied some little time : he took out his pocket dictionary and consulted it.

He was surprised at his own calmness. It seemed to him that he was really at last enjoying the work of giving himself up.

By and by the train from New York came, fuming and snorting and bell-ringing, up to the wooden platform. Joseph stood listlessly studying the faces of the passengers.

But suddenly he gave a shout, and hastened forward to meet a little man dressed in clothes much too large for him, and carrying a bundle done up in a mysterious cloth wrap-

per, which appeared as if it might once have been the flag
of a merchant vessel.

"Ben Zion!" cried Joseph, and he fairly hugged the
small pedler in the exuberance of his gladness at having
one sympathetic soul to make the return journey with him.

The pedler looked up at Joseph, and two big tears rolled
down his cheeks. But they curiously belied the angry
expression which made his red hair more bristly than usual,
and his mouth disclose a range of teeth which seemed anxious to snap at somebody.

"Reb Joseph! alive and well, and by the bones of Abraham! in spite of all these dreadful things, still the strongest
of all us poor leaders! Well, well, this is a meeting, as the
wolves said when they met the emperor; and at such a
time!" And he laid down the bundle and shook Joseph's
two hands until they ached.

Although Joseph was little in the humor for laughter, he
could not help smiling at the quaint figure of the pedler,
and at the almost reverential way in which Ben Zion scrutinized his face.

"And where were you going, Ben Zion?" he said.

"Where else, Reb Joseph, but to your colony, to get
every member of it except yourself to sign my petition."
And he pointed down to the bundle, adding quickly, with a
tremor in his voice, —

"I suppose you have heard the bad news. They said
among the sweaters that you had run away, but they
couldn't make us leaders believe that."

Ben Zion still cherished the belief that he was an effect·
ive labor-leader, and that without his valuable services the
work of Joseph could not have been brought to fruition.

"I have heard that I have to go back to prison, if that is
what you mean. But I wonder that some one from the
Union had not come sooner to let me know. The lawyer's

letter was not given to me until it was too late to do anything."

"Ah! now that explains things," said Ben Zion, his brow clearing up. "The lawyer said he heard that you had gone away somewhere, and then the little dark-faced fiddler — he was spreading stories last night, so I was told" —

"Stories! What stories?" said Joseph with a sudden harshness in his voice.

"Well, it seems that Bathsheba has been having fits, and that all of a sudden she stopped acting at the theatre, and sold a lot of her costumes. Then one day, when she thought her husband would be gone for some days, she packed everything off, and left him a letter telling him not to count on her any more, and that she was going away off where he would never hear of her. But it seems that the fiddler was jealous of her, and that he had been watching her for some days, as the bear watched the bees, getting little but stings for his pains. He had her followed, and the spy comes back and says that she bought a ticket for this station. 'Why, that's the station for Joseph's colony,' says the fiddler, and he goes and spreads it around that Bathsheba has perhaps gone away with you, and that neither of you will ever be heard of again" —

"The liar!"

"Agreed!" said Ben Zion. "But just wait until I put my paws on him, as the bear said of the fish that was making faces at him in the water. And nobody knows where that crazy Bathsheba is now. Heigh ho! She's travelling fast on the road that Baumeister's at the end of."

Joseph shuddered. But what did it matter to him? Would he not in a few hours be shut out from the world? What did anything matter now?

"And now, Reb Joseph, are you really going back? No — there! I thought never to ask you such a question. You'll have a few bad days among those cut-throats. But the governor can't refuse our petition. What do you think of this ? "

And plunging down into his bundle he drew forth a vast roll of paper, scribbled all over with Russian and Hebrew characters, interspersed here and there with English and German. " Won't that make his Excellency's eyes dance ? "

" They will not pardon me," said Joseph a little bitterly. " Freier and all the others will go up there to the governor's mansion with tears in their eyes, and tell him that the holy cause of capital is in danger from such rascals as I am ; and they will make me take my medicine, as they say in the ‹ Tombs.’ Let us say no more about it just now, for they say the train is coming."

On the way back to New York, Ben Zion unfolded the plan of Joseph's friends, and showed him that a formidable effort, in which the American press and public of the great city had interested itself, was on foot to obtain his pardon. " Your name is in every paper, Joseph : you are a great man," said the little pedler with unction.

They had taken an earlier train than that by which Bathsheba had travelled on the preceding day, and they arrived in New York toward four in the afternoon.

" Leave me now, Ben Zion ! " said Joseph, surprised that no officers were on hand at the station to seize him ; "and bring the people of the Union to meet me at the lawyer's office in an hour and a half."

Ben Zion looked wonderingly at him. " Don't be afraid," Joseph said. " Have I not told you that I will be there ? By the way, could you find that poor Shiphrah, and bring her to me there ? I have a message from Malcha to deliver to her, and they may be sending me up the river at any time."

" Shiphrah ! " stammered Ben Zion. " I found out where

she is, but they have been having typhus-fever down there
lately. They say the dead are piled up very thick in the
sweaters' tenements. I wouldn't like to go in there just
now, Reb Joseph, unless " —

"Never mind, Ben Zion." And a picture arose in
Joseph's memory of the horrible scenes which he had seen
among the wretched operatives in a "typhus ward." Misery! misery! Ever the same refrain. Typhus — the hunger fever, born of the crushing work, the insufficient
nourishment, — sometimes the total lack of it for days, — the
foul air and the promiscuity of the tenements turned into
forcing-houses. The Sweaters' Hell! Would it never be
swept out of existence? Was there any excuse for its tol-
eration in this new land of plenty, where fortunes were
made in a single year, and where labor could think and say
whatever it pleased? Was there not a Sweaters' Hell in
more than one of the great American cities? What had
these poor exiles done that they should be compelled to
starve and freeze in winter, and starve and roast in summer,
and to become the prey of typhus when their puny frames
were exhausted? Who could save them? Would their
cry for help be heard, or must they go down in the great
waters of misery, spurned and buffeted, as relentless Nature
has spurned and buffeted the weak since Time began?

"No, Ben Zion, never mind seeing Shiphrah to-night.
We can send a letter to her perhaps. Meet me in an hour
and a half with the others. Be punctual."

The pedler trotted off with his petition bundle under
his arm, and Joseph began to walk leisurely down town.
There was a bitter pleasure in this last walk before the
brand of the convicted criminal would be finally placed
upon him. Each commonplace sight and sound had a new
and unusual charm for him.

He went along Park Avenue, gazing at the spacious man-

sions with their huge entrances; at the elegant streets
crossing the avenue, each with its rows of palatial houses.
He peeped into a trim *coupé* in which two beautiful girls
were chatting and laughing, and he nodded pleasantly to a
man carrying a heavy bundle who jostled him and said,
" Excuse me."

Presently he came to the brow of the hill; and there he
met a procession of small Italian children, under the guidance of a sweet-faced woman, who had apparently been
taking them for an airing on some "saint's day."

The little girls, with their neatly braided hair, and the
boys, with their dreamy, poetic faces; the musical prattle of
pupils and teachers, and the air of contentment and security
which pervaded the whole procession, seemed to touch
some fountain of regret and longing in Joseph's heroic
bosom.

He thought of his own child, from whom he must now
be separated so cruelly for so long a time, and his eyes
grew dim.   A terrible tearing pain seized his heart; it was
as if some dread power were wrenching it from his breast.

He turned to look at the children again and again — at
their happy faces and their pretty dress.   And he murmured, "Our people will be like that some day — when I
have suffered enough for them."

He took up his cross and went on.

When Joseph reached the vicinity of his counsel's office,
which was in a shabby building near the "Tombs," he saw a
great crowd surging back and forth in obedience to the imperative waving of policemen's clubs.

He knew at once that his telegram must have scattered
the news of his arrival through the cloakmakers' quarter,
since Ben Zion had told him that some one went to the
lawyer's office daily from the Union; and his heart beat

tumultuously at the pleasant assurance that he was not entirely forgotten.

A few steps farther, and he felt a friendly grasp upon his arm. A well-remembered voice greeted him; an old woman seized his hand and kissed it. His cheeks were aflame now; he held his head up, and his spirits revived when he heard voices crying all around him in the rugged jargon, "Keep up, Joseph! Keep up! We will pull you through, and you will beat the sweaters yet."

And so perhaps he might! Who knew what strange happiness Fate might not have in store for him?

"*He* run away!" said another voice. "Never! The very idea was foolish. Of course it was one of Freier's lies. He will be out and tree old Freier, as the moujik treed the bear, before Passover comes. What was that lie about the actress? Of course it was all Freier's work! We'll pull that old devil to pieces yet! They say the governor has Joseph's pardon all made out, but that the sweaters are using plenty of influence against it. What luck that where they're going after death it'll be hot enough to make them sweat a little!" And then came a confused and growing roar, which finally broke into something very like a cheer, as Joseph entered the lawyer's office.

He found his counsel in great good-humor, and ready to wager large sums that Joseph "would be free in two or three days." But the young labor-leader's slight experience of prison routine made him less sanguine. He listened gravely to the recital of the efforts in progress on his behalf; and when he found that his fight had raised up for him friends in many an unexpected quarter, he felt profoundly calm.

And now came Ben Zion and the officers of the Union, puffing and blowing with haste and excitement, and there were hundreds of messages and dozens of handshakings; and just as a lynx-eyed man strolled in and remarked politely, "Mr. Zalmonah, I understand you've come to surrender," and Joseph had answered, "Certainly; I don't wish to put the State to any trouble," Ben Zion whispered, —

"I couldn't find any one who had seen Shiphrah lately. But who should I meet but the little dark-faced fiddler, as I was hurrying off to the Union; and after he had abused you, and said he hoped they'd set you to breaking stone up the river, he let me know that he was going to meet Shiphrah this very afternoon, as she had been doing some work for Bathsheba, and he had to fetch it. So I asked him to tell her to come and see me in the market to-morrow, and he grinned and said he would. Bah! he made me feel crawly, but I think he'll give the message, because it will offer him a chance to abuse you to Shiphrah. Yet he used to say that you were a hero!"

"This way, Mr. Zalmonah," said the lynx-eyed man ; and Joseph now had a confused notion that he was elbowed through the crowd, then hurried sharply to the right, into the "Tombs" prison, along a dark and narrow passage — and at last he realized that he had once more left the world behind him.

An hour later he was in the closely guarded, triply locked and barred section where the men under sentence were crowded together.

A keeper sat in a high seat close by a railing which would have resisted the shock of a thousand men. Two rows of cells, one above another on either side, were open, and the men who at night were locked in them were now walking up and down. Joseph thought of the wolf which he had once kept in a cage in Russia, as he saw them pacing fiercely, and muttering to themselves. A nameless terror awoke in him as he scanned the faces of these men.

He leaned against the perpendicular bars of the railing, and ventured to ask the keeper who they were.

"Good many on 'em's waitin' execution," said the keeper carelessly. "Some's on stays; some's to be moved up river soon. Got your stay yet?" he added not unkindly.

"N-no — I don't think so — in fact, I don't know what it is," answered Joseph, who was trembling violently now, and was compelled to cling to the railing for support. Murderers! He was surrounded by murderers! And these were his companions now — and perhaps for a long time to come. Surely Freier had triumphed, and the Sweaters' Hell would never be swept out of existence!

There was one young man with dark, handsome features and fine, bold carriage, walking to and fro, smoking a cigarette, and now and then stamping with one foot, as if in vexation. An unearthly and lurid gleam in his eyes made Joseph almost afraid of him.

The keeper noted his impression. "He's to be turned off April 8," he said. "He won't get no more stays, and he knows it. But they go on hopin' just the same," he concluded, taking a sharp look at Joseph, who was frightfully pale.

Joseph turned, walked to his cell, and fell down on his cot in a deep swoon.

In a day or two Shiphrah came to see Joseph; and when she presented herself at the railing he was shocked, so fearful had been the ravages of racking toil and foul air upon her slender frame. She moved and talked like an old woman; and her eyes had an apprehensive look, as if she feared the taskmaster behind her.

"Surely, my poor Shiphrah, I brought you out of the hands of the sweater for nothing. Why did you fall back into them so readily again?"

"I was starving," said the girl gloomily. "Father had nothing — and long before he died I had to go back. I knew this man. I get enough to eat. If it wasn't for typhus all round us I should be pretty comfortable."

Seventeen hours a day, and three dollars a week, refuse to eat, and a pile of unfinished garments to sleep on! Yet poor Shiphrah saw such terrible misery near her that by comparison she considered herself "pretty comfortable."

Shiphrah brought him the news that Bathsheba was still acting, and with success. Evidently she had repented of her wild intentions. Joseph was glad of this, although he had vowed that the woman should never have his thoughts more. "She is good to me," said Shiphrah. "I love her. I do some work for her, little by little, when I can steal time from the boss. She gives me theatre tickets. I have been twice: it is all the fun I have."

Then Joseph begged Shiphrah to accept Malcha's invitation to go and live in the colony, and he spoke of David. A thin red streak showed in one of Shiphrah's cheeks, but she resolutely declined. "I am no fit company for your people up there, especially for David," she said. "Let me work here till I die with a rush some day. That is all I ask."

Shiphrah's despairing declaration might be echoed by thousands upon thousands of poor victims in the Sweaters' Hell.

The days began to go swiftly. Joseph learned that New York was more and more deeply moved by his fate. Flowers, money, books, baskets of food, came to him. Newspapers talked of him daily. Politicians called on him. Malcha and David and Ben Zion came and went, bright-eyed and hopeful. The mysterious "stay" had been granted. The cry for Joseph's pardon, as for one sinned against, but not sinning, grew louder every day. Joseph found that he slept dreamlessly each night. His courage revived. One day when he was standing at the railing he startled the keeper by shaking the bars violently.

"I guess they'll come down for you pretty soon for good," said the rough fellow, smiling.

"I begin to think so too," remarked Joseph.

CHAPTER XXVIII

THE PASSOVER SUPPER

MALCHA carefully arranged the three cakes of the "unleavened bread" according to the formula, and smiled as she stooped to caress Zipporah, and to ask her if she remembered what she had to say this first night of the Passover.

"Yes, little mother," said the girl, clapping her hands joyfully. "See if I don't know it right! When the cup is filled with wine the second time, and the Seder dish is taken up from the table, then I say, 'Why is this night different from all other nights? Any other night we may eat leavened or unleavened bread, but on this night only unleavened bread. Any other night we may eat any species of herbs, but this night only bitter herbs. Any other night we do not dip even once, but on this night twice. On all the other nights we eat and drink, either sitting or leaning, but on this night we all lean.' . . . See, little mother, I have said it so often that I can't make a mistake! And then this is what all you grown-up folks must say; and I'm sure you'll forget some of it: 'Because we were slaves unto Pharaoh in Egypt, and the Eternal, our God! brought us forth from thence, with a mighty hand and an outstretched arm. And if the Most Holy, blessed be He! had not brought forth our ancestors from Egypt, we and our children and our children's children had still continued in bondage to the Pharaohs of Egypt. Therefore, although we were all wise, all of us having knowledge in the law, it nevertheless is incumbent upon us to discourse on the departure from Egypt; and all those who largely discourse of the departure from Egypt are to be praised.' "

"Of course they are," said a mellow, cheerful voice, which sent the warm blood rushing into Malcha's cheeks; "but do you know that sometimes I think we are not out of Egypt yet ? "

It was Joseph who came in, and placed his thin hand in parental benediction upon the small Zipporah's head — Joseph, freed from his captivity by the generous pardon of the Governor of the State, who had refused to see in the young labor-leader's act the crime which his enemies had attributed to him; Joseph, restored to his work, and revived and strengthened by the sympathy and helpfulness of hundreds of all classes and religions in the great city.

He had grown paler, and he stooped a little, as if his burden had been heavy to bear. But there was a radiance on the forehead, a sparkle in the eyes, and a firmness at the lips which indicated that he possessed all his old belief in his mission, and all his resolution in pursuing it.

"What, Joseph! " said Malcha reproachfully, "do you make light of the holy forms of our ancient religion ? "

He took his wife's head in his hands, looked at her smilingly a moment, then kissed her on her brow. "Didn't I tell you before we were married that I was a Reformed Jew ? " he said, with a twinkle in his eyes. "If you want to see Seder carried to extremes, just go into the flat on the other side of the passage. They are all Orthodox there, and they will go through the entire ceremony, if it takes them until sunrise. But come! you know that I love the old ways, and I will sit and listen. It will take my mind off from the horrible things I saw this afternoon."

"What were they, papa?" said Zipporah.

"There were so many of them that I cannot tell them all," said Joseph, sitting down and taking the child upon his knee. "But I will tell you what I saw in a miserable room on the third floor of a tenement house in Chrystie Street. Three pretty little children in rags, and gathered around a tin plate with a few boiled beans on it. That was the breakfast, dinner, and supper of those three starving, helpless ones. In a dark closet, without air, the mother lay dying of a slow fever; and the father is dying in a hospital, where our Union managed to get him sent. If it didn't make your heart bleed to look at the poor children, with the smallest one stretching out its lean hands and crying 'Oo! Oo!' because it didn't get enough to eat, you only had to look at the mother, without proper clothes to cover her, and not a cent in the world! And why? Because day by day, month by month, year by year, for seven long years, a sweater held in slavery the poor husband, — who was an operator and could work the machine well in the sweater's hell, — and paid him the wages of starvation for the work which three men ought hardly to have done! Why? Because the sweater coined the poor wretch's blood, drop by drop, and when he had it all in good red — yes, blood-red — gold safe in his own pocket, he kicked the useless operator into the street to die! He cheated him of his wages, he lied to him, he struck him! Oh! I say we are not out of Egypt yet!"

Zipporah's face was upturned, and she listened with lips quivering and eyes flashing. The women came out of the kitchen and crowded together at the door to hear. And an old patriarch hobbled forward from a warm corner, and put his wrinkled hand to his ear.

"But that was not all that I saw," continued Joseph. "I went out into Grand Street, and just as I was going to climb the "L" steps whom should I see but Freier. He didn't see me, and I was not anxious to enter into conversation with him. But I noticed how well he was dressed, and how he rolled along with that air of owning everything; and I saw his big white fingers loaded with rings, and his prosperous leer, and how he pulled his coat away for fear it would touch a poor devil of a cloakmaker who was loafing because one of Freier's sweaters had resented his independence. And I knew that it was out of one of Freier's shops that the poor used-up operative, whose children I had just seen starving, had been kicked, after he had been worked to death. Then it seemed to me that the air was filled with blood, and I hurried up and took my train, for fear that I might run after Freier and tell him what I thought of him!"

"Yes — yes," said a woman in the kitchen door; "Freier is a man-eater; and there are too many like him. But what can poor folks do? When one worker gives out, twenty of our poor refugees are howling for his place. The weak ones have to go to the wall."

Joseph's voice had risen to a strident key, while he was reciting the horrors which he had just seen. The women stood appalled and trembling, and they were beginning to cry, when the piping, quavering voice of the old patriarch was heard repeating one of the verses from the Passover ritual: "'For at every time enemies rise against us to annihilate us; but the Most Holy, blessed be He! hath delivered us out of their hands.'"

"Well, well!" said Joseph, sinking down on the little sofa in front of the Seder table, "don't let me worry you; but sometimes I feel the cruelty, the horrible wickedness, of the situation so that it lifts my soul to revolt. I wonder," he said with more gentleness, "if this was not the way poor Baumeister felt at times when he gabbled about his 'party of force'! But where are the others?"

"They are coming up-stairs now," said Zipporah. "I hear 'em." And she ran to open the door.

"Promise me that you will be calm to-night, Joseph," said Malcha in a whisper. "Remember that these good people will get frightened, for they are not used to your ways."

"I will roar no more," said Joseph, beckoning Zipporah to come and sit by him as the company assembled.

This was the first time Joseph and Malcha had met with some old friends, well-to-do merchants at home, but suddenly expelled from Moscow with only the wreck of their fortunes. The two brothers and their wives inhabited a small flat in a tenement house in Broome Street, and the tiny rooms were filled with the quaint old bits of furniture which they had brought from their Russian home.

They had been allowed a month in which to settle up their affairs before expulsion; and this gave them the chance which most of the exiles did not have — that of taking some of the household treasures with them. They had begged Joseph and Malcha and the child and David as a special favor to be with them on this first Passover night, and Malcha had delayed her return to the colony to accept this friendly invitation.

The two rooms of the flat were spick-and-span clean, and decorated with pictures and a few Hebrew books. The table was resplendent with clean linen, and in front of the elder of the two brothers were arranged on a glass dish the three unleavened cakes, covered separately; and the egg, the "haroseth," the salt water, the shankbone, the bitter herbs, and the parsley were placed on the consecrated cover.

A pillow was laid beside the officiator, who wore his hat; and opening the manual, after the guests were seated, he began rapidly to read the "sanctification" in a low voice.

Meantime the other brother filled the wine-glasses of

peculiar shape which had been procured expressly for the occasion ; and the women bustled to and from the kitchen, bringing things which had been forgotten, while the patriarch, with one hand to his ear, made gestures of approval or dissent with the other, according as the unction of the reading suited his fancy.

Slowly, yet not without a certain innocent and seemly mirth, the ancient ceremonial progressed. After the sanctification came the washing of the hands, then the taking of the parsley dipped in salt water. " You don't eat enough of it," said the good patriarch querulously. "A good Orthodox Jew would eat ten times as much as that."

" But, father, 'tis so mortal bitter," said one of the women.

" All the more reason to eat it, then ! " he piped.

Then came the careful breaking of the middle one of the three cakes, the saying of the service, the washing of the hands, and the breaking of the uppermost cake, after which the bitter herbs, horseradish, and vinegar were eaten in commemoration of the bitter work which the Israelites had to perform in Egypt.

" Give me a good handful," said Joseph, " so that I may not forget — even for a minute."

Then after the proper cups of wine had been served in the appropriate places in the service, and the haroseth and horseradish had left a bitter taste in every one's mouth, the supper was brought in. First came the soup, with the unleavened nödels swimming in it; then broiled fish, and finally some roast lamb and salad, of which Joseph ate slowly in his grave, preoccupied way, like one whose thoughts were thousands of miles away. But all at once he said quaintly, —

" If my cloakmakers should see me eating such a meal as this, they would say that the cause of organized labor is lost."

"Don't be too much their slave, Joseph," said the brother who was presiding. "You have suffered enough already. Persecution — prison — and hunger, I dare say, now and then, eh ? "

"Ah, well, I generally managed to get a crust and a sup of tea, except in the first days when I was living on apples, which are not half so filling as pickles, although they're more genteel eating."

"Sh-sh!" said the other brother, "some one is at the door."

"Well, you need not say sh-sh," said his wife; "we're not in Russia any longer, and there's nothing to be afraid of."

"True, true; I forget. See who it is."

"I suppose it is David," said Joseph. "He promised to come, although he said he might be late."

It was David, but he would not come in. He had an important message for Joseph — a message which could not wait. Would he come out at once ?

"Here, here, you are not eating enough of the middle cake!" cried the patriarch fretfully. "Bless me! what would the Orthodox think if they could see this ? "

While the two brothers were discussing with the patriarch the true method of serving the unleavened bread at that particular point in the repast, Joseph went out into the passage, seizing his hat as he went along.

"Promise to return in an hour, Joseph," cried Malcha, "no matter what it is."

"I promise," said Joseph; and when he was in the dark passage he felt his hand gripped tightly by David, and one of David's arms stole around him, and "stayed him up," as if he would need support.

"What is it, David ? " said Joseph, who felt a strange presentiment that at last he was to have news of Bathsheba —

the first since he had come victoriously out of the "Tombs," with the governor's pardon in his pocket, and ten thousand adoring cloakmakers at his heels.

"Come down-stairs quick, and out of the street," said David.

When they had crossed into another street where but few people were coming and going at that hour, David said, —

"I have a message from Bathsheba. She is dying. If she lives until midnight it will be a miracle."

"Well?" said Joseph. He felt his knees trembling.

"It is a verbal message; but you may be sure that it is correct, for Bathsheba made the woman who brought it to me repeat it many times before she was satisfied."

"Well?" said Joseph.

"It is this: 'I send to Joseph the kiss of reconciliation and peace. Let him think of me as one who first conspired against him, next worshipped him; and who, if she had not been cut down by the way, would have worked for him. And whatever he has done is right, and she alone has been blameworthy.'"

"Where is she?" said Joseph huskily.

"In Forsyth Street."

Joseph caught David by the arm. "Is it typhus?" he cried.

"Yes."

At this moment a figure darted out of the mists, and falling at Joseph's feet grasped him about the knees. "O Reb Joseph," it cried piteously, "promise me that you will not go to her; swear that you will not! It would be your death, and what could we do without you now? Promise!"

It was Ben Zion.

"Get up," said Joseph, "and don't make a spectacle of yourself. Do you suppose that I fear typhus? Have I not lived next to it, ate and drank among those who were soon to die of it, tended those who were dying of it? Look at me! I am typhus proof!"

"Perhaps so," said David, "but the innocent wife and child whom you have just left are not. Remember, 'Who sees the wife die has assisted at the destruction of the sanctuary itself.'"

"I am not going to Bathsheba, my friends. Why should you think that I am?"

"Because," said Ben Zion fiercely, "she is a witch, and who knows but she sent that message so that you would be tempted to go and see her, and catch your death there?"

"Be quiet!" said David. "Let me tell Bathsheba's story, and then if Joseph has a message to send, he must hasten to send it."

Ben Zion fell back, muttering, —

"Well, well! these be times indeed, as the fly said when the ox stepped on him! There are none too many of us labor-leaders now, and I am not going to see Joseph sacrificed for a silly, sentimental play-actress!"

"Bathsheba's husband deserted her," said David, taking Joseph by the arm, and walking with him up and down the quiet street. "They quarrelled while you were in the 'Tombs,' because he had learned that she had gone to see you at the colony, and he fancied that you had a plan for running away together."

Joseph said nothing. He was thinking of the exquisite and luminous vision which had hovered before him on the day when he had left the colony to deliver himself up; of the lovely face and the clouds of dusky hair, the lips and eyes which spoke of slumbering passion — those adoring eyes which had reproached him so cruelly when he had repulsed her on the night of the death of Miryam.

"Just then Shiphrah was sewing for Bathsheba from time to time, on her costumes. He knew it; and so he knew shortly before he decided to leave her that Shiphrah was surreptitiously working on a cloak for Bathsheba. One day recently Bathsheba, not suspecting that he was meditating a vengeance on her, said that she had not heard anything of Shiphrah for several days. 'I wish,' she said, 'that you would go and look up my cloak, for I shall want it at a performance in a week or so.'—'Agreed,' says the husband, and he goes off to the sweat-shop where Shiphrah works. When he gets there he finds it closed. 'Why is this?' he inquires. Because there was a typhus case there, and the Board of Health had closed the place, and condemned all the clothing there as infected, for a man had been struck down with typhus in the place. But he does not care for that; he has come after his property that has been paid for in advance, and he will have it; and finally — you know how our poor people are — they get frightened at his bluster, and yield. He gets into the place, and, under a pile of garments that just reeks with infection, he finds the theatrical cloak, which he recognizes from his wife's description. 'This is mine,' he says with an evil smile; and if the sweater comes back and makes a fuss, send him to me at this place,' and he gives a false address. Then he takes the cloak straight to Bathsheba, and says, 'Shiphrah was gone, but I managed to find it. Very pretty it is, and much good may it do you.' And that night he goes out, and hasn't been heard of since. They think he has gone West. Bathsheba tries on the cloak, and at the proper time she is struck down with typhus."

"Where is Shiphrah? and how did you learn all this?" said Joseph in a trembling voice.

"When Bathsheba found herself deserted she sent for me; but before I could come the typhus had declared itself, and the woman in whose house she lives had isolated her; packed her away — for fear the Board of Health would hear the story. Then Bathsheba sent me Shiphrah's address: I hurried to it and learned the story. Nothing was to be found of Shiphrah: she had disappeared, as they disappear in that sweater world; and the scared folk in the neighborhood say that the infected cloak was dangerous enough to kill fifty women."

"Did Bathsheba know of her husband's vengeance?"

"She suspected it when she was taken ill; and when she heard my story from the nurse, who has been true to her, she gave herself up as lost. And to-night is the end, Joseph. Will you send her a word, for she has come out of delirium, they say, and is now sinking swiftly."

"And why should anything stay me from going to her?" cried Joseph passionately.

Ben Zion sprang forward. "Reb Joseph," he said, "you'll have to kill me before you can go to that woman. She is a witch."

Joseph was silent for a long time. David, with his fine sympathies, Ben Zion, with his ruder ones, both felt that a terrible struggle was taking place in the great heart. But at last he spoke.

"Tell Bathsheba that I wish her eternal peace. Tell her that all is forgiven — and that she should be glad to go up out of Egypt into the promised land! No — no — not that; tell her peace — eternal peace."

His voice broke. David hurried him back toward the Broome street house.

"You have won your battle at last, Joseph," he said. And although Ben Zion did not say it he felt it.

Then they hastened away, and left him alone. It was better so.

He looked upward before he went into the house. The infinite stars were shining; the mist had vanished; the blue sky was beautifully serene — but so far — so very far away. Joseph stretched up his arms as if he were grasp-

ing at the immeasurable spaces; but they mocked him with
their vastness, they scorned his yearning.

In the darkened passage and up the unlit stairs he groped
his way back to the peaceful Passover festival. The
patriarch was declaiming garrulously about the exact period
at which the consecrated brandy should be tasted. But in
a corner Malcha and the women were talking about Baumeister and his sad fate. "Why not have his poor child
sent to the colony?" said Malcha. "It would be looked
after there."

"Ah, here is Joseph!" the women cried. "Ask his
advice about it."

"How pale you are, Joseph!" said Malcha. "You look
as if you had seen a ghost. Oh, I hope," she said in a
whisper, as he came closer, "that you haven't been near
any of those typhus people."

"Oh dear no! But you must remember that I have not
had much fresh air lately."

"Why, open the window," said one of the brothers.
"Father don't mind, do you, father?"

"Bless ye, no! Read on, son, read on," said the patriarch impatiently. And the reader, still pursuing the ceremonial, read, "'And the children of Israel sighed by
reason of the bondage, and they cried, and their complaint
came up unto God.'"

Joseph had moved to the opened window, and sat by it,
looking up at the stars. Half an hour afterwards, and
just as he was about to come away, it seemed to him that
all the stars grew dim, and he sprang up and uttered a
faint cry.

That was the moment when Bathsheba died.

THE END.